ALSO BY FRANCESCA FLORES

Diamond City

SHADOW

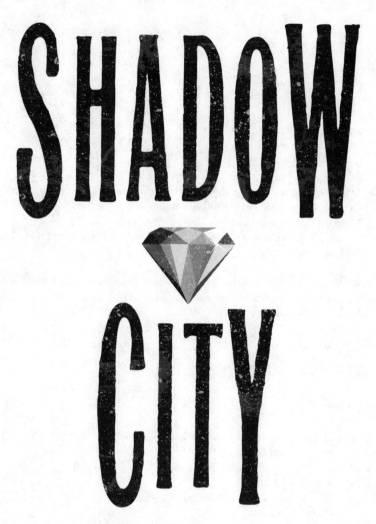

CITY

FRANCESCA FLORES

WEDNESDAY BOOKS
NEW YORK

First published in the United States by Wednesday Books, an imprint of St. Martin's Publishing Group

SHADOW CITY. Copyright © 2020 by Francesca Flores. All rights reserved. Printed in the United States of America. For information, address St. Martin's Publishing Group, 120 Broadway, New York, NY 10271.

www.wednesdaybooks.com

Library of Congress Cataloging-in-Publication Data

Names: Flores, Francesca, author.
Title: Shadow city / Francesca Flores.
Description: First edition. | New York : Wednesday Books, 2021. |
    Series: City of steel and diamond ; 2
Identifiers: LCCN 2020040132 | ISBN 9781250220486 (hardcover) |
    ISBN 9781250220493 (ebook)
Subjects: CYAC: Magic—Fiction. | Conspiracies—Fiction. |
    Betrayal—Fiction. | Fantasy.
Classification: LCC PZ7.1.F5943 Sh 2021 | DDC [Fic]—dc23
LC record available at https://lccn.loc.gov/2020040132

Our books may be purchased in bulk for promotional, educational, or business use. Please contact your local bookseller or the Macmillan Corporate and Premium Sales Department at 1-800-221-7945, extension 5442, or by email at MacmillanSpecialMarkets@macmillan.com.

First Edition: 2021

10 9 8 7 6 5 4 3 2 1

Dedicated to La Beesh

1

"Don't scream, and I might let you live."

Aina removed her blade from the spy's neck and spun her around so fast, the girl almost tripped. The spy flicked her gaze around the empty warehouse, to the shattered windows, to the main door twenty feet away, to the black market entrance where they'd both come from—and then to the dagger still in Aina's hand.

"You won't kill me," the girl said, her voice shallow despite the bold words. "You need as many of us as you can hold on to."

"Of what?" Aina scoffed. "Traitors?"

The word stung, a bitter poison on her tongue, but it was true. She and her colleague Tannis had fought to own all of Kosín's tradehouses—businesses that supplied criminal services to any paying client—but the victory meant nothing when some of the tradehouses didn't trust them and sent spies like this one.

"I'm just doing a job," the spy said in a rush.

The words echoed in Aina's mind. She'd given the same excuse countless times in her work as an assassin.

Aina's old boss, Kohl, had killed her parents on a simple job.

"Everyone is just doing a job," she spat out, making the spy wince, "but you, your boss, and everyone at the Thunder tradehouse is still a traitor." While she spoke, Teo appeared at the entrance to the black market, his broad shoulders taking up the entire doorway. "Why did your boss send you to spy on me tonight?"

The spy bent her knees and shot away toward the exit. Aina flung a knife at her and it skimmed against the girl's elbow, drawing blood but not stopping her. At the same time, Teo brought out a pistol and shot at the spy, but the bullet pinged off the side of the door as the spy ran outside.

Aina raced to the exit, Teo's footsteps echoing off the floor behind her. The thick, humid summer air hit them when they left the warehouse, the heat rising off concrete in waves that made Aina's breaths draw short. The towering gray factory buildings and textile mills cast sharp shadows along the street.

The spy was wrong about one thing: Aina would certainly kill her.

On top of the building across the street, movement flickered— the spy's leg slipping over the edge and onto the roof.

Aina followed, leaping to grab the rungs of the fire escape and hauling herself up. By the time she reached the roof, the spy had run to the other side and jumped across the gap to the next building. Aina sprinted after her, crossing to the next building in a running leap. The spy cast one terrified glance over her shoulder and ran faster, leading Aina into the Center of the city and veering south into the Stacks—Aina's home. Flashes of the silver and red crescent moons lit swathes of the rooftops from between the higher buildings around them.

Wind from the south blew in the river's stench, but even with the humid summer air, a chill slid down her spine. Usually, the lights from shops lit up this part of the city all day and night, the owners never missing an opportunity to earn more kors. But the farther they ran, the fewer lights there were, flickering out around them until soon, they'd be plunged into the darkness of the Stacks.

Last month, Aina had exposed how General Alsane Bautix, a member of the Sentinel—the country's governing oligarchy— was plotting an assassination against a foreign princess visiting the capital. He'd fled along with the Red Jackals gang and his biggest ally, Kohl. Desperate to regain power, Kohl and Bautix sent the Jackals to extort businesses in the south, killing anyone who refused to pay.

If she looked northward, there were electric lights, shops open at all hours, and Steels—wealthy industrialists—parading around in silk and diamonds. But the south was a sea of black, pin-pricked by only a few candles in windows, and growing more invisible to the rest of the city every day. She tried not to imagine the bodies on the ground there now, left to rot after the Jackals had dealt with them.

The spy veered south, and Aina ran faster not to lose sight of her. The spy could easily disappear in the cobweb network of cardboard and rusted metal houses. Aina shifted left, hauling herself up to the fourth floor of another building. She sprinted across the roof until she was parallel with and above the spy, who glanced over her shoulder to check for pursuit. A small, triumphant smile lit her features when the red moon's light touched her. Her pace slowed a little.

When Aina reached the end of the taller building's roof, she looked behind her to see Teo a building away, then turned back to the edge of the roof and dropped off smoothly. A deep breath of smoke-tinged night air filled her as she fixed her gaze on the view. The hills wound downward, pockmarked by the gray-and-rust houses ahead, until they met the barely visible greenish tinge of the river at the southern docks.

A moment later, she rolled to her feet on the third-story roof of the building below, quieting her breaths even though she was still panting from the run. A small chimney stood sentinel at the edge of the roof and cast a shadow over one side. She ducked behind it as the other girl drew closer on a parallel path. Soon the spy would have to step onto the roof where Aina waited.

For a moment, Aina breathed in the still air, allowing the shadows to drape over her face. The dark didn't scare her as much as it used to, but now it surrounded her and cloaked her in its depths as if to warn her that death was coming soon.

Kohl thrived in the dark. Aina stumbled through it, gasping for breath as clues slipped through her fingers like steam curling above a brass train.

Years ago, Kohl promised to give her a tradehouse of her own to manage one day. The hope that she'd have a real future had never been stronger, and now, her heart clenched at how foolishly she'd believed him. One mistake she'd made on a job last month, and he kicked her out, leaving her to be killed. She'd discovered his plans with Bautix, stopped them, and took the tradehouses for herself when he fled, but now he wanted them back.

The tradehouses were the only proof that her years on the streets after her parents' deaths weren't in vain. They were her success, her home, a sign of her ranking among the city's criminals that left her untouchable. A sign that she'd never be on the streets again, her only solace the paper bags of glue she'd nearly suffocated on. Her hand went to her lips, checking for some remnant of glue, that old fear returning and never leaving—she inhaled now to remind herself she could still breathe. A spy wasn't about to make her lose everything.

Still crouched behind the chimney, Aina held her breath as the spy reached this roof and approached. Her shadow stretched out before her, long and jagged on the concrete. Once she got close enough, Aina struck out with a punch to the gut. The girl exhaled sharply, falling back and doubling over as Aina stepped out in front of her. A snarl rose from the spy's lips, and she pulled a knife from her sleeve. Its blade glinted in the moonlight as she lunged forward. Aina shifted to the side and used the girl's own momentum to shove her away.

The spy's feet skidded across the rooftop. Her eyes widened in fear when she nearly toppled off the edge, but she threw her arms to the side to catch her balance. At the same time, movement from behind Aina, still in the shadows of the building overhead, caught her eye. At first, she thought it was Teo, but then she heard the click of a gun.

Aina rolled out of the way in a single breath, then took a dagger in one hand and a scythe in the other. Her pulse raced as her second attacker stepped into the light: another Thunder employee, this one second-in-command to their boss, Arman—Davide, if she remembered correctly. He must have been watching to make sure their spy got away safely.

A dull thud sounded behind her, but she didn't dare take her eyes off the two in front of her. A moment later, Teo walked up next to her. The wind whipped his waves of dark brown hair around his jaw as he lifted his own gun and faced the other Thunder employee.

Aina's thoughts raced, sweat trickling down the back of her neck. Against any other opponent, she would fight back without a second thought. Hesitation was a death sentence in Kosín.

But these were supposed to be her employees, and the thought of killing them left a bitter taste in her mouth. They were supposed to trust her, but maybe all their years working with Kohl had led them to trust no one but themselves. She couldn't blame them, but she couldn't let them get away with this. No real trade-house leader would.

The spy began to circle away from the edge of the roof, and Aina followed. The night air crowded around them, heat and humidity making her clothes stick to her skin with sweat. A buzz rose in Aina's ears, making all other sounds fall away, until the only thing left in the world was this fight on this rooftop.

"If you make one wrong move, Solís," Davide called over, not taking his eyes off Teo, "I'll blast your friend's head off. Arman's orders."

Teo let out a sharp laugh. "I'd like to see you try."

"Him, but not me?" Aina asked, wanting to keep them distracted. "I'm almost insulted, Davide. You don't think I'm worth your bullets, or is your aim really so bad that you'd just miss?"

He took his eyes off Teo for a moment, an angry retort at the tip of his tongue, and Teo shot out his kneecaps. Davide collapsed, crying out, his strangled yell the only sound in the Stacks, apart from the rats moving in the street below.

The spy gulped then, her eyes wide and bloodshot as she and Aina continued circling each other. Aina made sure her own steps drew her closer to the edge of the building.

"Aina?" Teo called over, his voice casual as though this were a stroll through a park. "Do you need this traitor alive?"

"Keep him there," she said. "I'll only be a minute."

Wind swept through the streets and the hair rose on the back of her neck. Her eyes flicked toward the three-story drop behind her.

Stay steady, she told herself.

Kohl had shown fear when she'd nearly pushed him out of a window last month and placed a blade under his heart. She would show none.

She crouched, angling her body so most of her weight was forward and under the shadow of the chimney. One hand moved to the brace of diamond-edged daggers across her chest, and the spy took the bait.

When she lunged forward, her eyes on Aina's knives, Aina hooked a foot around the girl's ankle and pushed.

The girl gasped, her eyes flicking down to see what had tripped her. Her arms windmilled, trying to grab on to something in the dark and failing. A small yelp left her lips but was swallowed by the wind, and a breath later, her body smacked against the ground three stories below. Aina spared her a brief moment of remorse, then turned to her second problem.

Davide's shouts still echoed off the buildings around them, cursing at them in multiple languages as he bled out on the roof. Aina walked over to him and Teo, who stepped aside to let her face Davide herself.

"Arman's orders," she said in a mocking tone. "You're forgetting one thing: I'm in charge."

He barely opened his mouth to beg when she slit open his throat. She stepped back so his blood wouldn't get on her boots, then moved toward the edge of the roof again. The girl's broken body was surrounded by a pool of golden light from one of the last few streetlamps heading south. Kohl wasn't Aina's boss anymore, but she'd always survived by his lessons: Be brutal and exact. Get rid of anyone threatening your position. Cut off loose ends.

As much as she hated him, he'd ruled the tradehouses with a steel-tight grip. She was newer and younger, and needed to hold on even harder.

She tensed when Teo placed a hand on her shoulder, then forced herself to relax. *He's not Kohl,* she reminded herself. Over the three years they'd known each other, Teo had stayed by her whenever she was injured or in danger, when Kohl kicked her out and the whole city wanted to kill her, before anyone feared or respected her.

His forehead creased in concern when he asked, "Which tradehouse were they from?"

"Thunder, like the other spies." In the loud, smoke-filled room of the black market moments before catching sight of the spy, Aina had told Teo about the threatening notes left in front of her and her employees when they were out on jobs. They weren't in Kohl's handwriting, but she suspected he was sending the Jackals to do it for him, to shake her confidence for whenever he would really strike. "She saw us asking around about Kohl in the market, and she probably heard me tell you about the notes too. The other tradehouses are loyal to us now, but if Arman found out that Kohl is actively trying to take back the Dom, he'd turn against us in an instant and try to get the others to do the same. Right now, Arman is looking for any weaknesses he can find."

"Traitors don't deserve mercy," Teo said, tilting his head toward the light of the silver moon, which lent a soft glow to his golden-brown skin. She breathed in, echoing his words in her head as he continued, "None of them do. Kohl, any of the tradehouses that want to challenge you, the Jackals working for Bautix, the Diamond Guards . . . We'll show them we're deadlier than all of them put together." Their eyes met and she felt that same fire building in him, that need to fight all those who threatened them and the refusal to be beaten down. But there was something else too; his gaze seared through her, a silent reminder of how they'd grown closer this past month—and how he wanted more between them than she could give him while Kohl still lived.

Brushing loose strands of black hair behind her ears, she broke their eye contact and looked toward the body on the roof.

"Let's leave them where Arman can find them," she said. Together they lifted Davide's body and carried it down the fire escape, the air growing quieter and pressing closer in the Stacks. Night deepened and the only other sounds besides their footsteps were the fleeting movements of rats and stray dogs on the dirt roads. But the faint sounds of voices, some threatening, some frightened, still reached them here from a few streets away.

Her limbs ached as she and Teo walked toward the body, and she knew she should rest, but any hour she slept was an hour in which Kohl could be moving against her.

"You know the Jackals are walking around the south like they own it all now," she said. "Raurie's uncle's tavern is close, and she's been eavesdropping on their conversations. Let's see if she's overheard something on where Kohl might be hiding."

She would use all the lessons Kohl had taught her as an assassin to hunt him down. She'd lie, blackmail, steal, and trick—she'd make him suffer, because death alone wouldn't be good enough. She'd kill, like she'd done many times while working for him, but this time, she'd kill him too.

A memory of Kohl pointing a gun at her head and then tossing it aside rushed to the front of her thoughts. The cold timbre of his voice every time he reminded her that he'd given her a home and could take it away whenever he wanted. The truth that he'd killed her parents, putting her on the streets in the first place. His fist delivering a blow to her face and then his fingers touching her hair softly.

She would keep this home she'd fought for and finally get his voice out of her head.

Soon, they'd face each other again, and this time, she'd win for good.

2

Night had settled in by the time they finished emptying the dead girl's pockets.

"You're very popular," Teo muttered to Aina while fishing through Davide's pockets next. "Even more people are trying to kill you than usual."

"I just hope the next person will wait until I've had a nap."

As she wiped off her bloodied knife with her scarf, she scanned every building for a sign of someone watching. A plastic bag swept by, caught in the wind, but that was the only sound besides her breathing and Teo's movements. Many shop owners had decided it was safer to hide at night, bolting their doors shut and boarding up windows. Homes were quiet, families drawn in for the night. They already starved every day, and now Kohl and Bautix's fight for the city robbed them of the chance to work and feed themselves. She gripped her knife harder, knuckles straining.

"There," Teo whispered, his copper eyes glinting under the

streetlamp as he looked up at her. "Almost looks like they had some bad luck in a mugging."

"Common enough in the Stacks," she said, flashing Teo a tense grin. "But I want Arman to know it was me. It's the only way he'll get in line."

He passed Aina half of the kors, which she pocketed, the satisfying clink of metal in her pocket reminding her she was safe and wouldn't be back on the streets anytime soon—she had more money than she'd ever had before, and she was still one of the deadliest people walking around Kosín.

Leaving the body behind, they rounded a corner and began to walk up a hill out of the Stacks, their boots crunching in the dirt on the narrow road. They kept their eyes peeled for any sign of danger, checking every alley they passed, their weapons on clear display. A few weeks ago, they could have passed through the Stacks without needing to be so on guard. Everyone knew who they were and not to mess with them.

But now, everyone feared the Jackals as much as they might fear her. Anyone in the Stacks would give up information on her if it could buy them protection from violence or extortion by the Jackals, whose ranks seemed to multiply by the day.

"The other tradehouses will trust you soon enough, once they realize you and Tannis are much better than Kohl," Teo said as they rounded a corner and descended a hill deeper into the Stacks. His voice had gone bitter, and in it she sensed the memory of how Kohl and Bautix's plans had gotten his mother killed by the Diamond Guards. But it vanished as quickly as it came, his eyes hardening as he said, "We can still stop them if we work fast enough."

They both looked southeast then, and Aina felt the familiar tension rising, the sense that they were scrambling and would fail if they made one mistake or fell one step behind Kohl and

Bautix. Dirt roads and run-down homes spread away before her, each one as familiar to her as the scars and bruises littering her body. The cloying, polluted air clung to her skin and slowly poisoned her lungs, but she would never trade it for the glittering, clean streets in other parts of the city. She imagined the Dom waiting for her at the river shore like it always had—as long as she could hold on to it.

It was the first tradehouse, started by Kohl in the wake of the civil war fourteen years ago, and now whoever ran the Dom managed all the tradehouses—they each paid commission to the boss of the Dom and got all their bribes and weapons through the Dom's careful negotiations. Since she was twelve, she'd trained there to learn to fight and protect herself, to reach for a future that would never be offered to her, like everyone in the south yearned to do. If she lost it, she'd have nothing.

They soon reached the tavern in the middle of the Stacks that Raurie's uncle owned. When they entered, smoke billowed out at them and Aina blinked, her eyes watering. Raurie, her uncle, and another employee took orders and prepared drinks at the bar. Since it had been so long since the civil war, most of the drunk patrons here wouldn't notice the small signs that the bar was run by Inosen—people faithful to the Mothers, the two goddesses the people of Sumerand traditionally believed in; the religion now banned since the end of the war where Inosen and Steels fought one another.

But Aina had been coming here long enough to see it: the red and silver curtains leading to the backrooms, the Mothers' colors; the names of their specialty drinks on the chalkboard menu that used words from the old holy language; the small drawing of a diamond, the Inosen's tool for blood magic, on the back of a notebook where they wrote tabs. It was a bold risk; if anyone else noticed and reported them to the Diamond Guards, they could easily be imprisoned.

As she and Teo weaved through the tables, she coughed on the stale scents of smoke and cheap firebrandy. With so many people gathered here in close quarters, the air grew hot, sticky, and hard to breathe. Most people skirted out of their way, recognizing Aina and Teo even while inebriated. She stared straight ahead as they walked, hoping no sign of fear showed on her face—that she was as formidable a leader as Kohl had been.

Someone waved to them through the press of people. Tannis and Ryuu sat in a booth in a tucked away corner, a small candle on the table illuminating their faces and the mugs of ale they each held. Tannis twirled her glass between her hands, her gold eyes calculating as Aina and Teo joined them. Throwing stars glinted at the holsters on Tannis's shoulders, and the candlelight made her blue hair more vibrant against her pale skin.

It was still odd to see Tannis among her friends when she'd pretended to work against them for so long, while fighting Kohl in her own way. But it had been easy to forgive her, when they'd both come from nothing and had fought their way to the top of Kohl's ranks. Now they ran the Dom together. "I don't like leaving the Dom alone too long," Tannis said, shifting her weight uneasily, then looked at Aina and Teo. "Did you learn anything at the black market?"

"We managed to pick up some new weapons, but no, we didn't find out anything about where Kohl might be," she said, meeting Tannis's apprehensive gaze. No one knew Kohl better than the two of them, nor how ugly things would get when he fought them for control of the Dom. "A spy from Thunder overheard us—and she had backup, Arman's second. They're not a problem anymore."

Silence fell at their table, and Aina's eyes darted toward the crowd to check for eavesdroppers. Even here, where alcohol flowed freely and everyone seemed relaxed enough, there was a marked change; people stayed in their groups, veering away from anyone they didn't know, eyes flicking worriedly to the door as if they expected Jackals to break it down and start shooting at any moment.

"They're testing us to see if we'll punish them or if we'll let them do whatever they want," Tannis said then, drawing Aina's attention back to the group. "Kohl wouldn't let them get away with this."

"We won't either," Aina said shortly. Two years ago, a tradehouse boss had gone around to the others and tried to get their support to take down Kohl. She'd been in the office when he found out about it; he'd gone deathly still, asked her to leave. The next day, that boss's head and arms were found floating in the river—no one ever found the rest of him.

Their job was to decide how much they wanted to be like the Blood King.

As they spoke, Ryuu tapped his fingers on the table and took in the tavern with a careful look in his umber eyes. His wavy black hair framed a narrow face with high cheekbones, and his fancy attire reminded Aina how strange it was that they were friends—he a Steel who'd inherited the biggest mining and construction empire in the country, and the rest of them criminals from the south of the city.

"Do you know what's going on?" Ryuu asked, crossing his arms and doing a decent job of trying to look comfortable. "Raurie asked us to come."

"She did?" Aina asked, looking toward the bar where Raurie poured a drink for a customer.

Ryuu gave a tense nod. "I was wondering if she found out

something about Kohl." He met her gaze then, his deep brown eyes lit with the same determination she felt to track down Kohl. Last month, Kohl had sent Aina to kill Ryuu's brother—that failed, and then they'd worked together against Bautix and Kohl—but eventually Kohl killed his brother himself.

Then Ryuu's outfit caught her eye—a suit with a red tie, gold watch glimmering against his bronze skin. "Why are you wearing a suit here of all places?"

Ryuu yawned and the bags under his eyes seemed to deepen. "Just had a meeting and didn't have time to change. Running a mining and construction empire takes away a lot of your free time, apparently. What's wrong with the suit? Does it make me stand out?"

"Yeah, that," Teo began, "and your gold watch, and your leather shoes—"

"We match now, my scarf and your tie," Aina said, lifting up one end of her scarf, which was far too hot to wear in summer, but she had a hard time letting go of it. The bloodstains that had turned it red were certainly memorable, even if they smelled like rust.

Ryuu grimaced. "My tie doesn't have blood on it, Aina. Do you want a new scarf? I can get you a new scarf." He paused, then added, "Please let me get you a new scarf."

"This is handmade artistry, Ryuu," she said with a grin.

"Took years of work," Teo added.

"Did you stab anyone today, Aina?" Ryuu asked then, leaning back from the end of the scarf she held out to him. "It smells exceedingly pungent."

"I did, thanks for noticing. But you really should hide that watch."

A minute later, Raurie stepped out from behind the bar to take her break. Aina waved as Raurie approached them, and

Ryuu slid a drink toward her as she sat down and gave them a bright smile. Chin-length black hair brushed against the ocher brown of her cheeks lit golden by the candlelight at their table. Last month, Raurie had joined them to stop Bautix and Kohl's plans.

"How is work tonight?" Tannis asked Raurie, her gold eyes lighting up as she leaned slightly across the table—they'd become friends since Raurie helped Tannis escape the Tower last month and recover from her wounds in an Inosen safe house. "When Kushik brought your message, he said you seemed anxious."

"I overheard a couple of people talking about a hideout nearby. I think they're new Jackals," Raurie said, then smirked. "Not as careful with their tongues. The hideout is in the warehouse district, at one of the textile factories. Bautix must have bribed one of the owners to give them space to sleep there."

"Did they say anything about Kohl?" Aina asked.

Raurie shook her head. "I overheard where it is, but they didn't say who's staying there. It's the best lead we've gotten so far." Then she nodded over her shoulder to the bar, where her uncle and a young girl still took drink orders. "See the new girl? Her family and a few others have joined our safe house, so we have people to help out here. I can leave early."

"You're all together in one safe house now?" Ryuu asked.

With a grim nod, Raurie said, "We still have that apartment you gave us, but right now it's safer to go underground. All the Diamond Guard captains who want to try to get Bautix's job are cracking down harder than ever on magic users and diamond smugglers. And if Bautix can take back power again by hurting Inosen, he'll do it."

"I don't understand, though," Teo said, leaning forward over the middle of the table to be heard above the loud, drunken voices nearby. "Why would he focus on the Inosen? Doesn't he want to take the Tower? I understand he's prejudiced, but killing the Inosen won't give him power."

"Won't it?" Raurie asked, tightening the purple silk shawl she always wore around her shoulders. "That's how he got it before, by killing King Verrain. Half the people in the city call him a hero for stopping the war. It's how he got his position, command-ing the Diamond Guards in the city and the whole military."

A moment of silence passed as they all took in what Raurie said. King Verrain had been an Inosen himself, but instead of embracing the Mothers' message of peace, he had used magic to kill, gathering his followers to help him shut down the factories since he viewed technology as a natural enemy of faith.

He gave a bad name to us all, her mother had whispered to her, while using the magic to heal a profusely bleeding boy, who'd come to them after getting into a fight, *but they're the ones who decided we're all the same, that none of us can be good; makes it easier for them to push us down.*

Businesses closing, bodies in the street, Inosen hiding in fear for their lives. Aina's shoulders tensed at the thought. It was as close to the feeling of civil war as Aina had felt since she was a child, despite some of her memories being hazy.

Everyone back then knew someone who had died. She looked around at her friends now, wondering if they'd all make it out of this if another war began. Each of them had fought for a chance at a future in this world, and none of them would go down easily . . . but she still didn't like to think of the possibility.

Aina let out a sharp exhale and looked up from the table as something caught her eye. The glint of candlelight on a glass mug reminded her of diamonds, the ones she'd used to smuggle to people like her parents. Power. Beauty. Magic that caused a civil war and brought death to thousands.

Magic that might be useful if she learned to use it now. Goose bumps rose on her arms at the thought. If she could learn to use the same magic as King Verrain, she could use it to fight Kohl and anyone else who tried to take the tradehouses from her.

But for now, she had a lead to follow. One that might take her directly to Kohl's hiding place.

"We should go," she said, standing and sliding two of her diamond-edged daggers into her sleeves for easy access—if Kohl was there, she'd need them.

When they left the tavern, the night had grown colder.
Hair clung to her skin with sweat from the heat inside the bar,
and after Aina brushed it away, she tensed, sensing eyes on her
from a distance. One hand went to a knife. A fluttering on the
ground caught her attention, and she inhaled sharply when she
spotted the piece of paper held down by a rock.

"Another note," Tannis whispered behind her.

As Aina bent to pick up the note, the others circled around
her, all of them looking toward the shadows between buildings
ahead, the rooftops, the windows, for some sign of who'd left it.

In a rushed handwriting that she didn't recognize, it said:

*You can keep fighting, Miss Solís, but Kosín will belong to General
Alsane Bautix again within one week. You're welcome to join the new
order if you fall in line, but first . . . he'll knock you down a few rungs
on the ladder.*

Tannis read it over her shoulder, her eyes hardening as she
did. Once Tannis finished reading, Aina curled the note into a

ball and tossed it over her shoulder—hoping that whoever left it was watching.

If Bautix managed to take back the city, he wouldn't stand for having someone in charge of the tradehouses who wasn't allied with him. Kohl's leadership had been beneficial for him, but hers was a thorn in his side. She looked over her shoulder, eastward toward the Dom, and her stomach twisted with nerves.

I won't let them down, she promised herself. *I won't let them fall to the claws of this city.*

Then she noticed the girl who'd been working behind the bar had slipped outside to join their group, closing the door softly behind her. She wore her wavy red-violet hair tied back in a loose ponytail, and freckles dotted her ivory Sumeranian features, but her eyes were the bright gold of Kaiyanis people. A bit of dirt was smudged on her nose and she picked at a frayed end of her shirt.

"Can I help you?" Aina asked, one hand settling on the handle of her scythe.

The girl cast one frightened look at the weapon, then turned to Raurie. "Raurie, is this about the Jackals you mentioned earlier? One of the other workers came back from their break, so your uncle said I could leave. Can I go with you?"

She said it all in one breath, a plea in her eyes as she waited for Raurie to reply. "I want you to come, Lill, but it's not just me who gets to decide," Raurie said, frowning, then she spoke to the group. "I told Lill she might be able to join us, but I didn't know all of you would show up. She's trustworthy, and I've never met anyone who hates the Jackals more than her, but there might be too many of us. I don't want us to get caught before we even get there. Maybe only a few of us should go."

"But we don't know how many Jackals there might be," Ryuu pointed out. "We don't want to be outnumbered either, and we want to take out as many of them as possible."

Aina paused, part of her wanting to agree with Raurie, while she also knew Ryuu made a good point. But time was wasting, so she made a decision.

"You can come with us, Lill. These factories are big, so we'll need a couple of us to keep watch to make sure no more Jackals come in while we're inside. Let's go already."

She and Raurie led the way west, while the others stayed close behind them. From the corner of her eye, Aina saw Lill approach Ryuu, her head tilted to the side.

"You're Ryuu Hirai," Lill said with a hint of curiosity.

"I thought you looked familiar," Ryuu said slowly, and then added with a desperate tone to his voice, "Our parents were friends, weren't they? Why did you leave our safe house near the mines? It's secure, I promise—"

"No, it's not," Lill cut him off. "The Jackals know about it. They have for years, actually, but we were too afraid to leave until now. The Inosen can only afford to side with one another until we see who ends up ruling this country. Sorry."

She shrugged, not looking sorry at all, and Aina held back a laugh as Ryuu's mouth fell open in shock.

As they walked, Raurie whispered the location to her and kept an eye out for any sign of the Jackals she'd seen earlier. Aina checked the location of each of her weapons—the two scythes strapped to her thighs, the brace of diamond-edged daggers across her chest, additional daggers in her sleeves, and a pouch of poison darts tied to her belt. Each one made her stronger, made her into a trained killer who'd proved herself in plenty of fights before.

Her confidence rose as they left the Stacks and crossed through the streets of the Center, heading west to the ware-house district. Under the quiet night, the creak of metal and the occasional gust of wind were the only sounds. Apart from two women who walked together across the road under streetlamps and a boy on a bike who sped past while humming to himself, they were the only pedestrians around. The buildings towered above them, the streets growing narrower and the stench of sewage building the farther they went. The steel mills, textile factories, and production plants all clustered together here, and though it usually emptied this late at night, something about the silence seemed eerier than usual.

This was familiar to her, stalking through the dark, noting every brush of the wind against her skin, every movement of shadow in the corners they passed. What was unfamiliar was walking with so many people—friends. Having them at her side now made her feel a little stronger, a little more protected, almost invincible. Almost like she could beat Kohl before he attacked.

"It smells out here," Tannis remarked, wrinkling her nose as they drew closer to the place Raurie had indicated.

"It always smells," Aina said with a shrug.

"Different now, though. Like something's rotting."

The scents of chemicals and smoke grew thicker in the air as they approached the factory. They gathered in a shadowed alley across the street, steam rising from a manhole in front of them, and took it in.

The textile mill was four stories, one of the biggest in the city, with Sumerand's symbol engraved above the main entrance: a sword and a pickaxe over a slab of rock. Tannis and Lill took places at either side of the building to watch for more Jackals, while Aina, Ryuu, Teo, and Raurie approached a side door. A stronger sewage scent reached them here while Teo picked the lock, and Aina buried her nose in her scarf.

When they stepped inside, the factory was empty of people, but the fumes of dyes and chemicals were still strong, etched into the walls and permeating the air.

"My mother worked in one like this," Teo said, his voice low with a bitter note. "No one can survive long, breathing in this stuff all day."

Aina placed a finger to her lips, then looked around the factory—three stories rose above, all work floors with machinery standing still and uniform like soldiers. Dread formed a pit in her stomach at the sight. Thousands of employees needed these jobs, hired by Steels who would just as soon let them die from the factory fumes; Inosen as well, whose Steels bosses would report them to Diamond Guards the minute they discovered who they were.

The only light came from fluorescent bulbs in a second-floor manager's office, which had a large window for managers and supervisors to watch the work floor. A narrow metal staircase without a railing ran along the right side of the wall, the only way to walk between each floor.

"You all have weapons?" Aina whispered, and when they nodded, she said, "Good. See the staircase? I think there's a basement."

They began walking down the stairs, sticking close to the wall to avoid tumbling over the railing-less side. Aina's anticipation rose as they did, her heart beating so loudly in her ears, she feared it would give them away.

It was nearly pitch-black down here, which she supposed made sense if they'd wanted to keep this hideout a secret. They must have set up some kind of bribe with the factory managers. The stairway creaked under their footsteps, and she winced each time, expecting a sleeping Jackal downstairs to wake up and start shooting at the staircase any moment now.

When they reached the bottom, she blinked a few times to adjust her eyes to the darkness. It was empty, their breathing the only sound. Her heart sank, but then she shook away the disappointment. Even if Kohl wasn't here, they could find something to help track him down.

A few of the windows above let in moonlight that illuminated the space. Unused or broken machinery spread around the room in a sort of maze. A single wooden door was in the far corner of the basement. Rows of cots lined two of the walls, dust swirling in the moonlight above them. In the dark corners were boxes of what might be supplies or weapons.

She pointed to one of the boxes, and Teo moved forward to check it. But before he got more than a few steps, the door in the corner creaked open.

Aina threw herself behind one of the tall textile machines that stood near the stairway. Teo squeezed in next to her a moment later while Raurie and Ryuu hid behind another machine.

Torchlight shone through the door as three men entered, their footsteps echoing off the basement floor. Through the door, Aina could make out the rocky, rough-hewn walls of a tunnel. Her hand gripped her knife so tightly, she thought she might break the handle, but Kohl wasn't part of the group. One of the men's sleeves were rolled up to show the tattoo of a Jackal's open jaw. They left the door open, and slow-moving footsteps sounded from farther down the tunnel—more people coming.

When Ryuu squeezed a little bit more behind the machine, his shoes squeaked on the floor and one of the Jackals looked up.

"Thought I heard something," he mumbled, his voice carrying in the quiet.

"Rats," said one of the other Jackals in a dismissive tone. "You got what we need from the Blood King?"

Aina stiffened at those words, leaning forward around the machine as far as she dared to see what this could be. The other Jackal nodded and flashed something in his pocket. Its smooth surface glinted in the torchlight, but he put it away so quickly, Aina couldn't tell what it was.

"How many more of these shipments will Bautix be doing?"

the third one hissed, casting a quick glance upward as if he feared someone could hear them. "Feels like we're getting a new one every other day."

"He has to wait for the smuggler from Kaiyan to return to act," the first one said. "These shipments, they're smaller parts of a whole that the smuggler is sending in before his return."

A minute of silence passed, punctuated only by labored breathing and the still-approaching footsteps coming from the tunnel. Then, four more men entered carrying two heavy boxes between them—and none of them bore Jackal tattoos. The Jackals stepped aside to let the men pass, then stood with their backs to the door they'd all come through.

The third Jackal's eyes flicked up once more, and this time, Aina followed his gaze to the manager's office on the second floor. Three figures had stepped into the light, and Aina cursed herself for not checking that room before. She squinted, trying to make them out, when one of the Jackals on this floor spoke again.

"You've all been very helpful, bringing this delivery," he announced to the men who'd carried in the crates. One of the crates was slightly open, and Aina could make out the edge of a grenade and the barrel of a gun. "I have your payment right here."

Then, he pulled out from his pocket what he'd shown the other Jackals before, something from Kohl. The glass sphere shone brightly under the torchlight, with a clear liquid inside, smoke rising off it and fogging the inside of the sphere. Aina's breath caught, and she beckoned the others to retreat with her toward the stairs leading out of the basement.

Before any of the men who'd brought the weapons could do more than lean forward to see what the Jackal was showing them, the Jackal threw the sphere on the ground and it shattered.

Smoke rose into the air as the Jackals vanished into the side door and slammed it shut behind them. A lock sounded.

"Run!" Aina whispered back to her friends as soon as they reached the steps.

"They tricked us, those goddess-forsaken bastards!" shouted one of the men who'd brought the weapons.

He ran to the door the Jackals had left through and began pounding on it, but it wouldn't break, even when he slammed his body into it. Risking a glance over her shoulder as they raced up the stairs, Aina watched as one of the other men collapsed on the floor. His eyes stared glass-like at the ceiling, the shadows of machinery towering over him while Kohl's poison choked the air.

"What kind of poison is that?" Raurie asked as the other two men reached the staircase and began racing toward them.

"Move!" one of the smugglers shouted behind Aina, push-ing so hard she almost fell off the stairs. Ryuu grabbed her by the elbow to stop her fall while Teo caught up to the smuggler, yanked him back from the top step, and shoved him off the side of the stairs. They reached the first floor, the whole factory dark except the light from the second-floor managers' office. The three people there began to turn away, and the glint of a diamond earring caught Aina's eye.

The fluorescent light revealed the man's face: a tightly coiled red beard, starkly pale skin on a chiseled face, and sharp blue eyes. "Bautix," Aina whispered as he lifted his chin at her in a taunting gesture.

She'd make him tell her where Kohl was hiding—and then she'd slit his throat. The last smuggler fled to the nearest door. He tried to shove it open, but something outside blocked the exit. They were trapped, and the poison would drift up to the factory's main floor in seconds if they didn't move. Aina raced to the next flight of stairs, with Teo, Ryuu, and Raurie right behind her. Teo fired into the window on the second floor. It shattered, spraying glass everywhere, and the three men inside ducked. But Bautix hardly looked shaken—he stood straight, facing them with an amused grimace on his face.

They reached the second floor just as Bautix vanished through a door in the back. The two men with him, most likely Jackals, lifted their guns.

Aina slammed her back into the wall, dodging the first shot. Ryuu fired back, one of his bullets hitting and instantly killing a Jackal.

Before the second Jackal could shoot them, Aina leapt through the window and knocked the gun out of his hand. It skidded across the floor, and Raurie put a knife to the man's throat a breath later. Aina raced out the door to find Bautix.

The door led to a hallway that passed through the back of-fices. The hallway was drafty, with all the windows open, and a sudden wind brought goose bumps to her skin. She raced down the hall, checking through each door, but there was no staircase to the other floors, and Bautix wasn't in any of the rooms. She ran to the fire escape instead, but didn't see him anywhere on it, nor on any of the surrounding streets.

She slammed her fist on the railing. It may have been years since he'd actually fought in Sumerand's army, but clearly the skills hadn't left him.

A moment later, Teo, Raurie, and Ryuu joined her on the fire escape, their shoes clanging against the metal surface. "Bautix is gone," Aina said, her voice harsh. "This was a waste of time. Kohl wasn't here, and now this hideout is compromised. They won't stay here anymore."

In silence, they left the warehouse by the fire escape and circled back to the front to meet Tannis and Lill. As they did, Kohl's words came back to Aina, calling her a broken blade that couldn't do its job and needed to be thrown out. She curled her hands into fists, knuckles straining.

"What would you do without me?" he'd asked one day several years ago when he'd spotted a grunt from a rival gang about to mug her in an alley off Lyra Avenue. Aina, only fourteen and still getting used to her training, hadn't seen the boy, but Kohl had found him almost instantly.

"I don't know," she'd muttered, unable to say why it had frustrated her so much at the time. Even then, she'd known agreeing with him was the safest choice.

She wished she could go back in time and change her answer, tell him she'd never needed him at all. If that boy had mugged her, she would have dealt with the consequences. If Kohl had never brought her into the Dom, she would have found her own path. She wouldn't have starved to death or suffocated on glue, alone in a back alley of Kosín.

She tried to convince herself of that now, but every time she came close to finding him, he vanished. Every time she had a clue, it proved fruitless.

Kohl had money, an entire gang working for him, and plenty of skill and weapons. She had all of that too, and they would continue running for each other's throats and just missing until one of them had something that would give them the upper hand.

Something to put her a step ahead of him, something Kohl himself had never even dared to do. Something to give her power that the rich, like Bautix, hated simply because it wasn't money and steel. Something the people of this city had always turned to when they had nothing else.

Her parents had used it to heal. She would use it to kill. She would beat Kohl at his own game.

Once they'd met with Tannis and Lill and retreated to an

alley nearby, Aina looked around at them all and voiced what everyone had feared since the civil war.

"I want to learn to use blood magic," she said, her voice a whisper yet freezing all of them in place. "To fight."

"You what?" Lill asked. "Are you even an Inosen?"

Their alley was empty, lit only by moonlight streaming in from the main road. Water dripped from a pipe into a puddle near the mouth of the alley, and a rat dug through garbage with tiny, jerking movements. No other sounds broke the quiet night, but the hair on the back of Aina's neck still rose. Anyone could be listening in Kosín.

But part of her no longer cared. Kohl and Bautix feared nothing, and neither would she.

"My parents were Inosen, and I used to be," she said in a harsh tone. "I know the magic is risky, but—"

"Yeah, anyone seen using it gets instantly killed by the Diamond Guards," Lill said, tossing her hands in the air.

"You think I can't handle any Diamond Guards who come after me?" Aina asked flatly, one hand gripping a knife out of frustration—and if Lill didn't shut up, she might use it on her. "I want to use the magic to fight, but even a tracking spell would be useful at this point. I can't kill anyone if I don't know where they are."

"I asked my aunt June about doing a tracking spell to find Bautix," Raurie said, crossing her arms, an uncomfortable look on her face. "She doesn't want to get involved in anything to do with this mess, and none of the Sacoren will agree to bless us to use magic—even for nonviolent reasons. They know we're angry enough to fight with it, if it came down to it."

"And you have every right to be angry," Ryuu said immediately. Lill narrowed her eyes at him, like she thought he might be acting nice as some sort of elaborate ruse.

"The magic puts a target on your back no matter what you're using it for," Teo spoke up, not bothering to lower his voice; it seemed to echo off the concrete walls around them. "But we walk around with targets on us every day; this is no different. And we need as many weapons as we can get to stand up to them. It's a good plan."

Raurie's gaze trailed northward then, and even with buildings blocking the view, Aina could tell Raurie was looking toward the Tower of Steel—the seat of all government and economics in the country of Sumerand, led by the four governors who comprised the Sentinel. Though none of them could see it from here, its presence always hung over the city like a shroud.

"They're also hoping the Sentinel will lift the ban on our religion, since Bautix isn't there anymore," Raurie said, the silver moon adding a soft glow to the brown skin of her cheeks. "But when has the Sentinel ever helped us?"

"Never," Aina agreed. "And if Bautix takes back the Tower, it won't matter what the rest of the Sentinel thinks. He'll kill them to rule on his own, and we won't stand a chance. If I can find a way to learn the magic, would you want to join?"

Silence fell on the group as everyone pondered the question, but Aina's determination only grew. She had no clue where to find a Sacoren—a priest for Inosen, like June's aunt, who could bless others with the ability to use blood magic—but she'd worry about that later.

After a long minute, Ryuu spoke up first. "I will."

Lill's eyes cut to him sharply, as if she couldn't believe what he'd said. "Why would you? You're not an Inosen, and it's not like Bautix would ever have a reason to fight you at your pretty mansion in Amethyst Hill. When was the last time you were punished for your beliefs, Steel boy?"

"When I lost my parents for them daring to help the people who shared their faith. I'll do whatever I can to help." He brushed back the black bangs that had fallen in front of his face and met Aina's eyes. Her heart ached for him—she remembered how they'd met, how they'd learned to trust each other while coming from completely different lives—and now she couldn't imagine not being friends with him. She couldn't blame Lill for doubting a Steel by default. But Ryuu had more than proved himself.

"Ryuu lost his whole family because of Bautix and Kohl," she said softly to Lill. "If there's any Steel we can trust, it's him."

Lill didn't reply, but her cheeks reddened a little as she backed down. Then she cleared her throat and said, "I'll do it. I want to fight the Jackals and Bautix."

"I'm sick of hiding and playing it safe," Raurie said, tearing her eyes away from the Tower and looking out at the streets around them. "My aunt is scared of what will happen if we fight back, but it's better than sitting and waiting for an attack, or hoping for the Sentinel to do anything for us. We have to help ourselves. I'm in."

They split up soon after that—Teo to his apartment north of Center, Ryuu to Amethyst Hill, and Raurie and Lill to the safe house, while Aina and Tannis walked back to the Dom together. They kept quiet as they walked, and Aina noticed Tannis hadn't said a word since Aina suggested learning blood magic. Her expression gave away nothing now either; her eyes were fixed on the horizon ahead, as if she were searching for the Dom.

The streets narrowed as they walked deeper into the Stacks, where slanted metal and cardboard homes stood so close together on the steep hills that it looked like they were stacked on top of one another. Though it was the place Aina felt most comfortable, her senses heightened now. All her life, she'd never seen it so quiet, so empty of life. The only people outside were those who had nowhere else to go. She began to count down the blocks toward reaching the Dom, a ritual she now did every night. In her dreams, it always disappeared in a puff of smoke, a mirage that had never really been there.

They turned down the next street and stopped in their tracks at the mouth of the road. Three bodies lay on the dirt road, their throats slit. The rust scent of blood choked the air. The wood-slab door of a nearby home swung open in the summer breeze with an eerie creak.

"More dead," Tannis said. "Bautix is having the Jackals kill anyone who doesn't want to work with them."

They took another road, the silver and red moons lighting the path ahead of them toward the eastern shore of the Minos River that circled the city. The whole way, Aina thought of Bautix's threat, his challenging smirk, the violence growing closer to the Dom every day—and it made her more determined to fight back.

When they were a few streets away from the Dom, Tannis pulled a crinkled piece of paper from her pocket. "For the past week, I've been spying on some Jackals who were giving letters to a janitor who works at the Tower. I cornered him earlier today and got this."

Aina took the note and read quickly. It didn't make much sense—it listed measurements and coordinates she didn't understand. But that wasn't what made her heart beat faster and her hands grow so clammy, she almost dropped the note.

"This is in Kohl's handwriting." She said the words softly, not sure how much this mattered. All the threatening notes that had been left in front of her employees throughout the city had been in varying handwriting she didn't recognize, like the one she'd seen earlier tonight. But something about this note was important, if Kohl had written it himself.

"Where's the janitor?" Aina asked, and Tannis raised an eyebrow. "You killed him, then. Did he give you any information before you did?"

Tannis gave a half-shrug, half-nod. "He couldn't read, so he didn't know what any of the previous letters said. The Jackals gave them to him to deliver to the Tower, but he didn't hand them off to any one person. He would leave them tied to the legs of a bench in the courtyard, or in cracks in the wall. The Jackals told him where to put them each time. Whatever is going on, it's clear there's a traitor in the Tower. Probably more than one. They could easily help Bautix find a way in when he decides to attack."

"If he attacks the Tower, he'll kill the rest of the Sentinel and rule by himself." The words made goose bumps rise on Aina's arms. "It will be a bloodbath. We won't only have Kohl to worry about anymore."

Neither of them said anything for a few minutes. The wind blew the scent of the river toward them, and the sound of crickets chirping reached her ears. Maybe Kohl wanted the Dom for himself, but Bautix would destroy it if the people inside weren't aligned with him. She gulped, suddenly wanting to run back home and check that it was still there.

"I don't care what happens to the Sentinel, though," Tannis

said, her voice as quiet as the steady flow of the river nearby.
"The Steels think Kaiyanis people are dirt in this country. They
think we're all killers and thieves—" Catching Aina's raised eyebrow, she clarified, "Okay, *I'm* a killer, and Mirran *is* a thief, but
most Kaiyanis aren't. I grew up in a fishing village. Just a lot of
poverty and slavery there."

Aina bit her lip while she considered a response. This was the
most Tannis had ever said about her past at once, and she was
already shutting down—shuttering the emotion on her face, staring straight ahead again. The moonlight brightened Tannis's hair
and glinted off the throwing stars and pistols she wore, so she
looked ethereal, like some kind of lethal fairy, and Aina caught
herself staring—she'd always found Tannis pretty.

"We've worked together for six years, but we haven't gotten
to know each other that well," Aina finally said. "I was afraid to
show loyalty to anyone but him, and you didn't want to trust a
single soul. And we both know that when working with Kohl, you
get used to hiding things."

When Tannis looked back at her, her gold eyes were bright
and cautious, and she clenched her jaw. If there was anyone else
who could understand what working with Kohl was like, it was
Tannis.

"When I was twelve," Aina continued, "I thanked him for
bringing me to the Dom. Every time I made a mistake after that,
he reminded me he could put me back on the streets whenever
he wanted. Any weakness you reveal, he uses it to manipulate
you, so you try to keep as much of yourself a secret as you can."
She drew in a quick breath, her hands trembling a little as she
dug them into her pockets. "But we shouldn't have to do that
with each other. You had to find your own way to Sumerand as
a child, didn't you?"

"I've always told people I smuggled myself onto a ship to come here as a child, but that's a lie," Tannis murmured, and when she spoke next, her words tumbled out like she'd been holding them in so long, they all needed to come out at once. "The day I was born, my father fell off a ladder at work and broke a leg. On my first birthday, he caught a plague sweeping down the eastern coast. He healed from that, but could still hardly work with his damaged leg. We starved a little more every year. On my fourth birthday, he fell ill to the same plague and died a few days later." She let out a laugh of disbelief. "My mother grew very . . . paranoid. She convinced herself it was my fault he died and my fault we were so poor. She thought of me as a plague." Her lips and voice shook as she forced out the next words, blue hair shrouding half her face from view. "When I was eight, she sold me to a slaver taking children to Kosín. I worked in the kitchen of a casino. Maybe a few months later, maybe a year, I don't know, I'd starved myself enough to slip through the bars on my room's window. I jumped from the third floor. It was winter, and the snow broke my fall. When I landed outside at the back door of the kitchens, I saw that the man guarding us had fallen asleep. I could have taken his keys. I could have saved more of the people they'd brought over. But I was a coward. I ran and left them there."

Aina felt a pang in her heart at those words and stepped closer to Tannis. She imagined herself as a child, running whenever someone else on the streets approached her even if they might have been able to help. Running from the scene of her parents' murder while their bodies were discarded.

"That's when you joined the Vultures?" Aina asked. "And then worked with Kohl?"

Tannis nodded. "When I was fifteen, I vowed to go back and break out anyone that I could. One day, I heard of a father and daughter. The father was a Sacoren; he'd lived here almost his whole life before he and his daughter were caught and made house servants for a rich Diamond Guard captain in Rose Court."

Aina nodded, the old stories coming back to her. "They used to offer captured Inosen either death, prison, or indenture that never really ends. So he offered himself and his daughter?"

"Yes, that's what he did. He never had his diamonds removed, and he and his daughter could live together in the house of that captain. But years after the war, they were still stuck there. I helped them escape, but the daughter was shot and killed in the process. After the father got settled in a new home, he met with me and said I could always come to him for help. And he said that if war ever strikes again, he would use his powers in the way Verrain had, the way he wished he had used them against the Diamond Guard when his daughter was killed. There was nothing he could do for her once the bullet hit her brain, but he still wished he'd fought back instead of ran." She sighed and met Aina's eyes. "Everyone in this city owes someone something, don't they? We're all running from some kind of guilt, trying to make up for it with deals and promises. But I don't see a point in fighting for the past anymore. The Dom is my home and my future. And if that means you want me to introduce you to this Sacoren, I will."

"Thank you," Aina said, trying to hide her shock at everything Tannis had told her. "Why didn't you mention anything about him earlier?"

Tannis's gold eyes softened, and her next words made Aina's heart race in a different way. "Maybe because I trust you. I didn't feel comfortable telling the truth of what happened to everyone, but . . . I wanted you to know. I know we both have a lot of dark spots in our past, but since we're leading the tradehouses together now, maybe we can help each other get rid of them."

Tannis moved closer, leaving only a few inches of space between them—and Aina didn't know how to reply. How many times had Kohl said kind words to her like Tannis just did, only to punish and taunt her later? She'd fallen for someone who only knew how to hurt her and had no idea how to move on from it. Every time she considered it, memories of Kohl came back and her throat closed up, her hands shook, her thoughts scattered. If she allowed anyone to touch her again, or anyone to kiss her, who was to say they wouldn't try to ensnare her next? Or that she wouldn't hurt them too? "Tannis," she began. "I don't know what—"

"It's okay, I get it," Tannis said quickly, stepping back. "I'll ask the Sacoren to meet us tomorrow, all right?" They walked the rest of the way to the Dom in silence, Tannis slightly ahead of her. Aina's ears burned the entire way back. What was wrong with her? Why couldn't she get over the pain Kohl had caused?

They soon reached the Dom and Aina breathed a small sigh in relief—it was still there. Willow trees stood out front, blocking anyone on the street from seeing through the barred windows of the two-story building. The silver moon washed out the white walls while the red moon's light gleamed against the oak door. Tannis walked in ahead of her, giving her one awkward grimace before going upstairs. The Dom was quiet at this hour, but well lit and warm. Tannis decorated in ways Kohl had never allowed. Pale yellow electric lights hung from the ceiling all the way down the hall in the shape of small stars, and a tall pot of flowers stood next to the staircase. Kohl had always kept the place cold and miserable, apart from his own office, all in an effort to keep his employees fighting to get what he had.

Aina entered the office a moment later. A candle cast a soft orange glow over the bookshelf, the chest of drawers, and the desk. She tensed like she always did at the sight of Kohl's old things strewn about, like he might be watching her from the face of the clock, the whorls on the wooden desk, or the window behind it. The small, porcelain horse that had belonged to her mother sat on the desk now, dust-covered and like a specter in the dark room. Candlelight played off it, glimmering on the ceramic-like fireflies' reflections over the river. She reached out, but halfway there, her fingers trembled and she let her hand fall back to her side.

If she touched it, she might remember her mother humming as she dusted the horse and everything else in their one-room home. If she picked it up, she'd remember Kohl holding it out to her without the slightest bit of remorse on his face; proof that he'd been her parents' murderer.

Her hand curled into a fist at her side. She wanted to slam the small statue into the wall and shatter it into a hundred pieces simply because Kohl had given it to her.

But it was the only thing she had left of her parents. The old copy of the Nos Inoken on their table, the dried yellow flowers her mother had liked to put in her hair, the wire dolls Aina had played with, the overalls her father had worn to work every day that carried his lemon and cedar wood scent—all of that was gone.

With a frustrated huff of air, she turned away from the desk, leaving the horse untouched like she did every night. She shrugged off her jacket and draped her bloodstained scarf over the back of the desk chair, which made it look like it was more her own than some remnant of Kohl's. It was getting too hot to wear them outside now, anyway. And maybe, seeing them in here would help her be less afraid of this room. Less afraid of ever being under his control again.

She went upstairs then, passing the room she shared with Tannis and Mirran, another employee who'd been in the Dom for years, and approached the bedroom where the recruits slept.

Johana, the youngest one whom Kohl had only brought in a year ago, would be on the roof doing an overnight watch of the surrounding area. The other recruits—Kushik and Markus—were two thirteen-year-old boys who'd lived at the Dom for a few years. Aina had started sending them on jobs without supervision as long as they stayed together, and now they were still awake, chatting and throwing knives at a target on the wall to keep themselves alert before heading out.

When she knocked on the door, they both snapped to attention and their knives dropped to the floor.

"Before you go on your job tonight, can you deliver a message?" she asked, and they both nodded, asking no questions as she instructed them to go to Ryuu's mansion, Teo's apartment, and the safe house where Raurie and Lill lived, and ask them all to meet outside the safe house at sunset the next day.

Once the recruits were well-trained enough, she'd let them go on jobs alone and assign them specific roles: Blades, who would be assassins like her and Tannis; Foxes, who were thieves like Mirran; and Shadows, who were spies like the one Aina had killed earlier tonight. She only hoped they would all live long enough to get those jobs in the first place.

She tried to sleep, but restfulness eluded her. The lead on the warehouse tonight hadn't led her to Kohl, and she was no closer to finding him than she was yesterday, yet her enemies only multiplied: Kohl, Bautix, the Jackals, even one of her own tradehouses. Half-awake, half-asleep, she dreamed of Kohl holding out her mother's porcelain horse to her, his voice mocking as he explained that he'd saved her life by taking her into the Dom.

I was just doing a job, Aina, he said over and over in the dream, holding out the small statue with his arm tattooed with the mark of his old gang. The vulture hung by a string of diamonds stared at her. The vulture came back to life, and the diamonds wrapped themselves around her throat, choking her while he laughed and whispered that he'd save her again if she begged him to.

Help me, she said in the dream, and when she woke up covered in sweat, she wondered how far she could really go without needing him.

5

Sunlight flashed through the training room window and shone on Markus's sweat-streaked face as he swung forward. Aina dodged his punch with a quick step to the side.

When he pivoted, the fear showed on his face: forehead creased in concentration, breath heavy and labored.

Aina struck out with the wooden stick she held. He dodged, but a little too late; it glanced off his side instead of jabbing him in the stomach. With his opposite hand, he moved to strike her newly open side, but she blocked it with her elbow.

Markus's next step brought him forward, but when Aina stuck out her leg, he tripped, sucking in air sharply. Aina grabbed him by the shoulder and hauled him upright, placing her wooden stick across his neck.

"Dead," she said, then stepped back.

"I need a break," he said, bending over to place his hands on his knees. Kushik and Johana both stepped forward, looking eager to take his spot in practice, but Aina held up her hand to stop them.

"Do you think an enemy will give you a break?" she asked. "If you're tired, go on the defensive and let your energy come back. When you're fighting for your life, it will." She nodded at Kushik and Johana. "What else could he have done better?"

"He got too close to you," Johana said in a rush.

"He was trying to land hits, but that left him open," Kushik added.

Markus stood up straight, wiped the hair away from his face, then sighed. "I won't be so reckless next time."

"I know," Aina said under her breath, but she knew that as long as they were doing this with wooden sticks, he wouldn't take it seriously. Kohl had only used them to train her for a month and then switched to real blades. The phantom pain returned, old scars reminding her of how harsh his training could get. Her hands curled into fists. She was trying to treat her employees more fairly, but what good was that when they could learn quicker if she pushed them? Taking a deep breath, she said, "Kushik, you're next."

While Markus and Johana moved to sit at the edge of the mats and Kushik stepped into the center, brimming with energy, Aina moved to the far wall where a rack of weapons hung. A small washbasin stood next to it with a grimy mirror above. She could see half of her face—wisps of black hair, the copper skin tone common of people from Mil Cimas, the scars and fading bruises that were always a part of her job, the sunken look of her eyes that she didn't think would ever go away after years addicted to glue. She still hadn't decided what kind of leader she would be, but she knew she'd only survived this long because Kohl hadn't gone easy on her. Dropping the wooden stick to the floor, she selected a long, curved blade from the rack.

Kushik swallowed hard when he watched her approach with it, and his earlier excitement ebbed—quickly replaced by the resigned determination she recognized in every recruit while training with Kohl's methods, a look she'd used to give herself in the mirror every night. She watched with disappointment swirling through her; hating that Kohl's way, in this regard, was probably the best.

"All of you need to step it up," she said in a hollow tone, re-membering the bodies she and Tannis had seen last night, the threats from Bautix, the spy from Thunder, the knowledge that Kohl would stop at nothing to get the Dom back. "I know none of you were probably even born during the last war. I was a child. But don't be surprised if another one starts up again." She took a deep breath, the sun in her eyes. "You need to learn to fight against real weapons while having none of your own, because you will be in that position at some point. You need to learn to kill with nothing but your hands, to stop people from doing the same to you. That's how you survive: keep drawing blood, show no weakness, or you'll be the one who's bleeding."

A nerve-filled silence followed her statement, but she gave them no time for it to soak in. Soon she would leave to meet the Sacoren that Tannis knew and learn the Mothers' magic—another weapon on top of the one she held.

She stood across from Kushik, blade held ready in her right hand. "Begin."

An hour later, Aina had left the Dom and approached the en-trance to the safe house, breathing in the summer air. The sun sent deep orange streaks westward over the Stacks, lighting the puddles on the dirt roads left from an afternoon rain.

Miles to the north, the Tower stood starkly against the orange and gray sky. Its black-rock spires touched the thick clouds that were sure to unleash another deluge tonight.

It will be a bloodbath. Tannis's words from yesterday came back to her now. If Bautix managed to kill all four members of the Sentinel and take over within a week like he'd promised, then they didn't have long at all to prepare for war.

She thought of Kohl, who would be helping Bautix try to take back the city, and disgust surged through her. Their battle for the city got so many innocent people, like the Inosen, killed.

Death wasn't enough of a punishment for Kohl. She'd kill him, but she'd find a way to make him pay for everything he'd done before she did.

She spotted Teo first, leaning against the side of a house with his arms crossed over his chest and staring southward. Raurie, Ryuu, Tannis, and Lill walked toward them from the safe house a block away. The path to the safe house was through a sewer entrance a block away, but since Raurie and Lill would be hiding this magic from the rest of the Inosen, they'd chosen to meet at a slight distance instead.

When she came up to Teo, he nodded toward Tannis and asked in a low voice, "Can you trust this man she knows?"

She shrugged one shoulder. "He owes her, which is as close to trust as you can get with most people in this city."

"Did anyone notice you leave?" she asked Raurie and Lill once the others reached them.

"Since everyone has moved in today, there are some supplies we're missing," Lill said. "They usually send the younger ones of us to go out and buy food and things, so we volunteered. We'll have to pick up supplies on the way back to cover ourselves."

Aina nodded. "Let's go then, so you don't have to take too long."

They walked out of the Stacks then and toward Lyra Avenue, the longest street in the city, which stretched from the eastern tip of the Stacks all the way through the immigrant neighborhood of the Wings and up north to Rose Court. With increased violence in the Stacks, the lower end of Lyra Avenue was unusually empty for summer. A few hawkers stood outside shops with tables full of wares, but their voices echoed off the towering walls of brick apartments on either side as Aina's group walked through.

A few blocks later, they reached the more crowded part of Lyra Avenue, and flashing lights greeted them. Different languages filled the air as tourists and locals crossed the street between shops, taverns, and casinos.

One of the tradehouses occupied the back of a currency exchange store, and both Aina and Tannis looked toward it now. Their youngest recruit had set up a stall on the street stocked with cheap souvenirs for tourists, but Aina knew they actually sold ammunition and pistols. Since she'd exposed Bautix's secret arms business last month and the Sentinel shut it down, it had grown more difficult to buy weapons in bulk in the city. His business had held a near monopoly on any firepower, but now smaller businesses could take advantage of the hole in the market. The boy jumped to his feet when he saw Aina and Tannis, then beckoned them over, eyes wide.

"What is it?" Aina asked once they got close enough.

"Diamond Guards," he muttered, then leaned forward and gestured toward a cheap jewelry store a few doors ahead.

He didn't have to say much more; a moment later, the door was kicked open and two guards hauled out a man with blood covering his face. One shoved him to his knees while the other tossed a handful of rough diamonds on the ground before slamming the butt of his gun into the man's face.

Tannis sighed next to her. "Three, two—"

A gunshot fired and the man fell forward, blood spilling from his head onto the pavement. A gaggle of tourists nearby screamed and backed away, probably regretting venturing down here from Rose Court.

Aina shook her head at the sight of the dead man. Since taking over the Dom, she hadn't needed to sell diamonds on the side anymore—her role as boss paid more than enough. But it was still hard to get rid of the bone-deep fear all smugglers lived with.

"Aina," Ryuu said through gritted teeth, and his eyes trailed ahead of them, toward the busier blocks of Lyra Avenue.

Another pair of Diamond Guards stood outside a bank a block away, watching them and whispering to each other. Aina swore under her breath. Enough of her group was heavily armed to draw attention, and they'd come from the direction of the Stacks—the guards always found reasons to harass people from the south of the city. Since Kohl had worked directly with Bautix, who'd commanded the Diamond Guards, he'd gotten plenty of special treatment. She and Tannis had their own bribes in place, but not with any of the guards she saw here.

She gestured for everyone to follow her lead, and they continued walking. Gaudy red and gold lights loomed ahead to welcome them to a row of casinos and burlesque theaters. Aina sensed the guards' eyes on their backs as they blended in with the busier crowds.

"Let's go in through the back," Tannis said, coming up next to them and nodding toward an alley. "The guards are following us."

Without another word, Tannis led the way to the alley service door for a casino decked in green with a red-brick apartment above it. While the others slipped inside, Aina watched for the Diamond Guards. Their heads bobbed above the rest of the crowd, and just as she stepped inside behind Teo, one turned in their direction. She jerked her head back from view, closed the door, and met the others in a large kitchen pantry.

When she nodded, they moved again, exiting through a kitchen—ignoring the cooks and waiters who looked up at them in confusion—and then left the double doors to step onto the main floor of the casino.

With hollow eyes and her jaw clenched tight, Tannis led them past gambling tables, women delivering drinks in short dresses, and card dealers calling out numbers and suits. Aina wondered, with a sinking feeling in her gut, if this was the place Tannis had been brought as a child.

They climbed a cordoned-off staircase and entered a long hallway. Some men and women stood outside the doors, whispering and beckoning to those who walked by. Broken glass strewed all along the carpet, which smelled faintly of urine and blood.

A child peeked out from behind her father's legs at one doorway, where he spoke in Kaiyanis to a few people huddled around the entrance with heavy backpacks and the glint of a blade at one of their belts. Tannis frowned, one hand trailing to a knife Aina knew she kept up her sleeve. Aina did the same, recognizing these men weren't mere tourists.

Tannis stopped in front of a door at the end of the hall and knocked softly. Everyone in the group had gone silent, though the floor creaked under their boots as they shifted their weight and waited.

At first, no one answered, so Tannis knocked again. Aina glanced behind them to make sure no one was watching too closely, but everyone in this hall was far too focused on their own pursuits to care what they were doing in this shady building. She doubted anything could surprise the people here.

A muffled shuffling noise came from beyond the door. A crack appeared as the door creaked open. The barrel of a gun poked through with a thin face above it, shrouded by a shock of blue hair and decorated with a line of three diamonds at the top. Every Sacoren received these three diamonds embedded in their forehead, marking that the Mothers had spoken to them, that they could lead worship services, interpret the Nos Inoken, and bless people to use magic. But unlike every other Sacoren Aina had ever met, this one didn't have a black arc tattooed in the same place as the diamonds.

Inosen caught worshiping the Mothers faced imprisonment, and those caught using magic were shot on sight. But the Diamond Guards often released Sacoren, after removing their diamonds and leaving tattoos in their place as a symbol that even the strongest among the Inosen were powerless against them. The Sacoren often repierced the diamonds themselves, but this man had never had them removed in the first place.

When the man locked eyes with Tannis, he opened the door and gestured them inside, then cast a sharp glance around the hallway before closing the door behind them. As they filed in, Tannis whispered with him in Kaiyanis for a moment and gestured toward the hall they'd come from. He answered quickly, with a dismissive shrug, then waved them all toward a sitting room adorned with tattered pillows and rugs.

"Amman oraske," he said to each of them as they entered—a common greeting among Inosen that meant "May the Mothers bless you."

"Amman min oraske," Aina said back, hearing Raurie, Lill, and Ryuu do the same. Tannis and Teo also said the words, but stumbled over them uncomfortably—neither of them had grown up with Inosen parents.

The Sacoren moved like a weasel, his movements jerky and furtive. The apartment was spotless, the floor even shining, but clearly lived in. She wondered when was the last time this man had walked outside. They each chose a pillow or an empty spot on the floor to sit on.

"Tannis told me you want to learn this magic." He spoke in such a low voice, Aina had to strain her ears to hear, and he twisted his hands in knots. "But not the normal way. You're not using it to heal, to create, to build love and peace like the Mothers wish."

"We're using it to fight," Aina said in a flat tone. She didn't see a point in hiding it, and she assumed he'd already guessed as much.

The man nodded, a knowing look in his eyes. "Verrain's methods can be useful, and in my opinion, are not evil by default. He originally wanted a compromise. He didn't want industry to take over the country, for faith to fall away—and he was right, wasn't he? How many people have forgotten the Mothers, or convinced themselves that the Mothers have abandoned Sumerand since the war? So Verrain shut down one factory, using this form of magic. But the Steels would not come to an agreement. They made him a villain and sent the army after him. And then yes, maybe he snapped and killed a lot of them, but his original intentions were good. Maybe he should have assassinated them one by one, quiet and quick—"

Tannis cleared her throat and gave the Sacoren an apologetic smile. "Sorry, Gevann, but we don't have too much time. Some of them live in the Inosen safe houses and will be asked questions if they're gone too long."

To the right of Tannis, Raurie and Lill both fidgeted nervously, and Gevann's eyes fell on them. He let out a long sigh. "You two have been Inosen your whole lives, I assume? Faithful to the Mothers, but your parents never let you receive the blessing to learn magic. It's too risky, leaves you open to being caught. But this type of blood magic, Verrain's usage of it, is even more dangerous . . . this magic will drain you."

"You know what else is draining?" Raurie said. "Hiding in fear all the time."

"We know this magic works differently, we know the risks, and

we're ready," Lill added, then nodded at the rest of the group—
Aina, Tannis, Teo, and Ryuu. "But they don't."

"What do you mean it drains you?" Aina asked, straining her
memory of her parents' use of the magic, but they'd only ever
used it in the normal way.

"There are a few spells the Mothers gave to us, listed out
clearly in the Nos Inoken, and that's what most Inosen will use in
their daily lives," Gevann explained, and when he reached toward
a chest of drawers nearby, the light through the window reflected
off the diamonds on his forehead. From a pile of books on top of
the chest, he picked up a tattered copy of the Nos Inoken. "You
know this holds all their teachings, all their hopes for us as their
children. The magic of blood and earth—using blood sacrificed
by the caster and diamonds from deep underground—is meant
to create unity."

"That's why the main spells work the way they do," Raurie
spoke up. "It works with blood and earth. Healing you from
blood loss, tracking spells, even creating things—people will use
the magic to fix their houses, for example, if it's made of earth or
materials from the ground. It's all under one spell."

"Amman inoke," Aina whispered. She'd heard it countless
times when her parents had used the magic to heal people in
their neighborhood. "'Amman' means the Mothers, and 'inoke'
calls them."

Lill nodded. "It's clearly explained in the Nos Inoken. But the
other spells, you have to look for—Verrain spent years combing
through the text and finding new ways to twist the magic. He
found spells that do the opposite of what the Mothers want:
making someone bleed instead of healing them, toppling a building or breaking swords in half, crumbling the earth and controlling it."

"The more you use it in this way, however," Gevann said in a warning tone, "the less you'll be able to use the normal spells. If you use it to kill, you might lose the ability to heal—even to heal yourself, and not only by magic; it could take longer for your body to heal normally as well. The Mothers allow us to make a choice, in that way. If you take a life, you lose a little of yours in return."

Aina, Teo, and Tannis all looked at one another. They'd each taken plenty of lives.

"It's also hard to focus after you use these spells," Raurie said. "Especially after making someone bleed. You won't bleed yourself, but you'll feel light-headed and weak like they do, until either they recover or they die."

"So what you're all saying is, make sure they die quickly so you can get on with business." Aina scoffed, but she couldn't deny this frightened her a little.

The Nos Inoken that Gevann still held drew her attention from the corner of her eye. The familiar red cover with silver text . . . ever since her parents died, it had been rare for her to see one up close. This magic was power, and that was what she wanted. Power was the only way to stay safe, the only reason she'd lived this long. She'd gather more of it around her until it became an invisible armor, and she'd never lose again.

"I'm ready," she said, and everyone else nodded or murmured in agreement. Without any more chatter, Gevann counted the people gathered in front of him, then disappeared to another room and returned a minute later carrying an armful of knives. Aina locked eyes with Ryuu next to her, and they both laughed under their breath. Everything about this man was a surprise.

While Gevann passed around knives in silence, Ryuu whispered to Aina, "Did you know there's a chance the Mothers might deny us if our faith isn't strong enough?"

She paused for a breath. "Wait, what?"

Ryuu grimaced. "The Sacoren is like a messenger between you and the Mothers, from what I know. It's the Mothers who decide to bless you. That's why people like Bautix, and most Steels, would never be able to use magic—it depends on your faith, and money is the only thing they believe in. Do you think the Mothers will agree to bless you?"

"They don't have any reason to," Aina said slowly, her heart sinking a little—she hadn't known there'd be some kind of test involved with this. "What about you?"

He shrugged, looking uneasy. "I hope the faith I do have will be enough. I need this to work." Then, lowering his voice and leaning toward her, he said, "My parents used their money and resources to help the Inosen, giving them places to hide, keeping them safe. They died for it. But I've done nothing, and even last month, when I tried to save my brother, that failed too. I need to do something to help."

His voice strained a little and his gaze broke away. He stared off toward the hallway, where the Sacoren rummaged through a chest of drawers, muttering under his breath.

"In my brother's will," Ryuu continued, "he left an addendum for me: to do whatever I could to destroy the Steels. All of them."

"While I commend your brother for hating the rich as much as I do," she said, frowning, "he can't mean your family too, can he? Your business?"

Since his brother's death, Ryuu had taken over their family business of mining diamonds and providing tools and machinery to construction companies, factories, and rail stations throughout the country. It was one of the most profitable businesses in all of Sumerand, and the work was showing; Ryuu's shoulders were tense in a way they hadn't been before, and there were bags under his eyes indicating he hadn't slept very well. When she'd first met him, she'd disliked him by default—but then he'd shown her he'd feared for his life as much as she had feared for her own at the time, and he'd believed both of them could be braver than they thought they were.

"I don't know," Ryuu admitted when the Sacoren returned. "But whatever happens, this magic is power against the Steels, something that stands apart from money and progress. I want to learn it, to do something to make up for failing them all."

"We'll learn it," Aina said slowly, placing a hand on his shoulder and waiting until he met her eyes—her heart aching at the uncertainty she saw there. "But none of what happened to your family is your fault, Ryuu. You don't have to beat yourself up over it."

The Sacoren Gevann now held a crystal chalice with a single diamond inside and cleared his throat to get their attention. The diamond mostly blended in with the cup, but Aina could spot a diamond from a hundred feet away. In his fist, he clenched more of the gems, and with his other hand, he picked up the copy of the Nos Inoken and flipped to a particular page.

"All right, well, the ceremony is quite simple, but you won't find it very appetizing." A smile flickered at his lips. "What you'll do is make a small cut on your upper arm as I walk by. I will collect your blood in this cup and wait until it touches the diamond. Then I will mark you and say the prayer to request the Mothers to bless you. You'll know if you've been accepted when the diamond fills with light. Your faith must be true. Note I say true, not strong. You must believe in the Mothers and their omnipotence, but you don't need to memorize the Nos Inoken or live your whole life without a sin. You are not expected to be perfect. Indeed, only the Mothers are perfect, and even Sacoren make errors in the Mothers' light." His jaw trembled slightly, his eyes losing their focus, but he shook himself out of it and finished explaining in a clear voice, "Once you've been accepted, you drink your blood that is inside the chalice; only a small taste is necessary. The ceremony will then be complete. Who wants to go first?"

"I will," Raurie said in a clear voice, already pulling up the sleeve on one arm.

She held the knife in her lap, utterly casual. The cedar brown of her eyes had lit up with fire, like amber gleaming in a bed of oak. Gevann approached Raurie, kneeling at her side while she made a cut on her arm with the smallest intake of breath. Blood dripped into the chalice and slid along its clear interior to coat the diamond at the center. The Sacoren began praying with complicated phrases in the old holy language that Aina only knew the very basics of. Raurie repeated the words under her breath in perfect time. The holy language was similar enough to the language of Marin, from where her grandparents had immigrated, that she understood it easily.

At the same time, the Sacoren dipped his finger into Raurie's blood and made a mark with it on her forehead in the shape of an arc, like the way the Sacoren wore their diamonds. Aina suddenly remembered what it represented. It was the arc of the bow carried by Kalaan, the goddess of love and war, and the curve of the harp carried by Isar, the goddess of hope and intellect. It was the simplest, yet clearest, sign of the Mothers.

A moment later, light shone through the chalice. The diamond appeared to be glowing, lit up like a small sun. As the light hit the crystal around it, a narrow rainbow stream painted the side of Raurie's face. She took the chalice in her hands, hesitating for the briefest second before tilting it back. She swallowed and lifted the cup away, her lips tinged with blood. She took a few deep breaths, then swallowed again and sat up straight.

The cut on her arm began to glow as well—a very thin, barely noticeable line of golden light. It shimmered for a moment, then faded away.

"There you are," Gevann said with a kind smile. "I hope you use this gift well, to be the beacon of the Mothers' hope in this misguided land and remind people the Mothers have never really left. You may clean up in the washroom down the hall." He looked at the others and rattled the diamond around in the chalice. "I'll wash this before moving on to the next person. We should finish quite soon."

The blessing worked the same for Lill, but when it was Tannis's turn, the diamond in the chalice remained dull. The whole room seemed to grow darker as they watched and waited, but after a full minute passed, Tannis handed the chalice back to Gevann with a grimace.

"No surprises there," she said with a shrug. "This religion isn't popular in the region of Kaiyan I grew up in."

Aina gulped as he moved on to Ryuu and Teo, not sure why she suddenly felt nervous. She'd spent most of her life trying to shove the Mothers' teachings out of her mind, knowing they'd condemn her for having taken so many lives. She'd never wanted their blessing until now, so why care? Suddenly, she imagined her parents' faces, filled with disappointment at who she'd become.

But whether her faith simply existed was another question . . . she'd seen magic work. She'd seen what happened to the people who believed in it. She'd spent hours in underground worship hideouts with her parents, weak candlelight illuminating the Mothers' words.

The blessing worked for Ryuu, but for Teo, the diamond remained dull.

He lifted one shoulder in a shrug, slight disappointment in his eyes. "It was worth a try, but my family is from Linash—I grew up hearing about a different god."

Gevann approached Aina then, and part of her wanted to tell him it would be a waste of time to try. But then she reminded herself why she was here: to gain a new power, something Kohl didn't have . . . yet another way to protect herself.

As she made the small cut on her arm, a chill spread through her. It suddenly felt like everyone in the room was watching her.

Her blood slid down the inside of the chalice, marking the diamond inside. Gevann's prayers filled her ears and seemed to grow louder as he drew the mark on her forehead with her blood. It was cold to the touch, making her tense up until his finger lifted away again.

Then she looked back at the chalice and gasped in disbelief. Like with Raurie, Ryuu, and Lill, the diamond glowed, reflecting in rainbow patterns through the glass. She took the chalice, forcing down her revulsion at the idea of drinking her own blood, then tilted it back. The coppery taste was wretched, but she forced herself to swallow it, pulling a face as she did.

"Were the Mothers taking a nap?" Tannis joked from across the room. "Are they aware of who they just blessed?"

Nobody had an answer. Aina shrugged, having no idea why the Mothers had agreed to bless her. She glanced down at the scar on her arm, shining with a brief light before fading away.

Maybe that was what they all were. Brief lights, shining with hope and making a mark on the world before they died. If there was anything she believed in, it was their ability to change the world their parents had left for them. Maybe that was why the Mothers had blessed her.

They finished then, thanked the Sacoren, and left. Night had fallen over Lyra Avenue, and with it came more heat and the ominous bank of slate-gray clouds overhead. Lill chatted casually with Ryuu, but Aina noticed how her gaze flicked to every corner, as if expecting a Diamond Guard to spot the small cuts on their arms from a distance and run over to arrest them.

While they shopped for the supplies that Raurie and Lill had promised to bring back to the safe house, Aina spoke with Raurie under the shadowed awning of the shop. They finalized a plan to meet the next evening to learn the spells they would use, quieting their voices whenever someone walked by them.

Fear charged the air, and Aina felt the hair rise on the back of her neck whenever a Diamond Guard walked near them or the wind blew sharply, long after everyone else went home and she and Tannis walked back to the Dom. She glanced at her healing cut, and a sense of power drowned out the fear.

A few minutes later, she and Tannis turned the corner and the Dom came into view.

Across the street, all the lights in the manor were on, illuminating figures on the roof. Two people were being dangled over the side. The exhilaration she'd briefly felt flickered out. She and Tannis slowed and, not taking their eyes off the Dom, withdrew their weapons. "Go," Aina whispered.

Tannis melted into the shadows, passing Aina a throwing star on the way.

6

Holding a scythe, Aina stepped out into the street. It was empty, the air tense and still. Everyone who lived in the area must have cleared out after they saw what was happening.

Mirran and Kushik had gone off together on a job for a client, so they weren't there. Johana and Markus were the ones being dangled by their collars over the roof of the manor with knives at their throats. When they saw her, their eyes widened and they squirmed in the grasps of their captors.

The heels of Aina's boots clicking across the pavement was the only sound as she approached the manor. Three other people stood on the roof; the two who held Johana and Markus, and another behind them. All bore the tattoo of a Jackal on their forearm.

Her eyes flicked to the windows then, pulse racing as she wondered if Kohl was already inside—if he'd burned her belongings, whetted a blade just for her.

A jolt of fear went through her, but she shoved it away and

sharpened her anger to the point of a knife. *Keep drawing blood, show no weakness, or you'll be the one who's bleeding.*

She recognized one of the Jackals. A tall, red-haired woman who held Johana in an iron-tight grip—she'd worked with the Jackals for years, maintaining a longer life span than almost any other gang member Aina had ever met.

"Good evening," Aina called up. "Your name is Kerys, isn't it? I didn't know we'd have visitors tonight or else I would have made you tea."

"We're not here for games," Kerys said, tightening her grip on Johana's collar so the girl began to choke, her face reddening as she kicked in midair. Aina gripped her knife tighter and willed Johana to hold on a little longer. "We have an offer for you, but not from Alsane Bautix. Do you think all these new people would have joined the Jackals on empty promises from someone who changes his hiding place every day? Someone who sends notes from the shadows when he's lost his power in this country?"

Aina froze, careful not to show any reaction on her face—did that mean Kohl wasn't waiting inside? Whatever they were here for, whatever this offer was, they clearly meant to threaten her into agreeing.

It made sense that Bautix's ranks weren't as fortified as he wanted them to be, especially with how Kohl had contributed to ruining his plans in the Tower last month. Kerys's words told her something else, though: Bautix was hiding, and he hadn't even shared his location with the Jackals.

"So who is this offer from?" she asked in a flat tone. There was really only one other person it could be, but it was hard to imagine him offering her anything, or sending anyone else to do it for him.

He never made compromises. He never showed mercy.

"The Blood King." Kerys's whisper was the only sound in the

quiet night. "If you take his job, your friends and your trade-house will be safe. Do you think he wants to be seen as second to Bautix if the disgraced general manages to take back power? Not a chance. Help him take down Bautix, and you'll both have everything you want."

Aina's breaths came shallowly as she tried to imagine Kohl's logic. He would never settle for second best, and if he stayed on Bautix's side, that's what he would always be. The Dom was his priority, as it was hers—they were each other's target. If he wanted to take down Bautix though . . . Images of the bodies she'd seen all over the Stacks flashed through her mind, getting closer and closer to the Dom every day. The note Bautix had left threatening her if she didn't join his side, his promise to take back the city, the poison he'd used in the warehouse almost killing her and all her friends. He was too dangerous to be left alive.

But Kohl was too dangerous to trust.

Her gaze flicked toward the Dom. She'd fought for this on her own, taken control of her own future. That was more than enough to prove she'd never needed him. "I've had enough of Kohl's promises and threats to last me a lifetime," she snapped. "He'd never let me walk free after I chased him out of the Dom, nearly killed him, and scared him into giving up Bautix's plans. And now you're telling me he's useless and can't take out Bautix without my help? Tell him that someone once told me to throw away things that don't work." She spat out those words, ignoring the sting as she remembered Kohl's voice calling her a useless Blade he had to get rid of. "You can tell Kohl to shove his offer up—"

"If threatening your employees isn't enough to show you how serious we are, we have collateral," Kerys spoke over her, her voice seeming to echo from the roof of the Dom. "Your friend, that handsome Linasian boy who lives north of Center. Teo, is it? Agree to work with the Blood King, or a messenger will run to a sniper with a rifle pointed at your friend's head, and tell him to shoot."

Aina squeezed the handle of her knife. *Teo. They had Teo.* His bright smile flashed in front of her eyes, and she imagined it disappearing forever. Her throat went dry.

A gunshot broke the night, and Aina flinched, imagining Teo under gunfire.

But then the Jackal standing behind the first two fell forward, a bullet hole in his head with Tannis behind him—she'd climbed onto the roof, blades and throwing stars gleaming, and now Tannis turned her gun on Kerys.

"Bring those two safely onto the roof and I'll reconsider killing you," came Tannis's harsh voice.

The other Jackal dug his blade a little deeper into Markus's neck, but Kerys shook her head once. Slowly, they brought Johana and Markus onto the roof, and Aina wondered why they weren't putting up more of a fight.

"Looks like you don't have a messenger anymore," she called up.

Kerys laughed, a chilling sound in the quiet night. "You think we only have one messenger? We thought you'd learned your lesson about backups at the Tower, but it looks like you're still making the same mistakes."

Aina locked eyes with Tannis, who gave her a barely perceptible nod. If Aina wanted to stop Teo from being killed, she'd have to do it herself. She took a deep breath before bending her knees into a slight crouch.

"You better hope your messenger can run faster than me."

She aimed the star Tannis had given her, its sharp, small blades glinting in the moonlight, and threw it. It slashed through the neck of the Jackal who'd been holding Markus. He grasped at the slit in his throat, then tripped over his own feet and tumbled off the roof.

Aina turned and ran. She sprinted up the hills that led out of the Stacks, her eyes on the roofs to check for a messenger to kill, but she saw no one. She had to rely on her speed and her knowledge of these streets, and trust that Tannis would be fine on her own against Kerys.

Now, Teo's life was the only thing that mattered.

She ran toward the Center, hearing Teo's voice telling her they could stand up to their enemies together.

What game was Kohl playing with her? He'd sent the Jackals instead of coming himself, and now she had to run through the city to stop Teo from being killed. Was it to make her panic and scramble so he could take the Dom, or would he step out from an alley and shoot her himself?

Streetlights glinted on windows and towering buildings as she shoved past pedestrians in the Center, ignoring the ones who yelled or pushed back. The streets grew narrower, more people pressing together. For the first time that night, with hundreds around her and the shadows of the buildings cloaking her, she allowed her fear to show on her face. All the nights she and Teo had spent together—drinking alone and laughing at their jobs, bandaging each other's wounds, sticking together even after Kohl kicked her out of the Dom and Teo's mother died—flashed through her mind.

She burst out of the crowded street and onto a row of apartments, gasping for breath—but there was no time to waste. When Teo's two-story apartment building came into view, she tucked away her fear again, scanning the area for a place where a sniper might be waiting.

Then she spotted it: a metallic glint on a balcony on the third floor of a restaurant across the street.

Bounding inside, she found a dining room on the first floor. A few stuttering candles on tables lit up the room, but there were no customers or employees. Incense burned somewhere out of sight, and all the walls were draped in red curtains. She blinked to adjust her eyes to the darkness, then moved toward the stairs leading to the second floor.

Just then, a man stood from his hiding spot behind a booth and shot at her. She pivoted, drawing in a quick breath as the bullet pinged off the wall next to her. As another bullet fired in her direction, she ducked and raced toward the stairs, the scent of smoke filling her lungs.

She took the steps two at a time, a rush of adrenaline pushing her forward, but halfway up, two more men stepped out from behind the curtains on the walls. Running at them in a crouch, she crashed into the knees of one of them, then disarmed the other and kicked him in the stomach. The first one stood again and his bulky arm wrapped around her throat—his sleeve slid up, revealing the Jackal tattoo on his forearm.

She slammed her head back into the Jackal's nose and wrenched herself free of his grasp. Blood rushed from his nose, spilling onto her neck and shoulders as she scrambled away from him. Racing up the stairs, she reached the next landing, the stairs to the third floor right in front of her—and then the click of a gun sounded behind her.

She ducked, the only thing she could do, but a dull pain coursed through her calf a moment later. Blood flowed down her leg as one shaking hand reached down to touch the wound. The bullet was lodged in deeply. Blood slicked her fingers when she drew her hand away.

Her eyes flicked up to the third floor. The sniper was going to kill Teo; there was no time to recover.

Wincing through the pain, Aina raced up to the third floor.

Footsteps pounded up the stairs behind her. Any second, some-one was going to shoot her again. All thoughts fled her mind except the need to get to the sniper before she was taken down.

She stumbled through the partially closed door onto the top floor of the restaurant, a dining room and bar with open glass doors that led to a balcony. It was quiet and empty except for the low howl of the wind and a shadowed figure standing at the balcony aiming a rifle toward an apartment window across the street. Her hand went to her knife when the man's head tilted to-ward the side, letting some of the moonlight hit it. All the breath left her body.

The man who'd killed her parents, left her on the streets to become destitute and addicted to glue, and then took her in to remake her into a weapon who owed him her life.

The man who'd told her she was worth something and then ripped away everything she'd been proud of—who'd taken her home from her twice and would stop at nothing to keep doing it.

Aiming a gun at Teo was the man who'd only ever hesitated to kill when it was her on the other side of the gun.

"I'll work with you!" she shouted, the words spilling out of her before she even knew what she was saying.

Kohl Pavel turned then, that smile she knew so well tugging at one side of his lips.

"I knew you'd see sense eventually, Aina."

The door slammed open behind her. The two Jackals who'd followed her up the stairs stormed into the room as Kohl stepped in from the balcony, set down his rifle, and walked toward her. She threw off one Jackal who tried to grab her, but the other latched on to her elbow. As she moved to grab his arm and break it, Kohl held up a hand.

"Stop," he said in a quiet tone. The Jackals relinquished her, but before they could leave, Kohl lifted a handgun from his belt holster and fired two quick shots to their heads. As their bodies thudded next to Aina, Kohl continued, "You really thought you could take my tradehouses from me and not pay a price."

The hint of amusement in his voice sent her over the edge. She stepped forward, one scythe swinging toward him. He caught her blade with one of his own, so quickly, she hadn't even seen him draw it. As she ground her weight into the floor, her knees buckled—the pain from the bullet wound finally catching up to her. Her vision wavered and, noticing her weakness, Kohl pushed back so her scythe flew out of her hand. She lifted her fists, but then her vision spun so badly, she nearly blacked out. Kohl grabbed her and shoved her into the nearest chair. She bit her tongue to draw the pain elsewhere, then looked down at her leg. The bullet was lodged in the back of her calf, blood spreading around it. It had struck at an angle and not gone completely through. It hadn't hit bone from what she could tell, but it still hurt like hell.

"Remember that your friend is sleeping in the apartment across the street, I have a rifle, and you can't run," he said, his voice scathing. "Stay there."

He closed the glass doors to the balcony, blocking off the howl of the wind, then walked toward the bar. As he rummaged underneath the counter, she watched him, wondering why he hadn't shot her yet. Since she was twelve, she'd seen Kohl nearly every day. His hair had grown in the past month, hanging toward his chin. His voice was still the cold, steel-like timbre she'd always known it to be. She wondered if his weaknesses were the same—if their month apart had made him more or less formidable.

She bit her lower lip to stop from screaming in frustration. He'd so easily disarmed her and thrown her across a room; like she was defenseless. Like she couldn't beat him. Her eyes flicked to the balcony, wishing Teo could sense what was happening from across the street, but a long minute passed, and she was still here with Kohl.

By the time he returned with pliers and an apron cut into long strips, her anger still hadn't abated.

"I don't need your help," she spat out.

"Really?" He smirked and raised an eyebrow. "Are you going to crawl across the street to Teo Matgan's apartment for help?"

"Like you sent your Jackals to ask me to help you?" She scoffed as he knelt and began to remove the bullet. As much as she hated the sight of him so close to her, she needed to get it out. To get her mind off it, she would keep him talking. "Was your master not watching tonight? Is that why you were able to sneak out of the kennel and meet me personally?"

Without bothering to warn her, he pressed down hard on her wound with the fabric. She hissed at the pain and clenched her fists on the arms of the chair.

"After everything that happened at the Tower, Bautix doesn't keep me as close anymore," Kohl said, a hint of bitterness in his voice. "I don't even know where he is right now. I have a few Jackals who are on my side, but the rest are still his and they think they're here on his job with me right now. I had to kill these two so they wouldn't tell the others I made them let you go. As for the rest, do you really think I'll let them survive the night?"

She narrowed her eyes at him as he unfurled the makeshift bandages. "Why are you telling me this?"

"If we're going to work together, you should know the circumstances."

"I didn't say we—"

"Yes, you did, actually—or do you not value your friend's life as much as I thought?" He tilted his head toward the rifle resting near the doors to the balcony.

If she looked at Kohl's face, she would want to punch him, so she shifted her focus to his hands. They began wrapping the bandages around her left calf, his fingers brushing against her skin with each rotation. With each touch, a shiver went through her, half with revulsion, half the old part of her that would have given anything for him to be this close to her. The tension she felt when he was near—that she knew he must feel too—came back in seconds, as if a month apart had done nothing to dampen it.

She narrowed her eyes at him, recalling the moment she'd held a knife to his heart and he'd actually shown fear. That had been the real Kohl; she wouldn't let him hide that now, no matter what deal he tried to make with her.

"Bautix has given me busy work. Recruiting Jackals, keeping up petty crimes to distract the Diamond Guards, finding safe places for the additional men he's hired to lay low."

"Additional men?" Aina asked.

"The Jackals rounded up some of those prisoners you freed last month and gave them an ultimatum; work for Bautix and be free, or be delivered back to the Tower. He also has hired guns from Kaiyan. If they help him take Sumerand for himself, he will fund the coup they're planning in their own country." He paused and his words sunk in, Aina remembering the armed Kaiyanis men they'd seen in the Sacoren's apartment building. "My job has been to make sure they don't get caught. Bautix still trusts me a lot more than he trusts most of the people he employs, but nowhere near as much as before."

"Is that why you want to take him down? Because you're not the favorite anymore?" she asked, drawing out the words to taunt him—but she couldn't hide her own curiosity.

"I am not his employee, Aina. We are two men who used to have similar goals of not getting in each other's way, but things are different now. He wants the government and the military. I want the streets and the fear of the people; I want them to know my name before I kill them, without me needing to say a word. I want them to step aside the moment they see my shadow. I will take whatever opportunity I can to gain this power. You know that." He tightened the bandages and then locked eyes with her, his gaze like shards of ice. "I've been working with Bautix since I was twelve—I know too much about his work. If he takes back the Tower for himself, he will try to destroy me. Right now, he needs my connections and I need his influence. But the minute one of us gets what we want"—he snapped his fingers—"our partnership will crack like kindling. My goal is to set it aflame before he does."

"And you think a partnership with me would work out any better?" she asked, unable to stop a laugh from escaping her lips.

He tilted his head toward her so that moonlight illuminated half his face, and his dark brown hair fell into his eyes. One side of his lips tugged upward in a smirk. Then he nodded toward the balcony he'd been aiming the gun from—moments away from shooting Teo.

"Why do you think I waited here instead of showing up at the Dom myself? Because I knew you were stubborn enough to try to run here and stop the assassination instead of simply agreeing to the terms my colleague gave you. And I wanted to watch that—see your face when you realized I was the sniper. You were willing to risk your friend's life to spare your reputation. We're more alike than you've ever admitted."

When he finished his sentence, she lifted her uninjured leg and kicked him in the face with her steel-toed boot.

"We are not the same," she said as he fell back.

He clutched his nose—which looked to be broken—and tried to stop the stream of blood with the unused bits of apron. She allowed herself a smile at the sight. He reset the bone with a crunching sound, tossed the bloodied cloth on the ground, then stood and faced her. He looked like he was two seconds away from choking her.

"You're still mad I took the Dom and bested you in a fight." She scoffed. "I know you want the Dom back, so what would make you want to work with me, of all people?"

As Kohl took a step closer, Aina stood and shifted behind the chair to at least have something between them.

Kohl placed his hands on the arms of the chair and leaned toward her, stopping when his face was only a few inches away from hers, but she didn't react at all, nor wince from the dull pain in her leg. A year after he'd brought her to the Dom, he'd given her a hammer and told her to break the fingers of a grunt at another tradehouse caught stealing kors from the commission owed to Kohl. She'd flinched after doing it, so as a punishment, he'd broken one of her fingers later that day and promised to break another if she didn't stop crying. She'd bit her tongue so hard it bled, if only to stop the tears.

"You should be grateful, Aina," he'd said, while placing her finger in a makeshift splint. "I train you harder than the others because I know you'll be a great Blade if you learn one thing: Blades feel nothing."

He'd trained her to show nothing, and that was the only way to face him now. "You already know that humiliation can only make a person more ruthless." His breath fell on her face, somehow cold even in the depths of summer. "More unashamed to do what needs to be done. Bautix will stop at nothing to get rid of you because you aren't under his control. But even I can't kill a man if I don't know where he is—that's where you come in. I'll use my position to find his spies, informants, anyone he relies on, and you'll kill them. If we can't find his hiding place, we need to weaken him enough that he crawls out of it. You're good with a knife, you're good with poisons, you're good at getting out of sticky situations. As far as the Dom, of course I want it back. But Bautix will come for both of us if we don't kill him first. Once he's out of the way, we can go back to fighting each other."

His words sank in, and the only sounds were their steady breaths and distant voices and footsteps from the street below. Images of the bodies found near the Dom, Bautix's promise of revenge, how they'd nearly gotten locked in the warehouse filled with poison, and the growing forces of the Jackals every day that meant her employees could barely walk down the street without getting threatened. Fighting Kohl, Bautix, the Jackals, and the Thunder tradehouse all at once only left her vulnerable.

She'd lose the tradehouses all on her own if she didn't stop Bautix. Panic rushed through her, a rapid beating of her pulse that blended with Kohl's next words.

"You worked for me. You saw most of our clients were from richer districts and that none of my employees grew up so privileged. I care about the people in the Stacks, just like you, and killing Bautix will help protect them all." Kohl began to walk away, past her and toward the door, but stopped. They stood next to each other, facing in opposite directions, their shoulders nearly touching, and she wondered if she could do it—how fast she could break his neck or stab him in the heart, if he would defend himself this time, if there was a backup, if she'd made another mistake. Yet the other half of her wondered something else.

Her desire to punish him for all he'd done would be difficult to quench. She didn't know if she was ready for the emptiness that would follow simply stabbing him—the loss of purpose. By pretending to be on his side, she could draw out his pain.

Kohl had been unable to turn his gun on her the night he'd killed her parents, because she'd reminded him of a childhood friend he'd killed by accident. He'd taken her to the Dom to assuage his guilt for killing her parents, yet the need to vanquish her and prove his own brutality to himself had never left him. But despite all his talk, she doubted he could ever bring himself to destroy his one remaining ounce of goodness.

She would use that against him, twist it into a weapon, like he'd taken her fear and made her need him, and like he'd used Teo against her. She despised it, this flicker of light in such a despicable man. She would make him wish he were as brutal as she. Make him regret sparing her and show him she'd always been stronger than him. Test his resiliency, force him to fight that urge to kill her, and douse that spark of decency until nothing was left and he became the monster he so clearly wanted to be. And then, finally, she would kill him.

Maybe she wasn't like the Blood King at all.

Maybe she was worse.

"I'll do it," she said simply.

A small, triumphant smile flickered at his lips for one moment, and something like relief flashed through his eyes.

"I'll get the information and you do the dirty work, just like old times," Kohl said.

Fighting the urge to kick him again, she said, "A smuggler from Kaiyan is bringing in a big weapons shipment soon, and sending in smaller ones ahead of time; Bautix's killing all the middlemen as soon as they make the deliveries. We need to stop him from getting any more weapons."

"We also need to stop his allies. There's a Diamond Guard traitor plotting entryways into the Tower, and I've had the Jackals pass notes to him, but I don't know who it is." He paused, and Aina remembered the note Tannis had shown her the night before. "Bautix covers his tracks well. I'll ask Kerys if she knows anything else about it."

"Kerys?" Aina asked, raising an eyebrow. "The Jackal you sent to threaten me?"

"Yes, that one. I'll find out what I can. How about we meet at our old place in a few days?"

She shook her head sharply. "I want this job done as soon as possible. We'll meet tomorrow at noon with whatever you can get."

For a moment, he glared at her, not seeming to take kindly to her ordering him around. She stared him down as he considered. Eventually, he shrugged, his casual demeanor sliding back in place.

"Tomorrow it is," he said, retrieving the rifle he'd left near the balcony doors and then walking back toward her. "And if you need to reach me for anything, I'm staying in a house near the southern docks, painted green. You'll know it when you see it."

"All right," she said. "We have a deal, Kohl."

Kohl turned so he faced her profile and his shadow fell over her. A curious smile shifted onto his lips, one that made her stiffen and remember all the times he'd drawn her in before.

"Do you remember one day, Aina, when you were eleven?" He spoke in a whisper, like revealing a secret. "It was the coldest winter this city had seen in either of our lifetimes. You woke up with a gift next to you. Do you still have that memory or did your addiction to glue rob you of it?"

It came to her like a rush of cold air in the dead of night.

She'd been stuck outside in the middle of winter. The snow glittered under the stars. Her shoes were filled with holes and were about to fall off. It had been a bitterly cold night, with dry wind chapping her lips and making her skin burn. It was one of those nights that she no longer cared about her life. If there was nowhere to lie down and be warm, then what was the point in anything at all?

The next morning, she woke up on a fire escape. A pair of shoes sat next to her. Though most people pretended she was invisible, someone she'd never met had finally shown kindness without waiting to see if she would thank them or return the favor. They'd wanted her to survive another night. Seeing that gift had made her want to keep fighting, because if a stranger had seen the value of her life, then maybe she deserved more than choking on glue, starving, or freezing to death. She'd worn those shoes every day for a year before Kohl took her in and gave her a new pair.

She drew in a shallow breath and turned to look at him.

"If it wasn't for me that winter," Kohl said, his gaze searing into her as if he were trying to read her mind, "would you have gotten frostbite? Would you have even lasted long enough to pull yourself away from glue?" Without letting her answer, he said, "One day, you're going to admit how much you need my help. I'll be waiting for that moment."

Once Kohl left, Aina only had to wait a moment until she
heard the sound of several quick gunshots fired, each one making
her grit her teeth. After a door below opened and shut with a
creaking noise, she walked down the stairs, taking in each dead
Jackal Kohl had left behind. Then she crossed the street and entered Teo's apartment building with Kohl's last words echoing in
her mind: *One day, you're going to admit how much you need my help.*

She shook off the chill that came with those words and knocked
on Teo's door. Footsteps came a few moments later and the door
swung open. Teo stood there in his nightclothes with a gun pointed
at her.

"Hello to you too," she said, limping past him into the apartment.

"Didn't know who it would be," Teo said, locking the door behind him and turning on the lights. "What happened to your leg?"

Instead of replying immediately, she turned to take in his new,
sparsely furnished apartment, even though she'd seen it a few

times already. She didn't know how to, or if she even should, explain what had happened—all she knew was that she'd needed to come see him. Her eyes flicked to the window, from where she could make out the balcony of the restaurant across the street. Kohl's wicked smile as he'd pointed the gun at Teo's window. Her shoulders tensed as she locked that image in her memory.

"Kohl sent some Jackals to the Dom to threaten us," she said, staring at the city lights through the window. "But he offered me a job. He wants to turn on Bautix and kill him, and wants my help."

"What did you say?" Teo asked quickly, and in his reflection, he wore the same worried look she'd seen countless times when she spoke to him of Kohl, the same concerned tone he used when he feared Kohl was hurting her.

A bitter taste rose in the back of her throat, and she swallowed it down. This agreement wasn't because she needed Kohl—it was how she would kill him and Bautix. But the more people who knew about her working with Kohl, the closer it would feel like going back to the past. She didn't need anyone underestimating her in this. She turned back around to face Teo.

"I told him I don't need his help." She brushed a loose strand of black hair behind her ears and avoided meeting Teo's eyes. "But Bautix is becoming a real problem; you know he doesn't want anyone in charge of the tradehouses who's not aligned with him. Kohl still wants the tradehouses, but as long as Bautix is in the way, I'm not his priority."

"So, you want to go after Bautix? We could just let them kill each other."

Aina scoffed, and she didn't have to fake what she said next, or the dread it made her feel. "For now. The Dom isn't safe as long as Bautix is around. Besides, Kohl may have killed my parents, but Bautix gave him the job."

Teo let out a sharp exhale. "And he's the one who told the Diamond Guards to hunt you down last month, the one who got my mother killed."

A rush of anger flowed through her, and she fought the urge to run outside right now and find Bautix. There was plenty of reason to hate him just as much as, if not more than, Kohl—so why had she only been focused on Kohl?

Her head spun and a sickened feeling built up inside. All the times he'd tricked and manipulated her had hurt, made her feel worthless and pathetic . . . but Bautix was the one behind these murders and ruining the city. Bautix was the one threatening her now. The thought came like a punch to the gut, raising questions of why every cruel word Kohl had ever said was imprinted on her mind; why it hurt so much when he'd never actually tried to kill her.

Was I just too weak to stand up to it all?

"Aina?" Teo asked. The circle of light from the ceiling lamp above gilded his brown skin, and his eyes were warm, making her want to go closer—farther from Kohl's chill. "I'm in. Kohl can wait. Bautix had the Jackals leave that note for you, didn't he? He might attack the Dom soon if we don't stop him. He's already terrorizing the south, and we know he'll kill the Inosen too if it gets him ahead. I'm sick of Steels like him, using us all as scape-goats while they fight one another for power. He doesn't expect any of us to fight back, but we'll prove him wrong."

Her thoughts slowly came back into focus, and her voice was clearer than she expected it would be. "Let's do it, then. We'll show them we're the real survivors in this city."

Their eyes met, and his blazed with that fire of revenge she knew so well. It drew her toward him, and she stopped inches before they touched. His breath caught as he looked down at her, but she didn't move any closer. Not while she was hiding the truth from him, like Kohl had done to her so many times. She wouldn't hurt Teo in the same way.

She sat at Teo's table as he made tea for them both, and tried not to let her eyes slide closed. As much as she wanted to get to work immediately, her body ached from the fighting and her race through the city to get here in time. She needed plenty of rest for tomorrow, when she would meet with Kohl again. And tomorrow night, she, Ryuu, and the Inosen would begin learning to use the Mothers' magic as a weapon. The Mothers' teachings had always said that life was precious. Her parents had fiercely believed that, but her mother had killed someone too—the first taking of a life that Aina had ever witnessed. She'd done it to protect them, to survive—something Aina understood all too well.

Aina had been seven. She'd curled into a ball under the kitchen table, as if the man her mother was treating wouldn't be able to see her. As if she were invisible and could melt away from this one-room home where her parents risked their lives and prayed for protection. As if she could hide from the light of the moons pouring through the window from the outside world, where the war had ended but people still killed one another every day.

Her mother had hummed in Milano under her breath as she brushed sweat and blood from the man's face with a cool washcloth. The man had no eyes and one of his hands had no fingers. Aina didn't know much about blood magic at the time, but she knew these were injuries her mother and father could never heal.

"I gave them up," the man said as if in disbelief. "I gave them up." His voice was scratchy and hoarse, as if the inside of his mouth had been burned.

He repeated the words over and over until Aina's mother's coaxing and patient voice finally got him to reveal who, exactly, he'd given up. He'd been taken for questioning by the Diamond Guards, and Inosen fighters had broken him out of prison, but not before he'd lost his eyes and the fingers of one hand during the interrogation. His knees were shattered and he'd only made it to her house because the Inosen had deposited him here, knowing her parents took care of injured people when they could. In the middle of his torture, he'd choked out the location of the Inosen safe house he'd lived in on Lyra Avenue. All the Inosen there were now dead, and if the Inosen fighters hadn't broken him out that night, he would have followed with his own execution the next morning.

"Kill me," he'd demanded of her mother.

Her mother had shaken her head, her eyes wide. She began whispering, and if Aina didn't know the words by heart already, she wouldn't have caught them at all: it was the Mothers' scripture from the Nos Inoken that currently sat under a cloth on the table above Aina.

"Aina, vete afuera," her mother had barked over, but before she could demand it again, the man took all her attention.

Aina didn't leave. She didn't blink or even breathe as she watched what happened next.

The man had begged her mother and shouted at her, his voice rising as he yelled out that there were Inosen hiding here and if her mother didn't want them to be given up too, she'd better kill him quickly. Her mother slapped him and held her hand over his mouth until he bit her. He called her terrible names, but also called her an angel, someone who understood mercy and when it was too late to save someone. It went on for at least an hour until he started threatening Aina, saying that if he survived the night, he wouldn't rest until he killed her as revenge on her mother. Aina kept her eyes fixed on him as her mother finally placed a pillow over his mouth and nose and pressed down.

When it was done, and when her mother asked a boy outside to get rid of the body, Aina moved from under the table. She placed her hands on the sheets where the man had died and wondered how her family could sleep there peacefully that night.

Her mother washed her hands, her face surprisingly calm, then sat beside Aina on the bed to undo her braids and brush her hair.

She leaned forward and kissed Aina on the cheek, then said, "Don't tell your father."

In the present, she shook her head. When her mother had killed that man, she'd set aside magic and used her hands, not wanting to use the Mothers' power for something deadly.

But Aina would.

As Teo sat down and passed her a cup of tea, she nodded toward a stack of boxes in the corner. He'd moved a month ago, yet most his things were still packed and gathering dust.

"I know I barged in uninvited tonight, but if you're going to have people over, you should probably decorate," she murmured. "Looks a bit barren. Any girls you bring over might guess you kill people for a living without you even having to tell them."

"Says the girl who walks around with a bloodied scarf." Teo laughed, then his voice softened. "You're the only girl who's come here, Aina."

He tapped his knuckles on the table as his eyes trailed toward the boxes. Her cheeks warmed at his words, but she didn't know what to say to that, so she looked at the boxes too. A wool blanket peeked out of the corner of one, and she could make out the edge of a landscape stitched onto the fabric in jewel tones and geometric shapes.

"I remember your mother's paintings," she said slowly. "She did some of them herself, didn't she? Like the blankets. All the steppe land, the plains, falcon riders."

As she spoke, he pulled a necklace from under his shirt. Only the gold chain was visible until he drew out the pendant. It was the same amber necklace his mother had often worn, with an image of Terroq, Linash's falcon god, etched onto the pendant.

"You know my parents were falcon riders—we call them *terrishan aleph*. Giant ones that they rode into battle in border wars for decades. They left and came here for me, without knowing how dangerous Sumerand would become. And you know how it is, growing up poor in Kosín after the war. There are only two choices: fear or be feared. Violence that never ends. I'm too far down that path to hope for anything else, but maybe the only way to stand up to the Steels is to be worse than them. I want to believe that will make a difference. But at the same time . . . that's what got her killed."

Leaning across the table, Aina reached for the pendant and brushed a finger over the falcon etching. Its gold eyes seemed to stare at her, as if the thing were alive, but it was the light gilding the curves and angles of the design. In the past few weeks, he'd avoided talking about his mother, and had shut down when she'd tried to comfort him before—he must have had this guilt and doubt running through his mind constantly.

"You know something?" she asked, her voice the only sound in the still night. "Your mother asked me to protect you when she couldn't. We can protect each other, and if violence is what we're good at, then we'll do whatever it takes to stand up to those who took our families and homes from us, and we'll stop them from doing it to anyone else. They don't stand a chance, Teo."

She let the pendant fall back to his chest, but Teo caught her hand in his before she could pull it back.

The night deepened around them. Aina knew she had to return to the Dom to let Tannis know what had happened. But right now, time froze, this moment etching itself into their history. When it was the two of them, nothing could penetrate the way they stared at each other, the heat between them, the way their thoughts seemed to pass to each other without needing to speak a word—the way thoughts did when you knew you were each other's best friend.

Then Teo lifted her hand to his lips and kissed the top of it. A light kiss, but one that still sent a blush to her cheeks. She kept her eyes averted from his, not trusting how she might react if she met his gaze. For a long moment, her thoughts roiled, a storm on two sides; one that wanted to draw closer to him and feel this connection between them grow, the other that reminded her she couldn't really love anyone until she got Kohl's voice out of her head—she'd only end up hurting them.

They stayed exactly like that for a long while after. He didn't kiss her hand again, and neither of them said a word.

"I have to get back to the Dom," she finally said, bringing their hands down to the table, where he let go first.

"Good night, Aina," he said when she stood and finally met his eyes. The light glinted off the copper color just as it had on the falcon pendant, and it was like the sun shone on her, even in the dead of night.

She tried to take a little of that warmth with her when she slipped outside and cast one more glance at the balcony where she'd agreed to work with Kohl.

The moment had broken, time moved again, and she was on her guard once more.

9

Teo's neighborhood, a few blocks north of the train station in the Center, was a rather quiet one—much different from his old place east of Lyra Avenue, which was almost as rough as the Stacks. Silence surrounded her, punctuated briefly whenever someone walked past her, but these were peaceful residents of the city.

Still, anger rose in her at the sight of them. How many of them in these richer districts still thought of Bautix as a war hero? In a way, he was smart to start building terror in the south. No one in the rest of the city ever cared what was happening in the Stacks until it affected them too, and by then, it would be too late for them to save themselves.

The lights faded as she moved south, but voices rose. Not the drunken voices that filled Lyra Avenue or the exuberant tones of tourists in Rose Court. These voices were hushed but panicked, low and forceful at the same time. Aina gripped a knife in each hand, knowing that her slight limp would make her look like an easy target.

Her footsteps quieted as she made her way down a hill into the Stacks, veering southeast toward the Dom. A few groups were huddled together on the road. As a child, she'd always avoided making friends, even with other children on the streets, because she never knew who to trust. Most of them had no faith left, not in the Mothers and not in one another.

But now people were grouping together more often, pushing aside their fear of one another to stand up to the Jackals as well as they could. She nodded to them as she passed, and while a few sent her a cautious wave or a nod, most avoided eye contact. As if even looking at her would put a mark on them.

She tried to temper her fury as she walked, but it kept building inside her—her side of the city didn't deserve to suffer because of Bautix's fight for power. The Inosen didn't deserve to suffer for it either. But that was exactly had had happened for years.

On the next road, now in the Dom's territory, she passed a boy a few years younger than her, sleeping in an alley under a cardboard box. As she left some silver kors next to him, small drops of water tapped on the cardboard. She held out a hand and caught a drop of rain on her palm too. When she stood, she noticed the boy wore no shoes. Her heart tugged with the memory of the pair of shoes she'd woken up to one cold winter morning when her hope had nearly run its course—the pair Kohl had left her.

Then, she clenched a hand into a fist at her side and kept walking down the dirt road that began to darken and turn to mud as the rain came down harder. Kohl had told her that story to unsettle her, like how he'd reminded her that he'd started the tradehouses to give opportunities to the people here.

That was yet another reason no one could know about her partnership with him: the tradehouses wouldn't trust her at all if they found out.

She could give hope to the people here as much as Kohl had said he wanted to—it started with treating her employees better than he ever had, and stopping Bautix from harming the south anymore.

Turning down the next road, she began to walk past a row of houses and small businesses, then stopped in her tracks. This was the Dom's territory. Usually, this street was lit with candles to mark which shops were open and which were closed. But now, boarded-up windows covered every building.

A door slammed open. Aina slowed, gripping her knives tightly. A woman yelped as she was dragged out of her home by two Jackals—obvious by the tattoo on their forearms. One of them, a girl a few years older than Aina, shoved the older woman to the ground.

"You've had a week," the Jackal said, her voice so cutting, the older woman winced. "Two thousand kors. Where are they?"

She held out a hand, beckoning with her fingers. The woman looked up at her, gasping for breath as the rain fell on her face and slicked her hair. But after a moment of staring up at the Jackal, her face hardened, mouth flattening to a thin line. She spat in the Jackal's hand.

The other Jackal, a man, whipped out a knife faster than the older woman could blink, but she didn't react; she'd made her choice.

Aina stepped forward and whistled. Both Jackals whipped around, hands going to their weapons, but when they saw her, they froze.

"You must both be new," she said, walking toward them with as casual a gait as she could manage. "Neither of you have asked for permission to even walk on these streets, let alone attack the people here."

She briefly met the older woman's eyes and gave her the smallest nod. As Aina slowed to a stop in front of the Jackals, the woman darted past them into her home and slammed the door shut.

"We're not new," the male Jackal said scathingly. "We've been doing this for weeks."

Aina raised an eyebrow. If they thought a few weeks was a long time, she didn't want to know what they thought was short. How many Jackals did Bautix have now? What had he promised them in exchange for shaking kors out of old women in the Stacks?

"How much money did you collect from these people today?" Aina asked. They looked at each other, frowning in confusion. "Go on, go to each door and give it back. Whoever does it fastest will get a quick death. Whoever is slowest . . ." She shrugged.

"You're injured," the girl Jackal said then, eyes lighting up as she nodded at Aina's bandaged leg. She flipped her knife in one hand and caught it. "The great Aina Solís, Queen of Blades, outnumbered in a dark alley."

"Queen of Blades?" she asked, bending her knees in a slight crouch. "I like the sound of that."

"Queen?" The other Jackal laughed, reaching for a gun in a holster at his hip. "More like the Blood King's bitch."

Aina flung her dagger straight into the Jackal's throat. As he dropped, blood spilling onto the dirt, the girl Jackal lunged for his fallen gun.

In two quick steps, Aina reached her and pushed her to the muddy ground. Pinning her down, she tilted the girl's head all the way back, knife at her throat.

"I'm a generous queen," she said then as the Jackal's eyes

widened in fear. "Give the money back to the people you took it from tonight, then tell all your friends to never step foot on my territory again, and I won't slit your throat."

She stood and kicked the Jackal away from her. The girl scrambled to her feet and ran to the nearest door, sliding kors under it in a clumsy rush.

A slow clapping sounded behind Aina, blending in with the rain that pelted the street. Hair rose on the back of her neck and her hand went to her knife once more. Turning, she schooled her features to show nothing, even though her pulse slowed at the sight of Arman Kraz, the boss of Thunder, gathered with the remaining members of his tradehouse—a girl and a boy around her age, and one younger boy whose nervous fidgeting told her he was still a recruit. By killing his second-in-command and his spy, Aina had cut his ranks down to four total. She grimaced at the sight; the last thing she wanted was to lose tradehouse employees, but when they did their best to spy on her and destabilize her and Tannis's rule, that was exactly what she would do.

"Good evening, Arman," she said in a chipper tone, her voice the loudest thing in the Stacks right now. "Happened to be taking a stroll and stumbled upon me?"

A tick went off in his lower jaw. "No, Miss Solís, I came here for you."

"Interesting," she said, shifting her weight casually to one side to seem completely unperturbed. "When I want to chat with someone, I usually knock on their door, ask if they're busy. I don't corner them on a dark road."

Arman raised an eyebrow then. "Do we frighten you? I thought you were our fearless leader." When she didn't reply immediately, he took several steps toward her, his employees hanging back. "Two of my employees have died in what seems to be a terrible accident. I want to know if I can trust you to watch out for the rest of them, or if you're too busy running around the city with Steels and Inosen doing Mothers-know-what instead of looking out for the tradehouses. I know your family's not from here, and you're too young to even remember what it was like during the war, but we don't take kindly to those who betray their own."

Her blood was boiling by the end of his sentence. If he was merely concerned about her keeping secrets and being friends with Ryuu, it would be a fair criticism. But Kohl had done whatever he'd wanted and no one in the tradehouses dared to question him. This was a challenge, not constructive feedback—and the small quirk at the corner of Arman's lips proved he was enjoying it.

She took a slight step back, looking up at him through her eyelashes and hunching her shoulders a little so she looked as weak as he thought she was.

"Well, Arman, what I'd say to you about that is—"

She slammed her fist into his face. Bone cracked. He stumbled back a step, blood coating his fingers as his hands went to his broken nose. While he tried to regain his footing, she shoved him to the ground and pinned him down, his face in the mud. His employees watched with open mouths, their hands going to their guns but none of them making a move.

"Are you listening carefully? Hopefully that knocked out some of your ego." She let out a huff of breath that fluttered the hair on the back of his head. "Every single thing I do is for the safety of the tradehouses. The Blood King is the one who ran to his Steel boss like a dog with its tail between its legs after I fought him, not me. Your attempts to undermine me are preventing me from protecting the tradehouses. Did you hear that? You are hurting your own business by doubting me. If you send a spy after me again, I will cut out your tongue. I hope this serves as a reminder of which tradehouse and which bosses actually hold the power here, and which bosses you should be loyal to. Your job is not to spy on me. Your job is to work for me."

With that, she stood and walked away, only pausing to take the knife from the dead Jackal's throat. She didn't bother to look back—after she'd humiliated Arman, shooting her with her back turned was the last thing he'd do. Nothing would make him look like more of a coward.

The lights in the Dom were still on when Aina returned. She wrung rainwater out of her hair before entering. When she did, she noticed the glow of candlelight spilling out from the office's open door, and walked toward it. Part of her was desperate to go to sleep, but she needed to find out what had happened at the Dom after she'd left, and she didn't know how well she'd sleep with her new arrangement with Kohl at the front of her thoughts.

Inside the office, Tannis sat on the floor in front of the desk, tossing a throwing star in the air repeatedly and catching it deftly between her fingers each time. A single candle's light glinted off the bottle of firebrandy she held in her other hand. When Aina knocked lightly on the doorframe, Tannis's head flicked up.

"What happened?" Tannis asked, her eyes going to the bandage around Aina's calf. "I was about to go looking for you."

A smile lifted one corner of Aina's lips at those words; Tannis had been worried about her. But her heart sank quickly after—she was about to lie. Aina sat on the floor across from Tannis, her muscles sore and her eyes heavy. She took a deep breath before speaking.

"Well, I just punched Arman Kraz in the face; he's still convinced he has some nobler reasons not to want us in charge, but really it's because we're girls who are younger than him and we're not Sumeranian. But he'll leave us alone for a while. When I left here earlier, I caught up with the messenger and more of Kohl's men cornered me. I fought them off, and I got information from one of them about what Bautix is doing." She looked at the carpet then, like she had every time she'd lied to Kohl about her whereabouts when she'd been selling diamonds on the side—hating herself for doing the same to Tannis. "What happened to the Jackal you cornered on the roof—Kerys?"

"You won't believe it." Tannis scoffed. "She knocked out Markus and fought me for a bit. I gave her a nasty cut, but she head-butted me, and when I fell back, she jumped off the roof."

Aina blinked. "I didn't see a body on the ground when I came in."

"She rolled right out of the landing and ran down the street, half-limping. I had Markus and Johana get rid of the other two," Tannis said, then smirked. "At least Kerys can run off and tell Kohl we're stronger than he thinks we are."

Aina gave a small laugh, trying to keep her features blank.

"We are," she said softly. She watched Tannis out of the corner of her eye for a moment, battling the guilt she felt. They'd both been mistreated by Kohl before and were supposed to stand up to him together. But this partnership was between her and Kohl alone. If she told Tannis, it would seem like she was going back to Kohl, like he was hurting her again instead of the other way around. She could handle him on her own—she had to prove to herself that she could.

"I'm worried Bautix is going to come for us next," she said, hoping to change the subject slightly. "You saw the note he left us."

Tannis shifted uncomfortably, her brow furrowed as she thought. "He will eventually. But now it seems like Kohl has turned on him."

"Exactly. That means Kohl isn't focused on us. We should fight the enemy we know is coming." When Tannis looked uncertain, Aina added, "The information I got is about those Kaiyanis men we saw in the Sacoren's apartment. Bautix brought them from overseas and, if they fight for him now, he'll help fund a coup they're planning."

Tannis's shoulders slumped and the light in her eyes dimmed. "They don't care what happens here, and he doesn't care what happens there. Allying makes sense for both sides. But I don't trust Bautix with them. He'll only take advantage and dispose of them when they're not useful."

The way she clenched her hands around the neck of the fire-brandy bottle told Aina she was more bothered by this than her words alone would indicate. Before she could stop herself, or wonder if it was the right move, she reached over and took Tannis's clenched hand, smoothing it out. Their eyes met over the bottle, and Aina's heart flipped at the warmth in Tannis's gaze. Aina wanted to tell her things would work out. But she had no idea if that were true, and she wasn't about to add another lie to her list.

But the way Tannis looked at Aina a moment later, her eyes bright, showed Aina there was more she wanted to say; more she wanted to share. Maybe Aina couldn't open up about her work with Kohl, but she could give Tannis an opportunity to share her thoughts—to show she could be there for her.

"Do you believe in their cause?" Aina asked, leaning next to Tannis against the desk.

"I don't know. There are more people there who support the king than those who don't. Those who don't support him hated the way his tyrant father ruled and they think he'll be the same, but he's only been ruling for a year. It's too early to tell, in my opinion. I think that their staging a coup will only bring more violence to the country." She let out a heavy sigh. "This is my home now, and I'll fight them and Bautix if they're a threat. Look at what happened tonight; I took you all to see Gevann, and then the Dom was attacked and the recruits were almost killed. I can't lose focus like that, and I can't care too much what happens to my old home. There's nothing I can do for them anyway," she finished, her voice tinged with a bitter regret.

"I know it must be difficult for you," Aina said in a low voice. "But the attack tonight wasn't your fault."

Tannis shook her head and straightened against the desk, like she pushed aside all those worries so easily. Aina's heart ached at the sight—shoving aside fears was something they'd both learned to do working with Kohl for so long.

"I can ask Mirran to help us look into places where they and the Jackals might be hiding; she's going on a job tonight, so I'll ask her before she leaves." Then Tannis passed the bottle of fire-brandy to Aina, their fingers brushing as she did. "You look like you need that. I'm going to get some sleep."

Once she left, Aina placed her lips on the rim of the bottle and was about to drink from it when the gleam of candlelight on her mother's white porcelain horse knickknack caught her eye. She let out a long sigh, a heavy sadness weighing on her chest. Maybe it was grief for the little girl she'd been when she'd last seen that horse, the girl who hadn't yet been hurt. Or maybe she wished she could feel her mother's warmth for a moment to replace the chill of Kohl's breath on her skin.

Reaching out, she picked up the horse for the first time since Kohl returned it to her. She ran a finger along the pink ribbon painted around its neck. The candlelight hit its side when she tilted it, revealing cracks lining the horse's body.

Frowning, Aina turned it over and found more cracks on its stomach. Kohl must have dropped it and put it back together. He'd called it his good luck charm, but he'd clearly broken it. So why had he kept it for so long?

No matter how brutal he was, some part of him still felt something toward her—even if it was only his old guilt for orphaning her.

When she met him tomorrow, she'd use that against him. She didn't need him at all; in the end, he'd be the one begging for mercy, and she would never be the frightened one again.

10

The next day, Aina woke to Mirran walking into the bedroom they shared with Tannis, who'd already left. Bags were under her eyes and she yawned as Aina sat up.

"How was your job last night?" Aina asked.

She shrugged while twining her long blue hair into a braid. "Stole a few thousand kors from some unsuspecting businessman at a fancy party, the usual. Some Jackals almost knifed me on the way home, also the usual."

Aina raised an eyebrow. "Where are they now?"

"In the river where I left them. I'm happy to stab anyone who's trying to stab me, but I'm worried about our recruits."

"Me too," Aina admitted, thinking of Kushik, Markus, and Johana. They were better at defending themselves than most other kids in the city, but the Jackals' attacks had only been growing more ruthless, and she couldn't help the spike of fear she felt for the three recruits. "Did Tannis ask you to look into the Jackal hideouts?"

Mirran nodded, then sat on the floor next to Aina's mattress. "I actually heard something from the men at the party last night. When they think you're a silly little girl, they don't really pay attention to what they're saying around you." With a smirk, she continued, "There's a Diamond Guard named Arin Fayes, have you heard of him?"

"He's a captain, isn't he?" Aina asked, dredging up from her memory what she knew of the man. "Works in the prison. I've heard one of his favorite hobbies is making the prisoners fight one another and taking bets on it."

"Yeah, that one. The party was on one of his boats in the northwest harbor. He also owns a few apartment buildings on Lyra Avenue, and he was whispering with some of his colleagues about how they were offering free rent to any tenants willing to hide people there and keep their mouths shut about it. I found out where all the apartments are."

From her pocket, she withdrew a folded-up piece of paper and then spread it out on the floor. It was a simple map of Lyra Avenue, showing the cross streets where the apartments could be found. Four of them. With Fayes offering free rent to anyone agreeing to house people from Kaiyan, he'd probably gotten a lot of volunteers. With Kohl's information that Bautix was hiring Kaiyanis rebels to fight for him . . . Her pulse raced at the sight of the map—this was more than a decent lead to start shutting down Bautix's plans.

"You're amazing, Mirran," she said, folding the map and tucking it inside the pouch of poison darts at her belt.

"I know," she said, leaning against the wall with her arms folded behind her head. "Can I have a raise?"

Aina took a gold kor out of her pocket and tossed it in the air. Mirran caught it easily and winked one of her own gold eyes.

* * *

The summer heat hit Aina like a brick to the face when she stepped outside. She brushed hair away from her eyes, finding it already sticky with sweat. It was barely noon, and the day would only get hotter.

Every time she turned a corner on her way to the Center, she glanced over her shoulder to check if anyone was following her. If any of the tradehouses found out she was working with Kohl, they would never trust her again; if Teo or Tannis found out, they'd realize she'd lied to them last night. The closer she got to the Center and the train station, the more alert she grew, checking the crowds around her for familiar faces.

Blending in with the hordes of passengers would shake off anyone tailing her. People ran past her to ticket booths and platforms, hauling heavy luggage in their arms and sweating in the crowded, sun-drenched station. With a nod to the bribed security guard, Aina slipped past the ticket barrier.

Unlocking the door to the darkened service stairwell, she made her way to the second floor.

When she neared the train station's tower, Kohl was already there. She kept her footsteps and breath quiet as she peered around the corner, wanting to watch him for a moment before speaking.

He waited for her on the edge of the windowsill, legs dangling over the side, his dark brown hair blown back by the wind. It was strange to see him so exposed, unaware she was there—she'd never had this opportunity while working for him, and something about it now felt personal, intimate. They'd spent hours here together when she was still training to become a Blade; he'd told her everything he knew about the city, and she'd grown used to his voice, his presence, all the secrets he kept. Half of her wanted to stand here and watch this man she'd spent years trying to figure out, while the other half wanted to shove him out of the window.

But she had to make him trust her again before killing him and proving to him that she'd never needed him at all. If she wanted her revenge, this job with him, to be worth it . . . she needed to be patient.

"I found out who the Diamond Guard traitor is," he said without turning, and she stiffened. How long had he known she was standing there? "He's been close to Bautix for years—they both came from army families and were stationed on the same base in the south. He's a captain, one of only four who works in the prison, and now he's helping Bautix build secret entrances into the Tower."

Crossing her arms as he turned to face her, she said, "Let me guess. Arin Fayes."

"How did you know that?" He raised one eyebrow as he stood to walk toward her.

"One of *my* employees found out he's also the one who owns the apartments on Lyra Avenue where all the Jackals and the Kaiyanis men are hiding."

"One of your employees for the next few weeks, you mean."

His gaze leveled at her and she stared back at him, refusing to blink or show any frustration at what he'd said. He'd come close enough that he blocked out the sunlight streaming through the window, leaving the half of the small room they stood in doused in shadow.

"If we can stop Bautix from getting any more weapons and take out Arin Fayes, we'll win this before he really starts fighting," she continued. His eyes flashed briefly at her words.

And then it'll just be you and me.

"I'm going to go look at the apartments today and see what I can learn."

After a brief pause, Kohl said, "I'm going with you."

"What?" she snapped. "I thought you wanted to lie low. Someone will see us."

He raised an eyebrow, then pulled a black kerchief from his pocket with a dramatic flourish. While she frowned at him, he tied it around the lower half of his face as a makeshift mask.

"You really think people won't recognize you like that?" she asked flatly.

"Not everyone has worked as close to me as you have for the past six years," he pointed out, his voice slightly muffled by the cloth. "The only Jackals I've personally spoken to are the ones on my side. Besides, you need me there, since half of the people we'll probably end up spying on are Kaiyanis, and I've learned their language. You haven't."

As he spoke, he tugged down the sleeves on his shirt to cover his Vulture tattoo, the bird hung by a string of diamonds, the marking of his old gang. He made a good point, but going to Lyra Avenue meant traversing half the city—there were too many chances someone would see them.

"My employees will recognize you if they see us together," she said in a low voice.

"What does that matter?" he asked in an icy tone. "If you're a good boss, they won't question you, and if they do, you'll put them in their place—won't you?" He paused. "Nice bosses get their throats slit, Aina, you should know that by now."

Aina gestured for him to follow her, turning so he couldn't see her expression. But her ears burned as she led the way down the stairs, back into the train station, and then out into the Center.

This is what he does, she reminded herself. His taunts wouldn't get to her if she stayed on her guard.

For the first ten minutes of their walk, she stayed ahead of Kohl, trying to put the crowds between them and checking every rooftop and alley for a sign of anyone who might see them together. He said nothing as they walked, but every time she glanced over her shoulder, he was at the same ten feet of distance, always watching her.

She decreased the distance between them as they approached Lyra Avenue, knowing it would be easier to blend in with the crowds once they reached the bustling district. As soon as they got there, they moved in perfect tandem, taking the same steps to avoid pedestrians and the hawk-like eyes of Diamond Guards patrolling the streets. She watched Kohl from the corner of her eye, finding it strange to work alongside him again now that they were equals.

She'd dreamed of being at his side for years, not taking orders, but truly working together. Before she'd learned to stop trusting him, she'd hoped that one day, he might see her as more than a colleague. Something of that old, naive hope sparked curiosity in her—how would he act toward her now? For a moment, as they meshed with the crowds of Lyra Avenue like shadows in the night, she let herself feel the brief exhilaration that came when you moved at the same speed as someone and worked with the same skill. In minutes, they slipped through a group of Marinian tourists and reached the casino where she'd gone last night.

Kohl tapped her on the shoulder and pointed to the alley next to the casino, where a fire escape led to the upper floors. Together, they stepped off the main road and into the alley. Wrinkling her nose against the scents of piss and garbage, Aina walked up to the fire escape and jumped to catch the lower rungs.

"That's a lot of apartments to search," Kohl said below her. "Four stories, six windows each floor. Let's look through the windows, then do a quick sweep of the halls."

She nodded, then lifted herself up onto the fire escape stairwell before climbing to the next floor. The window ledges were rather narrow, but would be enough to stand on. The difficult thing would be scaling between each window, using only the space between the bricks as footholds and handholds.

While she examined the distance between the fire escape and the first apartment window, Kohl started climbing over with an utterly relaxed expression on his face as if this were a stroll through a field. Cursing herself for hesitating, Aina found what purchase she could on the wall. She moved slower than she normally would, her bullet wound from yesterday throbbing when she put too much pressure on her left leg. She scaled her way over to the first apartment window and then glanced inside, gathering what details she could—it was just a family's apartment. An old woman napped in a chair. A door opened within the apartment and a younger woman walked out in house clothes. Aina quickly stepped to the other side of the window to avoid being seen.

It took an hour for her and Kohl to check all the windows, and by the time they finished, Aina was covered in sweat. Kohl, however, barely looked ruffled. When they met on the fire escape landing of the top floor, she held back a huff of frustration. This would have taken double the time if she were alone.

"See anything interesting?" she asked Kohl.

"Mostly families, but I saw some of the people Bautix hired from overseas. None of them said anything interesting while I had time to listen. You?"

"About the same. Let's check the halls."

They climbed into the top-floor hallway. Doors stood open, laughter and music filtering into the hall along with the scent of grilling meat. As they walked down it, people moved between apartments, families and friends visiting one another. A mix of languages filled the air; Aina caught snatches of Kaiyanis, Durozvy, and Marinian.

Aina and Kohl walked to the end of the hall and through a door into a winding stairwell. A chill hung in the dark, windowless stairwell, a welcome respite from the summer heat outside. A single flickering bulb hanging from the ceiling lit the way. The staircases were so narrow, they had to walk one at a time, their breaths and echoing footsteps the only sounds.

They'd barely reached the second set of stairs when the door on the landing above opened with a loud creak. Kohl came to an abrupt stop, and Aina almost tripped trying not to walk into him, except he spun around and caught her by the elbow. Her back pressed against the railing, and she barely breathed as she listened to the voices above speak in Kaiyanis. Three male voices, all of them loud and boisterous, with no care in the world if they were overheard.

Kohl was too close. Their boots touched on the stair, his chest was an inch or two from her shoulders, his chin at her eye level. As the Kaiyanis men descended the stairs, Kohl glanced down at her and she gulped, trying not to breathe in his scent—the same smoke-and-mint scent she'd used to take every opportunity to be near. She leaned back slightly on the railing to put distance between them.

The men's voices echoed as they approached, only one flight of stairs away now, and Kohl whispered, "Those are definitely some of the men Bautix hired, but all they're talking about is how great the burlesque clubs on Lyra Avenue are supposed to be." He raised an eyebrow at her and a blush overtook her face. She was about to shove past him when he said, "Follow my lead."

The men turned the corner then, so relaxed they didn't even notice Kohl and Aina standing there. But Kohl lifted a gun so fast, they had no time to react. Aina moved, drawing a knife. Kohl shoved the closest man away so he slammed into the wall, and fired into the head of the man behind him. At the same time, Aina launched a dagger into the throat of the third man.

As the two dead men slumped on the stairs, Aina pushed the surviving one to his knees. She placed a knife at his throat and turned him to face his dead colleagues. Kohl leaned toward him then and spoke in Kaiyanis, his voice a raspy whisper.

Though she only understood a few words, Kohl's voice was threatening enough in any language. His eyes flashed while the man choked out a reply, and then Kohl nodded at Aina. She swept her blade across the man's throat and let him drop.

As she stepped away from the body, Kohl said, "Bautix is having them prepare to escort a shipment of weapons this weekend, so they've been trying to enjoy the city's nightlife before then. Let's find out what else we can." Then he moved to walk down the stairs, but paused, turning back to face Aina with a self-satisfied smirk. "I told you it'd be good to have me here."

Grinding her teeth in frustration, she said, "We still have to sweep the hallways. Let's check alternating floors and meet downstairs."

Without waiting to see if he listened, she took quicker steps down the stairs and slipped into the next hallway, where he thankfully didn't follow.

They met on the ground floor, and having found nothing more, they made their way to the next apartment building. The heat pressed down on them as they skirted through the crowds, so humid it felt like trying to breathe underwater. She cast a glance at the clock tower of a bank at the end of the next block; it was already afternoon, and she had to get back to the Dom to meet Ryuu, Raurie, and Lill. She waved for Kohl to hurry up, and they soon reached the next building. They repeated what they'd done at the first one, moving slightly faster this time. That search yielded nothing, nor did the next one.

As they stopped under the fire escape of the fourth building, Kohl turned to her and, with a hint of mock concern in his voice, asked, "Did you want to stop?"

She brushed the sweat off her forehead, glaring at him out of the corner of her eye. He still barely had a hair out of place.

"I'm fine," she said through gritted teeth.

"Are you tired?" He reached out a hand and brushed back a lock of hair that had fallen from her ponytail.

When his hand touched her skin, she felt like an electric shock went through her, and she was thrust back into a memory. Last month, after she'd failed at a job, he'd cornered her in an alley, punched her in the face, and then touched her chin softly like this.

She flinched back and grabbed his hand, taking two of his fingers and bending them back dangerously far.

"Did you want me to break your fingers?" she snapped, nearly spitting the words in his face. "Don't touch me, Kohl."

She pushed his hand away from her and hauled herself up the ladder, resisting the urge to kick him in the face when he laughed a little. She was supposed to be making him uncomfortable, not the other way around.

"Hot-headed bosses also get their throats slit, Aina," he said in a threatening tone, so low she almost didn't hear. She stiffened for a moment on the ladder, then shoved his words aside and continued upward.

This last building went nearly the same way as the others, and Aina was close to giving up—until, at the first window of the third floor, she froze. Four people had gathered in the sitting room, and one of them had a Jackal tattoo on her forearm. The woman looked up then, and Aina pulled back from the window.

Hissing to Kohl, she caught his attention and waved for him

to come over. He did, gripping the pipe running down the wall with his hands while his feet rested above the bricks.

"Can't hear anything," he said, peering into the room along with her. "You stay here where you can see them, I'll go into the hall and try to listen at the door."

She nodded, her fingers aching from holding on to the wall. She inched one foot over to the windowsill to have a bit more purchase. Leaning closer, she tried to hear more of the Jackals' conversation. Their voices were mostly muffled with the closed window between her and them, but she caught something: "Day after tomorrow, I heard."

"At an unholy hour of the morning," another one groaned. "I'll have to take the first train out to the port."

One of them stood from their chair then and the squeaking sound drowned out the next words another one said. Aina's hands began to sweat on the bricks. Edging her foot farther onto the windowsill, she strained to hear more.

Then her boot hit the window.

She yanked her foot back, but the Jackal woman who'd almost seen her before jolted upright from her seat, a pistol in hand already.

Her next words came clearly: "Heard something out there, and I don't think it's a bird."

Aina grabbed on to the pipe Kohl had been holding earlier as the woman approached the window. Swinging herself around the other side of it, she gripped it with one hand and one foot, her other hand and foot scrambling to find purchase on the bricks, feeling very much like a cave spider. With her back to the wall, she could see the exact height of the three stories she'd fall if she lost her grip.

At that moment, a loud knock sounded on the door of the

apartment. Aina barely breathed, trying to calm her racing pulse as the Jackals answered the door. "Blood King," one of the Jackals greeted perfunctorily when they opened the door. "Didn't know you knew where to find us."

"There are many things I know that you don't," Kohl replied without a pause. "Check that the Kaiyanis rebels aren't enjoying Lyra Avenue's revelries too much. They're already sneaking out and probably getting seen by plenty of Diamond Guards who will be able to tell they're not simple tourists. Keep them in line." He paused then, and added, with a hint of bitterness in his voice that Aina thought only she might be able to recognize, "Bautix's orders."

As his words died out, Aina made her way over to the fire escape and climbed onto it.

The window opened then, and she jolted behind the steps. The Jackal woman who'd almost seen her stuck her head out of the window, one hand still gripping the gun. She glanced left and right, then slammed the window shut and drew down the blinds.

Aina swore as she leaned back on the railing. They'd almost shot her, and Kohl had been the one to save her by distracting them. She needed to do something to throw him off, to make him scramble for a reply.

When Kohl stepped out onto the fire escape a minute later, he finally looked bothered—he brushed back his dark hair, sweat on his forehead and shoulders tense. "Did you hear that? The shipment will be here in two days, at the southwestern coastal port. They'll be putting it on a cargo train."

"I'm going to stop it," she said, looking out at the rooftops visible ahead of them, the bars and brothels and casinos spreading all over Lyra Avenue, and toward the Stacks. A pall of black clouds hung over it all. "You in?"

"Wouldn't miss the chance to put Bautix in his place."

She locked eyes with him then, and for a moment, she imagined grabbing him and flinging off the fire escape. But instead, she said the one thing he wouldn't expect from her. "Thank you, Kohl. The Jackals would have seen me if you hadn't distracted them."

The words were like poison on the back of her tongue—admitting that he'd helped her. He froze, his eyes narrowed as he took in her words. She kept her features casual, unreadable. He could taunt and threaten her all he wanted, but she had a better weapon: making him trust her. And she was just getting started.

He held out his hand to help her up, and this time she took it.

11

The training room in the Dom looked different at night,
wind jostling tree branches into the windows, the only light
the small candle Aina had lit in the center of the room. Aina
watched the flames for a moment, remembering the torches in
the tunnels under the city that led to secret underground worship services, and a chill spread down her spine. Down there,
being quiet was the only way to stay alive.

Ryuu had arrived before anyone else, having left early from a
meeting with his company's advisors, and got here before Aina
had even made it back from her job with Kohl. While Tannis finished a shooting practice session with the recruits outside, Ryuu
and Aina waited for her, Teo, Raurie, and Lill in the training
room.

"Did you know," Ryuu asked, yawning where he stood near
the window, "that running a business empire is tiring?"

"Try running a criminal empire. Can you shut that window?
I don't want anyone to overhear."

Once he did, he asked, "Do you feel any different now that we have this magic? Not physically, but like you're a part of something now."

She walked toward him, biting her lip as she thought of a response. "I feel like learning this magic is actually making me closer to my parents. I'm using it as a weapon, and I doubt they'd approve, but it feels nice in a way."

"It does, doesn't it?" he asked with a small laugh. Black bangs fell over the side of his face as he stared out of the window, hands in his pockets. The leaves of the willow tree outside left shadowed patterns on Ryuu's face, and Aina felt at ease in a way she hadn't all day with Kohl. "Makes me feel like I'm doing something right. People like Kohl, Bautix, all the Steels, they don't care what happens to anyone from the south as long as their pockets are full. I see why my brother wanted me to shut down the Steels."

"But what does that mean to you?" she asked, leaning against the window across from him. "There will always be people with more money than other people. There will always be people who think anyone different than them is bad."

"I know," he said, his brow creased. "But it's what we're doing with that money that's the problem. My family has money now, but they started as poor miners in Natsuda over a hundred years ago. And sure, King Verrain brought a bad image down on the Inosen and his fight against the Steels made a war. But before that, he was the leader who advocated that Sumerand focus on steam engine production and funded the education of some of our best engineers. The past and the future aren't always in opposition; magic and technology can stand side by side. So while I know we can't actually get rid of the Steels, we can change what we choose to do with the power and money the Steels have." He sighed then, not meeting her eyes as he said, "I don't think I've done a very good job. But learning this magic and standing by the Inosen is a way to start."

She waited a moment before replying, knowing the guilt he felt was less about being a Steel and more about how he blamed himself for not being able to save his brother from Kohl.

"Do it because you know it's the right thing to do," she said slowly. "Not because you want to be their hero. I know that's not what you actually want, but if you're driven by guilt, that's what it will become. I know you still blame yourself for your brother's death, even though you shouldn't. Trust me on that."

Even though you can't trust me in other ways, she thought, guilt twisting through her. She leaned back, intending to put distance between them, when he reached out and took her hand.

"Thank you, Aina. I know we've both gotten a lot of new responsibilities lately, and it's easy to be too hard on yourself. But you and Tannis are doing a great job with the Dom. All the employees here are lucky to have you."

He gave her such a sincere smile, she actually believed it herself for a minute. He locked eyes with her, half of his hair mussed up and completely at ends with the finery of his suit. It made him look like a boy she might have met in the Stacks, not one of the richest people in the city. His words reminded her of how close they'd grown in the past month, how they both tried to show each other a little of their worlds. And though he'd grown up in a mansion, his childhood had been as lonely as hers.

The sun had vanished then, leaving him outlined in moonlight. For a moment, her heart stuttered, and she was thrust back into her past with Kohl—the nights with him at the train station, him standing in the moonlight, her in the shadows. They'd spend hours there, her shooting careful glances at him while he twisted his words to make her further committed to him. She shook the memories away and looked back at Ryuu.

She'd grown to value his friendship, but sometimes, when they were alone like this, she remembered that there'd been more between them—shy looks, deep conversations, sharing their hopes and fears. When she'd betrayed him last month, he'd been angry and told her they shouldn't speak anymore.

But then they'd made up and here they were, still close, their friendship stronger than ever—and now she had another secret.

Her stomach twisted with unease. Was Kohl right to say they were more alike than she'd ever admitted? She swallowed hard, finding a bitter taste in the back of her throat.

The more pain she felt from Kohl, the more pain she seemed to inflict on others. It was better for someone like her to be alone.

Footsteps outside the room made them both break apart, and a moment later, Tannis and Teo entered the training room followed by Raurie and Lill, who both wore jackets despite the heat.

"Sorry we're late," Lill said, walking toward the candle in the middle of the room with Raurie. "We had to make a good excuse to leave, and couldn't look like we were in too much of a hurry."

"But look what we got," Raurie said with a mischievous grin. She reached into the inner pocket of her jacket and withdrew a small handful of diamonds. Lill did the same, and with defiant expressions, they spilled them onto the floor next to the candle. They shone bright on some sides, dull on others, glinting in the candlelight as if daring one of them to take them.

As they all gathered around the candle and the strew of diamonds on the floor, Aina felt a surge of purpose; they were all here to stop Bautix for their own reasons; for revenge, to protect the tradehouses and the Stacks, to stand up for the Inosen. She knew they were only a few people, but with this magic at their hands and all the determination between them, she knew they stood a chance. Teo and Tannis sat a little farther away in the circle, Teo with his arms crossed and Tannis leaning back on her hands. Raurie, Ryuu, and Lill knelt around the candle, each of them fidgeting slightly.

"How much do you think we can learn in the next two days?" Aina asked, kneeling next to Ryuu.

"Two days?" he asked sharply. "Is Kohl planning something?"

"Did they leave another note?" Teo asked.

Aina shook her head. "Bautix. He's hiding Jackals and men he's hired from Kaiyan in these apartments on Lyra Avenue, and Mirran found out where they are. I went there today and overheard when his next shipment of weapons will be. Day after tomorrow, coming from the coast."

Silence followed her words, and a ripple of energy swept through the group as they all realized a chance to stop Bautix was so close. A twinge of guilt worked through her; she'd mostly told the truth, but she'd left out that Kohl had been with her today. If they stopped Bautix soon enough, it wouldn't even matter; Kohl would die at her hands, and no one would ever need to know she was working with him.

"We need to stop it," Lill said, clutching one of the diamonds in her fist. "If Bautix gets those weapons . . ."

"The Inosen won't stand a chance," Raurie said. "Not while most of them don't even want to learn magic; they're too afraid of retaliation. Imagine, being retaliated against for trying to defend yourself."

"He sees you as a means to an end," Tannis said in a bitter tone.

Turning to Ryuu, Aina asked, "Can you get train timetables for the coastal line and blueprints of the shipyards at the western ports?"

"Easily," he said with a nod. "I'll get them by tomorrow, and I'll see if I can get more diamonds for us to use so Raurie and Lill don't have to risk getting caught."

Lill looked like she wanted to protest, but Raurie nudged her with her elbow and said, "Thank you, Ryuu." Lill grimaced and mouthed thanks as Raurie reached for one of the diamonds.

She held it up, twirling it to catch the golden light so a rainbow fell across the brown skin of her cheeks and along the training mat below them. An eerie hush took over the room, and Aina could swear she stopped breathing. She thought of Kohl earlier today, his smug face as he taunted her; the Jackals wreaking havoc in the Stacks; Bautix's note threatening the Dom she and Tannis had fought for when they'd both had nothing else.

"Where do we start?" she whispered, her anticipation rising.

"Learn to draw blood from someone to weaken them," Raurie said. "And how to stop it, in case someone on our side is injured and we need to heal them."

Aina withdrew a knife from the brace across her chest, then held it out to Raurie. As Raurie took it, Aina recalled the night Kohl had first handed her a knife and told her he'd make her into something more than a girl from nothing

With this magic at their fingertips, they would all prove what people from nothing could really do.

"How much blood will it make them lose?" Aina asked, leaning forward slightly, her eyes fixed on the diamond. "How does it make them bleed?"

"When casting the spell, swipe the diamond through the air in the direction you want to make a cut," Lill said. "Your intention will help you guide the direction of the cut too. It will make them bleed both internally and externally, and they might also bleed from their eyes, nose, and mouth. How much they bleed depends on how much you want to hurt them, and you can control that too. Sometimes, if the spell is strong, their veins and arteries can burst and kill them. Verrain did that to some people," she added, biting her lower lip. "But our enemies won't shy away from violence, so neither should we."

After bringing the knife to her arm, making a small cut and holding a rough diamond to it, Raurie said in a steady voice, "Nagan inoke."

A moment later, the diamond glowed with an internal, soft golden light. Raurie held it level with Lill's face. The light shining through it cast a rainbow pattern on the floor, on Raurie's hand, and her bloodstained knife.

A moment later, Lill's nose began to bleed. A trickle of red fell from her lips. She paled visibly, drawing in a deep breath, and one hand darted to an inside pocket of her jacket to pull out a small cloth.

Aina nodded approvingly. "I like that one."

"Of course you do," Teo snorted, but then met her eye over the candlelight and grinned.

Raurie held a hand to her own head, as if she felt dizzy, but a moment later she shook it off. "See? Like Gevann said, it weakens you a little too. But you won't be bleeding, so as long as you can keep focused, it should be fine."

"Did you find this one in the Nos Inoken?" Ryuu asked.

Raurie nodded, then pulled a small copy of the holy book out of her jacket pocket, as tattered as the one Aina's parents had used. "Lill helped, since we both know a good amount of the holy language. But it's similar to Marinian, which I picked up as a child when my parents were still alive, so I don't have many problems reading it." Then she scowled slightly. "That's one reason they stamped out the holy language, fined anyone who spoke it; more people would probably learn this type of blood magic if they could read the Nos Inoken."

"We found as many as we could last night, and practiced a

bit when we could hide it from the other Inosen," Lill said. "But just learning the words isn't enough to be able to cast the spells."

"Is it harder somehow?" Tannis asked, frowning.

"You have to intend it," Lill said. "It's simple to summon healing spells because we naturally don't like to see people suffer. If our house is crumbling, it's easy to have the intention of seeing it fixed by magic because you want your house to be stable and whole. You barely even have to think about it. But it's much harder to intend to make someone bleed. You have to be honest with it. It can't be that you want to practice magic, because that's not the real intention. You have to actually want to hurt the person."

"How do you do it, then?" Teo asked.

"I have to . . ." Raurie sighed and looked over at Lill. "I have to think of something I don't like about Lill. She swipes my food off my plate when I'm not looking sometimes. It's a joke, and I usually catch her and she gives back the food, but I have to turn it into anger. I have to think how we can't waste our food, and it's selfish of her to do that, and that she's making me go hungry. I have to take something true and compound how hurtful it is in my mind, even if it's not really that bad. I can usually make the thoughts go away after practicing these spells, but I hope we don't end up actually hating each other along the way."

"Don't worry," Lill said, her voice slightly nasally with the handkerchief still held to her nose. "I'll still swipe your food, Raurie, no hard feelings from me."

Raurie laughed, but a hint of worry still glimmered in her eyes as she spun the used diamond between her fingers.

"This is a small taste of what the magic can do," Lill said, her eyes bright as she drew the cloth away from her face. Some of the rosiness had come back to her cheeks and blended with the red violet of her hair. "It's power over life and death."

"So, you've been able to hide it well?" Tannis asked, a frown pulling at her lips. "I know your aunt wouldn't approve."

"We have," Raurie answered, brushing her hair back from her face as she looked at Tannis. "If June knew, she would never let me leave the safe house. Or she'd kick me out. One of the two." After a pause, she said, "Ryuu and Aina, you two should try now."

She and Ryuu faced each other, each holding a knife and a diamond. Before they started, Aina opened her mouth, wanting to say something, but she couldn't figure out the words. They had to pretend to be mad at each other to practice this spell . . . so what would Ryuu think of for her?

Ryuu concentrated on Aina's face for a moment before bringing the knife to his upper arm. When his blood touched the diamond, he held it up in front of her face like Raurie had done to Lill and said in a shaky voice, "Nagan inoke."

A wet sensation touched her chin and a coppery taste filled her mouth. A drop of blood fell on her hand where it rested on her thigh, bright and starkly red. Teo handed her a cloth to wipe her face with, and she did, hoping the cloth hid the trembling in her hands.

"Ryuu . . ." she said slowly, her heart twisting in her chest. He'd placed the knife and the diamond down with a tight grimace, and met her eyes with something like a plea in them. She didn't even need to ask what he'd thought of; Kohl had sent her to kill his brother. She'd failed, and it was before she even knew Ryuu, but the fact would always remain that she'd tried to. As close as they'd grown over the past couple of months, he could still dredge up that memory if he wanted to.

"My turn," she said eventually, her voice slightly high-pitched. Then, before even lifting the blade to her arm, she said in a rush, "There's nothing I don't like about you, Ryuu. None of this is personal."

He nodded slowly, and the plea in his eyes faded a little as she drew her own blood. Perhaps the way to think of it would be how she considered her jobs as an assassin. Find purpose and act without hesitation. She would focus on Ryuu's status as a Steel; she could hate Steels, even if he was different from all the rest. His glimmering gold watch and silk tie certainly helped strengthen that image.

Taking a shallow breath, she focused with one purpose—to hurt someone—before saying, "Nagan inoke."

Her skin prickled, her cheeks warming with the blood rushing through her veins. A small gust of wind swept past her and she breathed in sharply at the sensation. Her hand was about level with Ryuu's shoulder—she drew a short line downward, blood dripping down her hand as she did.

A narrow cut formed on Ryuu's shoulder, and blood welled at it. A tingling, slightly piercing sensation came to her own shoulder, but nothing too bad—as she watched, though, the cut on Ryuu's shoulder opened wider. He paled, one hand going to the wound, and dark red blood coated his hand in seconds. Before anything worse could happen, Lill acted—she drew a diamond and her own knife in a flash, blood appearing on her arm faster than Aina could blink, and said, "Amman inoke" in a forceful tone.

The blood stopped flowing, but Ryuu swayed. Aina reached out to steady him, feeling nausea and dizziness rise through her too. She gulped, forcing it down. As she and Ryuu both sat back, her hands shook. She'd hurt plenty of people before . . . but never a friend.

"What happened?" Ryuu asked as he drew in a few deep gulps of air.

"I don't know," Raurie said slowly, brow furrowed as she looked at Aina. "Nothing like that happened when we practiced earlier."

"Ryuu, I'm sorry," she said, her own dizziness passing enough to speak. He finally looked up at her then, and a spark of uncertainty lit his eyes. She bit her lip, hating that she'd put it there. "I didn't think of anything that strong. I thought it wouldn't even work."

"Well, think of it this way," Teo said slowly, his head tilted to the side. "As an assassin, you're taught to shove feelings aside when killing someone; makes the job easier when you see yourself as a weapon, not a person. There's no time for wavering, you just act. Maybe the magic is like a knife in your hands, no matter who you're using it against. You're a better killer than any of the Inosen without magic, so with magic, you're even more effective."

"Different from those of us who don't go around stabbing people for a living, I suppose," Lill said with an attempt at a lighthearted voice. "It will be useful against the Jackals."

Aina twirled the knife in her hands, her pulse racing. If she could control this magic, she'd use it against Bautix, Kohl, and anyone who threatened them. . . . She'd be deadlier than any Blade that Kohl had ever imagined. The aftereffects weren't fun, but she could get used to it, like she'd gotten used to being an assassin.

"We can look for more spells," Raurie said. "Harder ones, but maybe you'll find them easy if they're violent. I know it can't feel good when you do that to a friend, but against an enemy, it will be good for you to know them."

"We should get back now," Lill said. "They didn't expect us to be gone this long. We'll come up with some excuse on the way."

A dull clang of metal on stone resounded from the hall, breaking Lill's last word. Aina's ears perked, one hand going to the handle of her scythe.

It could have been a recruit dropping something, perhaps a weapon in the armory. It could have been anything.

But she and Tannis stood, each of them gripping weapons. Everyone fell silent.

"What the hell was that?" Aina whispered, turning toward the open door of the training room. She pictured the Jackals she'd attacked last night, the one she let get away. All the ones who stalked the streets of the south, getting closer and closer to the Dom by the day.

A crackling sounded, and then a gust of air like what she'd felt when using the blood magic.

She ran toward the door with Tannis and skidded into the hall, covering her face as bright flames rose up in front of her.

12

Aina pivoted, slamming her back against the opposite wall as flames tracked up the one in front of her. Teo and Tannis stood with her in the doorway, covering their faces from the heat, with Raurie, Ryuu, and Lill behind them, the flickering orange light reflected in their wide eyes.

Squinting against the sear of the heat, Aina searched for the source of the fire. A metal cannister lay halfway down the hall, and tracks of oil soaked the floor. She drew in a slow breath without caring about the smoke she inhaled, suddenly finding it hard to move from this spot even with shouts around her and the roar of the flames.

At the end of the hall, a window creaked—a figure clad in dark clothing, only the tips of blue hair sticking out from under his hat, caught her eye for a moment, then leapt out of the window.

"Get out of here!" she shouted back at the others, inhaling

another mouthful of smoke as she did. "Go through the window in the training room. Tannis, get the recruits out."

Aina ran down the hall toward the window, skirting against the side of the wall that wasn't burning—yet. Sweat ran down her back, and as she moved toward the window, sparks snagged at her clothes. She tried to shake them off, but the heat only grew more intense, like she was being burned alive and hadn't realized it yet. The glass on the window ahead began to melt before her eyes.

Looking over her shoulder, she saw nothing but flames and the dark shapes their shadows cast. There was no going back that way. The Dom was being destroyed, and the people who'd done it were getting away.

Taking one short step back, she was tempted to close her eyes, but that wouldn't save her from the fire. She ran to the window and jumped, pressing off the sill with her boots.

Curling into a ball, she landed on dark, wet grass and rolled to the side, dousing the flames that caught on her clothes. Some of her skin still burned, and she hissed through the pain, but there wasn't much she could do about it now. She stood in the dark night outside the burning Dom.

It would have been pitch-black were it not for the fire and the slashes of the red and silver crescent moons in the sky. Three people sprinted away from the Dom, toward the street where they could disappear in the alleys of the Stacks.

Fury burning through her like the fire above, she raced after them across the grass. A window on the second floor shattered and glass rained down with sparks of flame. A shard of glass pierced her shoulder, but she ignored it and ran faster, raising a scythe with one hand as she closed in on them.

One of them turned then, and her scythe reflected in his wide eyes as she jumped toward him. He cried out, but his voice cut off when she slashed him from shoulder to hip.

She wrenched her scythe out of his skin and pushed him off with the edge of the blade. A gunshot fired next to her, hitting one of the others squarely in the back. With a quick glance over her shoulder, Aina spotted Teo running from the side of the house, his gun still raised. The man he'd shot fell to the ground, his blood spreading across the dirt road under the light of the flames.

Aina turned toward the last person just as they swung their own blade toward her face. Darting backward, Aina lifted her scythe again and faced the woman—the Jackal from the apartment she and Kohl had spied on earlier today, the one who'd almost caught Aina outside the window.

Plumes of smoke filtered into the sky as they faced each other, and the panicked shouts of bystanders who'd come outside of their homes across the street clashed with the roar of flames behind her. The Jackal swung toward Aina's side with her dagger, and Aina caught it with her scythe, pushing against her as the heat of the fire made sweat pour down her face and into her eyes. With a grunt, she forced the Jackal's dagger away, then swung toward the Jackal's unprotected side.

As the Jackal darted away, the blade missed her side but cut her thigh. She hissed in pain as blood poured down the side of her leg.

The Jackal snarled and shoved Aina back toward the fire, her knife slashing out; Aina barely dodged it in time and the blade seared across her arm. Pivoting, she grabbed the Jackal's arm and twisted it around her back, then shoved her down and pinned her to the ground in front of the Dom.

"Tell me where Bautix is hiding, and I'll make your death quick," she said, and slammed the Jackal's chin onto the ground.

The Jackal yelled obscenities at her through a bloodied mouth, but her voice was drowned out by a new roar of flames. The heat hit Aina in the face when she looked toward the Dom, drawn to it by a dreadful tug in her chest. All the windows were melted or shattered into nothing as the flames steadily claimed it all. She had no idea if everyone had gotten out alive—her friends, her employees. Everyone she'd said she would protect. She'd failed them all.

Then she did something she'd never done before with a target so close; her grip slackened, the burning Dom the only thing she could look at now.

"Aina!" called Teo's voice from somewhere nearby; it was impossible to see far in front of her with the building smoke. "It's going to fall!"

The flames had cut through the bark on one of the trees in front of the Dom and it broke in half, the rest of its trunk and heavy branches falling to the grass, shrouded in fire and smoke. The one closest to Aina began to fall too, an awful creaking sound coming from the bark.

The Jackal lifted her torso and slammed her head against Aina's chin, then wrenched free and scrambled to her feet.

Blood in her mouth, Aina rose and chased her. But the Jackal pulled out a gun and shot at Aina's feet, making her step back as a wall of heat reached her from behind. Aina threw her scythe with as much force as she could muster. The firelight caught its blade as it cut through the air and into the Jackal's neck.

Aina rolled to the side at the last second as the burning tree fell toward her.

Then Raurie appeared outlined by the flames, coming from the direction of the Dom and raising a knife to her own arm quickly. She shouted two words that sounded like the holy language, but Aina could hardly hear over the loud flames and the nearby shouts for help. A moment later, the ground under Aina shook. A large rock jutted out of the earth, spearing upward toward the falling tree and cracking it in half. The bottom half fell to the ground, and Aina rolled out of the way in time to avoid the top half.

Tannis pulled Raurie out of the way while Aina grabbed the scythe from the Jackal's body, then got to her feet. As they ran, she looked back, wanting to run into the Dom to save whatever was left, but knowing there was nothing to save.

The door of the Dom had collapsed, charred wood sending plumes of smoke into the air that stung and watered her eyes; the same door she'd entered countless times, when she'd first arrived here with holes in her shoes and no hope left, after every job Kohl had ever given her that brought her closer to owning her own tradehouse, to when she finally walked into the Dom and took it as her own.

Her first, irrational thought was that this had to have been Kohl's work. But as much as he wanted the Dom back, it might also be the only thing that man had ever loved. He would never attack it.

Only one person would dare. The realization hit her like a spark of flames searing through her veins, turning the shock and fear of the fire into ash, and leaving only fury in their place.

Bautix had set the Dom on fire.

13

As midnight approached, they reached the safe house, but Aina could barely remember the walk through the Stacks and into the tunnels under the city. Her vision was hazy, her thoughts sliding in and out of focus.

The Dom was gone. She'd lost her home again. She breathed in the still air of the tunnel, trying to make sense of what had happened. In all the years since Kohl had started the trade-houses, no one had dared attack the Dom—they knew it was full of trained killers, reputations honed through years of brutality.

So what did it mean that now, once Kohl was gone and she was in charge of it, someone finally dared to strike?

One day, you're going to admit how much you need my help, Kohl's voice echoed in her head.

"Aina, look at me." Teo's hands grabbed her shoulders, and she was jolted back to the present. His eyes were alight with fear, even with the fire far behind them. His forehead creased in concern as they stared at each other. "You're all alive. You're going to be okay. Kohl hasn't won."

"It wasn't Kohl. Bautix attacked the Dom. That note he left, he promised to knock us down. The Jackals' attacks have grown closer to us every day." Then she swallowed hard, finding the bitter taste of ash on her tongue. "Kohl would never destroy the Dom."

"He wouldn't," Tannis muttered in agreement. Aina had avoided looking at Tannis since they'd run from the fire—but now their eyes met, and she saw her own disappointment, the sense of failure, reflected there.

The whole group had slowed to a stop and huddled in the narrow tunnel. Aina's gaze went to the rock walls, the shadowy crevices. The Inosen held worship services underground to be close to the Mothers, who lived in the earth—the mountains and caves of Sumerand, the tunnels burrowing under Kosín. Aina felt a brief chill in the darkness underground, but it was welcome after the fire.

Tannis stood next to Mirran, their faces gray and ashen. The three recruits had gathered in front of them, covered in soot and sweat—Kushik, Johana, and Markus. Johana held her arm gingerly away from her and Aina's heart clenched at the angry red welt along her forearm. Ryuu, Raurie, and Lill stood at the front of the group, singe marks on their clothing and the scent of burned hair coming off them.

"The tradehouses are proof that people from the south can prosper without the help of the Steels," Tannis added. "Bautix doesn't want anyone to have that kind of hope unless he gives it to them."

"That's why he hates magic too," Lill said, holding a flare that lit up her violet hair like they were in the fire all over again. "It's power that he doesn't have; it can't be created with money or steel. He's convinced he made the world safer by killing Verrain, and that every time we stand up for ourselves, it's a threat. Anyone who wants to be seen as strong usually allies themselves with him, not against." Something darkened in her eyes as she said this, but she didn't elaborate.

"Then that means we still need to fight," Raurie whispered, then looked at Aina and Tannis. "Don't let this stop you; they expect you to give up now. But this is exactly the time to strike back, which means we'll need somewhere to practice the Mothers' magic. Somewhere all of us can learn the spells at once, without worrying the other Inosen will see and try to stop us."

"What about in Amethyst Hill?" Lill suggested. "At Ryuu's ridiculously large mansion with private security? I can't think of a better place."

"Sure," Ryuu said, nearly stuttering over the word in surprise. "Come tomorrow—we can use the time to prepare for the shipment. I thought you wanted nothing to do with anyone who isn't Inosen."

Lill shifted uneasily. "I don't know. You are now, I suppose, and you're all proving yourselves to be . . . not completely terrible."

Aina and Teo glanced at each other, eyebrows raised. "We are?" Teo asked.

Just then, whispers sounded from somewhere deeper in the tunnel, and they all went silent. Lill turned off her flare. Aina, Raurie, and Lill flattened themselves against the nearest shadowy wall and stopped breathing—an instinct Aina had honed by years hiding from patrolling Diamond Guards in these same tunnels with her parents.

"Wait," Lill said, gesturing that they could step out into the dim light again. "I think that's my dad."

A moment later, torchlight rounded the corner, followed by two people; a middle-aged Kaiyanis man and an older Milana woman. The torchlight illuminated the black tattoo arced across both of their foreheads with three small diamond piercings.

"Urill and Sofía," Raurie said with a sigh of relief as Lill stepped forward to hug her father, who must have been Urill. He had light skin, freckles, and gold eyes like Lill, even though he had the bright blue hair of Kaiyanis people while she didn't; she must have been half Sumeranian.

"We came to look for you," Sofía said, taking in the small group with trepidation in her eyes. Aina then recognized her as the same woman who'd healed her last month after the night at the Tower. "Are these your friends?"

Raurie nodded, then gestured at Urill and Sofía. "These are the two other Sacoren who live in our hideout. Sofía's family and three other families are here too."

"You've been gone for a long time," Urill said, casting a disapproving look at his daughter. "You could have told us you were going to meet your friends."

"That wasn't what kept us," Raurie said slowly. "Can they come in?"

Urill nodded, and then Sofía beckoned for the rest of them to follow her.

They proceeded down the long, dark tunnel until a wooden door in the crevice of a wall appeared; Aina would have missed it if Sofía hadn't stopped then and inserted a key in a small hole at the top of the door. It swung inward without a sound. All of them kept quiet as they entered, and a hush greeted them.

When they turned a corner and entered a main room flooded with candlelight, there were several audible sighs of relief. Raurie's aunt, June, waved them over and pulled Raurie into a hug when she got close enough. There were nearly twenty people, all huddled in small groups around low tables with meager supplies of food spread out—porridge, lentils, scattered nuts. Most of them cringed back from the newcomers, and Aina watched as one woman pushed a small child behind her, like she expected them to attack. For a moment, she imagined her parents among all the people here, trying to hide as death stalked them. But hiding had only gotten them killed.

"What took you so long?" asked Raurie's uncle, who stood next to June. Then his gaze shifted to the rest of the group. "What happened to you all?"

Aina stepped to the front of the group, making sure her weapons were out of sight, and then said, "Bautix attacked the Dom. He sent the Jackals and some men he hired from Kaiyan to do it. If he did this to us, he won't hesitate to do it to all of you—you need to be ready. This was a warm-up for him."

Raurie spoke then, the words tumbling out as if she suddenly couldn't hold them back anymore. "The magic of blood and earth would work to defend against any attacks. We should be prepared to use it."

June's mouth pressed into a thin line, weariness etched on her features. "If this is about learning King Verrain's evil powers, you can forget about it, Raurie. We will not resort to violence. That is what they do, not what the Mothers wish for us."

"So what's your plan?" Aina asked with a humorless laugh. "Sit here and wait to die?"

"He's doing what he does best: stir conflict, make it look like there's endless violence if he's not in charge," Tannis said. "He treats everyone in the south as his scapegoats, and that includes you. Raurie's right—you should learn how to defend yourselves."

Everyone in the safe house went quiet, looking apprehensively between Raurie and June as if they'd heard this argument before and didn't want to get involved. But Aina's anger only grew the longer the silence extended, because this kind of complacency was what allowed the Steels to win—like her focusing so much on hunting down Kohl made her miss that Bautix was still a threat.

"Well?" Aina prodded. "If he attacks—no, *when*—what will you do?"

"You can do whatever you want, Aina Solís, but violence does not come easily for all of us," June said, her jaw trembling as she turned to Raurie, who nervously tugged at a loose strand of her skirt. Remembering how much Raurie had fought with her, Teo, and Ryuu last month to stop Bautix's last plans, Aina wagered that June had no idea what her niece did with her free time. "Raurie, you're going to get arrested if you try it. Your parents died for their choice to fight back, and I'm not going to let you follow them. The Mothers will provide for us."

Aina snorted in disbelief and shook her head. That was exactly the kind of thing her parents had said before getting killed. It was exactly like how, as strong and skilled and prepared as she and all the people at the Dom were, it had still been attacked.

She squeezed her eyes shut, hoping to close herself off from the world for a moment, but instead of darkness, all she saw were flames.

"Besides the fact that we believe our magic should only be used for peaceful reasons, what would it do?" Urill asked in a kind, placating tone. "You know it can't contain fires."

But Raurie had called up the earth to cut through the flaming tree. Maybe the magic couldn't stop fires, but it could be useful in so many ways if they stopped being afraid of the consequences.

"You don't trust me to use it in the right way," Raurie said to her aunt in a harsh whisper. "Why don't you trust me?"

June reached over and placed a weathered hand on top of Raurie's trembling fist. "I'm trying to protect you, Raurie."

As their conversation died out, the other Inosen began to set up places for the Dom's employees to sleep. Mirran and Teo spoke to the recruits in a low, comforting tone, while Ryuu tried to convince the Sacoren that they would be safer in his house. His shoulders sank when they told him they would stay here—they couldn't trust his neighbors or guards and they might get caught on the walk there.

Aina helped Tannis carry blankets from a corner to the Dom's employees. Dark circles shadowed Tannis's gold eyes, which seemed to have dulled, like the light was extinguished from them. "When Kohl recruited me for the Dom," she said in a low voice to Aina, "I thought all my troubles were over. I thought I finally had a place to live that wouldn't disappear, and I know you did too. But every time you think you can stop being afraid, they remind you not to get complacent. Kohl, Bautix, the Steels—they always find ways to prove us wrong."

The truth of her words echoed painfully in Aina's thoughts. When she'd first come to the Dom, she'd had nightmares every day about it all disappearing. As they passed the blankets to the recruits, she saw the hope had trickled out of their eyes. They'd already accepted that the nightmare was real. And that was what people like them always did—faced the harsh hand they were dealt and learned to survive in their circumstances. Reach for more but expect little. Save no room for dreams.

The only reason she'd had the dream to one day own a trade-house, run the business, be a boss . . . was because Kohl had promised to let her. If he hadn't believed in her, she would have stayed the same—fearful, unambitious, addicted to glue. She would be dead already, if she hadn't had that hope pulling her along.

Her eyes trailed toward the door of the safe house, imagining the tunnel and the city above—and where Kohl might be now. If there was anyone who would feel the devastation she and Tannis did, it would be Kohl. Her heart clenched, and she wondered if he'd already heard about the fire.

If he had, he'd want to destroy Bautix as much as she did now. Fury rekindled in her, making her draw her shoulders back and lift her chin. Raurie was right: now was the time to strike back, not cower.

She turned to the Dom's employees—Mirran, Kushik, Johana, and Markus. They all still looked dejected, broken . . . but she wouldn't let them stay that way for long.

"We're going to get our revenge for this," she told them in a fierce voice. "When have we ever sat back and let the Steels do whatever they want to us? That's not what the Dom is. Get some sleep tonight so you're ready to work tomorrow."

The recruits began seeking out spots on the floor to sleep as Raurie walked over, wringing her hands together. When Tannis turned to face her, Raurie whispered, "Thank you, for pulling me away from the fire back there. After using the magic, it was hard to focus."

The tension in Tannis's shoulders lessened as she said, "Well, I don't want to give up either. Thank you for reminding me."

As they spoke and helped the recruits set up places to sleep, Aina slipped out the main door and back into the tunnel.

But right when she was about to turn a corner at the end of the tunnel, footsteps sounded behind her and she paused to see Teo jogging toward her. Her heart sank a little—she would have to tell another lie, about where she was headed now. In silence, they exited the tunnels onto a street in the Stacks with rain pelting down. Mist rose above the dirt roads like smoke. She breathed it in, trying to get the clean air into her lungs.

"It's probably too late for the rain to help," she said, squinting through the mist and the deep night in the direction of the Dom, but it was too far to see from here.

"I thought I was going to lose you back there," Teo said suddenly, his hands in his pockets. The mist settled on his dark waves of hair and golden-brown skin, the droplets sparkling like little diamonds. "At the fire."

His mouth opened like he wanted to say something else, but he held back. After another beat of silence, she stepped toward him and wrapped her arms around him in a tight hug.

"Thank you for calling out that warning to me," she whispered into his ear, her head against his shoulder as she stared out at the misty streets. "I wouldn't have seen that tree. I wouldn't have moved back far enough, and Raurie's spell wouldn't have done much to save me."

"Of course, Aina," he replied, hugging her back, his breath warm on her face. "We have to look out for each other—no one else will. I'd never let you get hurt."

"Me either," she whispered back, and for a long minute they stood there under the awning of a building, letting the rain build up around them while everything within their circle of warmth remained calm. She'd need that calm for when she let go of him.

"You can all stay at my apartment too," he whispered. "You don't have to go underground."

"I know," she said. "Thank you, Teo. I'll talk to Tannis about it and figure out our next steps." Then she shook her head slowly. "All this time, I was so focused on Kohl. It's pathetic, really, that he hurt me so much. What kind of leader am I supposed to be if I can't focus on real threats? What if we got caught in this attack on the Dom because I was paying attention to Kohl instead of Bautix?"

"You're not pathetic for that. Tannis and Mirran didn't see it coming either. And you're allowed to still feel hurt."

She drew away slightly, looking out toward the rain-slicked

streets ahead, but then he reached out to take her chin in his hand so she faced him.

"You're belittling what he did to you, but I was there. I saw how much it took out of you every time he would pull you in and then push you away again, how he kept you there with promises but never let you get too far. I saw you after he took all of your money and left you for dead. And I saw how, every single time, you went back. You've finally pulled away for good now. I don't want to lose—" His voice lowered to a whisper when he next spoke, his brown eyes softening. "Don't pretend it never happened, Aina."

"I can't forget it, Teo," she said, pulling back so his hand fell to his side. "That's impossible. But what I also can't forget is that it made me weak, and being weak only gets you killed. It gets your house burned down and leaves you with nothing. You know that. And if feeling all that pain leaves me easy prey, like it did all those years I worked with him, then I don't want it. All of those emotions, Kohl would never let them get in the way of his work. Tannis pushes them away too, and I'll learn to. I can't afford to feel that strongly." She paused, letting their eyes meet briefly before saying, "For anyone."

As the rain beat down and mist clouded around them, Teo said, "You're not weak, Aina. And I haven't given up on you."

She swallowed hard, still tasting ash in her mouth. "You should."

Turning away before he could stop her or ask where she was going, Aina disappeared into the cascading rain. Breathing it in deeply, she tried to banish the scent of smoke that seemed stuck to her now, in her nostrils, all over her hair and clothes, but it wouldn't leave.

Descending the hills deeper into the Stacks, her boots sliding on the mud, Aina walked farther south. The mist rose higher here, thickening and casting everything in a faint silver glow. In dips in the road, the rain formed large puddles, and she could already see it seeping under doorways into homes. The summer rains always devastated the south, sweeping through in heavy deluges almost every evening for a month. Everything down here would be flooded by morning, and by then, everyone would know the Dom had been attacked.

Her gaze turned north when she cut through an alley. Bautix wouldn't wait much longer before attacking the rest of the city.

As she kept walking, she caught the stench of the river on the air, as well as the copper scent of blood. Slowing, she strained her ears and heard fighting from a nearby road. The dull sound of a punch, someone stumbling in a puddle, the clash of metal on metal.

She slid through an alley to the next street, holding her breath as she took in the fight.

With blood splattered on his clothes, Kohl faced four men. Two bodies already lay in the mud, and even without much light, Aina could make out the Jackal tattoos on their forearms.

One of the remaining Jackals was close enough for Kohl to grab; he cracked the man's neck, but instead of letting him crumble, held him up as a shield when one of the other men shot at him. He then tossed the body to the side and delivered a punch to the jaw of the man who'd been stupid enough to shoot at him from close range.

Daggers slid into each of Kohl's hands. He struck at the men to either side of him, and blood flowed from their necks a moment later. The final Jackal, the one Kohl had punched in the jaw, now faced Kohl with his own blade drawn. Kohl tossed his own weapons to the mud and backed the man into the wall of the nearest home. The man's blade touched Kohl's chest, but fear flashed in his eyes.

"Blood King, I don't know anything, I—"

"That much is obvious." Kohl grabbed the man's wrist and with one push, forced the man's blade up into his own throat. The man's eyes widened as he choked on his blood. Kohl watched and waited until the man went still, then let him drop.

A moment of silence passed where the only sound was the rain beating against the dirt roads and corrugated metal roofs around them.

"I know you're there, Aina," Kohl said then, and Aina stepped into the road.

She took in the bodies around her as she walked up to Kohl, a thousand thoughts flickering through her mind. Plenty of bold people had tried to corner Kohl in dark alleys and didn't live long enough to regret it, but she doubted that was the case here. These men had been scared and tried to fight for their lives but failed. She suspected, with a twinge of unease, that he'd cornered them instead.

"They're all useless," he said, bending to pick up his daggers. "None of them know a thing."

He straightened and finally met her eyes. Her breath caught at the devastation she saw there; he must know about the Dom. He'd taken it out on these grunts who had probably only become Jackals a week ago and knew nothing of Bautix's plans. All of Kohl's lessons on how to be a Blade flashed through her thoughts. They killed with discretion, focusing on their target and no one else. Only people who tried to kill them, got in the way of their target, or saw them and might rat them out were liable to be killed as well. Blades felt nothing. A killing spree blinded by rage was not in their repertoire.

But right now, it was hard to care. A brief surge of justice swept through her. She'd been right to come here; he wanted Bautix dead as much as she did.

"We need to talk," she said, then turned south.

A few minutes later, they reached the southern river docks. Raindrops smacked against the black surface of the water, louder down here than up above. Examining the houses, she spotted a wooden one painted green and on a raised foundation—it was probably the best constructed house anywhere this far south. A light was visible through the front window. Kohl nodded and led the way, pulling a key from his pocket.

She glanced once more in the direction of the Dom. Some wildly hopeful part of her wondered if the rain had stopped the fire in time to salvage anything, but before she could let that hope grow too strong, Kohl opened the door and gestured for her to enter.

14

Aina stepped into Kohl's new home. Everything was wooden, the floor and walls and all the furniture, except for a sofa in the middle of the room. There was also a small table and chairs, and a basic kitchen. A few doors led off to other rooms, and the whole place was lit with candles rather than the electric lights Kohl had favored in the Dom. She supposed he didn't have anyone to impress here. The candles gave off a warm glow, making the house feel rather comfortable. Annoyance prickled through her at the thought. He didn't deserve this when the Dom was gone.

A moment of silence passed as they both moved toward the sofa. His shoulders were still tensed like he was about to break something.

"Kohl," she finally said, and they faced each other at the same time. "They burned it down."

His eyes drew her in, turmoil reflecting in the blue depths like a storm on the ocean. He held his jaw so tightly, she thought he'd break his teeth.

The Dom was destroyed.

The only home they'd both had after their parents died and they were left alone in the world.

At that point, she was convinced no one knew her better.

She placed her hand on the sofa and it rested between them—she didn't think much of it, just silently decreased the space between them.

Memories flooded her mind: standing at Kohl's side in the armory and wishing he'd take her hand right before he threatened her; punching her in the face and taking all her money, and then saying it was because he cared for her.

As if building a shield around her heart, she tucked away the memories, the emotions, and hid them in the back of her mind. They weren't that bad, really, and should only belong to her weaker, past self. None of it would help her beat Bautix or stand up to Kohl once this partnership ended. Being hurt by the past was a waste of time.

"It had to have been him," Kohl said, one hand curling into a fist above his knee. His eyes took on that steel-hard glare she knew meant he was imagining killing someone slowly. "I'm going to gut that man alive."

She nodded in silent agreement, then leaned back on the sofa, her eyes trailing to the wooden walls, half in shadow and half in candlelight. If the fire had happened here, the house would be gone in seconds.

"Where are you going to sleep tonight, Aina?" Kohl asked. "Where are the others going to sleep?"

"They have somewhere, and I'm not tired," she said, though her eyes felt raw and her limbs heavy. How could she sleep when Bautix was still alive?

"Me either," he said, standing. "Make yourself comfortable."

Without another word, he vanished into a side room. She

looked around again, noticing a few doors in the back of the house. For the Stacks, it was rather large, and she wondered who this place had belonged to. Years ago, fishing had been one of the biggest industries for the country, before the water got too polluted from factory waste and no one wanted to eat the fish there anymore. Perhaps this had belonged to someone in the industry.

One ajar door showed the edge of a bed covered in only sheets. It was far too hot in the summer, and especially humid down by the river, to need anything more. Wiping sweat from under her eye and pulling her hair into a higher ponytail, she stood and peered into the other rooms.

One, where Kohl sat sharpening knives, was a smaller version of the armory at the Dom. Her stomach twisted at the thought. All those weapons had cost hundreds of thousands of kors, and now they were gone.

The last door was mostly closed, but Kohl had said to make herself comfortable, so she pushed it open and walked inside. Lighting two candles on a chest of drawers, she took in the room and suddenly felt wide awake.

Before Kohl owned it, it might have been another bedroom or maybe a study. But now there were two small cauldrons on a low table with burners, and several shelves of ingredients in glass jars—powders, liquids, roots, herbs. It wasn't as well stocked as the poison room at the Dom had been, but close enough.

Walking over, she opened a few of the jars, breathing in herbal and floral scents, her knowledge coming to life. Then she remembered the poison Bautix's men had used at the factory the other day—Kohl's brew.

If there was anything they were equals at apart from stabbing people, it was poison brewing. Without knowing the ingredients he'd used and not wanting to ask him for help, she couldn't create an exact replica, but she could make something similar. Not wanting to sleep yet and see the fire repeat itself in her dreams, she set to work creating that poison and making a few she used regularly in her darts.

She was glad she'd come here, to see Kohl's own hatred of Bautix, his resolve to fight back—it fueled her own. But it also reminded her that he would stop at nothing to get what he wanted, no matter who he hurt in the process.

As she set up the ingredients for the poisons she would make, she recalled a night with Kohl in the city's only cemetery, behind the mansions of Amethyst Hill.

Cool mist had swept over the cemetery, past simple tombstones and grand mausoleums. Fall had arrived, and the muddy ground was strewn with gold, scarlet, and umber foliage that crunched under her boots as she followed Kohl.

They'd stopped in the middle of a row, and after a few minutes of silent shivering, she did what Kohl usually discouraged and asked a question.

"Why did you bring me out here?"

Her voice seemed too loud that evening. The outskirts of Kosín were much quieter, the air much cleaner and calmer than within the city. Her gaze trailed toward the mansions at a short distance and a scowl took over her face. Through the windows, she saw a fireplace blazing in one, multicolored lights strung in another, the edge of a bed draped in wool blankets.

He nodded at a tombstone, but said nothing. She noted, then, how his hands had curled into fists and how his blue eyes seemed a deeper sapphire than usual. His shoulders had slightly tensed up like they always did right before punching someone in the jaw.

She took an involuntary step backward, cursing herself for her fear, but she couldn't help the small paranoia rising through her—was this going to be her grave? Had she done something wrong and he'd brought her here to kill her?

In the four years she'd so far lived at the Dom with Kohl, she'd seen him kill two other employees—one for disloyalty and the other for incompetence. Her eyes flicked south, toward where the diamond mines were settled beyond the forest. Had he discovered her secret; her small dose of freedom? Her heart pounded a staccato rhythm in her chest.

Then she shook away the fear. It was stupid. Someone was already buried in this grave. And besides that, she wouldn't get a tombstone like this one. She would be thrown in the mass graves south, where her parents' bones were piled somewhere along with the rest of the corpses whose estates couldn't afford a more private plot of land.

"You remember I told you about my old boss?" Kohl finally said, his voice low but whip-sharp in the silence. "He's buried here."

Frowning, Aina stepped closer, pulling from her memory what he'd told her of his old boss—how the man had taken Kohl into his gang, the Vultures, in the years before the civil war with the promise that he'd help him break his parents out of prison. He'd lied and gotten Kohl arrested instead. By the time Kohl had managed to break out of the prison, his boss had been caught and killed while trying to smuggle himself out of the city.

"How did he get one of these fancy graves?"

Kohl tilted his head toward her and, with a smile that made her heart flip, said, "Money. You see, if you're a rich criminal, this city treats you the same as if you were an upstanding official who'd never broken a law in his life."

She let out a small scoff, then resisted the urge to kick the tombstone. That would definitely hurt her more than it.

"Sometimes I wonder, is there a limit to how terrible they'll let me be?" Kohl continued in a musing tone. "If I kidnap their loved ones for ransom, if I ruin their businesses, if I kill Steels walking down the street . . . will they still treat me like a king based on the kors in my bank accounts?"

She smirked. "Even the Steels call you the Blood King. They might fear you, but they still think of you as royalty."

He laughed a little, his hands now hanging casually at his sides. As usual, he wore no gloves and seemed unperturbed by the cold. Remembering she was wearing mittens, she slipped them off and tucked them in her jacket pocket. She wasn't like the Steels who needed every comfort and luxury.

"I want to test the limits of this city, see how much greed they have and how heartless they are. At what point will they stop respecting me out of fear and start despising me as a monster? At what point will I force them to admit that they have more morals than I do?"

She bit her lip, not quite knowing what to say to that. Instead, she cleared her throat and said, in a voice that rang out, something she thought he might approve of. "Once you test their limits, get a mausoleum here." She nodded at the tombstone of his old boss. "Build it over his grave."

He didn't laugh this time, but his eyes had glinted with amusement. Then he said, "You're more like me than you know."

Inside Kohl's wooden house, Aina gathered ingredients for the poison. Now she could better understand why he'd asked her those questions in that graveyard one cool, autumn evening. He'd wanted her to reassure him that he had no morals, that all his work was methodical and selfish. He hated any bit of mercy that crept into his actions—how he gave homes and jobs to orphans, how he'd spared her as a child when he could have killed her, how he'd had an opportunity to shoot her in the Tower last month but hadn't. Her mere survival meant, to him, that he wasn't as strong as he made himself out to be.

Once this partnership with him ended with Bautix's death,

Kohl would come for her and control of the tradehouses again, and she'd have to be prepared, no matter how connected to him she'd briefly felt tonight. The longer it took them to truly face each other, the more brutal he would be when the time finally came—and the more vicious she'd have to be in return.

She lit a fire under a clay pot, and as she waited for it to heat up, she noticed the label of a glass jar near the back of his shelf of ingredients. The text in Milano had caught her eye. Gently lifting the jar, she gasped when she saw the full name: la orquídea reclusa. Kohl's stores weren't as sparsely stocked as she'd thought.

The purple flower that grew near the northern mountains of Mil Cimas resembled a common moth orchid, but the petals were a deep shade of purple and the center bloodred. While the petals themselves could be eaten, the seeds and stems were deadly. Her mother had warned her about it when she was younger and they picked flowers in the fields east of the city, even though they wouldn't find the orchid here, all the way in Sumerand. But she'd seen it among the ingredients at the Dom, and now here.

The scrape of metal on metal from the other room assured her Kohl was still awake. Wind and rain beat against the walls of the house. Vines climbing along the window from outside cast shadows along her copper skin.

She pushed away the memory of the girl she'd been in the cemetery that day years ago, trying so hard to please him and be a good employee who believed every word he said, thinking she owed him her life just because he'd given her a place to live.

That girl was worthless and was no longer a part of her. That girl would never manage to kill him.

Once the fire was hot enough, she began mixing ingredients, preparing her usual poison darts that could kill or paralyze her target, as well as making her new poison with the orchid. It was a liquid that could be drunk or inhaled—taken in a very small dose, it would make anyone who ingested it or inhaled its fumes take ill, but a little more and they would die within twenty minutes.

When she finished, she poured what she'd brewed into a round, glass vial and corked it.

The satisfaction that swept through her was nearly intoxicating. There was something empowering in weakening or killing someone without ever touching them. Like an invisible hand reaching out from her and delivering the blow. It was strength and cowardice at once, but as long as it got the job done, she didn't quite care.

Lifting the vial, she stared at the liquids swirling together as the poison settled. She'd have to test it before making any more.

She might be a monster who found joy in creating murderous poisons, but she preferred to be intoxicated by the powerful feeling this gave her rather than by things that robbed her of power, like glue, or Kohl.

Maybe she would use it on him.

The sound of Kohl's knives scraping against each other had stopped. With quiet footsteps, she left the room with the poisons, tucking her new mixes into the pouch tied to her belt.

The door to the other room was still ajar, and instead of sharpening his knives, Kohl sat cleaning his guns, without a trace of exhaustion on his features.

She sat on the sofa again, propping her head up with her hand, and waited. But he didn't come back out. The only sounds were his quiet breaths, the river flowing by outside, and the dull beat of rain and wind against the windows. Her eyes slid shut in moments.

When she woke the next morning, her neck stiff, it was to the sound of clattering in the kitchen in front of her. Her dreams of flames and shadows licking the circle of trees that had collapsed around her faded away. Kohl came in from the kitchen then, carrying a bowl of porridge toward her.

She narrowed her eyes at him. "When do you sleep?"

"When do you eat?" he asked, shoving the bowl and a spoon into her hands before going to get his own.

"I went out last night and got information from a few Jackals," he said after a few minutes, and she briefly wondered if these Jackals were still breathing. "Arin Fayes has invited the Sentinel for drinks on his boat today. And he plans to hide a few Jackals on the boat as well."

She jolted upright, her thoughts racing. Bautix's next move was now, mere hours after attacking the Dom.

"Are they going to kill the Sentinel? Before Bautix's weapon shipment even gets here?" She stood, checking her weapons and adjusting the pouch at her waist that contained the poisons. Her fingers grazed the vial of the new poison she'd made last night, and she kept it close to the front of the pouch as she zipped it closed.

"The weapons will help him," Kohl said. "But if he kills the Sentinel now, he'll have a clear path to the Tower."

And the city will be his for the taking, she thought, the idea chilling her as she left without waiting to see if Kohl would follow.

15

The river's stench seemed to follow them as they walked north, clinging to their clothes and hair. Since it was still early, the heat hadn't risen yet, but the air was thick with humidity. On days like this, people in the Stacks usually spent more time inside, but today there were even fewer people on the streets than usual. Aina squinted against the bright sunlight, peering down each road they passed for some sign of people, but there was a particularly deadened tone to her part of the city today.

Her gaze turned in the direction of the Dom as they walked. She couldn't see it from here, with miles of homes between the eastern and western shores of the river, but she imagined it standing charred under the sun.

The few people who were outside gave her and Kohl a wide berth when they walked by, and in the scurries between the people stepping back and closing their doors, she caught whispers.

"My sister lives there, she said they used Verrain's blood magic to set the place on fire," a woman said to her neighbor, while they both hung out of their windows. When Aina shot them a sharp glance, they nearly jumped out of their skin and ducked under their windows.

Though Aina kept one hand on a knife and glared at anyone who whispered something similar, the hair rose on the back of her neck, and she began to sweat not only from the heat, but from nerves. The news about the fire had spread, but what she hadn't expected was that people had caught wind of Raurie using blood magic during the fire. They didn't have the details right, but they knew Verrain's form of the Mothers' magic was back—and they seemed to think that Inosen had caused the fire, when that wasn't even something the magic could do. The Inosen had no reason to attack the Dom. It made no sense, but if those were the rumors spreading, then that would mean nothing good for the Inosen.

She watched Kohl out of the corner of her eye, wondering if he'd overheard that the Inosen were involved, but he didn't look at her again until they reached the Center.

"See this?" he whispered, pointing to the windowsill of a bakery a block north of the train station.

"What? Dirt?"

He shook his head sharply and walked to the windowsill, beckoning her so they both stood in the shade beneath the shop's awning.

"I know you were a child in the last war," he said under his breath, so low she had to lean forward to hear. "But I was old enough to remember. Whenever my old boss had me deliver messages and weapons to the fighters on the side of the Steels, this marking was always nearby, to show their allegiance."

Kohl jabbed his finger at a small etching on the windowsill, and though Aina didn't know what it meant, she'd gotten chills at Kohl's words.

"It's a pickaxe, isn't it?" She frowned. "Like on Sumerand's seal."

"That's what it looks like, doesn't it? The sword and pickaxe are everywhere, so it's inconspicuous. But this is an arc, the Mothers' symbol, with a slash through it. It's a sign of those who blame the Inosen for the war, no matter if they fought for Verrain or were innocent. You know how Inosen will leave markings on their dead, or on themselves to indicate if a business or home is safe for Inosen?"

Aina nodded, thinking of all the small signs she'd seen at Raurie's uncle's tavern, and a pit of dread opened in her stomach. "This is a direct threat to the Inosen."

"And a sign of support for Bautix," he said, then added, "He gains more support every day that he causes chaos and blames it on someone else. If he kills the Sentinel today, his followers will rally behind him to lead."

Without another word, he moved back into the crowd and she hurried to catch up. Soon they reached Rose Court, and it was much hotter up here; the sun beat off the pavement in waves that caused the lights and windows to shimmer and glitter. Tourists crowded the streets so Aina and Kohl walked one at a time along the shop fronts. The tone here was remarkably different than the south; people shopped without a care, laughing and gossiping along the clean cobblestone streets, leaning on fountains with bowls of melting sweet ice in their hands. None of their houses or inns had been flooded or burned down last night.

Between all the bobbing heads, she caught snatches of the harbor and its luxury boats ahead, and with a twinge of unease, she realized the intelligence of Bautix's plan. First he attacked the south, farthest from the people here. Instead of working his way up through the other districts, his next attack would be right in the heart of one of the richest areas of the city; none of them cared about the Stacks, so they would never see it coming—especially not the Sentinel.

Halfway down the main road, Kohl's hand wrapped around her elbow and tugged her to a stop. "Do you remember years ago when we robbed one of these ships? Mirran did the actual stealing, we waited as backup on the docks below, and when we killed those Diamond Guards, you got those four diamond-edged daggers you like to carry."

"Yes," she said immediately, shaking off his hand and continuing to walk. She hadn't thought he would remember that night so clearly—how it had revealed how well they worked together, barely needing to say a word to understand what the other meant.

He stepped in front of her so she nearly walked right into him. Over his shoulders, she could make out the docks, the passengers embarking or disembarking from planks leading up to ships, and the guards scattered between each port.

"What was the most difficult part of that job?"

"It was easy enough for Mirran to get on the boat and steal from them," she said, shrugging. "The hard part was the guards. Not the ones on the boat, they were useless, but the Diamond Guards they called over."

He nodded. "Getting onto the boat will be easy. It's the aftermath we have to worry about. We'll need a distraction to lure away the guards and a boat to leave on."

"Good, you take care of that," she said, and when he raised an eyebrow, she added, "When we started this partnership, you said I would take care of the dirty work so they wouldn't catch you being a double-crosser. So you stay out of the way, and I'll take out the Jackals and hopefully Fayes himself too. Agreed?"

He stared at her for a long moment, a slight smirk tilting one side of his lips as if this were amusing to him. Then he nodded and swept out an arm, gesturing for her to go ahead.

"You are the boss of the tradehouses, after all," he said in a low tone as she walked past him. "For now."

Pretending she hadn't heard him, Aina headed to the pier opposite the one with Fayes's boat, while Kohl vanished into the crowd. Bobbing in the river, the boat was three stories high with an open top. The sleek white surface gleamed in the sun without a speck of dirt. Electric lamps and hanging lights shone in every window. She assumed the Jackals would hide on one of the lower levels until they got a signal to take out the Sentinel.

A ruckus on the shore caught her attention then—a large, onyx-and-gold decorated carriage broke apart the crowd, pulled by white horses with golden manes and led by an entourage of Diamond Guards with rifles slung across their chests.

She ran her fingers along the hilts of her knives, wondering how many Jackals she'd have to take out today. The Sentinel would surely bring Diamond Guards on board with them, as well. Fayes would know that, so he'd make sure the Jackals weren't outnumbered.

She wished she'd had time to find her friends to help with this. But she'd faced worse odds before, and the anticipation of a fight filled her with adrenaline now. The four members of the Sentinel—Mariya Okubo, Clement Eirhart, Roberto Gotaro, and Petro Diaso—exited the carriage and approached the stairs leading up to the ship, surrounded by Diamond Guards on all sides. There was no sign of Kohl—only dazed tourists and jaded locals watching the Sentinel's display of power.

"Welcome, friends!" a booming voice called out from the other side of the ship. Standing on her toes, Aina could make out the stocky figure of a blond, middle-aged man standing at the top of the ship's steps. With his broad shoulders, wearing a jet-black Diamond Guard vest and the silver epaulettes worn by captains, he had to be Arin Fayes. Taking out one of Bautix's top allies and ruining his plans today would just be the start of her revenge.

She scanned the pier quickly, searching for a way to get over there without drawing attention. If she didn't make it there now, she'd be too late. Swimming would be the least noticeable way—and it was only about ten feet across—but then her clothes would be laden with water and it would be more difficult to move as quickly as she needed.

Something swayed in the corner of her vision. To her left, a long rope hung from the side of the ship closest to her, tied to a hook atop the next level.

Without a second thought, she grabbed it, took a few steps back, and ran.

Gripping the rope, she jumped and swung over the water. At the height of the arc, she let go.

She landed on the dock harder than she'd hoped, wincing as her knees hit the wooden surface. Rolling, she hid behind the side of the boat. The rope swung back to where she'd found it.

Footsteps sounded from the other side. Standing and withdrawing a knife, she peered around the edge and then jerked her head back. A guard approached with a gun drawn, his eyes searching the area for whatever had made so much noise.

Quieting her breaths, she let him get close, and right before he turned the corner, she stepped to the side and slammed her elbow back into his nose. Pivoting, she swept her knife across his throat, then pushed him into the waters of the harbor. His blood stained the wooden docks.

"Manet?" called a voice, probably using the name of the guard she'd killed. Flattening herself against the side of the ship, she waited for his fellow to turn the corner. His eyes widened when he saw her, but before his hand could reach his gun, she lunged forward and drove her blade into his heart. She kicked him off the end of the dock so he fell backward into the water, blood billowing into the sea around him.

Before making any other move, she checked her surroundings for anyone watching, then took in the situation on the side of the boat. The Sentinel and their guards were making their way up the narrow stairwell onto the ship. The last one to enter was Mariya Okubo, the only woman of the group and the one to whom Aina had revealed Bautix's plans last month. Once she vanished into the interior, two guards took up posts at the bottom of the stairwell. With so much protection around the Sentinel, how exactly did Arin Fayes expect to kill them? She saw no other reason for him to have Jackals onboard if that wasn't his plan.

A door stood open next to her, likely the one these two guards she'd killed had been watching. On the docks, someone in a crew uniform approached the door, carrying a bag with loaves of bread sticking out of the top.

As soon as he walked inside, Aina followed.

Silver sconces on the wooden walls lit the narrow hallway with a dim glow. The boat bobbed in the water, making it difficult to balance as she followed the crew member to the only door. She stepped into a kitchen, with one chef chopping vegetables on the far side and a few kitchen waitstaff donning aprons and stacking tiny sandwiches on a large plate. None of them had noticed her standing in the doorway. Ducking, she ran in a crouch toward the door on the other side, staying below the counters so they wouldn't see her.

It was a storage room for cooking supplies and food, equally empty of Jackals as the kitchen had been. She darted through it and into the last room on the floor, where she found a collection of cots, probably for the crew to sleep in. The quiet of the ship unnerved her, the sound of her own breathing setting her on edge. Anything could be happening with Fayes and the Sentinel, and she'd have no idea. She strained her ears, hoping to catch some sign of Kohl's distraction outside, but nothing seemed out of the ordinary yet.

A staircase running along the wall, with a wooden railing and burgundy carpeting, led to the second level of the ship. She approached it, the first step creaking under the weight of her boots. Peering upward, she took in what she could before moving onward—it was the main floor of the ship, a door open to the right with a sliver of blue sky visible. That must have been where the Sentinel had come in.

Staying on the balls of her feet and in the shadows, she ascended the staircase, trying to make as little noise as possible on the creaking steps.

The second floor was one open room with a large dining table, but none of the Sentinel were here. Voices came from the third floor—the deck—with a staircase leading up to it on the opposite side of the ship. Behind her, a door stood ajar, revealing an office with a large window. Empty.

Where on this goddess-damned ship are the Jackals?

The boat suddenly shifted, hard enough that she almost lost her balance. She gulped. If this thing started sailing farther along the river, she didn't know how she'd get back. She knew the basics of swimming, but she'd never swum long distances before. The only solution was to work fast.

Footsteps pounded up the stairs behind her. Darting to the other side of the table, she crouched and hid behind its thick legs.

One of the waitstaff approached the door, and with a quick tug of the wires holding the staircase, withdrew it. It almost slammed into place in the doorway, but the waiter slowed it with his hand, easing it into place so it didn't make a sound.

Right before it closed, Aina heard a shout from the dock—the

Diamond Guards below. The waiter's sleeve slipped slightly as he locked the door shut, revealing half of a tattoo: a Jackal's snarling maw.

Before he could turn around, she leapt on top of the table, aimed her dagger and threw it into his throat. He made a strained choking sound as blood spilled freely, coating the clean white floor. She jumped off the table, then withdrew her dagger from his throat.

While dragging his blood-covered body to a corner, her mind raced. If the Jackals were all disguised as waitstaff, some were probably upstairs serving drinks. She couldn't waste time with the Jackals still downstairs—she had to get to the ones above as well as Fayes himself.

She raced to the stairwell, but halfway up, a loud boom shook the boat. It tilted sharply to one side and Aina slammed into the nearest wall, wincing as pain shot up her arm.

As the boat settled back in place, she looked over her shoulder and through the window of the office. A fire blazed on the docks with smoke billowing up from the carriage the Sentinel had arrived in. The horses that had been tethered to the front broke off, raising their front legs and squealing in panic as they tried to get away from the fire. People on the docks scattered, shouts rising up.

She let out a small laugh under her breath. Kohl's distractions were certainly effective. Without wasting another moment, Aina ran to the top floor, then stopped where a wall curved around the edge to the open top. Holding her breath, she peered around it.

A round table was set out, the beechwood finish of it gleaming under the harsh sun. All four members of the Sentinel had risen from their seats, Diamond Guards close at hand and alert. The Jackal waitstaff had paused halfway through pouring champagne into crystal glasses, and one overflowed, falling and shattering on the floor. They all stared open-mouthed at the docks as flames and smoke rose from the Sentinel's carriage.

Arin Fayes stood slightly back from the group, taking it all in—the fire he hadn't expected, the Sentinel who now realized something was wrong, the Diamond Guards ready to shoot anything that moved—and then, with a nonchalant shrug, he snapped his fingers.

The Jackals all withdrew their guns at once, aiming them at the governors' heads. The Diamond Guards drew their own weapons and a hush settled over the deck.

Aina flattened herself against the wall, keeping one eye on Arin Fayes as she loaded her blowgun with paralyzing poison darts. In quick succession, she blew into the gun, firing darts into arteries on the sides of the Jackals' necks. They dropped to the ground in seconds, and she stepped out from behind the wall.

The Diamond Guards turned their guns on her, and she rolled her eyes.

"Are you serious? I just did your job for you!"

A gunshot broke the tense silence, and Aina ducked, thinking Fayes had pulled out a weapon—but then she saw Gotaro, one of the Sentinel, fall backward with blood spilling from his temple.

"Get them downstairs and someone re-anchor the boat before we're stuck in the middle of the river," Aina hissed at the Diamond Guards still shielding the other Sentinel governors.

They paused for a moment, staring at her incredulously until Mariya Okubo barked at them, "Move already!"

Crouching, half the Diamond Guards circled the three surviving Sentinel governors and moved with them toward the stairs leading to the main floor. She really hoped one of them managed to stop the boat from floating out any farther. The docks were at least twenty feet away now. Panic lodged in her throat, but she didn't have time to think about it—the Jackals would arise from their paralysis in a couple of minutes, and there was still Arin Fayes to deal with.

"Things didn't exactly go to plan today, did they?" she asked, approaching him slowly.

He took her in with hazel eyes hardened by years of fighting, and she knew he was judging how much of an opponent she would be—she only gave him a second, then stepped forward with her dagger drawn. Feinting to the right, she struck toward the left, but he blocked her blade with a dagger that appeared in his hand in the blink of an eye.

Straining against the force of his weight, her boots began to slide along the slick surface of the dock. Bending her knees to get more purchase, she pressed forward, trying to force him back.

Suddenly, the night with Kohl, Tannis, and Mirran robbing a similar ship came back to her. When a Diamond Guard had held a knife to Mirran's throat, Kohl had distracted him so Aina could move behind him and deal a killing blow.

She didn't need his help now to win.

With a grunt, she pushed Fayes back so he slammed into the railing. Her knife had gotten caught on one of the buttons of his vest and it tore off, leaving strands of black thread behind. The button clinked across the smooth white deck and a folded piece of paper fell out of its back.

Just then, she noticed the rest of his buttons: the stitching around them was odd, as if someone unskilled had taken them off and then hastily sewed them back on.

And then it hit her: the notes the Jackals were passing to Fayes to plot secret entrances into the Tower.

Fayes struck her with a punch to the gut that forced her backward and knocked the air out of her. She rolled toward him on the deck with her knife drawn, plunged it into his ankle and then ripped it out. When he shouted in pain, she pinned him to the ground.

Her blade met his throat. "Give me your vest."

Struggling with her pinning him down, he shrugged out of the vest. Once it was off, she kicked it aside so he couldn't reach it, then bent over him again with her knife. But then, a bullet pinged off the railing and froze her in place.

Her eyes flicked toward the direction of the gunshot, and she spotted the sniper. On the top floor of the boat at the next port, the one Aina had come from, Bautix himself stood with a pistol drawn and a smirk on his face. He aimed his gun at her. She was close enough to Fayes, though, that he couldn't shoot without risking hitting his partner.

A surge of fury rose up in her at the sight of him, utterly fearless and unrepentant as he waited for any chance to shoot her too. The man who'd given the order to kill her parents, whose laws had killed and imprisoned the poor and the Inosen for years; the man who'd burned down the Dom.

Just wait, she thought, meeting his eyes. *You have no idea what's coming for you.*

Then she shrugged, as if admitting that he had the upper hand here. In one quick movement, she abandoned Fayes, grabbed the vest, and threw herself toward the stairwell as another bullet flew over her head.

But before she disappeared down the steps, she uncorked the fatal poison she kept in her pouch and rolled it along the deck. It landed next to one of the Jackals. Arin Fayes had slumped down next to the railing, trying to staunch the flow of blood at his ankle.

That would soon be the least of his problems.

Closing the door to the deck so none of the poison's fumes would reach them, she went halfway down the stairs and peered through a window at the other ship, then swore. Bautix was already gone from the deck.

Running down the last of the steps, she drew up short when she spotted the Sentinel and Diamond Guards gathered on the main floor. A crew member stood at the wheel, steering them back to shore, with a Diamond Guard aiming a gun at his head to get the job done faster.

Maybe she'd saved the three remaining governors' lives, but she didn't trust them not to turn on her or somehow blame her for what had happened. She had to get off this ship before any of them noticed her. Two of the windows on the opposite side of the boat were open, with just enough space that she might be able to squeeze through.

While the Diamond Guards were busy, she darted across the room to the windows, pausing once to glance back at the Sentinel. Mariya spotted her, her jaw tightening as she and Aina briefly locked eyes—like she was confused why Aina had bothered to save her. After rolling Fayes's vest into a ball with the buttons inward to protect the notes and then stuffing the vest under her shirt, Aina hauled herself through the window, held her breath, and dropped into the water with a loud splash.

It was cold even in the summer, and she fought hard against the weight of her clothes and weapons pulling her underneath. She broke the surface, gasping for breath and shoving wet strands of hair out of her face. The waves caused by the boat pushed her forward, and she almost slammed into one of the poles holding up the docks. She had to wrap herself around it not to get dragged back out into the water.

She took deep breaths, spitting the water out of her mouth, and watched as Fayes's boat re-docked. Her eyes flicked to the top floor, where his figure slumped against the railing—he hadn't moved at all, and none of the Jackals were standing either.

Dust still billowed along the docks from the explosion, with people running and shouting in different directions, Kohl's distraction providing plenty of chaos. Her hands tightened around the pole, breaking off bits of wood with her fingers. Bautix would have already disappeared into the fray.

"Aina," a voice said behind her, and she nearly fell off the pole.

Kohl was there, on a small boat he'd procured from Mothersknew-where. He held out his hand to pull her up, and once she was on the boat, they sailed away around the northern edge of the city.

"Bautix killed Gotaro," she said under her breath as the docks disappeared from sight.

There was a small pause from Kohl. And then he said, "He's started a war."

16

They traveled close to the shore, Kohl throwing Aina a
set of oars as they made their way around the city. The shadows
of the bridges and the grass at the shore would shield them from
view of anyone walking above, but Aina's nerves were still on
edge.

In the span of two days, Bautix had burned down the Dom
and killed one of the Sentinel. His threat to take back the city
in a week seemed all the more real now, and the importance
of stopping the shipment of weapons tomorrow only grew. Her
hands clenched around the oars. If she got out of this boat near a
bridge, she could head to Amethyst Hill now to meet her friends
and finish planning for tomorrow's shipment.

Or she could go to the Dom. Her head turned south, but she
tensed at the mere idea of seeing it now. What if there was really
nothing left? Her heart ached, and just as she was about to draw
into herself and ignore Kohl for the rest of this trip, he spoke.

"What else happened on there?" Kohl asked, his breath surprisingly close to her face—she couldn't see him, as he sat behind her rowing with his own set of oars, but he must have been close.

Before answering, she took in a deep breath of the fishy, polluted river air, grateful for the shadows that covered them and relieved some of the afternoon heat. The fight on the ship felt far away now, but Kohl's words rang true: Bautix had started a war, and this was only the beginning.

"Fayes was meant to lure them all to the deck, and the Jackals were there to keep them from running. Bautix himself shot Gotaro from the top of the ship at the next dock. I couldn't get to him, but I got the rest of the Sentinel downstairs, and I killed Fayes before getting off the ship."

"That's good," Kohl finally replied, monotone.

She craned her neck back to look at him, raising an eyebrow at his less-than-enthusiastic face. "I just took out one of Bautix's most valued allies. After we stop the shipment tomorrow, his plans will be ruined. He'll show himself again and we'll kill him."

"And once he finds out you killed Fayes, how will he retaliate?" Kohl snapped back, a tick going off in his jaw as he spoke. "I'm glad he's gone; it needed to happen eventually, but you underestimate Bautix's flair for revenge."

"He underestimates my flair for revenge," she hissed back at him. "I don't care how angry he is. I wasn't going to let him get away with attacking the Dom."

"I'm not saying you shouldn't have, but to be wary of what will come. Now he knows you're out to get his people. And if he can't get to you specifically, if you dodge him well enough with all your skills . . . who do you think he'll attack instead?"

A cold sweat built at her brow as she took in his words. They'd curved around the northeast corner of the city and the river spread south ahead of them, the lights of Rose Court left behind.

The answer to Kohl's question was ahead of them too. As if reading her mind, Kohl let go of one of his oars and the wooden tool splashed in the water. He stretched out his arm and pointed, his wrist resting lightly on her shoulder.

"The south," he whispered, and when she looked to the right, he'd leaned closer, his blue eyes glimmering in the sun. "Our home. The place we've both worked for years. Do you see why I want to win instead of him? He'll destroy it if he takes over the city. War is all that man knows. But once I take back the south, I'll lift it above all the rest."

His words left her with a chill. They both wanted the south. They both wanted it to thrive. They both wanted to rule the tradehouses, the Dom. The fact that they were really fighting each other, and that Bautix was just an obstacle in between, had never been clearer. She wondered if he felt the sudden tension rise between them, the knowledge that one would kill the other soon, even though they sat rowing a boat together in the sunlight now. But his face was as impassive as ever.

Apart from that, though, his words shook her. Bautix had already attacked the Dom. What would he do once he realized she killed Fayes?

"He can try as much as he wants," she said. "He's not getting the south. Where will you meet me for the shipment tomorrow?"

He leaned back then, taking up his oar again, and she was grateful he wasn't as close anymore.

"Smugglers usually bribe Diamond Guards directly when they want cargo placed on the trains, so I won't know where exactly the weapons will be until it's time. I'll ask the Jackals once we're on the train, and then I'll head to meet you. Wait for me in the dining car and we can get to the cargo from there."

She nodded, already thinking how to present this information to her friends when she met them tonight—and how she would manage to meet Kohl on the train without any of them noticing. A bitter taste rose in the back of her mouth at the idea of lying to them once again, but then she listened to Kohl's steady breaths behind her and reminded herself she wanted this partnership to only be between them. Killing him with her own hands, with no help, was the only option if she wanted to prove to herself she could stand without him.

"Bautix may be brutal and unpredictable, but if we stop this shipment and catch him off guard, we can end him." Kohl paused for a moment, then asked, "Did I ever tell you how I managed to get out of serving him at the Tower? How I got him to respect me when I was an escaped child inmate with no money or influence?"

"No," she muttered. "Stop here."

They both pushed hard with the oars to steer the boat toward the shore at the eastern edge of the Wings. It still bobbed along in the water, but was moving slowly enough that she'd be able to get out at a good spot.

She turned around to look at him. It was something she'd wondered for years, how Kohl had gone from prison inmate to founder of the tradehouses . . . but he didn't like to speak about his years before the Dom.

But maybe through the past, she could find some new weakness in him—something to use against him when the time came. Leaning forward and trying not to show too much curiosity in her eyes, she said, "I know you got in a fight and pushed your friend Clara off the balcony in the prison, and then you ran. Where did you go from there?"

"I ran through the Tower and found Bautix's quarters. I wasn't trying to find him specifically, just someone from the Sentinel."

"How did you get all the way there with no one catching you?"

she asked, remembering all the guards and servants she'd run into last month going from the underground prison to the first level of the Tower. "Don't they live at the very top of the Tower?"

He shrugged. "Got lucky with guard patrols and stuck to the right shadows, I suppose. I brought one of Bautix's own knives to his throat while he slept. I thought he'd be scared, but he opened his eyes and smiled like he was already expecting me. He congratulated me on managing to put him in such a precarious position and then offered me a drink."

"What's wrong with him?" Aina scoffed.

With a small chuckle, Kohl said, "When you get a lot of death threats, I suppose they start to become lackluster. So he served me a glass of wine and asked me to explain how I managed this feat. I told him I broke out of the prison, and then I got a bit more confident and told him how I used to gather information for my old boss and was one of the best at it."

He tapped his fingers against the side of the boat, clearly tense at the memory. Wondering why he was telling her this at all if it made him uncomfortable, Aina stayed silent, watching his small reactions—a darkening of his eyes, a small intake of breath before his next words.

"So then he told me he didn't like loose ends. He knew who my old boss was and that he'd learned plenty of Bautix's secrets during the war, so Bautix had him killed. But he remembered that my boss had an excellent spy on his side. I took the opportunity: I offered to get information for him like I did my old boss, if he let me go free."

"And that's when you started the Dom?"

Kohl shook his head. "That was when he told me that the wine he'd given me was poisoned, and that I would die in an hour unless I managed to find the infirmary and ask for the antidote. If I survived, he would hire me as a spy within the Tower's walls."

Aina's mouth fell open a little. She imagined a younger Kohl, hardly out of childhood, stumbling through the cold stone halls of the Tower, poison weakening him as he fought for one chance at survival. As much of a mess as she'd been at that age, addicted to glue and struggling to find any reason to keep trying, she didn't know if she would have made it.

"You survived," she said finally. "So then you worked for him."

"For a couple of years, yes. But I was better at figuring out secrets than Bautix wagered. I learned that he'd rigged those political murders of Steels to keep tension high during the war and profits rolling in through his arms sales. I learned he would do anything to hold on to power. But I was tired of being his rat in the Tower, so one night, I cornered him and poisoned him too. I told him I knew all his secrets and that I was leaving the Tower a free man. I left the antidote in a puddle in an empty cell on the lowest level of the prison. He had to crawl down there and drink it off the floor in front of all the prisoners."

He laughed a little then and, though it was the middle of a bright summer day, Aina suddenly felt like it was a cold winter morning.

"I find poison to be useful in mocking someone before death," he continued, his eyes wistful as he gazed at the gray apartments towering above them on the shore. "You want your victim to feel death coming from the inside—not something they can stop with a bandage. You want them to know you consider them so far beneath you that you won't even deign to fight them head on. And sometimes you want to rob them of their dignity before they die. Some call poison a coward's weapon, but I call it the best way to insult whomever is dying. And if you hold the antidote, that gives you even greater power over them. But stabbing someone?" He paused, letting out a low breath before saying, "That's personal. I think, to end someone with a knife through the heart, you have to love them a little. Or at the very least, respect or fear them enough that you know poison alone or a bullet through the back just won't give you the same satisfaction."

He turned to look at Aina, who said nothing. For a moment, she couldn't help feeling bad for him. Like her, his life had been controlled by someone else at a young age, someone who worked by threats and backstabbing.

"And then you started the Dom," she said.

"I did small jobs at first, leasing out criminals for hire. Bautix offered me a job a couple of years later. He told me he would let me do my work as I pleased in the city, as long as I kept discreet about his doings and did the occasional odd job for him. He's the one who gave me the idea to set up business in one of the old manors, you know. He learned to stay out of my way, I kept his secrets, and we still benefited each other. That first job he gave me was to spy on a worship service and take out any of the Inosen found there."

Aina's breath caught. That was the job where he'd found her and her parents. Glass shards seemed to pierce her heart at his words, but she forced herself to show no reaction—not to reveal how easily he could still get to her.

Just how weak she still was in front of him.

"I've told you this before," he finally said. "But that was the first job I was ever paid to kill someone, and only my second kill. If I told you how scared I was before going in, how much I wished my life had gone a different way, you wouldn't believe me."

She looked up then, wanting to tell him this changed nothing. He'd still killed her parents, left her on the streets, promised her a future and then ripped it away again. Nothing he said about fear or regret would change that.

"Right then, I knew I would owe Bautix my life forever if I didn't do something about it—I had no idea then that it would bring you here as well, facing the same enemy." The blue of his eyes deepened as he stared at her before saying, "I'll see you tomorrow, Aina. Soon enough, Bautix will be out of our way."

She kept her expression unreadable as she met his gaze, wondering who would falter first; who would offer the other an antidote or a blade to the heart.

17

After climbing the river shore, Aina retreated to an alley in the Wings and pried off the buttons from Fayes's vest to get to the notes inside. Leafing through them, she tried to dry the ones that had gotten wet, but they were already illegible. The ones that were still intact, though, gave enough information on the secret entrances into the Tower to be useful. Her nerves tingled at the thought. They might actually stand a chance.

After pocketing the notes and abandoning the vest in a dumpster, she turned south toward the Dom. A few hours still remained before she'd meet at Ryuu's mansion to practice more blood magic spells, and besides, she needed to see it. What kind of leader was she if she could never look her failures in the face?

As she walked, it began to rain again. The dirt roads of the Stacks quickly turned to mud under her shoes, and the sheets of rain falling marred her view so she could only see about five to ten feet in front of herself at any moment. Shielding her eyes with her hands, she walked faster to reach the Dom. She'd take one good long look and then leave—just enough to fuel her anger toward Bautix. Kohl would say to never let her personal feelings get in the way of a kill, even hatred toward that person, because weapons felt nothing, and that was when they were most effective. But she wanted Bautix to know he wasn't just another kill for her; this was revenge.

With a shaky exhale, she turned a corner and reached the long line of manors; about ten of them stood along the river shore, their windows dark, front doors falling off their hinges. Squatters stayed in most of them, but some were so out of shape that no one bothered; floors caving in, rat infestations. Once the rich who'd lived here decided they didn't want to live next to this lower part of the city where more and more low-wage workers were beginning to arrive, they'd turned to Amethyst Hill and never looked back.

The Dom lay in rubble near the southern end of the row of manors. The second floor was gone, scattered in heaps across singed grass, while the first floor was somewhat intact—the front wall had collapsed inward while the back and sides were beginning to buckle. It would fall soon too. An ache tugged at her heart, pulling her toward it through the cascading rain.

A few feet away, she halted, noticing someone else stood to the side of the Dom, arms crossed, her blue hair wet and sticking to the side of her face.

"Tannis?" Aina called, her voice nearly drowned out by the wind and the rain beating against the ground.

Tannis jolted, tearing her eyes away from the Dom. Once she spotted Aina, she walked over, saying nothing when she reached her—the devastation in her gold eyes was clear enough to not need words.

"It's worse than I thought," Aina said, crossing her arms and digging her nails into her skin. "Everyone in the Stacks will know about it by now."

"I'm surprised Arman hasn't sought us out yet to complain how this never would have happened with Kohl." Tannis grimaced, her voice bitter. "Where did you go last night, Aina?"

Aina opened her mouth to answer, then paused, unable to think of a proper excuse when the Dom looked like this right in front of her.

When she still said nothing, Tannis tugged her arm lightly. "Let's stand over there, out of the rain."

Still with her hand around Aina's arm, Tannis led them to the awning above the front door of another manor. When they reached it, Aina blinked the rainwater out of her eyes and considered what to say. She would tell everyone together about killing Fayes and his notes, but she wouldn't tell anyone she'd stayed at Kohl's new place last night. From the corner of her eye, she watched as Tannis leaned against the door next to her and squeezed the water out of her hair.

"It makes me so angry thinking that if Arman did come to mock us, he'd be right," Tannis said, her voice low and hard. "This wouldn't have happened if Kohl were in charge."

"Only because he was on Bautix's side," Aina said, then froze, knowing her words implied that he wasn't anymore. But when Tannis didn't look immediately suspicious, she continued, "Things would have been much harder for him if he didn't have that support."

"Maybe that's true," Tannis conceded. "I used to think of him as an older brother, you know? Back when we were in the Vultures together, and then when he asked me to join the Dom. As the tradehouses grew more successful, he would take every opportunity to make me fight for my place. Working for the Dom wasn't an invitation anymore, but a privilege. And I worked hard to keep that privilege, that's for sure, but it also proved to me how dangerous it is to trust anyone. It gives them power over you." Tannis let out a shaky breath, one of her hands curling into a fist where it still held her damp hair. "I'm grateful I have you here because I don't know if I'd be able to do this on my own. You need allies to succeed in this city, and I've never been good at that. I've spent most of my life trying to stand on my own and avoid getting close to people, knowing how they could use it against me. But I'm trying to let go of that fear."

When her words trailed off, Aina's heart ached. She knew what it felt like to fear trust.

"You come from nothing too," Tannis said, turning to face Aina directly, her words almost drowned out by a gust of wind. "And you've had to fight for everything you have. It makes it easier to trust you. Easier to like you."

The shade covered half of Tannis's face, leaving one eye molten-gold in appearance and the other like the glint of sunlight on water. Tannis reached up and brushed a strand of hair behind Aina's ear, her hand lingering there. Tannis's eyes flicked to her lips once, and a blush rose to Aina's cheeks.

It makes it easier to trust you . . . But Tannis couldn't trust her—she was working with Kohl.

The way he'd touched her chin or brushed her hair back from her face—always before delivering a threat or reminding her to be faithful to him—played in her thoughts over and over, tightening around her like a vise.

The person she could trust least in the world was herself.

"I know," she said, catching Tannis's hand and then bringing it down to their sides. "But I still can't trust anything I feel, as long as he's alive."

At least that was what she wanted to convince herself—but even if she killed him, the memories would still be there, and so would the fear. He would never stop haunting her.

Tannis grimaced, her eyes flashing with doubt. Then she shook her head and stepped away slightly. "Well, that's what you're learning this magic for, isn't it? Everyone else is probably at Ryuu's house already. Let's go meet them."

By the time Aina and Tannis reached Amethyst Hill, the rain had only turned more ferocious, the ground now slick mud beneath their feet. Tannis tried to speak to her a few times, but they couldn't even hear each other over the wind whipping downward from the hills ahead.

The guards at the gates of Amethyst Hill allowed them in without fuss, stating that Ryuu had told them he was expecting visitors that day. Since becoming friends with Ryuu, Aina had come here more often than she ever had in her life before, but this neighborhood full of Steels' mansions still unsettled her. The cobblestone path ahead led past mansions large enough to fit at least ten families comfortably inside. Ryuu's maple tree-lined mansion was at the very north end of Amethyst Hill, so they passed every other house on the way there. Normally, walking past such bold displays of wealth made her uneasy, but today the empty streets and the dark clouds blanketing it all made the whole scene strange—like walking through a dead city.

A maid led them through the marble halls and up to the second-floor library, where Ryuu, Raurie, Teo, and Lill waited for them. Cedar wood beams extended to the center of the ceiling, the wood scent permeating the space. She breathed it in, glad that it was much warmer here than outside. Before stepping farther into the library, she watched them all for a moment and steeled herself for hiding the truth about her work with Kohl once more.

"There you two are!" Raurie said, waving them over.

Then, at the same time that Lill asked, "Where did you go last night?" Ryuu asked, "Did you hear what happened?"

Pretending she didn't hear Lill, Aina took a deep breath and asked, "About Gotaro? I was there."

"Why would he kill Gotaro now?" Raurie asked. "He hasn't even gotten the weapons to take over the Tower yet."

"He's too confident." Teo scoffed. "He thinks because he attacked the Dom, he can take down anyone in the city."

Teo met Aina's eyes then and gave her a quick, slightly nervous smile. She returned one but couldn't help the guilt squirming through her as she remembered their conversation last night.

"Wait, Aina," Tannis said. "You said you were there? What happened?"

Shaking thoughts of Kohl from her mind, Aina said, "I found out who Bautix's contact in the Tower was. It was Arin Fayes, a Diamond Guard captain. I knew he'd be on his boat today, so I went after him, but I didn't know he was inviting the Sentinel there to try to assassinate them. I took out some of the Jackals he had with him, but Bautix still managed to shoot Gotaro. The rest of the Sentinel got off alive, and I killed Fayes too. Bautix will find out soon enough that I did it."

She wondered whether they could smell the scent of the river on her skin, Kohl's icy breath on her cheeks, and know she was lying to them. The thought sent more shame curling through her, but she reminded herself why she was doing it—this arrangement was between her and Kohl—and the thought of anyone helping her stand up to him instead of doing it on her own was more unbearable than the lies.

She refused to look like she'd gone back to him, like she was weak enough to be ensnared by him again. They were working together, that was all.

"I still can't believe Bautix killed one of the Sentinel just like that," Lill said, shivering slightly.

"He probably wants to show them he's not afraid of them," Teo said, his brow furrowed in thought. "It wouldn't send as much of a message if he killed them all at once. He wants them to be afraid before he kills them."

"So we should stop him before he manages anything worse," Aina said.

"I got everything we need for tomorrow," Ryuu said. "I'll go get it."

As he left, the group moved to the round table in the sunken center of the room.

"It's so odd being in a mansion after spending most of the last few years in cramped apartments or underground," Lill said, her voice echoing off the walls of the circular room as she stared, open-mouthed, around the grand library. Then she closed her mouth and looked at the floor, as though ashamed of herself for being impressed.

"I know the feeling," Aina murmured. "But there's no need to be ashamed about it. Ryuu wouldn't judge you; he judges himself more."

Lill gave an uneasy shrug as the two of them trailed at the back of the group. "He doesn't judge, but he doesn't understand either."

"I wouldn't be so sure about that, Lill."

Ryuu returned a few minutes later with several large, rolled-up papers tucked under his arms. Lill's words reminded Aina of yesterday evening at the Dom, when Aina had thought of the fact that Ryuu was a Steel in order to use the blood magic against him. But she knew circumstances didn't define a person; they were a part of you, but what you did with them was far more important. Her heart clenched as she looked at Ryuu, wanting to speak to him again about what had happened. But he didn't meet her eyes when he crossed the library and smoothed out a map of the docks across the table.

"Before we start," Aina said, withdrawing Fayes's notes from her pockets and spreading them over the map, "this is information about the secret entrances into the Tower that Bautix had Fayes building."

Tannis leaned across the table and began riffling through the notes. "Really? That's good information, Aina."

Ryuu had picked up a few of the notes and read them quickly, his brow creased. "I recognize the locations. Looks like a lot of them are passages that served old kings and queens in case they needed an escape. I thought they were all closed up during the war."

Aina nodded. "Fayes and however many other guards are in Bautix's pocket had been reopening them and also adding new ones. It looks like Bautix is planning to send people through multiple entrances, all at once, to have his men break into different parts of the Tower. There's also a note proving that Fayes is the one who helped Bautix track down some of the prisoners we freed and blackmail them into working for him."

"Does it say anything about where Bautix is hiding?" Teo asked.

"No, unfortunately," Aina muttered, her hand curling into a fist in frustration at how he'd gotten away today. "But the Tower should know about these entrances. Bautix won't wait much longer before striking."

"I don't know how you'll get it to them," Ryuu said slowly, twisting his fingers together as he stared at the letters. "After the assassination, the Tower is on lockdown. I'd even have to go through multiple stages of security if I wanted to talk to them."

"We'll find a way," Aina said, trying to inject confidence into her voice. "But this all makes tomorrow even more important. We have to stop Bautix's shipment so that he can't even try to get into the Tower."

Ryuu shifted aside Fayes's notes and said, "Trains from the southwestern port and the northwestern port leave every hour from each, alternating so there's a train every half-hour."

He drew two lines from both ports along the main railroad heading east toward Kosín, his long fingers making steady and precise marks with a charcoal pencil. He'd drawn the map of the rail lines himself, showing where they entered Kosín and marking major stations.

"They'll be coming from the southwest," Aina said, pointing to a label marking that station. "Is it a passenger train or cargo? Where are some places they might put the shipment?"

"It's a mix of passenger and cargo," Ryuu said, "but it's the first stop on the line, so there won't be too many people boarding. Just tourists or business travelers from overseas. The train is cheaper than taking the luxury ferry along the river, so people traveling on a budget will take this train. Smugglers are known to hide their wares in cargo boxes. There are only a few Diamond Guards who patrol the trains, and they're all bribed to look the other way. The ride lasts an hour from the coast to Kosín, so we'll have that time to find whatever they're putting on the train and stop it from reaching the city. And if we get a chance, we'll take the weapons for ourselves."

Aina glanced up at that, surprised at how devious his plan was. With a smile, he pulled a pouch from his pocket and passed it to Raurie. After she took it and opened it, she gasped and nearly dropped the bag.

"How many diamonds are in here?" she asked, her words nearly tripping over each other.

Ryuu shrugged. "I raided my parents' old closet and found a lot of clothes and jewelry with diamonds."

"We'll have to be careful tomorrow," Raurie said, cupping the bag of diamonds between her hands. "There will be more of a chance for people to see us using Verrain's magic if things get out of control on the train. I'm scared what will happen to the other Inosen if someone catches us."

"He's most likely planning an attack against the Inosen," Aina said, a bitter tone to her voice as she recalled the symbol Kohl had shown her in the Center earlier. "People are already spreading rumors that Inosen started the fire at the Dom. Bautix can use that to gain even more supporters."

"Aina's right," Lill said, her eyes cast downward. "You know there are Jackals who might know where we are, Raurie."

"If that's the case," Teo said, "then you need to leave the safe houses as soon as possible."

"Where to, though?" Raurie muttered. "There's a risk to us wherever we go."

Ryuu cleared his throat and gave Raurie and Lill a pointed look. "My house has thirty bedrooms."

"Anything we suggest, someone in our safe house will have a problem with," Lill said in a soft voice. "And your neighbors will report us if they see any of us."

"Not if you're careful," Ryuu said. "I'm not going to sit back and let you all get hurt if I can do something to stop it. Just know that the option is there; it always will be."

"I hope we won't always need it to be there." Lill sighed. "My mother abandoned us years ago, that's why it's only me and my dad. When my own mother wasn't trustworthy, how can I put my faith in someone else? And I know the rest of the Inosen feel the same; we're too afraid to trust anyone. It's nothing against you, Ryuu."

He grimaced slightly, as if he didn't really believe her, then said, "We should start practicing, then."

Teo and Tannis stayed at the table discussing the plan for tomorrow, while Aina, Raurie, Ryuu, and Lill gathered in a circle a short distance away, each of them holding a knife. Aina hoped Ryuu had a good excuse for why there was blood all over the library floor once this ended.

"I think we should start with healing spells, before we all have to pretend to hate each other," Raurie said with a grimace. "The important thing to remember is that this magic can only heal you from blood loss or diseases of the blood. It can't cure anything else. Like the other spells, you need a diamond, and it can only be used for this one spell."

"There are rumors, though, aren't there?" Ryuu asked. "Of people with strong enough faith and purpose that they're able to heal without diamonds or blood?"

Raurie gave an uneasy shrug. "There are stories of it in the Nos Inoken of people who gain that power after having some kind of divine experience, but it's hard to tell what's real. I've never heard of anyone in our lifetimes doing it, at least in Sumerand or Marin."

"To start, we should each make small cuts on our arms and see if we can stop the flow of blood," Lill said, passing diamonds around to each of them. "The cut should seal over too."

"Aina . . ." Raurie began slowly.

"I won't join the violent part," Aina said, putting her hands up as if in surrender. "I'd end up making a river in here."

Aina watched as they started, for some reason feeling nervous about this healing spell. She'd heard the words countless times, and it was easy, wasn't it? To want to heal someone. She'd get this right.

Everyone seemed to find it pretty simple, and when it was

Aina's turn, all her fear had dissipated. Lill drew a small cut on her own arm, and Aina raised the diamond she held, dotted with her own blood.

"Amman inoke," she whispered, staring at the cut on Lill's arm. The blood that had trickled out was beginning to dry on the freckled skin of Lill's arm, but the cut remained.

"That's odd," Lill said, peering closely at the diamond. "Nothing happened. Maybe you pronounced it wrong? Try again."

Frowning, Aina stared at the cut again and said in a clearer voice, "Amman inoke."

But as she watched, blood began to bubble at the edge of the cut, dripping once more toward the floor. She didn't even feel the exhilaration, wind rushing through her ears, skin tingling with magic, that she had the last time they practiced.

Lill reached over, taking the diamond from Aina, and performed the healing spell on herself—same diamond, same words. The cut healed over in moments.

"I have never heard of anyone struggle with healing before," Lill said, her gold eyes wide.

With a twist of guilt, Aina thought of how the magic had affected Ryuu the other day—hurting someone had come easily. Of course the Mothers would make healing difficult for her, she realized with a bitter irony. Her parents had been great healers, and all she did was kill. "I think the issue," Raurie began, her brow furrowed, "is that you're just trying to fix the problem. Like a puzzle that needs to be solved. You're not trying to heal the person."

"What's the difference?" Aina muttered under her breath, unable to conceal her disappointment. It wasn't as if she'd dreamed of becoming an assassin as a child. And now she couldn't even heal anyone with this magic when she wanted to. It was like the Mothers were making a joke out of her.

When no one had an answer, she shoved aside those bitter feelings and learned two new spells with Raurie, Ryuu, and Lill. The first was the spell Raurie had used to draw up a rock from the ground to stop the burning tree from falling on Aina.

"Shinek inoke," Raurie said slowly, and waited for them all to repeat it before saying, "It raises the earth. Shinek means 'to bring up.' And like the spell to draw blood, you can direct where it goes. I don't think we'll be able to practice that one here, but the opposite—the one Verrain used to collapse the factory buildings during the war—is 'Cayek inoke.' I think there's a way for us to try that one—Ryuu, do you mind if we break some things?"

Ryuu smirked. "Go for it."

For the next hour, they practiced breaking wooden chairs in half—cutting at different angles, making sure their cut was forceful enough to go all the way through—and then putting them back together with the normal spell, "Amman inoke." Aina was just relieved that all of these spells, unlike healing, worked for her.

After they finished that, the others began practicing the spell to draw blood once more. Aina itched to join, but she didn't want to end up hurting any of them, so she retreated to a wooden bench next to the rain-speckled window and twirled a small diamond in her fingers, casting rainbows on the wooden bench.

When some time had passed, Ryuu walked over to sit next to Aina on the bench. She tensed a little when he approached, but this time, he offered her a smile instead of a stiff nod.

"You know when I said the Inosen could stay here, the invitation is also open to everyone from the Dom."

"Thank you, Ryuu," Aina said, then looked to Tannis, who stood a few feet away and had looked over at those words. "But the tradehouses have never been in Amethyst Hill. We stay in the center of the city no matter what."

Tannis nodded in agreement. "Your people looked at the Dom today, didn't they?"

"Early this morning, they did," Ryuu said.

"They what?" Aina asked.

"After you left the safe house, Ryuu and I talked about it," Tannis said. "There are so many old manors there. If we get a new one up and running, it'll show the Dom is much more than a building. He won't get rid us that easily."

"We'll be able to get a new place set up for you really fast," Ryuu said.

"You didn't say anything earlier," Aina said to Tannis, a small spark of hope making her sit up straight.

Tannis shrugged. "Ryuu and I planned it together, so I waited until we met him to tell you."

"Thank you," Aina said, flicking her eyes down to the diamond in her hands. When Tannis walked back over to watch the Inosen practice, Aina said to Ryuu, "We'll be able to pay you—"

"Stop," he said sharply, holding up a hand. "Don't even think about it." Then he sighed, taking the diamond from her fingers and twirling it in the light. "I'm sorry, Aina, about what happened with the magic yesterday."

"I'm sorry too," she murmured, holding his gaze for a long moment. "Ryuu, I know there are some things between us that might not ever go away. What I almost did to your brother—what Kohl did to him—"

"You're not Kohl, though," he pointed out. "You didn't kill my brother."

But I'm working with him again, she thought but didn't say, pulling her legs up to her chest.

Apart from her other friends, Ryuu was the one who'd also suffered a loss at Kohl's hands. She cringed, her heart aching at the thought. She was working with the man who'd killed Ryuu's brother.

Without even consciously thinking about it, she shifted farther away from Ryuu on the bench. Yes, working with Kohl was a ploy to get to Bautix faster . . . and yes, she would kill Kohl once this was over. But she was still hiding it. She was still talking to Kohl, connecting with him in ways she'd promised herself she never would again—finding more and more ways they were alike.

Silence fell between them for a minute. She stared out at the library—the first place she and Ryuu had met—and noticed, then, that he was also watching Raurie and Lill practice blood magic. Lill yelped as the chair she was practicing on broke in half with a loud creak, and Ryuu laughed a little under his breath, his eyes on Lill the whole time.

Good, Aina thought, sinking back onto the bench. *He deserves someone far better than me.*

She should be alone. She drew in a deep breath, trying to quell the ache in her heart that opened at the thought. Since she'd started this partnership with Kohl, all she'd done was push away anyone else. A lump built in the back of her throat, and she turned slightly to the side so Ryuu couldn't tell that anything was wrong. The last time she'd felt this alone, even while surrounded by people, was when Kohl had been her boss.

But all she did was hurt people. She couldn't even do a healing spell. For someone who was just as terrible as Kohl, being alone was what she deserved.

After another minute of silence, Ryuu reached for something he'd hidden behind his back, then held out the porcelain horse from her mother. It was covered in ash, but remarkably still whole.

She took it from him, her fingers shaking slightly, and cupped it in both her hands—fearing it would fall apart if she wasn't careful.

"How?" she asked, her voice incredulous. "The fire gutted the whole place."

"We looked around for things that could be saved. Some shelves and the desk had collapsed in the office, and most of it burned, but this was trapped underneath so much stuff, I guess it escaped the flames. I don't know how it didn't shatter, though. It got lucky."

It's been a bit of a good luck charm to me over the years, Kohl had said.

"I know it's hard, losing the Dom like that," Ryuu said. "I don't know what I'd do if I lost the mines—so many people depend on you to hold it all together. You spend all your time trying to be as strong as they think you are, but you know it's not enough."

With a sigh, he stood and walked back to the middle of the library to practice. Aina stared out of the window at the rain-streaked grass. Maybe she should find Kohl now, spend another night in that cabin by the river.

But once Bautix was gone, she and Kohl would face each other, see who would strike first. And although it was inevitable, part of her almost didn't want to find out.

18

The next morning, barely an hour after dawn, Aina, Teo, Ryuu, Raurie, Tannis, and Lill got off the train at the port. Aina breathed in the fresh air, free of the pollution plaguing Kosín, and stared ahead at the pale blue sea for the first time.

She shook out her legs, which felt stiff after an hour of sitting on the train. She'd attempted to get up and walk around, but the shaking of the train along the tracks made her sit back down each time and wonder why anyone actually liked these things.

They'd almost missed the train to the ports that morning, since Diamond Guards had been enlisted as extra security in an effort to find the assassin who'd killed Gotaro. The Sentinel must have known it was Bautix, but didn't want any more support of him rising up in the wake of the attack, and so they played dumb. Rolling her eyes at how useless it was, Aina had led her friends through a side door held open by a bribed janitor, and they'd reached the train just in time.

"I like it out here," Teo said, breathing in the ocean breeze and letting his eyes close briefly. Aina fought down a smile, but admired how he looked so at ease just by being outside the city.

"I hate it," Tannis said, wrinkling her nose at the sight of the sea visible from the platform—the sea that separated Sumerand and Kaiyan. "Reminds me of Kaiyan, but smells slightly less like fish."

"You're so grumpy in the morning, Tannis," said Raurie, who'd been spinning her bracelet of small blue and purple stones to catch the light. Tannis frowned at her, but when Raurie shot her a bright smile, her features softened somewhat.

"Well, we won't be here for long," Aina said, looking toward the docks and ships ahead. Bautix's men likely had a covert method of getting the weapons to the train.

They all gathered in a circle on the platform, and Raurie passed small handfuls of diamonds to Aina, Ryuu, and Lill. Closing her hand in a fist, Aina could see flashes of the sun on each of the diamonds through her fingers. If Bautix was bringing in weapons as well as more hired guns from Kaiyan, and having Jackals supervise it all, there was every chance they could be outnumbered today. It was risky to use the magic where the other passengers on the train might see, but part of her didn't care; she'd make all of Bautix's men bleed if that was what it took to win.

Ryuu checked his watch and said, "We should get on the opposite platform now. The train back to the city will leave soon."

"And then we just have to find the weapons, steal as many as we can, destroy the rest, and try not to get killed while doing it," Lill said with a smirk. "Solid plan."

They moved to the end of the platform where a rusted red staircase led to the other side and lined up along with the regular passengers. Dozens of people had gathered with their luggage, bleary-eyed and blinking in the sunlight as they waited for the train in front of them to open its doors.

A few minutes later, train attendants unlocked the doors and gestured for passengers to board, helping lift heavier luggage and directing traffic. Aina searched the platform as they did, trying to make out some sign of Kohl through all the bobbing heads, even though she knew he'd be out of sight. Right before boarding, she noted which car was marked on the outside as the dining car—about ten cars up from the one she was entering, closer to the back of the train.

"We only have an hour, so we should split up," Aina whispered to the group. "We'll take forever if we don't. When you want to use your magic, remember to stay out of sight. Let's meet on the roof of the dining car in thirty minutes to see what we've found, all right?"

That had to be enough time to find the weapons and regroup, especially with Kohl's help. She noticed their skeptical looks but pretended not to. This was the fastest way to get the job done.

They broke off then, and Aina moved farther along the line of cars. Looking over her shoulder, she checked that the others were far enough away, then boarded. Stepping aside from the passengers squeezing past her to reach their seats, Aina stood in a corner of the luggage storage area, one hand on the handle of her scythe. A family took one frantic look at her before hurrying away with their children.

A few minutes later, the train lurched out of the station. A low rumble of voices rose up from the passengers, mingling with the creak of the train's wheels on the tracks below them.

She moved then, walking fast down the aisle and stepping through the vestibule between cars and into the next one. The countryside flicked by the windows as the train picked up speed—wheat fields, pastures, and a winding mountain spine that curved along the coast and then inland just south of Kosín. She held on to the walls and backs of seats as she traversed the halls. Some cars were private with a glass door separating the narrow hall, while others were public with double rows of seats and a hall in the middle. Every time the train lurched with a turn or the wheels bumped against rocks on the tracks, her heart jumped into her throat. The ride out to the coast—her first time ever on a train—had been frightening too, but at least she'd been seated for the entire trip.

By the time she reached the dining car, her nerves were on edge. That had taken at least ten minutes out of the half hour she had. Catching her reflection in the window on the door of the dining car, Aina quickly fixed her hair into place and forced her features into an unreadable expression. She wouldn't let Kohl see a bumpy train ride had rattled her.

Kohl stood at the counter, sipping from a drink, as she walked in. Other passengers at the small tables and booths in this car looked up at her and then quickly away once they spotted her weapons. Kohl hadn't seen her yet, so she watched his profile, taking in the tense set of his shoulders. A tick went off in his lower jaw, which he clenched tightly.

She leaned her weight on the floor, making it creak a few steps behind him, but he didn't even turn. He always noticed when someone approached him.

In this moment of vulnerability, she watched him, wondering what was going on in his head. Early morning sunlight flicked through the windows, light and shadow over and over. Whenever the light hit, it painted gold on his pale cheeks, lightened his oak-brown hair, and made him seem closer to the man she'd used to hope he could be rather than the monster he was.

The voices of the other people in the dining car filled her ears with a buzzing sound, mixing with the rumble of the train until it felt like it was just the two of them here. After a moment, he peered into his drink and then lifted the cup again, downing it all in one gulp.

As he lowered it, he finally noticed her there and raised his glass as if toasting her. His eyes were bloodshot, like he hadn't slept at all. Aina narrowed her eyes as she sat on the edge of a stool next to him.

"Are you drunk, Kohl?" she asked. "If so, you're going to wait right here and not ruin—"

"I know where the cargo is," he said in a flat tone, placing the glass down. He lifted a face mask over his mouth and nose like he'd used as a disguise when they'd scaled Fayes's apartment buildings. "Let's go."

Together, they walked back through the train at a quicker pace than before. Kohl moved fast without any sign of stumbling or uncertainty. The whole time, though, Aina felt jumpy. There was the rocking train and the creaking of its wheels, and when she looked out of the window to see the train traversed a bridge with a straight drop into the mountain valley below, she wondered why anyone would ever willingly put themselves on this metal death trap.

The train turned sharply then, and she slid into the nearest wall. Kohl had caught himself before falling, and she glared at him from behind. Nothing ever seemed to bother him. Except . . .

If I told you how scared I was before going in, you wouldn't believe me. His words about the night of her parents' murder came back to her, making her stomach twist uneasily. One of the main lessons he'd always told his employees was that guilt didn't exist for them because they were tools: Blades did what blades did best, Shadows hid, and Foxes thieved. Embracing that was how to survive. He'd taught her how to shut down the guilt instead of letting it poison her, but he hadn't had anyone to teach him that lesson.

She exhaled sharply in annoyance. He'd probably told her that to make her care for him again. But she wouldn't let his words lure her in like that anymore.

They'd traversed two more cars and were nearing the end of the train when, beyond the door ahead into the small vestibule between cars, a familiar voice caught her attention.

"Kohl!" she hissed, and when he looked around, she yanked him through the doors of the private compartment just as Raurie and Tannis stepped into the hall.

They landed in a crouch, the door slamming closed behind them, and gasps rose up from the group of Steels gathered in this compartment.

Reaching for Kohl's gun, she withdrew it and pointed it toward the room.

"First person who screams gets shot."

All their mouths closed at once, and they froze where they sat. She didn't care about them as long as they stayed quiet, so she kept the gun level on them but strained her ears to hear Raurie and Tannis in the hall lining the compartment.

"But if things don't work out," Raurie said in a low voice, continuing a conversation they must have been having since the group split up. In her clenched fist, Aina could make out the glint of a diamond. "Then my and Lill's lies are for nothing. My aunt would have every right to kick me out, never speak to me again, if we put them all in danger and have nothing to show for it."

Tannis stopped next to her by the window, her brow furrowed as she said, "Well, if that happens—which I don't think it will— talk to me. I wouldn't shut you out. I know you're doing this for the right reasons, and you're not alone. We all decided to go down this path together."

"Thank you, Tannis. And you're not alone either, as much as you think you are. You don't have to hide what you're feeling all the time, you know."

They continued on to the next compartment, while Kohl, who'd been peering over the edge of the window as well, gave

Aina a sly smirk and whispered, "So no one knows about us working together. That's interesting. Are you keeping me a secret, Aina?"

"Shut up, Kohl," she said, turning the gun on him. There was a collective sigh of relief from the Steels behind them.

She wasn't really aiming it at him, though. It touched his collarbone, and the silver barrel reflected in the blue of his eyes, lightening them even more. He reached up between them, his fingers trailing her wrist and then resting atop her hand before she passed the handle of the gun back to him. A shiver swept through her, one that reminded her of the times he'd gotten close or touched her before while he was still the boss of the Dom—how she'd always wanted more from him. He kept his eyes on her face the whole time, and she refused to look away or blink. Was he testing her for some reason, as a way to unnerve her?

Or maybe her plan was working . . . maybe he was beginning to trust her again.

Without another word, they both stood and stepped into the hall, leaving the shocked group of Steels behind them. They walked fast then, soon reaching the rear end of the train where the cargo was stored.

Silence fell in this part of the train. There were only a few passengers, mostly solo travelers reading newspapers or sleeping in their seats

Before entering the third cargo car, Kohl held a finger to his lips. Then he slid open the door to the next car and waved her in. Shafts of light shone through the windows onto the dusty boxes strewn throughout this car.

"Where are they keeping the rebels they're smuggling in?" she asked.

Kohl shrugged, his face fixed forward. "Probably posing as passengers. It's good they're not here, or we'd have a problem."

Then he pointed to a box, and Aina walked up to it, her pulse racing as she lifted the lid of the box.

"Diamonds?" Kohl asked in confusion.

Frowning, Aina lifted a handful of the translucent gems and let them slide through her fingers, clinking together as they landed. Then she exhaled softly.

"Not diamonds. Rhinestones."

They both looked up, their breaths cutting short so the only sound was the rumble of the train beneath them.

"The shipment's fake," she whispered, one hand already going to a knife. The Jackals wouldn't leave a box of rhinestones on a train and do nothing else.

The door to the next car slid open, and three people stepped through, each one raising a gun.

19

A bullet struck the wall next to Aina as she ducked and rolled behind the crate of rhinestones. Kohl shot back, striking one of the Jackals in the head. In the next breath, Aina stood from behind the crate and flung her knife into one of their throats. She leaped from behind the crate toward the last Jackal with another dagger in hand and, as he turned his gun on her, ducked and plunged her blade into his stomach.

As he doubled over, she knocked his gun out of his hand and then pulled out the dagger. Blood cascaded down her arms.

"Aina," Kohl hissed, grabbing her by the elbow. "More are coming, from both directions." She strained her ears to hear footsteps pounding toward them from the same compartment these Jackals had come from. Through the window to the compartment in the opposite direction, she could make out a line of people walking down the aisle toward them. Passengers gasped and jolted out of the way when they saw the Jackals were armed.

Without wasting another moment, she and Kohl sped into

the space between the train cars. Holding his arm out to stop Aina from going any farther, Kohl jerked his head toward the roof. Aina's stomach plummeted at the thought of escaping from the Jackals on the roof, but they'd be trapped and heavily outnumbered below. Taking a deep breath, she followed, placing her hands on the rusty ladder fixed to the side of the train. As she climbed, she refused to look behind her to the rolling hills flashing past them. If she fell, there'd be no coming back from that.

But right before she reached the roof, a grunt below made her look down. One of the Jackals had reached Kohl, but Kohl slammed his fist into the man's jaw so hard, his head banged against the ladder, then Kohl shoved him off the side of the train. The man's shout was lost in the wind.

Kohl began climbing behind her, and a moment later, they both reached the train roof. She bent her knees to keep her balance. A fierce wind blew from the force of the train's speed, nearly pushing her back. The wind had knocked the string out of her ponytail, leaving her hair to whip around her face. For a moment, she saw nothing but black hair and the flashing colors of the landscape speeding by.

Then a hand grabbed her shoulder from behind. She slammed her head back into their nose and spun around to see a Jackal with a bloodied face. Grabbing him by the shoulders, she hurled him off the side of the train toward the rock-strewn hill. She skidded to a stop at the edge, heart in her throat.

A hand latched around her arm and yanked her back to the center of the roof. Shaking it off, she lifted a knife and went into a defensive crouch, but then saw it was Kohl who'd pulled her back.

He gestured to the opposite end of the roof. She followed, running and leaping onto the next compartment with her pulse pounding in her ears. They both turned to face the roof they'd come from, and exhilaration swept through her. Standing on the roof of the train as rolling hills sped past them, holding her ground with weapons in hand, diamonds in her pocket, and Kohl fighting at her side—she felt invincible.

And then the train turned with a shriek of its wheels. A yelp left her throat as she slipped, and her hands scrabbled for purchase on the roof. It was thankfully flat, and she caught herself before sliding off the side. A few feet ahead of her, Kohl crouched to hold his balance. Panic flashed briefly through his eyes and then vanished, a murderous glare returning as he straightened to face the Jackals.

The Jackals surged toward them from the next roof, the two remaining ones they'd seen in the storage car and three more following.

Aina leapt to her feet as the Jackals jumped onto her compartment's roof, a bullet striking the spot where she'd just been. She ducked from his next shot and rolled to the right, sliding her knife into the heart of another Jackal who'd jumped onto the roof.

Another of the Jackals swung a hammer toward her head. Her scythe arced upward, catching it inches from her face. A gunshot sounded and the Jackal fell, bleeding from his head. Kohl stood a few feet away, turning his gun from that Jackal to the next.

More footsteps pounded behind them. Thinking there might be more Jackals coming, Aina left Kohl to deal with the first ones. But then she saw Ryuu, Teo, Tannis, Raurie, and Lill racing across the roof toward them. Her heart sank briefly—Tannis, at least, would recognize Kohl in moments even with the mask he wore.

She pivoted away from him, putting distance between them and hoping that she could lose him in the fray of the fight. If they thought he was here as an enemy, her work with him could remain a secret.

More Jackals, and the fighters Bautix had hired from Kaiyan, hurtled onto the roof ahead; at least ten of them but too many to count. Bodies blurred together and all sound reduced to shouts, the sharp whistle of wind, gunshots, and metal clashing against metal; all that was left was to strike and survive. She slashed her knife through the throat of a Jackal who'd come up behind her. His blood spilled on the roof, making her steps slippery as she skirted around the side of the fighters. Gunshots sounded from every corner of the roof, but there was no way to tell where they were coming from before they fired. She didn't even know if her friends were alive.

More blood splattered the train roof, not only from the fighting, but from Raurie and Lill using blood magic to fight back. They stood apart from the rest, but the Jackals still came for them. Raurie held a diamond, her legs shaking as she stepped back to avoid an approaching Jackal with a knife raised to strike. She whispered another spell and the Jackal stumbled back, blood streaming out of his eyes and bubbling at his mouth. He collapsed a moment later, and Raurie stepped back, staring wide-eyed at the man she'd killed. One of the Kaiyanis fighters approached her from behind, but Tannis launched a throwing star into his throat before he could reach Raurie.

Just then, a Jackal pivoted toward Aina with a knife. She grabbed him by the wrist and pulled his arm straight out, then slammed her boot behind his elbow. As he screamed, she spun him around and plunged her knife into his gut.

As he dropped, a flash of red caught her eye, and there, at the edge of this roof, stood Kerys. The Jackal woman didn't attack anyone, but stood at the head of the group, her eyes scanning them all as if searching for someone.

Lill had stepped away from Raurie, closer to the fray, seemingly frozen in place as she stared at something ahead of her. Aina called out to her, but Lill didn't react at all.

"Lill!" Ryuu shouted, then lunged toward her at the same time a shot rang out.

Lill screamed as they both rolled toward the edge of the train, but they stopped before they could fall off, and Ryuu lifted a pistol to fire at the Jackal who'd shot Lill. Blood continued to coat the roof of the train, but Aina could no longer tell whose it was.

Aina turned to face the Jackals once more, her own fury pushing her forward now—she'd already lost the Dom. She wasn't about to lose her friends too. Two Jackals approached her, cornering her at the very edge of the roof, one with a knife and the other with a gun. There wasn't an easy way out . . . but neither of them knew she could use blood magic.

She reached for a diamond and made a cut on her arm faster than the Jackals could realize what she was doing. As she lifted the diamond, she thought of all the people in the Stacks Bautix had sent the Jackals to kill—the lives he didn't care about losing as long as they weren't Steels.

"Nagan inoke," she whispered, and swept the diamond diagonally in front of herself. In an instant, deep cuts formed, ribbon-like, along their skin, starting from their shoulders, and down across their chests. Blood spilled from the cuts, down their torsos and legs—they trembled where they stood. Their eyes turned a deep red, blood filling them, and at the same time, Aina's knees buckled.

She fought to stay upright, even though her vision blurred and threatened to black out. It felt like small needles were pricking her skin. Finally, the men collapsed in puddles of their own blood, and her own side effects ebbed away. She tossed that diamond to the side and as she looked up, spotted Kohl slashing a knife across one Jackal's throat and shooting another of the rebels in the head in the same breath. The fighting had mostly cleared out. Once those two men collapsed at Kohl's feet, only a few more Jackals remained—she caught sight of a couple of them, including Kerys, disappearing down the ladder they'd all come from.

Raurie and Ryuu had gathered around Lill, whose torso was covered in blood. Her face had gone pale, standing out starkly against her violet hair and freckles. Ryuu held an arm around Lill's shoulders as Raurie fumbled a diamond in her hands, the healing spell already at her lips. When nothing happened and Lill's eyes began to slide closed, Raurie thrust the diamond at Ryuu for him to try instead.

Teo faced one of the last Jackals, his gun raised. But once he got rid of the Jackal, he would turn to see Aina standing across from Kohl.

"Get out," she said under her breath, stepping toward him and swinging one of her knives at his torso. If it looked like she were fighting him, maybe she could still keep her secrets. He sidestepped her with ease, blocked her next strike, and knocked her weapon out of her hand.

She pivoted away, and as she did, caught sight of the last Jackal aiming a gun at her. A shot fired into his head a moment later and he dropped. Looking over her shoulder, she saw Kohl lowering his gun.

The train bucked, a hard turn that made a yelp leave Aina's throat as she scrabbled for purchase on the smooth brass roof. The wind slammed against her ears as she lay there, gritting her teeth with the effort it took to hold on.

And then a shout caught Aina's attention; a shout from someone she'd never heard cry out in her entire life.

Spinning around, she didn't see Kohl anywhere. But then he shouted again and the sound broke through her shock. She scrambled toward the edge of the train. He hung from the window below, his knuckles straining with the effort to hold himself up. The train sped along a bridge at least fifty feet above a winding, churning river filled with rocks.

She reached down, and one of his hands wrapped around her wrist. Then he grabbed her other hand, and she held all his weight. Sweat dripped onto her forehead as she grounded herself on the roof to avoid slipping off and making them both tumble into the river below.

His life was literally in her hands. Her mind went blank except the two choices in front of her: pull him up or let him fall. "Aina," he said, his wide eyes meeting hers.

It would be so easy. All she had to do was let go, and Kohl would plummet to his death. The scene was so similar to how she'd nearly killed him in the Tower last month that her breath caught. They were always in these positions of one almost killing the other and having a choice before them.

His words from yesterday came back to her then: *Once I take back the south, I'll lift it above the rest.* Her breath caught in her throat at the memory, but she shoved it aside.

His hands slipped a little. "Aina!" he called again, his voice sharper against her ears than even the gusting wind.

But he didn't say please. He didn't beg. He didn't even try to tell her she needed him. All he did was say her name.

He wasn't pleading in the way she wanted him to, like he had at the Tower last month when she'd placed her knife under his heart. Then, he'd shown fear—she'd proven herself to him. But now? He considered Bautix the worse enemy, and she was just a nuisance. Her heart hardened. She hadn't made him fear her enough yet.

Only I get to kill him.

Kohl tripping off a train wasn't good enough. Simply letting go of his hands wasn't good enough. Would anything ever be, though?

She suddenly remembered when he'd sat across from her at a tavern and told her the place would be bombed if she didn't leave with him right then. He'd dragged her out of it alive, for his own reasons, but still alive.

Shoving all those confusing thoughts out of her head, she hauled Kohl over the side of the train. He collapsed next to her, taking deep gulps of air, as if he hadn't expected to be breathing anymore. His mask had fallen off, lost somewhere in the wind, so his face was revealed.

The click of a gun sounded behind her. Slowly, Aina turned.

But it was Teo, and the gun wasn't pointed at her. He aimed it at Kohl's head.

"Get away from her."

Ryuu had stood and moved next to Teo, alternating between glaring at Kohl and frowning at Aina. Her heart sank, and she tried to speak, but couldn't get any words out to explain what she'd done. For a moment, Aina didn't move—having no idea what to say, not even really understanding why she'd pulled Kohl up over the side.

When Kohl didn't move, Teo said, "The only reason I haven't killed you yet is because I want Aina to have the honor. But I have no problem with injuring you."

His finger touched the trigger as he aimed the gun at Kohl's arm instead. Before he could do anything else, Aina placed herself between them.

Raising her eyes to meet Teo's, she said, "Don't."

20

Teo stared at her for a long moment, his eyes widening.
She didn't even blink as she stared back, willing him to understand, to forgive her.

"You went back to him," he finally said, his voice nearly lost on the wind.

"No, Teo, I—"

Before she could finish her sentence, Ryuu moved. He took Teo's gun and, eyes blazing, fired.

Aina ducked, but a sharp intake of breath behind her told her Kohl had been hit. He strode past her in one smooth movement and his fist flew at Ryuu's face.

Ryuu fell, one hand going to his jaw. Lunging to Ryuu's side, Aina looked up as Kohl stood over them both.

"You put up much more of a fight than your brother," Kohl said, paying no mind to the bullet wound on his shoulder and the blood that leaked down his chest.

"Get out of here," Aina yelled, grabbing the gun Ryuu had dropped and standing to aim it at Kohl. "Leave."

Kohl turned to Aina with curiosity lighting his eyes. Now that she'd saved his life, did he see her as a coward? Weak? The word played over and over in her mind, infecting her with how true it might be. She lifted her chin, clearing her expression of any emotion, any hint of what she might be thinking.

Let him think she'd saved him on purpose, that it was part of her plan. She wouldn't let him realize that saving him had been a spur-of-the-moment decision she could hardly explain to herself.

Without another word, he turned and left, his blood trailing a path down the roof of the train.

As he walked past her, Tannis shot a disgusted look at Kohl and said, "I'd say it's nice to see you, but I'm trying not to hide my real feelings anymore."

Teo and Ryuu left soon after, neither of them sparing Aina a glance as they did. Raurie and Lill followed, and Ryuu stopped to help Lill walk. A smear of blood was left behind on the roof where Lill had been.

The train barreled on toward Kosín and the air turned colder, making Aina shiver where she stood on the roof. The city grew closer in the distance, all bronze and gold in the midday sun and so different from the grassy landscapes around them. It seemed completely at odds with how bleak the day had become.

Tannis approached her then, disappointment etched on her features as the wind pushed her blue hair in waves around her shoulder. But at least she didn't look like she wanted to shove Aina off the side of the train.

"Tannis, I—"

"I lied to you last month about my work with Kohl," Tannis said in a soft tone. "Though we weren't running a business together then. I want to hear what your reasons are, but let's join the others first."

They left together and moved down the ladder on the side of the train. The inside of the compartment was starkly calm and quiet after the roar of the wind above. The passengers in this compartment cast her an anxious glance, tensing when she entered the room. They'd already been moving to other seats, casting a wide berth between themselves and Lill, Raurie, Teo, Tannis, and Ryuu, who were all covered in blood to varying degrees.

Aina scanned them quickly, checking for injuries. Teo was tying a makeshift bandage around his upper arm. Tannis, Raurie, and Ryuu had scratches and cuts, but nothing serious. The wound on Lill's neck had already sealed over, but copious amounts of blood still coated her upper body. With Raurie and Ryuu helping her, Lill took shaky steps to a seat and lowered herself into it with shallow breaths.

Then Aina noticed the diamonds still clutched in Lill and Raurie's hands. Inhaling sharply, she looked toward the passengers who'd moved to the other end of the compartment. None of them spoke or looked toward them, but they might have seen something.

"I saw more people leaving when I came in," Tannis said, crossing her arms and leaning against the booth where Raurie and Lill had sat. "Unless you want to hunt them all down right now, it's too late. We were loud enough up there that anyone in the surrounding cars could have heard."

Aina nodded stiffly, knowing she was right, then walked toward the passengers at the end of the car. They all flinched back in their seats when she drew near to them, their eyes flicking to the blood coating her shirt and her weapons.

"Leave," she said in a flat tone, and they nearly tripped over themselves trying to get out of the compartment.

Teo and Ryuu were seated across from each other at a table in the center of the car, and neither of them looked at Aina as she sat in the opposite row with Tannis, Raurie, and Lill. Teo stared out the window, tapping the fingers of one hand on the table between him and Ryuu. Every single tap felt like an accusation directed at her, and she knew she deserved each one. Ryuu turned his head toward her, and the pure venom in his eyes made her back up on her seat. He kept his hands clenched together on the table, knuckles straining.

As much as she wished she could go back in time and tell them the truth, the fact remained that they wouldn't have gotten this far without her fake partnership with Kohl.

"Raurie, what's wrong?" Tannis asked suddenly, reaching over and placing her hand on Raurie's overturned palm. Raurie jumped a little, blinking back tears that hadn't been there a few minutes ago. But she didn't move her hand away.

"I couldn't . . . I've never actually wanted to hurt someone before, but I had to stop the Jackal coming at me." The blood on her hands seemed to stand out on her palms then, under the harsh light in the train car. "I know it had to be done, but I didn't know how fast it would work. Or how brutal the magic would be when I really wanted to use it. I just wanted to hurt him, not necessarily kill him, but I wasn't able to control how strong the attack was. I grew up in the Stacks; I've had to fight for myself for a long time, and I've seen plenty of death, but . . . I've never killed anyone before."

Aina and Tannis sent each other a quick look, and Aina knew they were both remembering the first time they'd killed—and how Kohl had taught them to think of it. That they were a weapon doing what weapons did best, and the real blame rested with whomever had hired them as an assassin. Feeling any guilt only left room for errors. But Raurie wasn't an assassin-in-training. She didn't have Kohl whispering away the guilt and reminding them he had no room in his tradehouse for people who questioned their jobs.

"I didn't want to kill anyone today either," Tannis said. "It's never something I want to do. But we get wrapped up in things we don't choose or want sometimes, and we have to make the best of it . . . even if we have regrets."

"They were trying to hurt us, so we hurt them instead," Aina added. "You already know it's the only way to stay safe in this city."

Tannis nodded. "But you're doing it for something greater than survival; you're fighting for what you believe in. We try to avoid killing in our jobs, only doing it when necessary. And today it was necessary."

Raurie said nothing, just stared at the table between them as silence fell. Lill finally lowered her hand from her neck and leaned back in the seat, tears at the corners of her gold eyes. The blood on her neck and torso had begun to dry, but still looked gruesome.

"How are you doing, Lill?" Ryuu asked, standing from his table across the aisle and walking toward them.

"Alive, I guess," she muttered.

"You froze up there on the roof," Ryuu said, leaning on the edge of the bench. "Did something happen? Were you scared?"

"I'm not scared," Lill said in a harsh tone, then she winced and sent Ryuu an apologetic look. "Thank you for helping me back there. No, it's . . . something else." She looked toward Raurie then, who nodded as if encouraging her to speak.

"My mother used to live in the safe house too, and she was a faithful Inosen back when I was a child. She left because she fell in love. With someone who wasn't my father. She loved him be-fore, but the war changed things—made her scared. Some people only want to stick around where power and safety are, and the Inosen were losing both. Did you ever wonder how Bautix got the Jackals on his side? Or why we got scared of the safe house near the mines being targeted?" When they said nothing, Lill cleared her throat and said, "That was my mother on the roof. She fell for Bautix, and she got in with the Jackals. Eventually they trusted her enough to follow her lead when she took them to work for Bautix. I didn't know I'd ever see her again, so I wasn't prepared to face her. I'm sorry I put us in danger by doing so."

"It's okay, Lill," Ryuu said. "You didn't know she would be there. Which Jackal is she?"

Lill blinked back tears before saying, "She's the red-haired Sumeranian one. Her name is Kerys."

Aina startled a little at hearing that. Lill's mother was on Bau-tix's side? But Kerys was also working with Kohl. Which one was it really? Or did they both pull her between them, trying to force her to pick one side or the other? Aina felt a twinge of empathy with her at that.

But if Kerys was pretending to be on Kohl's side, she would have told Bautix about their plan to intercept the shipment and leave a fake one here. She might be the reason they'd failed at this mission. And if this had been a fake shipment, then where was the real one?

"Your mother is truly on Bautix's side?" she asked, and Lill shrank back in her seat at the words, like they stung. "She wouldn't switch sides or waver in that, would she?"

"I don't know," Lill said. "I haven't spoken to her in years. She seemed sure of him when she abandoned us. He was strong, and we were Inosen. We were the weak ones in the war; we couldn't give her the life she wanted."

Her voice stayed steady as she spoke, and Aina realized she must have thought them over and over again until it was the only truth she acknowledged.

Aina looked over her shoulder as if expecting to see Kohl standing behind her, waiting to hear this information about Kerys and start planning how to recover from this failure. Her mind already spun with ideas, from tracking down this current shipment, to torturing Kerys into telling them Bautix's current location.

But that would all have to wait. Teo was still ignoring her, and no one else would look her in the eye for longer than a second. Guilt twisted her heart—how would any of them trust her after this? She wouldn't blame them if they never did again. But she had to at least try to explain. Letting out a heavy sigh, she stood and faced them all.

"He also wants to kill Bautix," she said. "For his own selfish reasons, of course. But using his information has gotten us closer to our goal than anything else. Do you think I want to be around him? He killed my parents. I'm only partnering with him until Bautix is dead. I am sorry I didn't tell any of you, but I did this for all of you. I did it for everyone who lives in the Stacks, and for the Inosen, since Bautix thinks he can use us to regain power. I did it for you, Tannis, so we could beat Kohl and prove we're more than capable of keeping the Dom and running the trade-houses. I did it for you, Ryuu, because I know what it feels like to lose your family to him." Then she turned to Teo, who kept his gaze averted. "I did it for you. He had a rifle aimed at your window while you were sleeping. I got there in time to say I would work with him, to spare your life. Because I'd rather work next to the man who ruined my life than watch you die at his hands."

Her voice trembled on the last words. She pushed away from her seat and walked to where the luggage was stored in the cabin, then sat down and stared out of the window. The rumble of the train helped steady her breaths and calm her.

She'd saved Kohl. It would have been so easy to loosen his grip from the side of the train. To watch him plummet to his death. It scared her that she hadn't. She thought of the night she'd stayed in his house at the southern docks, the time they'd spent on the little boat yesterday when he'd told her his past. She'd been getting too close to him lately.

Whatever this new weakness was, she would get rid of it. Like all the other weaknesses and softness and pathetic aspects of herself that she'd shed since her parents' death, she would cut off this one too. She had to be strong if she wanted to live, and granting your enemies mercy was not strength.

Keep drawing blood, show no weakness, or you'll be the one who's bleeding. She repeated the words like a mantra to herself in her thoughts.

Twenty minutes later, the train pulled into the station with a loud creak of its wheels. Aina stared at the floor of the car as people around her gathered their luggage and disembarked.

The flash of a familiar face outside the window caught her eye. Kohl walked away on the train platform, his hands in his pockets and his gaze fixed on the city ahead. Once he disappeared from sight, she stood and turned to face the rest of the car.

Tannis, Raurie, and Lill were still there, but there was no sign of Teo or Ryuu. She tried to pretend that didn't hurt, but maybe she still deserved their anger. One apology wouldn't be good enough. "They went to the safe house ahead of us," Raurie said. "Said they needed time to think."

Tannis passed Aina a wet cloth and nodded at her arm, and Aina used the cloth to wipe away the dried blood from using magic. Her eyes flicked toward the platform outside, wondering how many of the passengers had overheard their fight.

They barely said another word as they moved to the train platform and then made their way out of the station. Half the people walking by pushed past them on their way to the ticket booths, and the other half moved toward the exit along with them. Since Diamond Guards were still checking every person who walked into the station, long lines had formed outside, disgruntled passengers sweating in the heat and complaining they would miss their trains.

As they pushed through the crowd to reach the exit, Aina caught whispers of blood magic. Right in front of her, Raurie and Lill stopped in place and shot each other a panicked glance.

It took them another minute to reach the exit, stepping through the glass doors into the square. The sun beat down hard on them as they walked across the square, but even with the heat, Aina felt a chill.

Halfway across the square, an older couple nearby stared at their group for a long moment, whispering to each other. Tannis glared and flashed the silver edge of a dagger, making them hurry away.

"Don't worry," Aina said, trying to keep her voice level as she faced Raurie and Lill. "Pretend this is a normal day. We'll get you back safely."

They both nodded, then moved on, Aina in front of them and Tannis behind. She kept her eyes on the people around them, watching to see if anyone else began talking about them.

"Diamond Guards down that street," Tannis whispered, nodding with her chin to the road they were about to cross to. "Let's take a longer way around."

But no matter which way they took, they passed Diamond Guards, and Aina heard more mutterings of magic, more whispers spreading through the city at an alarming rate. Her pulse pounded as they walked, and she impulsively rubbed her arm where the cut from using magic was, even though her sleeve covered it. She swallowed hard, finding her throat dry. Not only had they failed to stop the shipment of weapons, but . . . they might have just put a target on all the Inosen by using the old form of magic. When Aina saw June waiting for them in a shadowed alley across from the entrance to the sewers minutes later, she knew it wouldn't be good. June rarely came up from the safe houses unless it was necessary. Her arms were crossed, the diamonds on her forehead glittering under the sunlight.

"She knows," Raurie whispered, clenching her hands together.

When they approached, June simply said, "Hand over the diamonds."

Raurie froze for a long moment and opened her mouth with a confused expression on her face, but June swiped a hand through the air as if cutting through her excuses.

"Don't act like you're clueless. Hand them over." As Raurie and Lill both grimaced and then reached for the inside pockets where they kept the diamonds, June continued in a murmur, "Tales of bleeding men falling from the roof of a train and people holding diamonds like weapons. We had two girls missing from the safe house today who slipped out before dawn and didn't even leave with a proper excuse. You were obvious and reckless. Everyone knows Verrain's magic is back now. Come with me, and hope that the tunnel isn't bombed while we're walking through it."

21

When they gathered in the dimly lit, cool underground safe house—thankfully, the roof of the tunnel did not collapse while they were walking—and saw all the frightened faces, Aina's heart sank. Urill pulled Lill into a tight hug, and said nothing when they let go, relief in his eyes but his mouth flattened to a thin line. He, June, and Sofía sat across from Raurie and Lill at a table. June folded her hands in her lap, waiting for them to speak.

At the same time, Tannis retreated to a corner to sit between Teo and Ryuu. Ryuu looked up once and gave Aina a small nod, but Teo still didn't look in her direction. She needed to apologize to them, but right now, her focus was on the Inosen. If more anti-Inosen sentiment rose in the city and Bautix used that to his advantage, all the people here would suffer for her choice to learn this magic. She moved toward the table then and sat across from the Sacoren as well, between Raurie and Lill. "It's my fault that these rumors are spreading. I'm the one who suggested we learn blood magic."

"But we had to do something," Lill said under her breath, looking between Aina and her father with a plea in her eyes.

Instead of replying to either of them, June turned to her niece with tears in her eyes. "Words cannot describe how disappointed I am that you hid this from me, Raurie. We're family—not just us, but every Inosen here. Using Verrain's magic puts every single one of us at risk."

"It's not Verrain's magic," Raurie said quickly. "It's the Mothers' magic. They gave it to us—"

"That doesn't change how they see us," Urill spoke up. "Lill, you know better than this. If people hear rumors of Inosen making men bleed in the streets, they're never going to let us follow our beliefs freely. We will always be underground."

"The people of this country love to blame anyone for their problems but themselves," Sofía added. "Using this magic that they hate, out in the open, will be an excuse for them to treat us the same as they always have."

"You say you want to fight back, Raurie," June said, "but you're forgetting to be smart along the way, and you're forgetting that I am the person who raised you after your parents let their own bravery get in the way of their common sense. They were caught and killed. I refuse to let the same happen to you. Let your use of this magic die as a rumor on these streets and nothing more."

As the Sacoren left them and Tannis walked over, Raurie's hand went to her wrist, turning her bracelet over and over so the little stones caught in the cavern's dim light.

"I don't know if I can blindly trust the magic just because the Mothers allow us to use it," she said, with unshed tears in her eyes. "Especially after killing someone with it. I couldn't heal Lill after, Ryuu had to do it because the spell wouldn't work for me. We're supposed to show respect for life, and because I didn't, the Mothers didn't let me heal Lill. She almost died. And I don't want to put the rest of the Inosen at risk." She twirled a frayed end of the purple shawl she always wore, then said, "You know this shawl is my mother's? It's the only thing I have left from them. Your parents died for their magic too, Aina. Doesn't part of you just wish they'd stayed safe?"

Silence fell after her words, but Aina didn't know how to reply. If the Mothers wanted them to live peacefully, maybe they should have given everyone a fair chance at life. She couldn't imagine it, the faith that the people in this safe house had, the faith her parents had had despite how much they'd struggled.

"We can't give up now," Lill said.

"You can do whatever you feel is best, Raurie," Tannis said slowly. "But only if it's really what you think; don't let Bautix scare you. You've always believed in your convictions more than anyone I've ever met. Don't let them shake that out of you."

"It's like you told us after the Dom burned down," Aina added, her voice growing soft and her heart clenching at the memory. "This is where they expect you to give up; don't give them the satisfaction. And Bautix won't rest now that he has this shipment of weapons."

He'll destroy it if he takes over the city. She remembered Kohl's words from the day on the boat when he'd whispered that Bautix would find a way to retaliate by attacking the home they both wanted to protect. That included places like this safe house, where the Inosen hid. And by using this magic and drawing attention to the Inosen, she might have doomed them. A chill swept down her spine, knowing Bautix's threat to take back the city within a week was now a very real possibility.

She remembered something else then: that night at the warehouse, they'd overheard the Jackals talking about Bautix's upcoming weapons shipment. There would be smaller shipments prior to the return of the smuggler from Kaiyan. She frowned, wondering whether this had been the big shipment or if there were still more to come. Kohl would be able to find out.

As if reading her mind, Tannis said to Aina, "Maybe it was the best way, siding with Kohl temporarily. Working with him will get Bautix out of our lives faster. I don't blame you for making that judgment. But you should have told me, Aina. Are you the boss of the Dom, or are we?"

A sharp silence fell after her words, and Aina felt like every eye in the room was on her, even though most people had retreated to their own small groups and hushed conversations. Shame curled through her, and she hated herself for damaging Tannis's trust in her—they were supposed to be partners; they were supposed to understand each other and be equals in running the Dom . . . but Aina had broken that. She forced herself to meet Tannis's eyes before speaking.

"We are," Aina finally said. "The reason I didn't tell you isn't because I think I'm the only boss. It's just that . . . I wanted to face him on my own. I still do. I'm sorry, Tannis."

Tannis's eyes softened. "You can do that, but remember I'm on your side. And tell me when things are happening."

"I will, I promise," Aina said with a grimace. "First, we need to find out Bautix's next steps; if he has another shipment of weapons coming, or if he'll attack with what he has now." She could look for Kohl, see what he'd learned . . . but she still couldn't make sense of why she'd saved him earlier, and didn't want to see him again until she did. "I'll find some Jackals to get information out of."

Tannis nodded. "You do that. I'll ask if Mirran has heard anything, and I'll send the recruits to the tradehouses to get information from them."

Then, Aina looked toward Teo and Ryuu, her throat going dry. Before she did anything else, she needed to apologize to them. Ryuu turned in her direction as she approached, but Teo's gaze was fixed somewhere in the distance. There was the same tension in his shoulders that was always there after he saw her with Kohl, even when she'd still worked with him, and the same hardness to his eyes that came so much more often after his mother's death.

Ryuu took a deep breath, and when he let it out, his hair fluttered away from his face. "I could tell something was off, Aina, when you separated from us on the train. But I had no idea what it was." Then he spoke directly to Teo when he added, "I don't think we would have gotten the lead on this shipment at all without Aina doing this, even though we failed to stop it. And she got those notes about the secret entrances into the Tower because of her work with Pavel. It was probably safest for her to keep quiet about it. Even though she lied to us. Many times."

Aina winced, but then Ryuu smirked to show he was joking. When Teo spoke, Aina's eyes flicked to him, and she held her breath, hoping he didn't hate her now.

"I don't like that you kept it from us," Teo said slowly, staring at the ground as he spoke. "It's already hard enough to trust anyone in this city, Aina. We should be able to trust one another."

"We can't fight among ourselves, though," Ryuu said. "We need to stand together if we want to stand a chance against Bautix. None of us would be alive right now if we weren't all looking out for each other." Then he chuckled. "Least of all you, Aina. You're in a shoot-out almost every day."

She rolled her eyes. "It's other people who are starting the shoot-outs, and they happen to catch me in the middle of them, okay? I'm peaceful by nature."

He let out a snort of laughter. "Okay, sure, I believe you."

A moment of silence passed, where she felt a brief spark of relief, before she said, "You could take your own advice too. Stop putting the world on your shoulders when the world isn't even asking you to."

"It feels like it is, though. It'll keep feeling like that until this is all over." Ryuu shifted uncomfortably, frowning. "I know it couldn't have been easy to side with him, but we all do what we think we have to do to stay safe; we keep secrets, we put on a strong face so our weaknesses can't be used against us. I know you made the choice that seemed best at the time. But if you're not careful, it'll be very easy for him to hurt you again."

"The partnership will only last as long as it takes us to kill Bautix," Aina said, hoping Teo would meet her eyes, but he didn't. "I won't work with Kohl anymore after that. Once we kill Bautix, we'll both want the tradehouses—we'll be enemies again. But until then, we'll keep this partnership alive. It's been getting us further than anything else."

Shaking his head, Teo stood and walked past them and into the tunnel that led out of the safe house. She let him go for a minute, doubt freezing her in place—part of her knew he was right to be mad at her and that if any forgiveness was to come, it should be in his own time.

But as he'd walked by and she'd caught his eucalyptus scent on the air, saw the way his shoulders tensed when he passed her, she feared this might be the last time she'd ever see him. Jolting out of her indecision, she ran after him into the tunnel, her footsteps echoing off the rock walls.

He stared straight ahead as she slowed to walk next to him. "You could have told me, Aina," Teo murmured, making Aina's heart sink—her reasons for not telling anyone all seemed to fall away, weak and meaningless, as he continued, "What do you think would have been so bad about telling me, or any of us? Manipulating you—or anyone around him—is that man's favorite hobby. I know you want to prove that he can't do that anymore and that he doesn't affect you. But it doesn't work like that. Your anger at him, your frustration with yourself, seems to be the only thing guiding you now, and it's going to hurt you."

He started to move past her, but she stepped in front of him. He almost walked into her, and stopped just short, staring down at her with those deep brown eyes she'd gotten to know so well. Those eyes that she trusted more than any others. Those eyes that seemed like they'd never trust her again.

"You're one to talk," she said, her voice unsteady. By the way his hands curled into fists at his side, she could tell her words stung. "Your anger drives you as much as it does me. And if it leads me to work with him, I can handle it, Teo. He doesn't hurt me like he did before. I won't let him."

"I want to believe you, but I don't trust him, Aina." He reached for her hand and pulled her a little closer, making her pulse race as her hand came to rest on his chest. "Not him, not the Diamond Guards who killed my mother, not the Sentinel who would let it happen again. All they do is take advantage of us, and I don't want to lose you to them too. I thought we were standing up to them together, not working with our enemies behind each other's backs. You're my best friend, Aina, and you're still the person I love. I want to trust you. I want *you*. But you don't see me that way."

Her thoughts scattered as he finished speaking, his breath still warm on her face—he'd pulled her to within a few inches of him, so if she leaned forward even a little, her chin would touch his shoulder. He wanted her. He loved her, words he'd never said before but that she knew were as real as the breath in her lungs, as true as the solid rock of the ground beneath their feet. She gripped the fabric of his shirt in her hand, turning his words over in her head.

"Who said I don't see you that way?" she whispered, meeting

his eyes—but they were unrelenting. When he next spoke, he enunciated each word in a way that cut.

"Because you still love Kohl."

"I don't love him. I'm going to kill him," she said, shoving away to break their closeness. Her voice was low and harsh but somehow sounded like a child telling their parents they were all grown up and could handle anything without knowing what waited for them.

"Why?" Teo asked, his voice hard and challenging.

A thousand reasons came to her mind and fell away a breath later. He'd killed her parents. He'd lied to her and manipulated her and made her feel like she owed him her life for years, getting her to do anything he wanted to prove she deserved to live.

But Bautix had been the one who'd hired Kohl to kill her parents. And Kohl had manipulated her, but she'd been weak and naive enough to fall for it all. Her hands curled into fists, nails pressing into her skin.

"The Dom was the first home both of us really had after our parents' deaths," she said, her voice much less steady than she'd hoped for. "We both want the tradehouses more than anything else. If he tries to fight me for them, which I know he will once Bautix is dead, then I'll kill him."

"But what if he doesn't?" Teo replied immediately. "What if he'd rather you work under him instead?"

"I'll never go back to that." The words came automatically, so sure in her mind she didn't even have to think about them. She straightened, pulling her shoulders back and hoping her certainty was clear in her eyes.

"From here, it looks like you already have," Teo said softly. "It feels the same as it did then."

"Like what?" she asked, her voice as frail as smoke in the wind.

"Like every time you talk to him, you fade away a little more.

Whenever it happens, you're still the girl I've known for years, but transparent somehow, like you're becoming a shadow of him rather than staying yourself."

Teo walked away then, leaving her cold and alone in the tunnel.

22

After struggling for hours to fall asleep on a cot in the safe house, Aina slept for longer than she had in weeks. She woke abruptly the next afternoon; something hard under her pillow had begun pressing into her cheek. Reaching under it, she pulled out her mother's small porcelain horse statue, which she'd left there the night before trying to stop the shipment and had forgotten about until now.

Her conversation with Teo last night came crashing back into her thoughts, how he'd challenged her and accused her of loving Kohl. She would prove she didn't, and that she was ready to fight him when the time came; she had to get rid of anything sentimental about him. Without another thought, she knocked her mother's porcelain horse off the side of the bed. It shattered at her feet, the little pieces skidding over the rock floor, some hitting into the other mattresses around her. Her shoulders tensed and she gripped the side of the bed. Her employees from the Dom and the Inosen glanced over at her, but she ignored their stares and knelt on the floor amid the shattered porcelain.

Folded-up pieces of paper lay next to pieces of the broken horse. Her pulse raced as she reached for them. The cracks that had been on the horse's surface, clearly glued back together—had Kohl broken the horse on purpose, multiple times, to put a new note inside each time?

Her hands trembled as she opened them, laying them all out on the rocky floor and arranging them according to the dates in each corner. Kohl had signed each one and written her name next to the date on most of them. She let out a long breath, wondering if it would be better to burn them all now without ever reading them. But when he'd returned the statue to her last month, had he meant for her to find these notes? She needed to know what they said, and she could do so without letting him get to her. One hand reached toward the earliest one, and she began reading.

Each word was a shard of ice through her heart.

I let you escape. I could have chased you. You were right on the roof. But I couldn't bring myself to kill you, not when you look so much like Clara. Not when you were so terrified. Your parents are dead, and that's what he wanted. Surely he won't care if I allow one child to live. Someone has to be the future of this doomed country, don't they? I hope you enjoy your freedom, girl, even though it came with a price.

Clara. It always came back to her, the first person Kohl had killed. He regretted killing her, and so he'd frozen when the time came to kill Aina. He wrote this letter like it had been a conscious choice he'd made, but Aina closed her eyes now and pictured it. Like Lill freezing up on the train in front of her mother, Kohl had gone numb when he saw Aina's face—his legs rooted to the ground as she fled her parents' murder scene.

The second note stared up at her, marked with a date roughly two years later.

The first time I saw you after that night, it was like seeing a ghost. You nearly looked like one anyway. Your face was gray like a corpse, a bag of glue stuck to your nose and mouth where you lay facedown on the street. I didn't have to pull it away from you, but I did. I paid one of my informants to track you down, give you a clean job, and find out your name for me. You're a survivor. I hope you take that job, and I hope I'll learn your name.

She had taken that job. She remembered waking up the next morning, angry that someone had stolen her bag of glue in the middle of the night. But then a man approached her saying he would pay her to deliver packages of laundered money from the shops in the Center to his boss, with no strings attached. She'd been young enough not to be suspicious of that.

The next note, a year later.

Aina, you keep throwing your own life in the gutter. Why don't you have that job anymore? I wish I could send you this letter, but I know you don't have an address. You have a pair of shoes now, though. You're welcome.

Another year later, when she was twelve—the night he saved her from the bombing. She let out a long, shuddering breath as she read the two short sentences over and over.

You're better off in the Dom than dead in the wreckage of some bombing that has nothing to do with you. If anyone's going to kill you, it'll be me.

There were only four left, but she didn't know if she could get through them. Shaking her head, she unfolded the next one and read slowly.

This morning you asked me if you could open your own trade-house. You know I'd do anything to get you to stop trying to overdose.

Or maybe you don't know that, Aina. I hope you know now. Once you're ready, I'll give you everything you want.

That one hit hard. She bit down on her bottom lip. He'd been determined to give her the tradehouse she wanted, but as soon as her mistakes threatened his reputation, he threw her out. He'd punched her in the face, taken all her money, and left her at the Jackals' mercy. He only cared about her as long as she proved herself worthy of that care.

You killed your first man today, the next note read.

You're shaking less than I did when I killed Clara. Maybe because you didn't know the man personally. Sometimes I wonder if I let you live because I wanted to or because I'm too weak to end you. I hope we won't have to find out. I like this limbo between us, of neither of us knowing what the other truly wants.

The next note, written last year when she was seventeen, made a blush rise on her cheeks that both confused and angered her.

I saw you with your friend in a tavern. You were too drunk to notice I was in the same room. But he moved your hair out of your face, and he looked like he wanted to kiss you, but he stopped himself. That fool is hopelessly in love with you. I wanted to kill him right then, Aina. He doesn't know you like I do.

The last note was written only about two months ago, after she'd failed to kill Kouta Hirai.

I hate to see you go, Aina. But I had to make a choice between the empire I've built for myself, the protection it affords, the way it empowers this community—and the one girl who makes me weak in a city where you can only afford to be strong.

She reread the notes again, knowing she should be angry at Kohl—but instead, relief washed over her. She hadn't imagined what he felt for her—she hadn't just been crazy and hopeless and pathetic the past six years. It was like a weight lifted off her; she might never forgive him for all he'd done, but a small spark of hope lit in her—maybe one day she could forgive herself.

These notes were proof that he might be as weak as her, and that she was more than a match for him. And perhaps she could use them against him.

She tucked the notes into the pouch with her poison darts and left the safe house. The air was hot and dry outside, and there was no sign of puddles on the ground; the afternoon rain must not have come yet.

Last night, she'd told Tannis she would get information from the Jackals about Bautix's next steps—and to find out if he had any more weapons shipments coming. It would be easy enough to find some Jackals in the Stacks and beat the truth out of them, but most of the ones Bautix had put in the south were grunts who knew nothing. She needed Jackals who were high up and closer to Bautix, like Lill's mother, Kerys.

As she breathed in the smoke-tinged air, her eyes trailed over the muddy hills leading out of the Stacks. It was far from here, but the tallest buildings of Lyra Avenue were still visible at the crest of the hill. The answer came easily to her then: she'd go to the Jackals' hideout in Fayes's apartment and hope they were there now.

A half hour later, she reached the side of the building and began climbing. She soon reached the third floor and the window she'd found last time. With her hands clinging to the windowsill and the tips of her shoes digging into the narrow holds between bricks, she peered inside.

Three Jackals played a game of cards and drank together. Another sat off to the side, her legs crossed and one foot tapping the floor restlessly. Kerys.

A moment later, Kerys barked at the other Jackals to hurry up, then jerked her head to the hallway leading to the other rooms.

With reluctant looks, the other Jackals picked up their drinks and headed to a room halfway down the hall, leaving the door slightly ajar.

Hardly breathing to avoid making any noise, Aina lifted herself over the windowsill and into the room. On the balls of her feet, she moved to the corner and crouched down next to a chest of drawers, willing her pulse to slow so she could hear.

"He'll need poison for all three of them," came a Jackal's voice. "Will he even have it ready in time?"

"Don't doubt Alsane," came Kerys's voice. "He'll sneak into the Tower himself and pretend to have negotiations with the Sentinel, but he'll poison them. It would have been easier with Fayes still alive and his connections in place, but Alsane will manage. He has a plan for his men to sneak into the Tower while his meeting with the Sentinel is underway."

"I hope so. To do the job without Fayes, Bautix needs a good plan."

"He knows what he's doing," Kerys snapped, her voice leaving no room for argument. "You don't need all the details. Now, tell me. How many men will you have at the ports? They need to be ready to receive the smuggler in three days."

Aina's eyes widened. The main smuggler still hadn't arrived from Kaiyan. She listened closely, but the man replying only gave numbers: fifty. If they had fifty men just to meet this smuggler, that must mean there would be an even bigger shipment than before. Probably not only weapons, but also hired fighters.

A moment later, chairs were pushed back with a squeak on the floor of the other room; the meeting had ended. Aina flattened herself to the wall behind the chest as the Jackals made their way out of the apartment.

Her thoughts raced with what she'd heard. Bautix was planning to poison the whole Sentinel, infiltrating the Tower to do it.

He knew Fayes was dead, but he still seemed confident—with the men and weapons he was bringing in, he'd be more than a match for the Diamond Guards in the Tower.

She moved to sneak out of the apartment again, but a few feet from the window, the air shifted behind her and an arm wrapped around her throat. She jammed her elbow into her attacker's stomach and spun to face Kerys aiming a gun at her.

"Hear anything interesting?"

"Care to introduce me to this smuggler of yours?" Aina replied.

It was best to let her think Aina had only heard the end of the conversation. As Kerys considered her words, Aina took a moment to look more closely at her. Instead of the usual hard blaze, tears rested at the corners of her eyes.

"She's working with you all," she said. "She shouldn't be."

"You mean Lill, your daughter?" Aina asked after a pause. "What else should she be doing in this great world you and Bautix made together? Should she hide and wait for one of your Jackal friends to attack?"

With a sharp shake of her head, Kerys spat out, "You have no idea what you're talking about. All I wanted was a chance at survival—you understand that, don't you? No matter what the Mothers promise, there's no guarantee we'll survive in this city. Lill was no safer with or without me there. I can't change how much I hurt her in the past, and all of them, by leaving. But I will never put my daughter in danger."

"You already have," Aina scoffed. "And every day that you continue to work with Bautix, you still do. So, I assume it was you who ratted out our plan to him about trying to stop the shipment. Kohl shouldn't have trusted you."

A brief, sad smile flickered on Kerys's features. She took a deep breath before saying anything else, her gun still aimed at

Aina's face. "The safe houses in the city aren't safe. The only reason I haven't killed you right now is because I want you to get my daughter out of them."

"Does Bautix know where they are?" Aina asked, a sinking feeling in her stomach. "What is he planning?"

"I told Alsane the location of some old ones that aren't in use anymore, but I wasn't the only Jackal informing him," Kerys said in a terse voice. "He has enough people working for him that he can scour every corner of the city and find their hiding places. He's going to kill all of the Inosen."

As she spoke, Aina was already moving toward the window. The sky had gone overcast, the sun hidden behind deep gray clouds that gave the city a dull tone. Leaning halfway out of the window, Aina looked toward the south of the city, then back at Kerys.

"I'll get them out."

"Tonight," Kerys barked. "Now."

Without waiting another breath, Aina slipped out of the window.

23

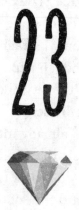

Aina raced through the tunnels, nearly running into walls as her eyes adjusted to the darkness. But she had to get to the safe house soon, or it would be too late.

Years ago, while she and her parents had sneaked through these same tunnels, there'd been a night when they'd had to out-run Diamond Guards hunting for Inosen in the secret worship centers underground. Her mother had knelt down, taken Aina's face in her hands, and whispered that they were playing a game.

"Whoever stays quiet the longest before we get out of the tunnel will win a prize." She glanced over her shoulder, where Aina's father gestured for them to hurry, to leave the little nook where they'd briefly hidden. "Not just your voice, but your feet too. Try not to make a sound, and I'll buy you any sweet thing you want."

Aina nodded, pretending she was so easily fooled—but she knew what was happening. She'd seen people killed for the same things her parents did. She knew what they risked. This wasn't a game, and she wouldn't treat it as one. But for her mother's sake, she hid the real fear burrowing into her bones and nodded excitedly.

"Sweet ice," she whispered, and that was the last word she said before grabbing her mother's hand and following her father's lead through the tunnels, careening into the walls like she did now and wondering if the Mothers could really hear them down here like the Sacoren always said. That was the first time they'd done it, and it wouldn't be the last—but all those times, as soon as she'd said, "sweet ice," that meant they were on their way to safety.

Minutes later, her fists slammed into the door of the safe house. She knocked loudly, louder than she should have—she definitely would have lost the game her mother had played—but she didn't care. They had to get out now, or they never would.

There was a small hole in the door where someone could peer through, and Aina waited as a gold eye blinked at her before opening the door. "Aina!" Lill exclaimed, ushering her inside. "What's going on?"

She glanced around the room once, taking them all in—most of them were chatting in small groups or reading in quiet corners. The Dom's employees, however, stood as soon as they saw her.

"You have to leave," she said, so quickly she thought they might not have understood her. "Bautix. He's going to attack all of the safe houses in the city." When they didn't do anything, she threw her hands in the air and shouted, "What are you waiting for? Move!"

Tannis, Mirran, Kushik, Markus, and Johana grabbed their weapons and moved to stand next to Aina a breath later. Some of the younger Inosen half-rose from their seats, but seemed unsure what to do, their eyes going to their parents and the three Sacoren gathered near the fire—June, Urill, and Sofía.

"How do you know?" June asked.

Lill met Aina's eyes, as if she could somehow predict what Aina would say—and she shook her head a fraction of an inch, her skin paling under her freckles.

"I got good information out of a Jackal," she said instead of Kerys's name, not wanting to bring up the painful reminder that Lill's mother was a traitor. "I don't know what kind of attack he's planning, but I know it's something big. You need to get out of here."

"We're as safe here as we are anywhere," Sofía said, her hands folded together in front of her. "Where would we go?"

"The safe houses in the city aren't safe," Aina said, looking directly at Lill as she added, "but there's another one, just outside of the city."

Her words sank in, and the rest of the group finally started moving, grabbing one or two things and throwing them into small burlap sacks, ready in moments. Maybe they'd been slow to react, but they were used to upheaval, disaster, and moving on.

"What about the other safe houses?" Urill asked. "Have you warned them yet?"

"I only found out about the attack twenty minutes ago," Aina said, shaking her head. "I don't know when it will happen."

"Then we need to send people to each of the other safe houses to warn them and get them to the mines safely," June said, her voice taking on a tone of command.

"How many other safe houses are there?" Aina asked.

"Five more, one in each district," Raurie answered, standing. "I'll go." Her voice left no room for doubt, and though June frowned slightly at Raurie's words, she didn't argue.

"I'll go to one too," Tannis said. Mirran, Lill, and one of the other younger Inosen all agreed to split up and go to each safe house. Urill looked like he was about to protest Lill leaving, but she merely gave him a determined nod before slipping out of a back door along with the others.

"I'll go with the rest of you," Aina said, nodding at those who remained—Kushik, Markus, Johana, and the rest of the Inosen.

Aina led the way out of the main door, heading back through the tunnel she'd come from, and she wondered for a moment how many situations like this her parents had dealt with—if this kind of bone-deep panic was what the Inosen had felt during the war. It wasn't like when she went on jobs; usually adrenaline urged her on, her skills and strength shielding her from any fear that might make her mess up. But this was different. They were in a tunnel, they were hunted as a group, like mice being led to a trap. If they didn't find air, they'd die under here—and the attack hadn't even started yet.

But just when she was wondering when Bautix would finally strike, the earth shook beneath them, tremors that knocked them into the walls. Aina winced as her face hit the tunnel wall, a rock scraping her cheek sharply. A couple of the Inosen behind her cried out.

Aina hardly breathed. Dust billowed from the tunnel ahead, making her cough and her eyes water. Another tremor shook them, a second explosion—she caught her balance then, her hands held out to both sides of the tunnel wall. People clung to her, Inosen holding on to her arms and waist as if she could actually do anything about a bomb.

She unstuck her mouth, dry and nearly sealed shut from the heavy cloud of dust that had passed over them, and said, "Maybe we should go the other—"

The tunnel collapsing ahead drowned out her next words—rocks fell from the ceiling, closing the way ahead, and the rest of the tunnel began to follow suit, clouds of dust rushing toward them. The Inosen ran back in the direction they'd come. Aina followed at the back of the group with her hands over her head as if that would protect her from a falling rock.

Then the memory of the night of the fire flashed through her mind—the beam, falling toward her, Raurie holding a diamond in the light of the flames, a rock jutting out of the earth to save Aina from being crushed.

They reached the safe house again and raced toward the back door, but Aina withdrew a knife and one of the remaining diamonds Raurie had given her yesterday. With shaking hands, she made a quick cut on her upper arm and tried to recall the spells they'd learned so far.

This room was a bit more stable than the rest of the tunnel, so she had more time—but if she was unlucky, the tunnel would crash down on both sides around her and bury her in this safe house. The old game would be over, but she'd go quiet very fast.

For a moment, fear gripped her that maybe the Mothers wouldn't let her use the magic again, like how Raurie hadn't been able to heal Lill on the roof of the train after using the magic to kill.

But then Teo's words came back to her: *the magic is like a knife in your hands.* Shoving aside her doubts, she concentrated on the tunnel floor ahead with the razor-like focus of a Blade. That would be the only way to get everyone out of here alive.

"Shinek inoke," she said, sweeping her hand upward with as much force as she would when swinging a knife.

The earth rose in front of her, grating and screeching like metal sliding against metal. She slid backward as a ramp rose out of the floor of the safe house, its sharp tip extended toward the ceiling.

She stumbled backward as the ceiling was gutted, the ramp carving a path through it like it was no thicker than blood.

Forced through the back door as the ramp continued to rise, Aina looked over her shoulder, blinking the dust out of her eyes to see that the Inosen stared back at what was happening with their mouths open in awe.

When Aina looked back at the ramp, relief surging through her that it had worked, she was nearly blinded by the light spilling through the hole in the ceiling.

But it wasn't sunlight—it was flames, licking at the buildings visible through the hole. Bautix must have planted bombs in the buildings lined above the tunnel, not caring who was caught in the crossfire as long as the Inosen were buried beneath.

"Come on!" Kushik yelled, and he, Markus, and Johana gestured for the Inosen to run up the ramp. Aina led, a dagger in each hand as she came onto the street.

It was a blaze of fire, carnage, and madness as the buildings around them burned. Aina froze for a moment, the fire searing through her resolve and sending her back to the night she'd lost the Dom. For a moment, she wondered where Kohl was now—if he feared losing their home as much as she did. People screamed, running away from falling debris and collapsing walls. The late afternoon sky was slate-gray and shrouded with clouds of ash.

A gust of wind swept that ash toward her as she waited for the Inosen to come up the ramp, and she shielded her face with her hands, forced to crouch in the rubble until it passed. A wave of heat passed over her and she remembered leaping out of the window of the Dom, her clothes singed with flames and the windows melting before her. For a second she feared she would be lit aflame right where she stood.

But then the wind passed, and when she opened her eyes, she was safe—for now. Fire still blazed around her, she could barely see more than five feet ahead due to the cloying smoke, and the road was a maze of fallen walls, isolated fires, and collapsed ground.

The Inosen stumbled out into the street around her, wide-eyed at the wreckage. Aina gestured, barely knowing what street she was on, but at least she was sure of the direction—ahead was north. She just needed to get them off this street that ran directly above the tunnel.

She led the way, veering right through an alley past a building that was still intact—if they could reach the next block, they might avoid any more attacks. Kushik, Markus, and Johana took the sides and rear of the group, each of them holding pistols that they'd only recently gotten used to using.

She heard the next explosion before it hit. Like metal screeching directly in her ears, followed by a strange quiet like snow falling over an empty street. Then the world shattered.

Hands over her head, Aina let herself roll with the burst of hot wind that followed behind her. She could do nothing for the Inosen now except hope they hadn't been next to the building when the explosion rocked it.

Her back slammed into a wall a moment later. She wasn't burning alive, so she allowed herself a moment to rest there, eyes squeezed shut, her body aching. When Kohl had saved her from the bombing of the tavern when she was twelve, they'd landed in a pile of snow to cushion their fall. The cold and wet had helped smother some of the flames, easing the aftereffects of that particular explosion.

In the heat of summer right now, there would be no such relief.

She opened her eyes again, her eyelashes white with ash, and saw her city burning.

Shadowy figures rushed toward her, their shapes and features barely discernible, just black shapes moving through white clouds.

As she staggered to her feet, the others came into view—some of the Inosen who'd been with her, June among them. Aina spotted Markus stumbling out of the wreckage, but couldn't make out any sign of Kushik or Johana. Her heart clenched at the thought that they might be trapped there, but staying here to search would only risk the lives of the survivors even more.

"They all know the way to the mines," Urill choked out, his hands on his knees when he reached the group. Then he gestured at the smoke and dust clouds surrounding them. "There's no way we'll find them in this, so we need to go."

They walked another block, still veering northeast, when two more Diamond Guards rushed in their direction, their gleaming buckles and pistols making them stand out among the panicked pedestrians. It was a little easier to see here, one block away from where the most damage was, and there was a moment when they stood across the street from the Diamond Guards, staring at one another. The diamonds and silver on their clothes glittered in the dim light, and then their eyes flicked to their group—where June, Urill, and Sofía wore diamonds in arcs on their foreheads.

Aina opened her mouth to say something, anything to get them to hurry to the scene of chaos and actually do something. But then the Diamond Guards raised their guns and fired.

24

Aina flung a knife into one of the guard's throats. The other one turned his gun to Aina instead, and she rolled toward him as a shot fired. She flung his arm to the side and plunged one of her scythes into his stomach. He choked on his own blood and collapsed to his knees as she pulled it out.

Turning back to the group, Aina saw them gathered in a small circle around someone who had fallen. When she got closer, she saw Urill on the ground, his blue hair stained with his own blood and his gold eyes, so like Lill's staring up at the smoke-ridden sky.

"There's nothing we can do," Sofía said, her voice thick with tears as she reached forward to close Urill's eyes. "Not even magic could save him now."

"We'll find him again once this is over," June said, her own tears falling on her cheeks in trails. Then, in the white ash that coated his forehead, she drew a small arc, and Aina remembered her mother often doing that with coal dust on the Inosen who were brought to her but died before she could heal them. *To help the Mothers find them,* she'd said when Aina had first asked what it was.

"Help me move him somewhere out of sight," June said once she finished.

"I'll do it," Aina said, then nodded toward a boarded-up store across the street. "That store is empty, so I'll leave him in there. I'll loosen one of the boards on the door for you to get in later. You all need to get to the mines as fast as you can. Those Diamond Guards don't belong to the Tower anymore—they're Bautix's, and I bet you he's given them orders to finally turn, and to kill you all if they find you. Go, I'll catch up."

As they stood to leave, June took one of Aina's hands and squeezed it. "Amman oraske, Aina."

"Amman min oraske," she replied, the words flowing from her immediately. *May the Mothers bless you too.*

After they left and she'd carried Urill's body into the store, Aina's gaze trailed north. She had no idea how many more buildings Bautix would bomb, but if he kept going, then Teo's apartment might be in the line of fire. Without wasting another minute, she ran toward his street.

A few blocks away, the heat of the fires had mostly left her, but smoke and ash were still thick in the air. Out of the white clouds ahead, a figure walked toward her, and she squinted, hoping it was him—when he called her name. Her heart leapt and she raced toward him.

"Aina!" Teo ran the last few steps toward her, becoming visible when he was just a few feet away, and pulled her to his chest in a tight hug—she knew it was temporary, that he'd go back to being angry at her once they were safe again—but she breathed in his scent anyway and tried to hold his warmth to her when they pulled apart again. "What are you doing over here?"

"I had to get the Inosen out of the safe houses." She gestured toward the fires behind them. "Bautix did this. I got them out in time, but I had to come get you—if the bombings keep going, your apartment will get hit."

Teo bit his lip as he stared at the flames ahead, the sky shrouded with smoke. "That's why I came, I heard the explosions and when I looked out of my window, I saw where they were. I knew the safe house would get hit."

She breathed a sigh of relief at his words; maybe things weren't perfect between them, but they'd both come for each other now. And they'd make it out of this alive.

"The Inosen are headed to the safe house at the mines right now," she said quickly. "We should go there too, but I want to check something first."

He nodded, gesturing for her to lead the way, and she glanced at the buildings around them first before deciding—a theater was nearby, the tallest building in this part of the city at three stories high. From there, she'd be able to see a good amount of the city above the flames and smoke; she could see how much more of it was burning, and how much chance the Inosen in other safe houses had to survive.

The theater only opened in the evening for performances, so the door was locked. She hacked through the lock in seconds with her scythe and pushed the door open into the dark interior.

Before heading to a set of carpeted stairs on the left, she breathed in the clear, cool air of the theater, blinking white ash from her eyes and shaking some of it out of her sleeves. It was odd, how calm and quiet this place was while chaos reigned outside.

She and Teo walked side by side up the stairs, the theater opening on their right with a shadowed stage in the distance.

At the top of the stairs, Aina stepped through a set of velvet curtains onto a balcony and looked out at the city.

They were level with the smoke now, so she wasn't able to see as much as she'd hoped, but she could still take in more than from the ground.

The fires spread south, only for about a quarter mile, even though it had felt like she'd traversed half the city since leaving the tunnels. From here, she could make out Rose Court north. There were fewer fires there—perhaps Bautix didn't want to risk killing too many Steels—but the warehouse district, visible beyond the landmark of the train station, was aflame just as much as the Stacks and the Center.

Squinting, she looked up at the sky, expecting her eyes to water from the smoke. But it wasn't all smoke—thick dark clouds had amassed there too, promising rain that couldn't come fast enough.

The fires, she noticed then, weren't headed straight north. They curved a snake-like, diagonal path through the city. And that meant they wouldn't hit Teo's apartment, which was more directly north. That meant . . .

Teo realized it at the same time she did.

"Aina." He gripped her arm above the elbow, his eyes wide.

The same silence, like steadily falling snow, descended over them. Panic rushing through her, Aina reached up, tugging on the curtain, and Teo helped her pull it down. Carrying the billowing velvet, they ran to the balcony.

"Sweet ice," she whispered, closing her eyes for a brief moment right before the theater exploded beneath them.

The blast propelled them outside, nothing but white-hot air behind them. As they leapt off the edge of the balcony, she grabbed on to Teo's waist, holding on with all her strength as he held both sides of the curtain out like a tent around them. The air caught it for a moment, carrying them to the ground, but as the heat and force of the explosion behind them roared, the curtain turned to cinders in his hands.

They let go of each other then, their hands over their heads as they dropped the last ten feet to the hard ground. Debris fell around them as they tumbled, rolling across the street while heat seared in the air around them.

Her eyes opened briefly, in time to see more wood and stone falling toward her. She gripped her hands tighter around her head—right before she blacked out.

She didn't know how long she was passed out, but when she woke, it was to someone tapping her cheek repeatedly. Through bleary vision, she looked up at Teo and noticed a stream of blood coating one side of his face.

And then she noticed it wasn't Teo tapping her cheek over and over—it was droplets of rain. The sky had opened, and rain fell, darkening everything around them. Mist rose steadily in the wake of the flames.

Teo held out a hand to her, pulling her out of the rubble. They stood for a moment on shaking legs, neither of them saying a word, then turned to run to the edge of the city.

25

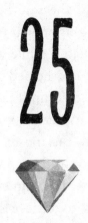

The next morning in the safe house in the mines, the quiet was nearly unbearable to Aina. Her ears still rang from the explosions. Her body ached, but her mind was alert. She hadn't gotten much sleep, since every time she closed her eyes, she only saw fire and destruction. It brought her back to the night of the fire at the Dom. Bautix kept spreading his attacks wider and wider, destroying every home she knew. The city still stood, smoldering and gasping for breath, but for how long?

She had to go back to the city and make him pay.

But first, she'd wait for Ryuu to return to make sure the Inosen had everything they needed. The place had dusty crates stacked along the walls, likely having been an underground storage unit for the mines before it was turned into a safe house during the old war. Cots lined the walls and a few small tables stood around the open space. On one of the tables was a tiny statue of the Mothers, covered in dust. The chipped paint made it hard to see details, but she noted their long hair, Isar's harp held across her chest and Kalaan's bow and arrows slung over her back.

A wooden door was at the back of the safe house, leading deeper into the mines, while the exit was up a flight of stairs on the opposite side. Luckily, the safe house had been unlocked when they'd come last night, and so the Inosen had been able to tend to injuries immediately while waiting for Ryuu to bring food and supplies. Raurie had helped, but she didn't touch any diamonds while she worked. Tannis had assisted her by passing her bandages and alcohol to clean wounds.

Aina felt much closer to the Inosen now, closer to the memory of her parents and who she'd been when she was younger. A lump built in her throat as she counted how few of them were left. Those who'd been sent to retrieve the Inosen from other safe houses hadn't been very successful; only about half had managed to save anyone at all.

Lill had avoided speaking to anyone after learning of her father's death, and sat in the corner across from Aina and Teo, her hair and face coated in ash, her eyes as blank as those of the dead they'd left behind. Every time Aina had woken during the night, she hadn't seen either of them sleeping. Now, Teo watched Lill for a long moment, and when he turned to Aina, she was surprised to see tears in his eyes. After his mother's death, she'd only seen him cry once—at the very scene of it. Her heart ached as she wondered how much of it he kept shut inside. She reached out, intending to comfort him, but then he stood.

"I'm going to check on my apartment and see if I can find any more Inosen," he said in a clear voice as he blinked those few tears away. "Will you be fine here?"

She nodded, and he left a moment later, passing Ryuu on his way out. Ryuu entered along with a couple of maids from his mansion, all three of them carrying baskets of supplies and food.

The scent of roasted meat and fresh fruit reached Aina, and her stomach rumbled, but she would wait for the Inosen to eat before taking any for herself. After they settled the baskets on a cot in the center of the room, Ryuu looked at Lill, a worried crease forming on his forehead, and then walked toward Aina.

"Raurie told me you suggested they all come here," he said. "Thank you for that."

"Of course." She smiled at him. "It's the best place for them to be, for now. And I know you'd invite them to stay in the main house if we could trust your neighbors. Maybe the Dom's employees will stay there, though. We've already crowded the Inosen enough."

"And what about you? I know you haven't really rested."

She shrugged, fending off any thoughts of sleep. "I'm fine. I'm more worried about the Inosen."

At the same time, they looked toward Lill, who sat with her knees pulled up to her chest. In a whisper, Ryuu asked, "Has she spoken to anyone yet? She should eat something, at least."

When Aina shook her head, Ryuu sighed and then walked toward Lill. Aina didn't want to eavesdrop, but their strained whispers carried across the room where everyone else was mostly quietly working.

"Lill," Ryuu said, kneeling next to her. He leaned toward her as if to give her a hug, but stopped when she looked up at him, her eyes fierce despite the tears resting there. "This was all Bautix's doing, but you'll be safe here and—"

"Stop," she breathed out, and Ryuu's words halted abruptly. "I appreciate you opening the safe house to us and bringing us supplies, but you can't fix everything, Ryuu. We're not safe until Bautix is dead and people who don't think like him are in power. That's the only way this will be fixed: making them bleed as much as they do us. That's what we learned this magic for, isn't it?"

When she finished speaking, her eyes trailed toward the ceiling to stop her tears from falling. Ryuu paused for a beat, looking at the floor between them before saying, "On that train, I shot Kohl Pavel. The person who killed my brother, Lill. I know what the need for revenge feels like, and I know it fixes nothing. It might make you feel better for one moment, but all your old doubts and fears come back in the next. Don't let the desire for revenge take you over, Lill."

She tilted her head back down and tears tracked down the white ash still on her cheeks. Ryuu hugged her, his black bangs falling in his face.

Aina stood then and walked to the three recruits, who'd arrived shortly after she had last night, covered in soot. They all shared a cot now while they ate breakfast, Johana's little fingers sticky with the juice of a mango. When Aina reached them, they all straightened and waited for her to speak.

Instead she bent down to give them each a long hug. "I'm glad you all made it back yesterday," she said, her voice gruff. "Thank you for helping get everyone away from the bombings. Get as much rest as you need, all right?"

"Thank you," Kushik and Markus mumbled, surprise lighting their eyes—they probably had never gotten much gratitude from Kohl when he was their boss.

"You get some rest too, boss," Johana said, and Aina nodded but didn't reply.

She left the safe house shortly after—the only way to solve any of their problems was to stop Bautix. She couldn't do that from here, and certainly not by resting. Ryuu might have a point about revenge not fixing much, but as long as Bautix tried his best to kill them all, she'd keep fighting back.

She headed back to Kosín, breathing in the crisp scent of the forest around the mines, and knowing she would smell only death when she entered the city. Even after the downpour last night, a hint of smoke still hung in the air, growing sharper the closer she got.

An eerie quiet permeated the empty streets as she walked through the east of Kosín. Clouds partially obscured the sun, but whenever they moved, sunlight revealed the gruesome scene in stark detail. White ash coated entire streets like untouched snow while gray limbs and streaks of blood stood out among the rubble. Something wet touched her cheek and when she lifted a hand to it, she found more tears she hadn't realized she'd shed. She'd seen a lot of death in her life, but nothing like this—nothing that showed such complete disrespect for life. She walked slowly, making sure she took in every broken body and fallen building, to breathe in the rancid air so she wouldn't forget it. It was part of her, this city, whether it was whole and safe or burning and dead.

The civil war was the last time the city had been so quiet. Her parents had kept her inside and so she'd missed what had really been happening. But she'd seen their terror, had known things were bad even though she couldn't see it herself. Now that she did, she knew she could let nothing stop her—not the fact that they'd failed to stop Bautix's weapons shipment, and not these attacks that only made people afraid. All of this was a reason to not rest, to fight Bautix until he was nothing. Even if no one else joined her, she'd do whatever she could to stop him, whether that meant using the brute force she'd honed for years or the new blood magic at her fingertips. She'd prove what a girl from nothing could really do.

Before she realized where she was walking, she'd arrived at the edge of the Center square, opposite the train station. She let out a small sigh. Of course this was where she'd been going. It was the place to look out on the city and feel like she was some bigger part of it than she truly was. And if she wanted to see the damage done, this would be the best place.

But there was something odd strewn across the ground—bits of wood, arranged in a purposeful way. From the scent of smoke lingering on them, she guessed they were bits of buildings that had been blown apart in Bautix's rampage. With a pit of dread building in her chest, she skirted around it and entered the train station.

It was empty, closed in the wake of the attacks, with ticket stands and platforms abandoned. Walking through here was like traversing the ruins of a silent, ancient city. Her breaths and foot-steps were the only sounds as she made her way to the stairwell that would lead to the tower.

When she reached out to turn the doorknob, though, it opened from the inside with a creak. She bent her knees, a knife in one hand—but then Kohl stepped through the door.

"Aina," he said, his voice tinged with relief, his bloodshot eyes widening. "You're safe." She'd stepped back slightly, trying to con-ceal her surprise at his reaction as her knife hand lowered to her side. "I saw you coming from the edge of the square. You have to see something."

On leaden legs, she followed him up the stairs to the tower like she had countless times when he'd still owned the Dom. For the first time since then, she felt like they were actually working together; they were both appalled by what Bautix had done. She watched him from behind as they approached the window, mid-day light casting gold on his stoic features. The letters he'd left for her in her mother's statue flowed through her thoughts now, and it was suddenly easy to believe he'd worried for her safety during the explosions; easy to believe he'd never stopped caring. She let out a low breath as he beckoned her forward, not knowing what to do with that knowledge but knowing that her heart ached at it, and that Teo's words came back to her now: *Because you still love Kohl.*

She shook away the thought and coughed on the smoke as the outside air filled her lungs once more. Kohl pointed to the wooden beams arranged on the ground below.

There were hundreds of them, pilfered from the buildings that had burned, arranged in letters and words and a single sentence that sent a chill through her whole body:

Let it be known that our goal is to progress, not to regress.

Kohl let out a long, slow breath before speaking. "I watched as the Diamond Guards assembled this sentence, not caring at all who saw them. None of them tried to stop the fires or save anyone. They're his."

"How many?" Aina asked in a hollow voice.

"I counted ninety. Who knows how many more he hasn't yet revealed?"

Aina shook her head slowly. "As long as he can convince people that there's chaos without him, that the city would be safer if he were in charge, he'll have supporters."

Kohl let out a humorless laugh. "And that's why he won't ever completely destroy the Stacks. He needs to keep poor people around. He needs the people who are always trying to latch on to the closest thing resembling safety."

She turned away from the scene to face Kohl. "He's planning another shipment the day after tomorrow. He is one step ahead of us, as he proved by putting the fake shipment on that train, and now with these attacks. We can't let him get any more ahead of us than he already is."

Kohl turned back to the window and she noticed the edge of a bandage peeking through the neck of his shirt and covering the bullet wound on his shoulder. He rolled his shoulder back and grunted in pain, and Aina smirked a little. Ryuu had gotten in a good shot.

Kohl's eyes trailed toward the Stacks then. The ghosts of flames danced in those eyes, and he went so still, she thought he'd stopped breathing.

"He tricked us. He must have found out our plan somehow and planted the decoy on our train while getting the real shipment in some other way, maybe on the train from the northwest port rather than the southwest."

"Your friend Kerys can't be trusted," Aina added, crossing her arms. "She and Bautix are together, did you know? She's been pretending to be on your side. How do you know she hasn't told him about everything you're planning?"

Kohl bit down on his lip as he gazed out at the city. "Because I'd be dead now if she had. Kerys always has her own plans going on—she doesn't tell him everything." Then, with a harsh sigh, he said, "The station is closed right now, but they'll open it as soon as they can; they need to make money off the railroad they spent years building. I can find out what port Bautix is planning to send the next shipment from. He's also planning to bring in more fighters to help him take over the Tower."

"Good, but don't tell her anything about it, just in case. The shipment isn't the only thing we have to worry about. He's planning to poison the Sentinel."

"I'm aware," he said suddenly, his hands gripping the edge of the windowsill so hard, his knuckles turned white—reminding her of how he'd dangled from the edge of the train, his hands the only thing hanging on. "None of the Jackals realized I was on the train that day, so Bautix doesn't suspect me yet, but he's still in hiding and only sends messages at random. This morning, he sent a Jackal to ask me to brew the poison for him. He'll pretend to want to negotiate, but he'll slip the Sentinel poison while his men come through the secret entrances to take the Tower. Can you brew the poison, and make antidotes as well by the day of the shipment?"

She nodded, her thoughts racing and the thrill of a new plan settling over her. "We'll poison him instead. If he's pretending to have a negotiation with them, he'll have a drink of whatever he serves them so it won't look suspicious. Convince him to put the poison in his cup too, and give him an antidote. But it will be fake. We'll give the real antidote to the rest of the Sentinel, and Bautix can die in front of them while we stop his second weapons shipment from ever reaching the city. Turn his plan on its head. I'll find a way to tell the Sentinel what's happening." Her eyes trailed north toward the Tower, and she considered Fayes's notes, still tucked in her pocket. There'd only be one way into the Tower now—Fayes's secret tunnels. She'd never imagined working with the Sentinel before, but if it would stop Bautix, she'd do it.

Kohl nodded, then one side of his lips tilted upward in a smirk. "The first time he tried to kill me, he did it with poison. Now? The last time we see each other, I want to use the same weapon. I can only hope I'll get to watch him drink it."

The words sent a chill down her spine. They would both do anything to get what they wanted, and even though she'd saved his life on the train, he would still come after her. So then, what did it matter, those notes he'd written, the relief in his eyes when he saw she was safe?

Will I still go after him? she wondered, and his hands tightened over the windowsill again as if to mock her.

Kohl met her eyes with a surprising softness in his own, and said, "I never thanked you for not letting me fall to my death on the train. For a moment, I really thought you would do it. Step on my hands, maybe. Slice through my fingers. Simply let me hang there until my grip slipped and you could laugh as I fell over the edge. For a long time, I thought that was what you wanted most of all."

She swallowed hard, trying to keep her face clear of emotion. "You don't know what I want, Kohl."

As long as he still wanted the Dom, the plan was on; she couldn't let him see that doubts and questions had sprung up in her thoughts. That was a weakness he might latch on to in order to win, and she could afford no weakness now.

But as she walked away, the letters from the horse came to the front of her thoughts again. He had weaknesses too. Tilting her head toward him so the sunlight hit her face, she unstuck her throat and asked, "You could have come after me in the Tower and killed me before I ruined Bautix's plans last month, Kohl. Why didn't you?"

A long pause passed before he answered, and she held her breath throughout it. His eyes flashed briefly with some emotion she couldn't read. For a moment, she was certain he would ignore her.

"You've been an influence on my life since I was fourteen, Aina," he said, his voice quiet as the ash falling on the city. "I fear knowing what my life would be like without that influence."

As soon as his words trailed off, she turned away and walked down the stairs as fast as she could, not taking a full breath again until she reached the lobby of the train station.

So Kohl feared something, after all.

And maybe, when she'd saved him on the train, it was because she too feared knowing what her life would be like without him in it.

26

Once Aina reached Rose Court—which was, unsurprisingly, already back to normal business even after the fires, the rich not caring what happened farther south—she approached the harbor where she and Kohl had escaped from Fayes's ship. When she reached the docks, she scanned the area for Diamond Guards.

It was mostly empty except for dock workers and ship crew. Some sat on the edge of the docks, legs swinging over the river as they passed a bottle of firebrandy between them.

None of them paid attention to her. She supposed the Diamond Guards weren't here because the traitors no longer needed to pretend to do their jobs, and the ones who weren't traitors were too busy dealing with the aftermath of the fire to stand around.

Before heading to find a boat, Aina glanced behind her. The rain yesterday had smothered most of the fire, but smoke still curled into the air from the damaged buildings farther south.

"Where will you go?" one of the crew employees sitting at the edge of the dock called then, and Aina turned to face them, the hair on the back of her neck prickling.

"What do you mean?" she asked.

"We're talking about where we'll go when another war starts," another of the men said before taking a swig from the firebrandy.

Noting that he said "when" and not "if," Aina swallowed hard before answering. "I'm staying right here."

They shook their heads slowly, as if she were a fool. But she wouldn't abandon Kosín or Sumerand. Someone had to be here once the war ended, when the rain would wash away the scent of dead bodies and the sky would clear.

"Well, where are you going now?" another one asked. "They've blocked ship travel out of the city while they try to sort out this mess."

Aina reached into her pocket, withdrew a gold kor and turned it, letting sunlight catch on it.

"I need a small boat. Not to go out of the city. Just around it."

One of the men raised his hand in the air and she tossed the coin to him. He gestured for her to follow him and led the way down three more piers until they came to a grouping of four small boats with two oars each.

"I'll bring it back tonight," she said, and without another word climbed into the boat and took up the oars. He grunted as if he didn't believe her, but he and the other men seemed not to care about anything other than their eventual escape, and her gold kor would certainly help him in that.

She wiped sweat from her brow before picking up the oars and beginning to row north, resuming the path she and Kohl had taken the other day. His face flashed in her thoughts then, his relief that she had survived . . . and then she pushed it away.

Wondering what to do about Kohl wouldn't help her now, and she'd need all her focus to make it to the Tower safely.

A half hour later, when she was in the shadows of the bridge leading to the Tower, she reached into her pockets and withdrew the notes from Fayes. A couple of them were singed on the edges from the explosions, the weak paper catching quickly, but they were still legible. As Ryuu had said, it would be nearly impossible to get into the Tower by simply requesting an audience with the Sentinel, even for someone with his status. And after the explosions yesterday, the security would be even tighter.

If she was going to show these notes to the Sentinel and convince them to do something about them, the best way would be to prove that they worked.

Taking a deep breath, she picked up the oars again and rowed toward the other shore of the river. There was nowhere to grab on to and pull oneself to land; it was a sheer drop, at least twenty feet. Whoever decided to choose this path in or out of the Tower had no other options and would simply have to hope the currents of the river that day weren't strong enough to pull them under.

From her pocket, she withdrew a small flare to cut through the shadows cast by the shore and the bridge above. The secret entrance she searched for was a fold in the wall, one that you wouldn't find unless you were looking for it. Using the flare, she searched each crack in the wall, every curve, moving downriver about twenty feet to search there as well.

Finally, after about an hour of searching, she found a deep crack in the wall. She stuffed her flare back in her pocket and rowed toward it.

She could fit in there—and it would be a tight squeeze—but her boat certainly wouldn't. She took off her shirt and trousers until she was in her underclothes, and rolled them into a ball that she could hold above her head. The last thing she wanted was wet clothing slowing her down.

As she reached the secret passage and perched at the edge of her boat, the sun flashed a sliver of light into the entrance, revealing it briefly. She looked over her shoulder once more at the buildings she could see from here, at the smoke still curling into the sky.

The city was coming apart at the seams, cracks and crevices opening in the walls and the ground where people like her could slip through and take advantage; kidnap the bones of the city and construct it in their own image; revel in the chaos and forge their new successes in the flames like a blacksmith making a sword for heroes.

With everything in her, she would fight to make sure the wrong people weren't the ones who did that. She held her breath and jumped off the boat.

The cold pierced her skin, making her teeth chatter immediately. One hand holding her clothes above her head, she used the other to push herself forward through the water and then claw at the cliff walls until she wound her way inside a narrow passage.

She swam in complete darkness, her breath and the ebb of water the only sounds. After long minutes, the walls around her widened and her shoes touched sand. Scrabbling for purchase, she walked as quickly as she could in the water, and eventually hit a wall.

Feeling her way across this cavern wall, she began turning inward, deeper into the cave, and up ahead, light flickered against the walls.

Moving faster, she soon left the water entirely as the path continued gradually upward. A new tunnel opened with a single torch in a bracket on the wall. Another torch hung from the wall twenty feet down. As she approached it, the sound of water sloshing against cave walls reached her. She soon reached the second torch and saw that the floor vanished into a cavern so deep, the light barely revealed anything. A rusted ladder led downward.

She breathed in deeply, hoping she wouldn't run out of oxygen in this cavern, and then began climbing down the ladder one-handed. Her other hand still held her clothes in a ball above her head. All of this reminded her of traversing the tunnels beneath the city last month with Teo, Ryuu, and Raurie to find Kouta, before any of them knew that Bautix was the real enemy.

The ladder stopped abruptly at the same time that her feet met water.

Looking over her shoulder and squinting through the faint light provided by torch above, she saw another dark crevice in the opposite wall and hoped that would be the exit.

She descended the last few rungs and entered the cavern water. Teeth chattering, she swam as fast as she could to the other side. It was already colder here than outside, and her lungs began to seize with the effort to draw breath. Briefly glancing into the water, her limbs looked gray as the corpses she'd seen strewn about the city streets.

Pushing through the last few feet of freezing water, she tossed her clothes onto the rock and began to pull herself up onto the small ledge. Then she noticed that the light didn't reach all the way into the crevice. Rocks had fallen into it, possibly from the force of the explosions throughout the city the day before.

The cavern grew deathly quiet as she considered what to do. She could leave, but their plan to stop Bautix would fall apart. He would break into the Tower with ease, kill the Sentinel, and take the country for himself. And if she didn't do this, who would?

Frustration curled through her at the thought. The Sentinel had never helped her when she was a child and death approached her on the streets, a bag of glue threatening to choke her. They'd never given her a way to support herself, like Kohl had. Yet here she was helping them when it was the last thing they deserved.

But they wanted the same thing—safety, for themselves and their country. Just like she knew Kohl wanted to help the south too, and they were working together, so she would go to the Sentinel now. Putting aside her bitterness toward them, she withdrew a knife from her pile of clothes as well as a diamond from the stash Raurie had given her, then shoved the clothes to the side of the crevice to make room. She made a small cut on her arm, blood leaking onto the diamond and into the water. It sank down in little droplets toward the cavern floor. Holding up the diamond toward the fallen rocks, she whispered, "Cayek inoke."

A small rock fell, and the others trembled slightly. She swore, her voice echoing around the cavern once more. If that was all the spell could accomplish, then that had been a waste of a diamond.

Her limbs had begun to feel numb. Coming here alone might not have been the smartest idea. Reaching for the rocky ledge, she began to pull herself out of the water—when a rumble sounded from ahead.

The rocks separated, one cascading over the other, smaller ones first and then the ones as large as her head lodged near the bottom of the crevice. She scrambled backward on the ledge and her foot slipped on the slick rock. Heart in her throat, she fell back into the water with a hard slap against its surface.

She held her breath just in time and opened her eyes to clear water lit by the torch above. Turning herself around, she swam toward the light, the cold making her limbs tight and stiff, but the surface was so close—

Rocks from the crevice slammed into the water one at a time. Aina flung her arms over her head. A few rocks glanced off her arms and shoulders, but when she tried to pivot out of the way, one of the rocks slammed into her upper back. Gasping, she sucked in a gulp of water.

It seared down her throat, putting fire in her lungs. She spun around, trying to find the surface or a flicker of torchlight, but suddenly there seemed to be light everywhere and nowhere at once. There was no way to tell what was below her or above.

Panic flooded through her and she suddenly felt certain she would die here. But maybe, with all the death on her hands, she deserved it. Light seared across her vision, and for a moment she thought it was fire. But it was a pale silver light, with a red tinge behind it. Something about it reminded her of the fireworks brought in by Steels once a year for the end of summer. She'd gone to that event every year with her parents, cowering behind her father's legs whenever the loud noise took over the night, but marveling at the patterns of light in the dark sky all the same.

This time, the patterns coalesced into shapes, the curved figures of two women with hair that reached their ankles. One of them had bright silver hair, the other crimson red. Aina calmed, her breath coming naturally as if she spent all her time underwater. Her mouth opened a little and no water rushed to fill her lungs. She could tread easily, no longer panicking to reach the surface. She couldn't explain it, but she was safe here now.

"What is happening?" she asked, feeling like she might be talking to herself. Then, a suspicion entered her thoughts—whatever was happening, it wasn't normal. Her mouth went dry even though she was surrounded by water. "Are you the Mothers?" she finally asked the two moving lights in front of her.

"You're our daughter," they said, their voices chorusing and echoing in Aina's ears like the melody of a harp. If that didn't confirm they were the Mothers, nothing would. "Remember what we teach."

Aina frowned, not really wanting to remember their lessons because everything they taught would condemn her; their most common teaching was that all life was precious. Her entire existence went against that.

"Why?" she asked, her voice challenging.

"Because you, and all the people of this land, are in pain," their voices chorused once more, and suddenly the figures in front of her grew so bright, Aina shielded her eyes with her hand. "You will fail unless you learn to face the real enemy. Embrace your weakness, or else you'll succumb to it."

She bit her lip, having no clue what they meant. Weakness? Why would she want to embrace that? She couldn't afford any kind of weakness.

"Wait!" she said, but they were already fading away, bright light reducing to shadows in the dark cave waters. At the same time, their effect on the cavern water fell away; water flooded into her mouth and she clamped her mouth shut to avoid taking in any more of it.

Swimming to the surface again, she spat out the water and pulled herself onto the rocky ledge ahead. She sat there sucking in gulps of air for long moments before moving again. The path ahead was clear, all the rocks that had been blocking it effectively cleared out of the way.

She should be dead. She wasn't.

But the Mothers lived in the earth, in caves like these—it made sense for them to be here, of all places, and they'd stopped her from drowning. But why had they appeared to her? She was nothing like the real Inosen—like Raurie, Lill, June, her own parents. She left a path of destruction everywhere she went. Yet their words tugged at her: *Because you, and all the people of this land, are in pain.* For a moment, she felt the same, deep sadness she had while traversing the ruined city.

She pulled on her clothes again, reveling in every touch of warmth. After putting them all back on, she knelt on the rocky ledge and stared out at the cavern water for another few moments.

If Teo were here, she wouldn't feel so cold. They would help each other stay warm, and if one of them succumbed to the cold, the other would find a way to go on.

But if Kohl were here, they'd freeze to death together. Even if they never brought a knife to each other's throats, they'd still end up killing each other slowly.

The words in his notes came back to her: *Sometimes I wonder if I let you live because I wanted to or because I'm too weak to end you. I hope we won't have to find out.*

She no longer knew if she wanted to find out either.

Until then, she had to face the real enemy, like the Mothers had said.

Using the wall to push herself to her feet, she continued on the path toward the Tower.

27

Light flashed ahead in short bursts as she climbed a set of steps dug into the tunnel floor just beyond the cavern. She stopped counting after one hundred steps, her legs burning with the exertion. One more torch hung halfway up the set of stairs, and by its light she checked Fayes's notes, trying not to dampen them too much with her wet hands. Whoever had written the note had drawn the stairs leading outside, with arrows pointing up. She didn't know what the arrows meant, but she had a hunch, and a pit of dread opened in her stomach.

Steeling herself, she walked up the rest of the stairs. Wind blew in steady gusts past the opening, which was tall enough for her to walk through hunched over. Goose bumps rose on her skin at the sudden chill in the air from the wind ahead. All she could see through the opening was sky; no trees were visible from this height. Moving to the edge of the opening, she peered over, then looked up the side of the Tower wall, and then whipped her head back inside, her pulse racing.

"You have got to be kidding me," she muttered to herself, her voice disappearing in the gusts of wind.

She was at least one hundred feet in the air, facing the plains north of the Tower. Handholds and footholds were gouged into the Tower's surface, completely unnoticeable unless you were the one scaling it. No entrance above was visible.

Quickly drying her hands on her clothes, she hesitated for a moment. She wasn't afraid of heights, but one hundred feet above a flat ground with barely anything to hold on to was no joke. Her limbs still ached from the run through the city yesterday and jumping out of the theater. She gulped, not knowing if she'd be able to hold on long enough to make it up this treacherous path.

Then, turning back to the opening, she tried not to think about what she was going to do. Whenever she'd taught Johana, Markus, and Kushik to scale the city's walls, fear was the first thing to get rid of. It could crumble even the most skilled and knock them to their deaths. Instead of fear, she kept Bautix at the front of her thoughts; the man who'd destroyed half the city and would do more if she didn't warn the Sentinel.

As she climbed, carefully deciding which holds she would reach for next before even moving, she kept her eyes peeled for some sign of the outer defenses of the Tower. She noted Diamond Guards standing at intervals all around the bottom of the Tower, with multiple gathered in clusters where there must have been doors. She couldn't have made it through any of those doors without being caught, if she'd approached at ground level.

The handholds curved around the side of the building and she breathed a sigh of relief when she saw a crack in the wall ten feet above. Once she reached it, she crawled inside and collapsed against the wall. Every one of her muscles ached, and all she wanted was to pass out.

This path was as narrow as the first one, but at least there was no water. Now she had to be somewhere in the middle of the Tower's thirty floors, based on the height from the ground. Diamond Guards would show up soon, especially once she entered the main halls. Keeping her steps and breath as quiet as possible, she traversed the hall and came to a narrow door. No light peered through the cracks; the room on the other side was dark. Pressing her ear to the crack on the side of the door, she strained her ears, but heard nothing. When she was sure the room ahead was empty, she pushed the door open.

It nearly hit into another door in a very cramped space. Frowning, she looked up and down to see if she should climb to anything, but there was only the other door ahead. No sounds or light came from beyond. Shrugging, she pushed open that door too and stepped into an empty locker room.

A locker at the very back had been painted a deep emerald color to blend in with the wall. The floor was white tile, and her footsteps echoed across it as she darted through the room. From the uniforms hanging over the benches and open locker doors, she assumed this was for Diamond Guards. When she reached the exit, she stood on her toes to look through a small window set in the door, and saw a hallway somewhere in the middle of the Tower.

Slipping out of the locker room, she glanced to each side, pondering where to start. Mariya Okubo was the only member of the Sentinel she'd ever been on slightly good terms with, since Mariya knew that Aina, Ryuu, Raurie, and Teo had come to the Tower last month to expose Bautix's plans to murder a foreign princess. If anyone would listen to her and Kohl's plan to stop Bautix again, it would be Mariya. But with the assassination of Gotaro and the attack on the city, Mariya might not even want to talk to her.

Unless Aina gave her no choice.

Choosing to go left, she walked down the hall at a steady pace. All the Sentinel's personal quarters were on the top two floors of the Tower. All she had to do was find a staircase and avoid any Diamond Guards.

When she turned the corner, a door stood open ten feet down the hall, with a stairwell visible halfway through. Boots clicking against the marble floor approached from the opposite end of the hall, probably a Diamond Guard. She slipped into the stairwell before they could turn the corner, then ascended the stairs as quickly as she could. Ten minutes later, she arrived at the second-to-last floor. Bending over with her hands on her knees, she took a few deep gulps of air.

A window was cut into the door, and peering through, she noticed how empty these top floors were. Instead of a hallway, it was a circular, open floor with four doors interspersed around the curving walls—one of them with a window cut into it like this one, probably leading to the stairwell on the opposite side of the Tower. No one guarded the other three doors.

Just then, the door to the opposite stairwell creaked open. Eirhart, one of the surviving Sentinel governors, stepped through along with an escort of two Diamond Guards with rifles slung across their chests. Eirhart led the way to one of the doors, which must have been his personal quarters, and entered alone. The Diamond Guards took up a post outside.

Stepping back from the door, she continued up to the highest floor. These were definitely the Sentinel's rooms, but she wanted to draw as little attention as possible now that she'd nearly reached her goal. She would check the last floor before starting a fight with these two guards.

The final floor was empty as well, but this one only had three doors set around the circular walls: the door to the opposite stairwell ahead, and two more. She walked toward one of them, quieting her steps so they wouldn't echo across the marble floor. An obsidian plaque hung on the door she approached, but instead of Alsane Bautix's name being etched into it, diamonds were studded to spell out his name. Aina rolled her eyes at the sight. The Sentinel likely hadn't bothered to change it since no one had yet been hired to fill his position.

She walked toward the other door and exhaled in relief when she saw Mariya Okubo's name. Instead of diamonds and obsidian, there was a simple brass plaque with her name etched across it. Aina turned the doorknob and entered.

She'd expected luxury, but this was surprisingly bare bones. Forest-green carpet lined the floors and shimmering gold curtains hung halfway draped across the windows. In the office, there was only a desk with a chair, while the sitting room had a fireplace, a sofa, and a low table with a plate of fresh, colorful fruit. No decorations covered the surfaces, no paintings or statues lined the walls. The fire blazed low now, keeping the room warm. Even though it was summer, a chill permeated these higher floors, so she supposed the Sentinel kept their fires blazing year-round.

Only a lamp, a single pen, and a framed photograph stood on top of the desk. All the drawers were locked, as she discovered when she tried to open them. Mariya was much more organized than Aina had expected, and definitely not as luxurious as most Steels.

Aina glanced out of the floor-to-ceiling windows behind the desk. In the distance, the city had the look of a war zone already, with crumbling buildings and smoke billowing above to blot out the sun. At least the Sentinel was forced to watch whatever destruction occurred in the city from these lofty heights.

Turning away from the view, her gaze landed on the photograph on the desk. Sunlight from outside shone on it, highlighting the image of a Natsudan girl with the same round face and long black hair as Mariya. She looked a few years younger than Aina, with the view of trees and a river behind her. She was smiling, her eyes bright but wary. Aina picked up the frame, wondering if this was Mariya's daughter, or maybe a younger sister. If so, where was she?

The door began to creak open and Aina darted behind one of the sofas in the sitting area, the picture frame still in her hands. She peered around the edge of it, watching Mariya enter and wave away the Diamond Guards who'd escorted her to her door. She shrugged off a white blazer and kicked off her shoes, leaving her in a blouse and a long skirt. Her eyes, with dark bags underneath and lines like spiderwebs at the sides, peered out of the window, and Aina could see the curling smoke over the city reflected in the glassy, deep brown color.

As Mariya stepped toward her desk, she frowned and stopped in her tracks, as if she'd already noticed something was amiss. Her ears perked like a rabbit being hunted, and she turned to face the rest of the room. Deciding this was as good a time as any to reveal herself, Aina stood. Mariya startled, taking a step back, and opened her mouth.

"Is this your daughter?" Aina asked quickly. The sight of the photograph made Mariya's words catch in her throat, and Aina was just grateful she hadn't called for the guards outside her door. "Is she dead?"

Mariya flinched at her words, and Aina knew they were harsh, but she had to keep Mariya's focus on her instead of the guards outside until she could explain why she was here.

After a long pause, Mariya spoke, the words breaking out of her in short, clipped tones. "My husband took her to Natsuda the year the war started. He knew I had to stay here, with my position being what it is, but we wanted our daughter to be away from it all. She was a baby when the war began. I've only seen her twice since." She cleared her throat, her shoulders tense, her eyes glimmering a little with unshed tears. "Recent events in our country have not done anything to persuade my husband to bring her back."

"And you wouldn't go there to be with them?" Aina asked, walking back to the desk and placing the photograph where it had been.

"This is my home, and I have a duty to protect it," Mariya said simply.

At least I chose the right person to come to, Aina thought, then turned to face her. "Do you know how I got in here? Bautix has built secret entrances into the Tower." She reached into her pocket and pulled out the notes. "I used one of them and no one saw me. You'll need these to seal up as many entrances as you can before he brings in his men through them."

Mariya stepped forward in one smooth stride and took the notes, holding them gingerly like they were some kind of weapon instead of information.

"How did you find these?"

"The Blood King and I are working on taking out Bautix, and we found a rat in the Tower." As Mariya's eyes narrowed sharply at the mention of the Blood King, Aina continued, "You remember that day your colleague got assassinated, and I saved the rest of you because your guards are useless? I killed Arin Fayes on that ship, and I got these notes off him. He's been constructing these entrances into the Tower for Bautix."

Mariya let out a long sigh as she riffled through the notes. For a moment, the crinkling and shuffling of notes were the only sounds as she read a few of them. Then Mariya looked up her shrewdly. "Thank you for getting us this information. It's very useful. But I know that the Blood King has been working with Bautix for years. Is he on your side now?"

Biting her lip, Aina didn't quite know what to say to that. "We're both against Bautix, at least," she finally answered. "He's pretending to still be on Bautix's side to get information."

Mariya nodded once. "We won't be able to close all the entrances in time, but we can close some and at least post guards at the others. There's also the matter of the Kaiyanis rebels Bautix has hired and promised to help with the coup of their king. Did you know about them?" When Aina nodded, Mariya sighed and said, "Their king advised me to watch the ports for a sign of them, and we've caught some, but we must have missed others. He's sending soldiers to help out. But he expects a favor in return. He wants the Kaiyanis Inosen who are still imprisoned here to be sent back as a sign of good will. If the soldiers arrive at the port and see no one ready to be sent back, they're instructed to leave immediately."

Thinking of Tannis and the Sacoren she'd introduced them to, Aina asked, "And you're doing it?"

"We've checked the prison, but only a few are still alive," Mariya said with a slow shake of her head. "It would be a joke if we only sent three people; the soldiers would turn around and leave."

"Only a few are still alive?" Aina repeated, unable to keep the anger from her voice. "And whose fault is that? Don't say Bautix. Maybe he's the one who made the laws to arrest every Inosen, but all of you stood back and let him."

Mariya clenched the notes in her hand, not saying anything for a long moment. "I can acknowledge that there is room for change, and that I should have done more to stop it. Years ago, we made the Inosen an enemy because that made it easier to stop Verrain from destroying the country."

"From what I know, he and a few others attacked one factory, and then you sent the entire army after him and everyone who shared his religion," Aina scoffed. "You Steels worship money and industry so much, you'll stamp out anyone in its way. Maybe you've learned something since then, but maybe you're just desperate and are saying what you think I want to hear. I'll make a deal with you, Mariya. I'll find enough Kaiyanis Inosen to send to the ports and I'll tell you what I know of Bautix's final plan, if you and the rest of the Sentinel free every Inosen in prison and lift the ban on their religion."

Mariya nodded stiffly. "We have a deal. But you must know we're outnumbered—we've had to dismiss any Diamond Guard we suspected might still have connections to Bautix. Whatever you know of Bautix's plans, I'm not sure we'll be able to stand up to them. The fighting will only become more intense soon. What we need most of all is time and people we can trust, but we're not getting either."

"I'll send reinforcements from my tradehouses to be your security here," Aina said slowly, already dreading the arguments she would likely have with them about it. None of them liked the Sentinel, but they all liked having a place to live and sleep, so she'd find a way to make them comply. "Bautix is planning to stage negotiations with you and poison you all instead while his men sneak through the secret entrances. I'm preparing the poisons as well as antidotes. The Blood King and I will get the antidotes to you. You'll keep the real ones for yourselves, and Bautix will have a fake. He'll drink the fake one and succumb to the poison while you all live."

"That's too risky," Mariya said then, shaking her head. "Inviting the enemy into our home."

"That's why it works: Let him think he's winning, and then you take advantage. If you don't invite him, then he'll find a way in and catch you off guard. Better to keep him where you can see him."

"And if he figures it out before we can even try?"

"We have a fail-safe. If his plans change, he'll need weapons and fighters to take over the Tower. I'll go to the ports to stop his last shipment of weapons and take out Bautix's men there. The Kaiyanis will be able to pass through, so you'll have more soldiers to help, and Bautix won't get his firepower. This will all happen the day after tomorrow."

"You have the Blood King's confirmation on all this?" When Aina nodded, Mariya said, "I can only hope he wants Bautix dead as much as we do."

Aina's gaze trailed toward the window. She looked toward the south of the city and remembered the ghost of the flames in Kohl's eyes.

"He does," she said finally. Then, remembering the caves she'd gone through and the climb up the side of the Tower, she said, "One more thing, tell your guards not to shoot me on the way out. I'm going through the front door this time."

28

The next morning, Aina woke to the sounds of someone moving around on the bed across from hers. She was slow to open her eyes, her whole body aching from everything that had happened in the past two days: the bombings throughout the city, jumping from the theater window with Teo, and traversing the caverns to the Tower.

Yesterday, she'd told Tannis, Teo, Ryuu, Raurie, and Lill about Bautix's plan to poison the Sentinel and how she'd sneaked into the Tower to warn Mariya—right before closing her eyes and falling asleep immediately.

Had the Mothers really appeared to her, or had those rocks hit her hard enough that she'd imagined it?

"Aina?" came Tannis's voice from nearby, and Aina opened her eyes to see that Tannis was already dressed for the day. "I spoke to Ryuu this morning. He said we can move into the new manor. Mirran and the recruits will come once they wake up and he gives them the news, but I can't wait any longer. Come with me?"

Aina pushed back the sheets and stood, for a moment wondering if she'd misheard Tannis. "He fixed it up already?" Weak morning sunlight shone through the floor-to-ceiling windows—she couldn't see the city from here, but she imagined it, still smoking and in rubble. "When did he find the time?"

Tannis laughed, then gestured around the expansive bedroom Ryuu had offered them. "When you have this much money, time isn't really an obstacle."

She shot Aina a bright smile, and Aina returned one, her spirits lifted for the first time in a while. If they could start over, build a new Dom . . . a spark of hope shot through her, daring her to think maybe they could still win this.

As Tannis strapped on her throwing stars and knives, Aina watched her for a few moments, hoping her friends noticed she was now trying to share more with them about her plans.

What she'd told no one, though, were her doubts about killing Kohl. Uneasiness rose through her at the thought—for so long, the desire to kill him had driven her, only for her to question it now. But until Bautix was dead, there was no use in thinking about it.

"Come on, get up!" Tannis said, rolling her eyes with impatience.

"Okay, okay," Aina said, finally standing. "Let's go home."

They soon left the Hirai mansion, taking the long path toward the gates of Amethyst Hill. The path was silent and no one stood outside their homes. It was early in the morning, but she wondered if the bombings had had anything to do with it. If the Steels were finally afraid that Bautix would come for them too. The drawn curtains on all the windows of two of the mansions they passed made her think that might be the case. A small surge of satisfaction swept through her—now they finally knew what it meant to fear for their lives. But then her own anticipation rose.

If even the Steels feared what Bautix would do, then none of them were in an optimistic position.

When they passed through the gate out of Amethyst Hill and the first view of Kosín's gray skyline appeared, Aina spotted the Tower in the distance and realized there was something she hadn't mentioned yet to Tannis.

"Last night, I told Mariya we could get the tradehouses to help defend the Tower tomorrow night," she said slowly, watching Tannis's reaction as they walked along the dirt path leading toward the bridge into the city. "We're all trying to survive, and I know most of the bosses have brains enough to understand that. Arman Kraz, on the other hand . . ."

"So the Sentinel needs our help?" Tannis scoffed. "They were never this interested before. How do we know they won't turn on us immediately?"

"We don't," Aina said, shrugging. "But I needed to tell them about the secret entrances unless I wanted Bautix to waltz into the Tower and take it. And they need something from us too . . . that's what I wanted to talk to you about."

Tannis stopped walking and turned to face Aina, crossing her arms. "Did you volunteer me for something without telling me?"

Aina cringed, but she couldn't blame Tannis for how much she'd hidden from her. But behind the anger, disappointment tinged Tannis's voice, and that stung more than any yelling or fighting would.

"No, I promise I didn't."

After Aina explained the situation with the Kaiyanis king wanting prisoners returned in exchange for sending soldiers, Tannis blinked a few times, then unfolded her arms. "Well, I didn't expect that," she finally said. Then her voice turned hard again. "What does that have to do with me?"

A beat of silence passed while Aina considered how to answer. The wind rustled the trees around them and a sudden chill spread up her arms, reminding her of the cold underground lake she'd passed through yesterday, where the Mothers had told her to focus on the real enemy.

"You told me how that Sacoren, Gevann, was forced to work for a Diamond Guard captain to avoid prison or execution. The Tower barely has anyone in the prison itself to send back, but I bet there are a lot of people like Gevann who need help."

Tannis shifted uneasily, biting her lip as she thought. "I'd rather help us. Fight against the people who want to hurt the trade-houses. This is my home, Aina. Maybe I feel bad for my past, but I don't . . ."

"You don't want to do anything about it?" Aina asked, nodding—she'd expected that answer. "I know that feeling. It's scary to even think of facing your past. That's why the Dom is a safe place for so many of us. It takes us away from all the rest of it. It's something we can focus on and fight for. I won't force you to. I can ask the other tradehouses for volunteers, if you'll help with information. But it's something to think about."

Tannis gave a stiff nod. "We can feel out the tradehouses when we visit tonight and see who we might trust to do it. Thank you for asking me first, Aina."

"We're a team," Aina said, then took a deep breath. "I know things have changed between us since I lied, but there's still no one I'd rather run the Dom with."

"Like I said, I've lied to you too," Tannis said, shaking her head. "Neither of us is a decent person, and that's one thing I always liked about you. We know what it's like to stand in this world alone. We both know what it's like to have someone try to take our home from us and to fight against them. We've always been on the same side, and there's no one else I want to run the tradehouses with either." She sighed then and tilted her face toward the sun. "I liked you, Aina, as more than a friend. But I'm starting to think it's not enough to like someone just because you have the same bad experiences. I've never had many friends, have only ever trusted a few people, but since we've been fighting Bautix, working with the Inosen, like—"

Her voice cut off for a moment, a blush rising on her cheeks.

"Like Raurie?" Aina asked, her voice soft. She'd noticed the two of them getting closer—heard their conversation on the train. She felt a little remorse at that, knowing that her lies, her hesitation, and the memories of Kohl that always held her back were the reasons she'd pushed everyone away.

A breeze swept by them, lifting the waves of blue hair off Tannis's shoulders. She exhaled and her shoulders dropped, the tension going out of her gold eyes. "Like Raurie, yes."

Aina gave her a warm smile, feeling a strange sense of relief— and she thought of Teo. If there was anyone who lifted her up, made her want to be open and vulnerable, it was him. The only question was whether she'd pushed him away too. Her heart twinged at the thought, but there was no point thinking of it now.

"Let's go to the new Dom," she said finally. "I'll need a few hours to make the poison and antidotes for Bautix and the Sentinel before we head out to the tradehouses."

An hour later, when they reached the last street before the row of manors along the river, Aina forced herself to look at the remnants of the Dom. Her heart clenched at the sight; it was a pile of charred walls and broken furniture. She let out a long breath, sealing the image in her memory—she would never forget it. But now they had a new manor to live in, a new place to call the Dom, and it would stand just as strong for the south of the city as the old one had.

"It's that one," Tannis said, pointing to a manor three houses north of the Dom. They walked to the front door, which looked brand new compared to what she was used to seeing on these manors. Ryuu had replaced the old door with smooth white wood and a crystal knocker. "Do you think everything might be decked out in gold now, since Ryuu's been in charge?" Tannis asked. "People are going to try to rob us every night."

"I hope not," Aina muttered as she led the way in. She gasped, and as Tannis pushed past her to get in, Aina whispered, "Not gold, but it's really pretty."

Maybe Ryuu didn't like the business side of running his family's empire, but he certainly had the artistic and architectural flair for the construction they were involved in. Even though he hadn't done the actual construction himself, his touch of design was all over the place. The floor had diamond-shaped jade tiles outlined in tiny crystals. The walls were a smooth, deep green with silver metallic vines encasing electric lights all along. The staircase ahead also had jade steps with the same pattern as the floor, and a crystal banister along the side.

"He really went all out," Tannis said, shaking her head in awe. "I suppose this is what he comes up with when he's procrastinating on meetings."

Aina walked toward the office, pleased that this manor had a similar layout to the old Dom. She would have been happy with dirt floors and candles, as long as it could be their tradehouse and it was safe to live in, but she wouldn't complain about this makeover.

When they entered the office, Aina took one moment to stare open-mouthed at the rose quartz and gold flooring, walls, and furniture before she noticed the door to the poison-brewing room was open.

"I'll get started," she told Tannis, ingredients and techniques coming to her already—she'd remake the poison she'd used on Fayes, as well as antidotes.

Tannis went upstairs then, and Aina got to work, only taking a brief moment to admire the new silver and crystal instruments Ryuu had supplied her with, the white tile floors so clean and bright, she could almost see her reflection in them.

She worked for at least an hour, losing track of time. Four vials of poison, three antidotes, and a mixture of milky water that would be presented to Bautix as the fake antidote.

While the poison was colorless with a faint smoke that rose off it, the antidote was murkier and thicker. Since they each used different parts of la orquídea reclusa flower, they shared a subtle scent. It smelled like Kosín. A hint of rust, smoke, and river stench.

Shaking her head to clear it, as if she'd imagined the scent, she stoppered all the vials and then lined them up on the table.

She would let Bautix know he was powerless before death— the poison gave the victim twenty final minutes before they succumbed. Twenty minutes for him to see that he'd lost, to see that she'd overpowered him without even needing to touch him.

When she began putting away the ingredients, the door to the room creaked open.

Expecting Tannis, Aina said, "I'll be ready in a few—"

"Hi, Aina." Teo stood in the doorway with his hands in his pocket. His deep brown eyes took her in with a cautious smile.

For a moment, she stiffened, not saying anything or making a move toward him. They hadn't had a real conversation alone since their argument after he'd learned she was working with Kohl—when he'd called her the person he loved.

Her heart felt lighter at the memory, even though it was tinged with regret from keeping the truth from him. But two days ago, when they'd run to each other during the bombings and leapt out of a theater window and somehow both survived, it seemed like nothing had changed between them. Last night at the safe house when she'd told everyone the new plan, he hadn't spoken much, but he also hadn't taken his eyes off her.

A small bit of hope bloomed in her heart, and she walked toward him.

"Do you want to go up to the roof with me, Teo?"

Please say yes, she thought. *Please don't give up on me.*

He nodded, not saying anything, but it was still something. As they walked up to the second floor, he blinked as if all the new decorations were too bright to look at. They climbed onto a ladder attached outside one of the bedroom windows and stepped onto the roof. There were a thousand things she wanted to say to him, but when they looked out at the city, all of them briefly left her.

Ash still coated many of the streets. Scorched, blackened roads were scattered through the Stacks and what she could see of the Center. Collapsed buildings at the edge of the Center threatened to topple down the hills into the Stacks. No more smoke lingered above the city, but the scent of it remained, filling her lungs as she breathed in next to Teo.

"It looks . . ."

"Like a nightmare," he finished for her, shaking his head. And the mere sound of his voice relieved her so much, she didn't care what they were talking about. She just wanted him to speak to her again. He'd tilted his head slightly to the side as he examined the city ahead of them, and lifted a hand to point to a nearby street. Reluctantly tearing her gaze away from him, Aina looked in the direction he pointed. A group of workers loaded rubble onto the back of a wagon. "It will get better, though. Your plan to work with the Sentinel is a good one, you know. I never thought I'd agree with that, but I also never thought I'd see the entire city bombed. I want this place to have a future."

He bit his lower lip for a moment as if holding back what he wanted to say. Then he turned to her and crossed his arms in front of his chest. The movement reminded her so much of Tannis earlier in the day, dread filled her. Of course things weren't back to normal between them; she'd ruined that.

"You were right, when you said I've been driven by my anger. I focused on that instead of really feeling the pain from my mother's death, or actually trying to make sense of the guilt I feel because of it," he said, then took in a deep breath before continuing, as if his next words cost him a great effort. "It made me vengeful and stopped me from having hope about anything for the future, that anything we do makes a difference. Every time you go back to Kohl, you fall down that same self-destructive path, and it looks like you're going to disappear; lose yourself without ever really having the future you've always wanted. I think there's a way out of this, that the choices we had to make to survive won't stay with us forever. That we can do better than anyone expects of us—my mother always had faith that I could, and I want to believe I deserve that too. Most of my guilt and my doubts have gone away, but some of my doubts have gotten worse. And it hurts that they're about you."

Her heart twisted at those words, a physical pain in her chest. The guardedness of his eyes drew her toward him. She placed a hand on one of his arms, lightly so that he could move away if he wanted.

"I'm not keeping anything a secret anymore," she said. A crease formed in his brow, but a hopeful glint lit up his eyes for a moment, and she wanted to hold it there forever so he would never worry or doubt or fear ever again. "I kept the truth from everyone because I wanted to be able to face him all on my own. I felt like I would look pathetic if everyone knew, but . . . that's not true, and you deserved the truth before. I don't know what will happen after Bautix is dead—if Kohl will try to fight me or not. But whatever happens, I want you on my side." Her voice went quiet as she spoke, an embarrassed blush creeping up her cheeks. "If you'll be there."

"I don't know what to think of that, Aina," he said. "When you told me you didn't know what you wanted, I believed you. But then you went back to Kohl and hid it from all of us. If I'm going to be at your side, that should be something we both know for sure that we want."

He reached out a hand and placed it on her chin, tilting her head up and making her breaths slow and her pulse race. The sun turned his eyes a molten gold that she didn't look away from. The chaos in the city fell away. Even the Dom disappeared. All she really knew was that she no longer wanted Teo to doubt her.

Taking his other hand in her own and twining their fingers together, she said, "When we first met, we didn't know if we could trust each other, but we didn't leave each other alone. I helped you win a fight when you were outnumbered, and you bandaged my wounds after. We didn't need each other, but we chose to be there, and from that day on, I knew I could trust you. The last thing I want is for you to lose that trust in me. There's a lot we both have to be afraid of right now, but I don't want to be afraid with you."

He stepped forward so they were almost touching, his face blocking out the sun so it cast a halo of light around his dark waves of hair. He shifted slightly, and then their shoulders touched. Suddenly they were inches apart, his breath warm on her face. She lifted a hand to cup his jaw and hoped he wouldn't move away.

When he didn't, she whispered, "What do you want, Teo?"

"The same thing I've always wanted," he said, his eyes flicking to her lips once, so close to his own. "What do you want, Aina?"

Without wasting another moment, she placed her hands on both sides of his head and pulled him close. But before their lips could touch, he placed a finger lightly on her lips to stop her.

"I want to trust you, Aina," he said, his voice almost breaking in a way that made her heart ache. "I wish there were a way you could prove to me that I can."

Her breath caught in her throat as she tried to come up with a reply. She wanted to prove it to him—she would. But she didn't know how.

"Aina!" a voice called.

They broke apart, Aina's heart racing as she flicked her head around to see who had called her.

It was Tannis, standing on the ladder rungs that led up to the roof. "Sorry to interrupt!" she said with an apologetic grimace. "We should go to the other tradehouses now."

29

As Aina and Tannis left the second-to-last tradehouse in the warehouse district, they both turned toward the Center, and Aina sensed Tannis's dread rising too. It had taken all day to convince the other tradehouses to work with the Sentinel, and they'd saved Thunder for last.

"At least the other ones have agreed to help," Aina said, unable to keep the bitterness from her voice. "We'll still be outnumbered against Bautix's men, but it's better than nothing."

"It's a good start," Tannis agreed, nodding slowly as they walked, the setting sun sending red light all around them. "I'm glad they'll be at the Tower tomorrow night, but I don't know about asking them to help with Kaiyanis prisoners." She drew in a deep breath, and Aina turned to look at her, worried she might suggest abandoning the whole plan. But then she said, "There are plenty of politicians who work in the Tower and have assistants and maids there who are actually Kaiyanis Inosen blackmailed into serving them to keep their religion a secret. Mirran and I will find out where they work in the Tower and get them out. We can go in at the same time the tradehouses do, since the Sentinel already knows they're coming; if Mariya Okubo really wants us to get the Inosen out and to the ports, she'll tell the guards to leave us alone."

Aina bit her lip, trying to hold back her relief from showing on her face. "You'll be able to figure this all out by tomorrow? Where they all are?"

"I have my sources," Tannis said. "I thought I could pretend the past doesn't exist, but . . . I don't want to push it away anymore. Not the memories, not the guilt. And they deserve whatever help they can get." She straightened, her shoulders back and a new determination glinting in her eyes. "I know we can make Arman listen to us. But we'll stop Bautix tomorrow with or without Arman's help." They walked onward toward the Thunder tradehouse in the Center, and Aina felt a surge of confidence. The challenges that lay between her and Bautix's defeat suddenly seemed small. When they reached the tradehouse, she knocked out a code on the back door, knowing that nothing Arman said would derail them.

One of the younger recruits, the boy Aina recognized from the night Arman and his men had cornered her in the Stacks, opened the door. His eyes widened when Aina and Tannis entered the tradehouse without a word.

"Tell Arman to come out and meet us," she said, and the boy scampered away to fetch his boss.

Minutes later, the same boy served them drinks in the office at a desk across from Arman Kraz, who'd placed down a cigar on a saucer to greet them. He still had a bruise on the side of his temple from where she'd punched him. A small smirk tilted the side of her lips at the sight.

Not bothering to take a sip of her drink, Aina said, "I don't want to waste either of our time, so we'll make this quick."

"I have a guess," Arman Kraz said, sticking the cigar back in his mouth with a pop of his lips. A smoke ring unfurled toward her face. "The Sentinel is a mess and doesn't know what to do since the Diamond Guards have turned, and now they want our help defending the city."

"Imagine what we'll have once it's over," Tannis said as Aina crossed her arms and tried to hide her frustration at how quickly he'd figured this out. "We can ask the Sentinel for anything we want."

"We don't ask," he said harshly, his eyes narrowing as he stared at them. "We watch this city fall and we take advantage of the mess that's left afterward. That's how the tradehouses started and how they should have always been."

"They've also always survived on bribes and favors," Aina said, talking over his last few words. "And the tradehouses were only formed after the war, not during. We're trying to save our asses during the actual fighting because if you haven't noticed, we're in another war right now. If Bautix kills the Sentinel and takes over, he'll come for us immediately, and he'll have the entire army to do it with. He's the one who attacked the Dom. If you think he doesn't see us as a threat worth paying attention to, then you underestimate our entire institution."

A thick silence fell between the three of them as Arman took in her words. Even as they sunk in, though, something about his eyes still looked defiant, like he would search for any way to anger them and make them show weakness. It reminded her so much of Kohl that she almost rolled her eyes.

"Tomorrow, you and the other tradehouses will go to the Tower with me and Mirran," Tannis said. "She and I will have our own jobs in the Tower, while your job will be to help protect it when Bautix strikes."

Arman jerked his head at Aina. "And you?"

She raised an eyebrow. "None of your goddess-damned business."

Arman shook his head so the smoke coming from his cigar spun erratically in front of him. "I like you, Solís. And I know you've stepped into some big shoes. You've done the best you can, despite how little experience you actually have. But promise me something: If you somehow stop this city from falling apart . . . we will continue to thrive in the chaos. That's how the tradehouses were born. The chaos is what we take advantage of. We don't exist because the Sentinel decides to do us a favor. Don't do too good a job of getting rid of the chaos, or else we'll have nothing left. Do you want to be a factory rat or do you prefer being in charge of your own life?"

A silence followed, and she took in his words, knowing how true they were. The tradehouses were a sign of what people from the Stacks could become with no permission or blessings from the Steels who wanted to keep them poor. But Arman was more similar to the Steels than he would ever admit; he resisted change as much as they did.

And while Aina was still figuring out what kind of tradehouse leader she wanted to be, she knew that change was something they all needed.

She met Tannis's gaze from the corner of her eyes and knew she felt the same—that the tradehouses meant more than just chaos.

"Maybe we take care of the city for them since they've messed it all up," she finally said to Arman. "But that means we're the ones who have control over what it turns into at the end of all this."

He clasped his hands together and leaned back in his chair, a pensive smile on his face. "All right. We'll go to the Tower tomorrow night, and I'll wait for you to prove that to me."

The next day, as fat gray clouds hung low in the sky threatening rain, Aina approached the train station in the Center with Tannis. It had reopened late last night, though it was emptier than she was accustomed to seeing it.

So were the streets around them. People still went to work, but no one dallied in the streets or spoke to one another. Leather shoes clacked along the pavement around them, but the only voices were hurried whispers rather than the usual din.

"I'll make this quick," Aina said, lifting up the bag she held with the poisons and antidotes for Kohl. "See you all on the train."

"Good luck with him," Tannis said with a grimace before turning around to walk through the main doors of the station.

Knowing that Tannis meant Kohl, Aina steeled herself before going to meet him. She had all the pieces of the plan in place, the Dom, and as for Teo . . . at least he was talking to her. The only thing to decide was what to do with Kohl. She wouldn't let him rattle her like the last time they'd spoken to each other and he'd said he feared living without her . . . or think about the way his eyes had softened in relief when he saw she'd survived Bautix's attacks, or the notes he'd left her proving he'd always cared.

Teo's words echoed in her mind then: *Every time you go back to Kohl, you fall down that same self-destructive path.*

She shook the thought away and took a deep breath before entering the station café, which was filled with tired travelers and people who needed a place for quiet conversation. She'd expected to meet him in the tower of the train station, but that morning, a note had appeared under the Dom's door asking her to meet him here instead.

When she entered, a small bell clanging above the door to announce her arrival, she figured out why: He stood near the counter and held up a drink as she approached.

"Toast me, Aina," he said in an enigmatic tone.

Narrowing her eyes at him, she took the drink. "What are we toasting?"

"Our impending victory, of course," he said with the quick flash of a smile. He raised his own glass and clinked it against hers. "I assume you're ready."

She nodded, and after taking a sip of her drink, passed him the poisons under the darkened counter—four poisons, three antidotes, and one fake antidote. When he took the last of the vials, he clasped his hands around one of hers. Her breath caught, but she tried not to show anything on her face. Just like when they'd worked together, she never knew what direction he would take; if he'd try to hold her hand or break her arm.

But when she looked up and met his normally sharp blue eyes, they'd softened somewhat. She remembered the letters in the horse. Had they really come from this man in front of her, who'd threatened her more times than she could count? His feelings for her had always been muddled, always confusing, always a mess, like hers had always been for him.

"Thank you," Kohl said, his voice nearly lost in the rumble of a train leaving the station. "Now we're nearly ready. I couldn't have done this job without you, Aina."

She stilled for a moment, not having expected him to admit that. As he put the vials inside a pack on the seat next to him, she took another sip of her drink and leaned against the counter, facing the rest of the café. He turned to do the same, and she watched him out of the corner of her eye, wondering how much of what he showed her was real and how much was a mask.

"The smuggler's ship will be docked at pier four," Kohl continued. "And I instructed one of the Jackals on my side to leave a small boat on the side of pier eleven for your friends to reach the back of the ship. I'll give the poisons to a Jackal who will transfer them to Bautix, and I'll get the antidotes to the Sentinel so the plan at the Tower can pull through."

She pictured the plan playing out, Bautix's death and the city safe. Where would they all go from there? The apparition of the Mothers in the cave—which she still suspected might have had more to do with getting hit by those rocks than actually seeing the Mothers—came back to her now. Even if it had just been her imagination, their words rang through her thoughts now.

Remember what we teach, they'd said. *Because you, and all the people of this land, are in pain.*

"You were right about the benefits of poison," she said after a pause. "It shows how much power you have over the person you kill. But it's also a way of keeping your hands clean, at least for a while. Do you know what I mean?"

He laughed a little at that. "Yes, I know what you mean, Aina." He tilted his head toward her, smiling at the confusion on her face, then said, "I would have thought the way I've treated you should prove that I didn't always want to be a killer."

The way you've treated me? Holding back a sarcastic comment on that, she crossed her arms and said, "You don't want to be a killer—you want to be the best, most fearsome, most accomplished murderer and criminal this city has ever imagined. It's the only way you can live with yourself, isn't it?"

"You've got me all figured out, haven't you?"

"I saw the notes," she said abruptly, watching his features for any sign of what he thought. "The ones you left inside the horse. They tell your story well enough."

"You found them," Kohl said, letting out a long breath. "You know, then, that only two things have ever mattered to me."

He met her eyes, and her heart stuttered a little. Teo was right—she was less of herself around him, and she couldn't forget the things he'd done to her, no matter what he might feel for her.

"You've wanted to get rid of me for years, Kohl," she said, hoping he would simply agree—it would make her choice so much easier. "You've just never admitted it to yourself, because I'm the only proof you might have a soul of some sort."

"What's the other thing that matters to me?" he asked, speaking over her last words in a rush.

"The Dom," she said after a pause. "The Stacks and the people who live there."

"And you took it from me. If I've ever wanted to get rid of you, that's why." He leaned toward her where she rested against the counter, his cold words and ice-blue eyes pinning her in place. "You took my life's work, and without that, doesn't that mean there's only one thing left I care about?" Then he leaned closer, and for a moment, she thought he was going to try to kiss her— the one thing she'd dreamed about for years. Some twisted part of her still wondered what that would be like, but another part of her rose up in disgust. Then his hand drifted to her chin, and he ran a finger across her lower lip. It was cold, like the wintry feel of his breath on her cheeks.

It was nothing like Teo.

He pulled away, and instead of the usual amused smile he wore whenever he unnerved her, deep pain flashed in his eyes that she couldn't figure out.

She ran her tongue over her lips, noticing a slightly metallic taste as she did. Taking the glass of firebrandy, she took a long swig to clear away the taste of him too.

As he turned and walked away, she exhaled, tense and breathless against the counter. The voices of the people in the café and the rumble of trains in the station behind her filled her ears. Kohl opened the door and it swung shut behind him, little bell clanging above.

There was a cycle of revenge in this city, one where everyone was either debtor or collector. When people were hurting, they hurt other people in return. She'd taken his home from him, just like he'd done to her. The thought was like a punch to the gut. For so long, all she'd wanted was to get revenge on him. But that only continued the cycle and made her as bad as him.

She couldn't forgive him, but she no longer wanted to kill him.

30

When Aina reached the train platform a few minutes later, she spotted Teo, Ryuu, Lill, and Mirran in front of the large brass train that would take them to the ports. Looking up toward the roof, she shuddered a little, hoping any fights she got into today wouldn't be on a moving vehicle.

Before she reached them though, she heard a familiar voice to her right. Tannis and Raurie stood in the doorway to one of the station waiting rooms.

"I'm really glad you and Lill were able to make it today," Tannis said.

"And miss all the fun? Never," Raurie said, drawing out a laugh from Tannis.

Aina was about to move on, not wanting to eavesdrop, but Tannis's next words caught her attention.

"I was also worried I wouldn't be able to see you before going to the Tower," she said in a haltingly nervous tone. "I'm usually never afraid before missions; I don't think about the idea of failing because it's not an option. But with this one, I fear failing more than I have with anything else."

"You won't fail," Raurie said in a reassuring tone, brushing a strand of Tannis's blue hair behind her ears. "What makes you so sure you will?"

"I always seem to mess up everything," Tannis said, shaking her head sadly. "I've spent as long as possible trying to ignore my past and my guilt, focus only on the Dom—ignoring the problems affecting my people in this city just because I'd gotten away from it myself. And now that I'm finally deciding not to do that anymore, it's scary thinking it might backfire."

Raurie rolled her eyes. "And what have I told you about giving up? Remember when you had to remind me not to do the same? It's worthless. Why would you do that when you can do so much for the people you care about?"

"You're annoyingly encouraging."

Raurie shrugged with a playful expression. "You'll have to get used to it."

"Good thing I like challenges," Tannis said, then leaned forward to kiss Raurie.

Aina turned away then, her ears hot. She hadn't really wanted to listen in, but she couldn't help herself—Tannis deserved some happiness.

As she approached the others, Teo saw her first, and the smile he gave her was brighter than the sun. Her cheeks burned at the memory of almost kissing him yesterday. She wanted to believe she deserved some happiness too—but her heart sank a little and she wondered how she would ever prove to Teo that he could trust her again.

She looked over her shoulder toward the clock hanging over

the platform—only a few minutes before the train would open for boarding. Then she turned to Ryuu and pulled him into a hug. "Ryuu, thank you. The new manor looks beautiful."

"Maybe too beautiful; people will definitely try to rob us more often," Mirran said with a grimace. "But seriously, thank you."

"It was the least I could do," he said with a shrug, but Aina still noticed the pride in his eyes as Tannis and Raurie joined them.

"We should go," Mirran said to Tannis in a low voice. "We'll have to start early to get the Kaiyanis out unnoticed and to a place where we can escort them all."

"You're right," Tannis said. "Aina, make sure the ports are safe by the time we get there. I don't want to lose any of the people we're helping."

The two of them left with a quick wave, Tannis's eyes lingering on Raurie for another long moment. Minutes later, the rest of them boarded the train and searched for an empty compartment as it sped away toward the coast and left the clouds of the city behind. Sunlit fields began to flash by in the windows. Aina walked at the front of the group, with Lill right behind her.

"About your mother . . ." Aina began slowly.

Lill gave her a sharp look. "Was she the one who told you that Bautix would attack? I saw you look at me when you were telling us."

Aina nodded. "She wanted me to get you out of the city, because she knew it would happen."

"If she cared, then where has she been all this time? She just wants to avoid feeling guilty if I die because of her choices."

"I didn't say she cared," Aina said, falling back to walk next to Lill in the narrow hall. "I don't know what she feels. But she didn't want you to get caught in it. There's a chance she's thinking about changing sides."

"I don't know about all that. I've already agreed to this crazy plan of yours with the Sentinel. That's enough trust for one day." Lill went quiet for a long moment. "I used to be so afraid of living underground. It was so dark and I felt suffocated. I've always been afraid of ghosts, and one of the others was messing with me one day and told me the ghosts of all those who died in the civil war haunt the city from its tunnels. I was always afraid of the mines collapsing on us too. So many forgotten bones and secret passages and hidden stories there. I didn't want to join them. I feel better now, even here, just because we're above ground. And being with all of you."

"It's much better than being afraid alone," Aina said, knowing that was something she often did; tackling problems on her own rather than ever admitting she needed help.

"Afraid or angry? Both?" Lill shook her head. "I'm tired of being angry and afraid all the time; I'm tired of being alone. I want this to be the last of it."

Minutes later and halfway down the train, they found an empty compartment and gathered around the table together.

"Did you two have to sneak out again?" Ryuu asked Raurie and Lill once they'd all been seated.

"Not this time," Raurie said while Lill shook her head. "June and I talked about it last night. For the longest time, I thought she underestimated me . . . but she only wanted to keep me safe. She'd already lost her sister—my mom—fighting for Inosen rights. She doesn't want to lose me too. But she admits we need to do something, and that using the Mothers' magic might be the only way. If anything, she thinks the ports will be safer than the city—so I think she's actually glad I'll be gone, but somewhere I can still help."

"I'm glad you two made up," Teo said. "I don't think anywhere is safe anymore, though."

"It never has been for us," Lill added. "You just pick from multiple bad options and hope the one you chose is best."

Aina blinked. "Like being friends with us?"

"Yeah," Lill said with a wink. "But I made the right choice with that one."

Ryuu smiled back at her as he pulled out a map of the ports, and then they began their last stages of planning. Sunlight flickered through the windows, illuminating the map as Aina pointed out the best vantage points to take out the Jackals.

"The shipment will come from the northwestern port this time, it's confirmed," Aina said. "We assume most of the Jackals will be concentrated around there, but it won't hurt for us to have eyes everywhere. Raurie and Lill should go with Ryuu and look for the weapons—take as many as you can and throw the rest out to sea. Teo and I will search for the smuggler and take out any Jackals we see, and we'll look for the weapons too."

Once they finished planning, she sat next to Teo for the rest of the train ride. The whole way there, she tried to shake off the memory of Kohl touching her lips, but it clung to her like a heavy cloak.

A sharp wind gusted over from the ocean as Aina stepped off the train an hour later at the southwestern port. The sound of boats bobbing in the water blended with their breathing. It was deadly quiet here, with none of the usual clamor from sailors or passengers. The silence made her tense, one hand going to a knife already.

"That way," Ryuu said, pointing northward.

They walked past the piers, the sun shining so brightly, it was difficult to see ahead without squinting. Aina looked everywhere for a sign of the Jackals: behind the ships bobbing in the water, amid crates stacked along each pier, in the shadows of warehouses and sheds spread along the port. The farther they walked with no sign of the Jackals, the more on edge she became.

"There," Aina said, pointing to a small boat bobbing in the water next to pier eleven, the one that marked the split between the northwestern port and the southwestern port. "Like Kohl said."

Ryuu, Raurie, and Lill climbed into the boat, grabbing sets of oars as they did. A sharp breeze gusted down the docks and made their boat wobble in the water. All three of them tensed, and Aina couldn't blame them.

"You'll make it to the storage entrance of the ship if you go up behind it," Aina said, reminding them of the plan. "We'll take out as many Jackals as we can at the front and enter there. We'll regroup on the deck in an hour and then leave."

"Good luck," Ryuu said, dropping his oars into the water to push the boat onward.

"Not taking any chances now," Teo said, withdrawing two guns from the holsters at his belt and holding one in each hand. "Even if we haven't seen them yet, I bet they know we're here."

With a tight grimace, she nodded. Like before any fight, adrenaline flooded through her, spurring her onward down the piers with Teo at her side. But right now the sharp edge of fear struck through the confidence she usually felt. Any moment now back in the city, Kohl would be giving the poisons and fake antidote to Bautix. She imagined Bautix's smug smile as he slithered through one of the secret entrances into the Tower. If she stopped his men and weapons shipment from getting through the ports, Bautix wouldn't have the backup and firepower he needed to take over the Tower. But if they failed, his men would outnumber every Diamond Guard left in the Tower, and he'd win without even needing to poison anyone.

When they reached pier seven, a gunshot rang out. Aina leapt out of the way as a bullet flew past her and into the metal side of a shed behind her. Teo fired in the direction of the attacker, behind a collection of storage crates at the edge of pier six, and someone fell to the ground with a thud.

She and Teo ran toward the crate in a crouch, then took cover. Her breath came quickly, her eyes darting to every potential hiding place at the piers ahead. Shadows moved at some of them, and she halfway lifted her dagger, ready to throw it into the throat of the first Jackal she spotted.

"If they didn't know we were here before, they definitely do now," Teo said, wiping sweat off his forehead.

She drew in a deep breath and stood. "Let's go meet them, then."

"I'll cover you."

She nodded and, without wasting another moment, jumped up from behind the crate. Approaching the fifth pier at a run, she drew close to the warehouse at the pier. Heads peered through the windows, raising rifles that shone in the sunlight. Bullets slammed against the pier, wooden docks exploding at her feet as she ran. Teo returned fire as he ran behind her. Bodies fell from the windows of the warehouse, landing with loud thuds on the docks or smacking against the water.

The remaining Jackals in the windows fell back, none of them wanting to join their colleagues.

Turning to see how close Teo was, she spotted a Jackal approaching them from behind and lifting his gun to aim at Teo's head.

She launched her dagger into his throat. Teo tensed as it flew by him, and looked back as the Jackal fell to the ground with blood spilling over the docks.

"Get to pier four!" she called to Teo as she ran to retrieve her dagger. Anticipating another attack from the Jackals at the window, she pivoted away as a bullet landed where her foot had been. Heart in her throat, she raced toward the crate Teo hid behind at the edge of pier four.

A tall, wooden ship bobbed in the water ahead, its sails waving in the afternoon wind. The Kaiyanis flag, pale blue with a white lily in the center, flew on one of the masts. More crates were stacked all along the pier. Straining her ears, Aina heard the cock of a gun. It was a bottleneck leading up to the ship's entrance; the Jackals wanted them to try. Her pulse raced in anticipation to the challenge. One look at Teo told her he was ready to run for it, guns blazing. They would either get trapped in here, or do the trapping themselves.

She withdrew her blowgun, loaded a poison dart, and held three others ready to go. Her other hand gripped the handle of one of her scythes.

Teo nodded at her as he withdrew a second gun, and then mouthed, "You take the right, I'll take the left."

They moved in sync then, neither needing to confer with the other what they were doing, and elation filled her despite the fact that they were probably going to be shot full of holes. They would win this yet.

When she and Teo worked together, nothing could stop them.

At the edge of one crate, the wooden dock creaked under a footstep, and Aina pivoted, blowing into her blowgun just as a Jackal stepped out from behind the crate. The dart hit his neck and he stumbled toward her. She swept her foot behind his knees to knock him to the ground. He'd be dead in a minute. The click of a gun sounded to her right.

She ducked as the bullet fired, then barreled forward before the Jackal could load the gun again and slammed into his waist. She swept her scythe across his chest, then pivoted to avoid the next fighter who came running out from behind a crate. Her scythe swung into his neck and she pushed until it nearly took off his head. He dropped to the ground, drowning in his own blood.

Yanking her scythe free and ignoring the blood dripping down it, Aina raced forward. Twenty more feet, and she'd reach the ship.

Her eyes flicked toward Teo, who'd just shot a Jackal flying at him from behind a crate on his side, but as she did, an arm reached out from behind the crate closest to her and slammed into her throat. As she stumbled back, another Jackal lifted her up by the collar. He slammed her into the crate, the breath getting knocked out of her with the force of it. His knife appeared at her neck.

Grabbing his hand, she began to push back, her feet scrabbling for purchase on the crate to lean into the knife even more. Sweat dripping into her eyes, she pushed the knife toward him instead. With one more forceful push, she sliced it through his throat.

As he fell back, blood pouring over his clothes and onto the dock, Aina lurched to her feet and nearly slipped in the blood.

Across the pier, Teo shot another Jackal. One more approached behind him, and Aina flung a knife at him before he could reach Teo.

With one more quick glance around at all the bodies, she and Teo ran forward, encountering no more Jackals as they approached the gangplank.

They raced up it onto the empty deck, and Teo pointed to a staircase that led to the lower levels.

The thrill of winning a fight worked through her, spurring her onward to follow Teo down the stairs. They were so close; all they had to do was kill the smuggler and get rid of the weapons. She could almost taste their victory, like the salt of the sea ahead.

It was dark inside the ship, lit only with a few oil lamps hanging on the walls. Blinking to adjust their eyes, they began to search through narrow, labyrinthine halls. They passed empty offices and storage rooms, with no sign of any more Jackals. It grew so quiet, she could hear her own heartbeat.

"The weapons will probably be on the lowest level," Aina said, glancing around as they reached an intersection of four hallways. Her footsteps approaching Teo made the floor creak. "The smuggler above."

"We'll find him," Teo assured her. "Let's look for another staircase."

They chose one of the hallways and raced down it, searching for a staircase that might take them to the highest level of the ship. When they finally found one, they ascended to the next floor, their footsteps the only sound. They reached the next landing and turned the corner. But the light of a flare ahead caught her attention. Someone passed in front of it, their shadow extending like a scythe across the floor.

Three Jackals stepped around the next corner, guns aimed at Aina and Teo's heads.

31

Aina braced herself, knowing she'd have to take a hit, and lifted her blowgun. As she fired out the first dart, a bullet struck her upper arm. Teo shot the middle Jackal between the eyes as Aina shot a dart into the neck of the last one.

As soon as he collapsed, she leaned against the wall, clutching her arm and hissing as a dull, throbbing pain spread down her arm and along her chest. Glancing down, her vision blurring, she tried to squeeze her hand into a fist, but the fingers wouldn't move.

"Aina," Teo said, placing his fingers gingerly on her arm. A crease formed on his forehead as he pulled bandages from the pack strung over his back. Her arm shook on its own and her head spun, suddenly dizzy.

"We should keep going," she said through gritted teeth.

But Teo ignored her, removing the bullet and bandaging the wound. She watched him, her nerves settling and the rapid beat of her pulse slowing as she did. Not long ago, Kohl had taken care of a bullet wound for her too. But this was so different from Kohl. When Teo touched her, his fingers were soft and gentle enough that she hardly felt them. Or maybe it was the numbing sensation spreading through her arm.

When Teo finished bandaging her wound, she grabbed his hand with her other hand, twining their fingers together. The ship fell quiet around them, so she could almost pretend no more danger would find them.

"I'm not leaving you," he said, smiling as he squeezed her hand. Her heart swelled, first with warmth at his words and then with sadness—she'd fought alongside him so many times, yet not until now did she really fear for him, even though she was the one injured. Like with the Inosen being targeted because of her choice to use magic, her friends were now all on this ship because she and Kohl had planned it.

As if reading her mind, Teo placed a hand on her chin so she would meet his eyes, and said, "We can still win this."

"I know," she said, her voice shaky. "But there are more Jackals than I expected."

"There are fifty total, right?"

"At the piers," she said. "I don't think that number included however many people the smuggler has on this ship."

"Let's get moving, then."

There was a strain in his voice as he spoke, anticipating—as she did—how much fighting still lay ahead of them. But the only option was to keep moving forward, and hope that Raurie, Lill, and Ryuu weren't facing as much difficulty on their part of the ship.

They traversed the next two halls, peering into every room for some sign of the smuggler, and finally found him in an office close to the wheelhouse. He was turned away from them, rummaging through a drawer. Keeping her movements as quiet as she could, Aina lifted her blowgun, fired a dart into his neck, and pulled the door closed behind her. A moment passed, and then the smuggler shouted from within and began yanking on the door to open it, but Aina and Teo managed to hold it shut. Soon after, the man's grip relinquished, Aina nodded to Teo, and they pushed open the door.

The smuggler knelt on the floor, weak and shaking as the poison worked through him. Knowing he didn't have long, she grabbed him and pinned him to the floor with her knife at his throat. He coughed up blood and his eyes widened at the sight of the blade against his skin. "I have an antidote," she whispered, and like a puppet, he slackened in her arms, ready to do anything she said. "All your pain will go away. But you have to tell me: How many men have you brought in to fight for Bautix? And where are the weapons? Speak fast or the poison will kill you."

The words tumbled out, so fast she could barely catch them all. "All I do is bring in the people he's hiring from Kaiyan, all right?"

"And what about the weapons?" she asked.

Sweat covered his skin, making her blade slide easily over his throat. His eyes bulged as he marked its progress.

"I have those too. I get them in Duroz, then I pick up the hired men from Kaiyan. They're on the bottom floor of the ship, and when they get to the city, they're led through the mine tunnels to wherever Bautix is storing them. I don't know where he puts them after that or what he's planning to do with them. The man's so desperate, he practically threw kors at me, but he's not stupid—he doesn't tell me anything more."

"Good to know," Aina whispered as she swept her knife across his throat. "You won't be a problem anymore."

As his blood spilled over the floor, Teo grimaced. "You didn't really have an antidote, did you?"

Shrugging, Aina said, "I told him his pain would go away. Come on."

They left the room and turned down the next hall, stepping over the bodies of the Jackals they'd killed. When they reached a staircase, they raced down two sets of stairs, looking in each room they passed for a sign of the weapons or for any glimpse of Ryuu, Raurie, and Lill.

But as they rounded a corner, a Jackal met them, his knife striking out. Teo grunted and doubled over as the blade thrust through his side. Aina shoved the Jackal back and punched him in the jaw—his head slammed off the wall, and before he could recover, she cut his throat. The moment he collapsed, his blood slicking the floor, Aina dropped to her knees at Teo's side.

"I'm fine," Teo said, his breath hitching. "We need to find the weapons, Aina."

Blood seeped from his wound, and he tried to staunch it by pressing his hand on it. Sweat dotted his forehead and his next few breaths came shallow. She withdrew more bandages from the pack he carried and used some of the fabric to press down on the wound.

She swallowed hard, her throat dry. Her left arm had gone nearly numb, the fingers of that hand stiff when she tried to move them. Neither of them would last much longer if the Jackals found them again. Her confidence began to slip away like water from cupped hands and she imagined them failing, shot to death on this ship, Bautix taking over the Tower.

"Let's keep moving," she whispered after she'd wrapped bandages around him as well as she could.

As they continued onward, the scent of smoke grew in the air. Her breath caught in her throat as she remembered the Dom burning before her, the bombings through the city shaking the earth. She gripped Teo's sleeve with the stiff fingers of her left hand. Pulling him close, she asked, "Do you hear that?"

Something crackled nearby, a sound that had grown familiar: the spark of flames preparing to spread. Her eyes flicked to the wooden walls around them and she pictured them burning, melting to charred husks and burying her and Teo here. This place would be devoured in minutes if there were a fire on the ship.

She and Teo exchanged a panicked glance, then looked down the hall to see a door ajar. The hallway curved around a corner at the end. Straining her ears, she heard no footsteps or other signs that Ryuu, Raurie, or Lill might be close. There was only the faint crackling noise coming from somewhere nearby, and the growing scent of smoke in the air.

"Let's check that room, then get out of here," she said, then coughed on the smoke. "If there's a fire, that'll take care of the weapons better than we could."

As they moved toward the room, she wondered why the Jackals would set their own ship on fire—unless they'd already gotten the weapons off and her plan had failed. She shook away the thought, not even wanting to consider it.

But when they entered the room, a few crates stood scattered, with one flickering lamp illuminating them. She quickly knelt in front of one. Lifting the lid, she almost laughed in relief. Grenades and guns stared up at her.

"Found it," she said, turning to look at Teo. He leaned against the wall, his hand still pressing down on his wound. His face had paled slightly, and instead of replying, he bit his lip and nodded.

"Teo," she said, going to him. "Let's grab as many of the weapons as we can—the fire will take care of the rest." She fumbled for a diamond in the pouch at her belt, the fingers of her left hand shaking as she withdrew it. "I'll try to stop the blood flow."

She murmured a quick prayer to the Mothers. *Please let me do this. Please help Teo.*

But before she could draw a cut on her arm, the door swung closed. A bolt latched in place. A Jackal's smirking face appeared in the slit of a window, then vanished.

"Aina, there's . . ." Teo's voice faded, too weak to finish the sentence, but he pointed toward the floor next to the crate.

A sheen of liquid had gathered in a puddle on the ground. Heart pounding somewhere in her throat, Aina peered around the crate. Two smashed vials lay on the ground, broken bits of glass interspersed in the spilled liquid—a liquid that looked far too familiar. Her breath caught in her throat, but she still breathed in the scent, a scent she knew better than any other: the acrid rust-and-copper scent of Kosín.

"The poison."

She'd hardly breathed out the words when Teo collapsed next to her.

32

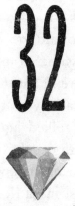

The stench of smoke grew thick in the air now, making her eyes water as she dropped next to Teo. Or was that an effect of the poison? Her heart seized, her thoughts raced—no, that wasn't an effect of it, she would know. She'd brewed it, after all. For some reason, the poison wasn't hurting her.

But as she turned Teo over, she saw the effects. The veins stood out on his neck. His breath came in short, shallow gasps. If he didn't get the antidote, he would die in twenty minutes. Her thoughts went hazy, her heart stuttering as she watched him.

The realization struck her, then, like a punch to the face: Kohl had tricked them.

Her hands shook as she lifted Teo into a sitting position. Forget the weapons. She'd pry open the door, they'd get out of here and find Kohl, and force him to give them the antidote.

"Come on, Teo, let's go." She wrapped her right arm around his waist to bring him upward. Her left hand couldn't get a good grip on him anywhere, the fingers twitching whenever she tried to close them. Gulping, she tried not to think of it and concentrated on lifting Teo.

But his legs trembled when he was halfway to standing and he collapsed. Her knees slammed hard on the wooden floor as she fell with him. The crackle of flames from somewhere in the ship grew louder then, and her throat went dry. Her thoughts scattered, and it took a moment to focus on what Teo said next.

"It's poison, isn't it?" His voice was a frail copy of what it should be, hoarse and scratchy as if he'd been yelling for hours. When she nodded, he let out a sharp laugh, like he should have known this would happen to him. "What will it do to me? How long do I have?"

The anatomy of the poison she'd created crashed into her, Kohl's voice in her head telling her all the effects in a methodical tone. It would devour Teo's lungs and heart, eating through them like acid. Her mouth opened, but she couldn't get the words out. The only thing that left her was a hollow sob.

"Please," she whispered, imagining the Mothers appearing to her in the cave under the Tower. She withdrew her knife and made a cut on her arm, coating the diamond with the blood. She knew this spell could only stop blood loss, not cure anything else, but maybe if she begged, the Mothers would listen.

"You're not going to die," she told Teo, tears trickling down her cheeks as she stared into his eyes—eyes that had only ever shown her kindness, eyes she knew better than anyone else—that now took on the resigned look of every person she'd faced who knew they were about to die . . . and he wasn't even trying to fight it.

"Amman inoke," she whispered, holding the diamond closer to his face as if that would help.

"It won't fix this," he whispered, his voice a harsh rattle as his eyes lost focus.

Dropping the diamond and the knife, she tried to haul him to his feet again. He slid on the liquid from the poison, nearly bringing her down again. Smoke filtered into the room through the cracks on the door, making her eyes water and her breaths shallow. She wondered how long until the fire blazed through here and claimed them both.

As Teo leaned on her, his eyes started to close. Tapping him on the face to make him open them again, she walked slowly toward the door with him.

"Almost there," she said, coughing on the smoke that had now grown so thick, she could barely see through it to the door handle. After leaning him against the door, she began hacking at the lock with one of her scythes. Metal clanged against metal, and she coughed harder with each swing. Sweat built all down her back, and she knew it wasn't just from the exertion—the air was heating up drastically, turning the ship into an oven.

The next swing of her scythe, the lock broke and fell to the floor with a clatter. The door swung open, and a wall of heat hit her so fiercely, she stepped back. At the same time, Teo swayed and fell facedown onto the cabin floor.

Dropping next to him, she grabbed his wrist, her hand nearly sliding off with the sweat that had built up on it. A pulse still beat, but so slowly she thought, for a moment, he was already gone. His breaths came in ragged inhalations, like each one caused him pain.

I did this to him, she thought, the words repeating on refrain as she turned him onto his side. This boy who'd known her for years, who'd bandaged her wounds when they barely knew each other and had been her friend ever since. She'd promised his mother she would protect him, and now her poison was working through his veins and organs, killing him slowly.

All because she'd trusted Kohl.

Of course the Mothers wouldn't let her heal Teo; she'd killed with their magic, gone against everything they taught. She should be the one with poison in her veins now, not him.

After she tapped his face a few more times, he reopened his eyes. With her help, he was able to get into a sitting position, but his arms trembled so badly, he nearly collapsed again. A trickle of blood appeared at his lips.

"Do you have the antidote?" he asked, one word at a time and in a whisper so low she barely heard.

"If Kohl . . . I don't think—"

"He tricked us," Teo gasped out, his eyes unfocused as he spoke.

The realization weighed heavily on her chest, squeezing her heart and lungs, making it hard to breathe. After she'd given him the poison and antidotes, he must have given some of the poisons to a Jackal to plant on the ship and lock them in this room. He'd probably already given Bautix the rest of the poison and thought he'd successfully killed her and Teo.

"There's still time for you," Teo said.

Halfway through his sentence, Aina was already shaking her head. "I won't leave you—"

"Aina, please," Teo said, his voice sounding like the useless prayer she'd sent to the Mothers. One of his hands fumbled for a dagger from the brace across her chest. He placed the hilt in her hands, and when he looked up at her with a plea in his eyes, she nearly dropped the knife.

Though the ship burned around them, her whole body went cold.

"I won't do that, Teo," Aina said.

But with a surprisingly strong grip, he grabbed her wrist and brought the knife to his chest.

"Either the fire will claim me, or the poison will," he gasped out, each word sending a stab of fear through her heart. "Make it quick, Aina. Make it painless."

"No," she whispered, unable to believe he would ask this of her.

"You have to get back to the city. I don't need to be there, Aina. But either you're making it out of this alive, or neither of us are, and I won't pull you down with me like that. You'll live, and you can save a lot more people than you give yourself credit for. The city needs you."

His other hand had moved to the back of her head, his fingers shaking. Her tears blurred his face in front of her and she blinked them away furiously, refusing to miss any last glimpse of him. Wishing she could sear his face into her memory.

"I'm not letting you die here with me, Aina," Teo said, his voice so soft through the crackle of flames nearby that she had to lean close to hear him. "I'll bring your knife to my own heart if it means you get out of here faster. You only have a few minutes. Please, Aina. I trust you."

She told him no over and over again through her sobs, but her hands brought the knife to his chest anyway, one slow inch at a time. She had to prove to him, in his final moments, that he could trust her—that there was someone left in the world he could count on, someone who would be there for him, even for something as terrible as this. The tip rested on his shirt. It bumped against his skin.

She leaned forward over the knife and kissed him. His hand tightened in her hair, and the other trailed down her face to her neck. He kissed her back, softly and slowly, their lips parting now and then to let out the smallest breaths. But then he slowed, and his fingers in her hair loosened, his grip too weak.

She wished she could stay here in his arms forever and that

the fire would never reach them. But there was no forever for people like them.

There never had been.

Pulling away slightly, she blinked away her tears, letting them stare into each other's eyes for one long moment.

And then she drove the knife in.

A choking sound came out of him, and more blood trickled from his mouth. Her hands slipped on the blood that left his chest. As his eyes lost focus, she pulled out the knife and he fell forward, his head landing on her shoulder.

The heat of the flames grew so close, the smoke so thick in the air, she knew she only had minutes to make it out of here.

She gently moved his head to the ground. Tears blurred her vision again, but she didn't blink them away, refusing to have her last memory of him be this. Instead, it would be the kiss they shared, the trust in his eyes as he placed the knife in her hands.

She didn't look back. She ran through the door and stumbled down the hall through the smoke. It had grown so thick, she barely managed to find the staircase. Now that she was in the thick of it, she could tell the flames came from above rather than below. Bounding up the stairs, she expected the floor above to fall down on her any moment. Cinders fell onto her head, singeing her skin where they landed.

As she reached the next landing and rounded the corner, she nearly ran into Ryuu. In the hall beyond him, flames devoured the wood, licking up the walls and searing through the floor. As she watched, floorboards caved in, the fire eating through it all and flames racing to the floor below—where Teo was.

"Aina, we have to go," Ryuu said, his own face strained and covered in sweat from the heat. "Where's Teo?"

Hearing his name was like a sharp punch to the chest. She

rose her eyes toward Ryuu's, hoping he understood without her having to say it.

Teo's dead. I killed him.

Something shuttered in Ryuu's eyes, then he blinked and began to pull her away. He understood.

33

The hall ahead of them collapsed on one side, a burst of smoke and flame nearly knocking Aina and Ryuu off their feet. Stumbling into the wall behind them, they covered their heads to avoid getting burned by cinders that flew toward them in a cloud.

Peering through the haze of smoke, Aina could make out a light ahead that wasn't the roaring flames.

"We should run for it," she said, and Ryuu nodded stiffly. Aina moved in front of him and, without wasting another second, ran down the hall with her arms covering her head.

Heat seared along her arms, flames grasping at her clothes as she raced down the side of the wall that was still intact. The heat grew so intense, she feared her skin would melt.

Seconds later, she skidded onto the pier outside and Ryuu nearly slid into her as he followed.

Coughing smoke out of her lungs, Aina bent over, hands on her knees. Her throat was scorched dry, her thoughts jumbled together. For a moment, she convinced herself this was a nightmare.

When one lone Jackal stepped into the center of the pier ahead of them and pointed a gun at them, she didn't even try to move away.

Ryuu slammed roughly into her, knocking her to the hard, wooden pier. He lifted his own gun and fired at the Jackal, hitting him in the center of his forehead.

As Ryuu stood, Aina placed her hands on the dock to push herself up. Her left arm still shook as she did. When she stood, she looked down at her bloody handprints on the docks—Teo's blood. The setting sun behind the ship and the growing flames sent red and orange light across the blood, making it brighter, more accusatory. A bitter taste built in the back of Aina's mouth, and she thought she'd vomit before Ryuu pulled her away a moment later.

As they ran from the burning ship, Ryuu kept one arm around her shoulders as if he could tell she needed the support. Together, they left the ports, walked across the train tracks where the station's employees stared wide-eyed at the fire blazing above the ship, and headed across the plains toward a copse of trees ahead.

The whole way, she barely felt herself walking, her limbs seeming too numb to move, her thoughts too scattered to tell her body which direction to go. But somehow they made it. The trees closed around them, a cool darkness that Aina wanted to sink into. The spaces between the trees deep with the approach of night were even more mercifully dark. No flames hid between them.

She breathed in the scents of the trees to banish the smoke in her lungs, but then stopped short, her breath catching in her throat as she remembered walking through the forests on the outskirts of Kosín with Teo. He loved the trees, the dirt beneath his feet, the wind carrying the scent of eucalyptus. Why was she allowed to breathe such fresh air when he couldn't?

A small clearing opened ahead as they walked, moonlight forming a white pool at its center. She dropped to her knees there, her hands gripping the wild weeds and grass. Ryuu sat next to her, leaned his head against a tree trunk, and stared at the pocket of sky above.

"Where are Raurie and Lill?" she asked, her voice surprisingly clear. She'd expected it to sound raw and broken.

"We got separated when the fire started and some Jackals found us. I thought maybe I'd find them on my way to look for the weapons, but there was no sign of them. Then I ran into you. I don't know what happened to them." He paused for a moment, and devastation shook his voice when he continued, "It was a setup. It couldn't have been anyone but Kohl."

But Aina merely blinked at his words. He didn't know the half of it. He knew Teo was dead, but he didn't know how. Her poison and her knives, Teo's blood and his last breaths. Raising a hand to her lips, she touched them, remembering their first and final kiss. How had he succumbed to poison and she hadn't?

As she considered it, Ryuu watched her, his eyes soft with concern. She scoffed under her breath. "I don't know how you can sit there and not want to yell at me right now. I'm the one who trusted him."

"I don't blame you for trusting him. I blame him for taking advantage of that." He sighed then, seeming merely resigned—as if he should have predicted this outcome and now simply had to suffer it with her.

"After two months of spending all your time with people from the Stacks, you've really gotten used to having low expectations," she said with a humorless laugh. "He didn't just set the Jackals on us. When we found the smuggler, he told us the weapons were downstairs. A door was open, with a light on. Looking back, we should have known something was wrong, but we were both injured and . . . Kohl took some of the poisons I gave him and got them onto the ship. A Jackal locked us in that room, and the poison, it was going to kill Teo. He asked me to . . ." She gestured weakly at the brace of knives strapped to her chest, and understanding dawned in Ryuu's eyes. When her lips trembled, he reached forward and pulled her into a hug.

"I'm sorry, Aina," he said in a gruff voice. "I know that does nothing—it never helped me when people said sorry for my parents or my brother. But I am sorry about what Kohl did. I know you didn't want to trust him again, and I know you were being careful."

"It's not just that I trusted him," she said with a sigh, staring into the forest. "I was so stubborn, so determined to prove he could never hurt me again . . . it only made it easier for him to do exactly that." Her words choked up for a moment, but she pushed through, trying to make sense of it all. "It's strange, though, isn't it? I was in the same room. The poison should have killed me too."

And then it hit her. She gasped, her whole body tensing as she remembered Kohl approaching her in the café, touching her lips softly and then walking away.

"Kohl gave me the antidote before I got on the train, so the poison spared me," she breathed. "I didn't realize it until now." And when she'd kissed Teo before driving her knife into his heart, was there any remnant of the antidote on her lips? Could it work like that with how much time that had passed since she'd ingested it herself? Ingredients and mixtures ran through her thoughts, but everything was a jumbled mess. All she remembered right now was Teo collapsing before her.

But even if the antidote on her lips could have saved him, the knife had killed him. Even if the knife somehow missed his heart, a mistake she'd never made before, the fire tearing through the ship right now would have ended him.

And through it all, Kohl came back to her. He'd wanted her to survive this and realize he'd given her the antidote—would probably expect her to thank him for saving her. Her hands curled around blades of grass, squeezing so tightly, they ripped from the ground.

Mere hours after she'd decided she didn't need to kill him anymore, he betrayed her. Teo's words came back to her then, reminding her how she'd always gone back to Kohl even after he'd hurt her and reminding her not to forget it. She gulped, finding her throat dry and sore. She'd thought Kohl couldn't hurt her anymore, that the only pain he'd caused was when she was too weak to stand up to him. But that wasn't how it worked. "I'm not surprised that Kohl turned on us," Ryuu said slowly, still holding her steady. "But I am surprised that he did it now, before Bautix has been killed. Why not let us do the dirty work of getting Bautix out of the way and then try to turn on us?"

"Unless he thinks he doesn't need us anymore," Aina whispered. "He only worked with us because he thought he had to. He wanted us out of the city, which means he thinks he can win this fight on his own."

Everything about it rang achingly familiar to her, and it felt like a fist clenched around her heart. They had so much more in common than she'd ever allowed herself to admit. Constantly fighting to outwit their enemies, doing whatever it took to survive and be safe despite the cost. She knew, in her heart, that she was cast in his shadow.

And it was impossible to escape your shadow.

For once, that seemed not like a drawback or a fatal flaw, not like something she had to run away from. For once, it seemed like the most comforting thing in the world, because it was suddenly painfully obvious that there was no such thing as safety to fight for in the first place.

"We'll go back to Kosín now," she said, a new plan forming in her scattered thoughts. "There's something I need to do."

34

"A train is scheduled to leave soon," Ryuu said, glancing at his watch and then through the trees in the direction of the station.

"Let's go, then." Aina stood and began leading the way out of the forest. The closer they got to the edge of the trees, the harder it was to hold at bay her memories of what had happened on that ship. She took a deep breath, steeling herself for what she would see.

Night had truly fallen and the lights of the train were fireflies in the distance. Voices reached them from here, people boarding the train and pointing at the fire. The smoke unfurling into the air blocked out the stars, ash building thickly in a way that made her throat itch. The boat had mostly sunk.

She felt a pull toward it, a part of her that wanted to run onto the ship and find Teo. But it was too late—he was sinking into the water, and she'd never see him again. Tears pricked at the corners of her eyes, but she didn't blink them away. She kept her eyes on the ship, not wanting to lose sight of it until it was truly gone.

"Is this the last train of the night?" Aina asked as they walked across the dark swathes of grass with the wind at their backs.

"There are a few more," said Ryuu, but then he grimaced. "If they don't shut down the station because of the fire."

"We can't wait around for the next one," she said. "Who knows what Kohl and Bautix are doing while we're gone?"

There was still a chance that if Tannis and Mirran got here, they could make the trade-off, sending the Kaiyanis prisoners back to their country and bringing the Kaiyanis soldiers to the city to fight—if they had survived. But she banished that thought as quickly as it came—she didn't even know what had happened to Raurie and Lill. There were so many things that could have gone wrong, but if she started thinking all of them were dead, she didn't know how she'd do what needed to be done once she returned to the city.

A horn sounded from the train. With a quick glance at each other, she and Ryuu began running, the wind spurring them onward.

The train began to pull away from the platform as they were thirty feet off. As they ran, she pointed to the back of the train, where a sliding door was open with the barest hint of light peeking through.

"There's always another way in," she shouted to Ryuu, her voice almost lost in the rushing wind and the creak of the train wheels.

Her adrenaline raced as they sprinted across the grass. The train was still moving slowly, and while she'd never considered jumping onto a moving one before . . . if they reached it in time, there was nothing to do but try.

If they failed to get back to the city in time, Bautix would win and the city would be lost. Kohl would take the south. He said he cared about the south, but he'd also said that about her, and he never ceased to find ways to hurt her if she didn't do exactly what he wanted. If the south fell into his hands, she didn't know how long it would last.

They began running along the tracks at around the halfway point of the train. It started picking up speed, and Ryuu shouted that they were close. Glancing over her shoulder, Aina saw the open door of the last compartment outlined in the red moon's light. She ran faster, and in seconds, it was in front of her and she leaped.

She strained her muscles to hold on to the ladder at the side of the compartment, her shoulders aching with the sudden pull. As wind whipped her hair out of her eyes, Ryuu landed next to her, his teeth gritted as he fought to hold on.

A second later, Aina was yanked inside by a burly arm around her waist. A knife went to her throat at the same time that the wind stopped roaring in her ears.

"One hundred kors," grunted the man holding her as another thug yanked Ryuu inside and did the same.

Aina nearly laughed. This was the least threatening knife-to-the-throat experience she'd had in months. She reached into her pocket for the money and tossed it on the floor.

The man dropped her and she brushed off her clothes, her pulse racing with the exhilaration of the race to the train, the jump onto it. But as she peered out of the door toward the ports and the still-burning boat at the far-off pier, the exhilaration vanished. She was doing what Teo wanted, going back to the city, surviving, fighting for all the people like him who'd never really had a chance to change their own destinies . . . but it was by leaving him behind. A lump built in the back of her throat, emotion threatening to well up—she clenched one hand around the rusted door to stop herself from leaping off the train.

She watched it all disappear with Ryuu next to her. Their shadows chased them, stretching long on the grass as the train sped away.

When they stepped off the train an hour later, a storm reigned over Kosín. The sky flashed black and silver with lightning and thick dark clouds. Aina breathed in the fresh scent. Most people hated when it stormed so ferociously—she definitely had as a child when she'd slept on the streets—but now, she loved the rain. It chased away the fires threatening to consume them all; it reduced the tinge of pollution in the air and the grit on the streets; it was a sign that all the bad things might be washed away.

Everyone paused on the platform, as if they weren't sure whether continuing onward was the best option. Ryuu frowned, peering ahead through the small group of passengers that had disembarked the train and then stopped in their tracks. She felt it too; the square ahead, with King Verrain's statue in the center of it, was crowded as usual, but with an eerie pall of silence and fear over the people gathered there. When the lightning flashed, a stack of smoke unfurling from a building a block away caught her eye. The crackling sound of a fire nearby reached her when the next rumble of thunder died down. They'd had no idea what state the city would be in now that they'd come back, but the next shrill scream that broke the night gave her a hint.

A group of Diamond Guards had gathered in the center of the square on a platform, with the crowd surrounding them. Between rumbles of thunder as she and Ryuu traversed the square, Aina caught snatches of what they were saying. "All who choose to fight for our freedom will be compensated," one of the men shouted, his hands cupping his mouth to project his voice. His partner handed a rifle to a man in the crowd.

"For Bautix? They think they're fighting for a hero." Aina

scoffed. "But he'd just as soon kill them all if they helped him get what he wants."

Ryuu shook his head slowly as they turned a corner and the square disappeared from view. "It's easy for him to convince them they'd be safest following him, that the city is only in war when he's not in charge."

"When you have nothing, all you want is something real," Aina said, in such a low voice she didn't know if he heard her. As they reached the next intersection, the sounds of screams and the crackle of fire growing louder the deeper they walked into the city, they both slowed.

"I should go," Ryuu said, his gaze trailing east toward the mines. "I need to check that the safe house is secure. Where are you headed?"

"Home," she said, briefly meeting his eyes. For the first time, she wished she didn't have to face her troubles alone—she wished he could go with her. But the Dom was hers to protect, no matter how difficult.

As Ryuu set off, she watched him for a moment, hoping he would make it there in one piece. Then she drew in a quick breath and checked which weapons she had on her.

There was only one place Kohl would be now.

With light footsteps, she passed a street at the edge of the Center where a fire still raged, undeterred by the rain. People had run out of their homes and businesses, glancing back over their shoulders at a group of men who blocked the other exit of the street. Peering closely, Aina caught sight of a Jackal tattoo on one of their forearms, and her blood ran cold. She picked up her pace to the Stacks, nearly getting run over by an older woman with three diamonds pierced in an arc on her forehead. She held a few possessions in her hands, her eyes flicking back to the fire she'd fled.

As Aina walked down the hill into the Stacks, the hair rose on the back of her neck. She turned east after walking south for a few minutes, and as she continued, the Tower caught her eye, its surface illuminated every time lightning flashed across the sky. People ran past her, breaking the windows of small shops and grabbing anything inside they could carry. She kept to the shadows, not wanting to draw attention to herself.

About a mile from the Dom, she walked by a group of people huddled around a fire on a relatively quiet street, shielding the flames with their bodies and passing around a bottle of firebrandy.

"All their bodies hanging from the bridge," one of the men said in a slightly derisive tone, his eyes wide in amused disbelief. "Except Mariya Okubo, that is."

Aina slowed, straining her ears to hear them and keeping her gaze forward so they wouldn't know she was listening.

"Where'd she go?" asked one of the women at the fire.

"Either she escaped or she's a hostage," the first man replied with a shrug.

"Or, maybe she's in on it with Bautix," another of the men said in a gravelly voice. "They say he came in through the prison and bribed the inmates to fight for him."

Aina's heart raced as she continued. Bautix had taken the Tower, and most of the Sentinel was dead. Were Tannis and Mirran still alive? What about the fighters from the tradehouses? And where were Raurie and Lill?

She could do nothing for them now, but she wouldn't push thoughts of them away. She held the image of Teo's last moments at the front of her mind, reminding herself what she was here for. Now she had only one job, and it was to get to Kohl.

She couldn't go with her knives drawn or fierceness in her eyes. She'd used to think anything else was weakness, but like the Mothers had said in the cave under the Tower, she needed to learn to embrace that weakness.

She would be strong, but not with Kohl's strength—she'd use the same strength she'd used to survive her parents' death and the same she'd used to plunge her knife into Teo's heart. The same strength she'd always had, and that Teo had always known was in her.

A full storm was in effect now, and her hair clung wet to her face. As she pushed it out of her eyes, a shrill scream reached her ears. She crouched near a house and peered around the corner.

What she saw next happened so quickly, she barely drew a knife in time to help. A couple of tall, burly men had found the Sacoren woman Aina had seen fleeing earlier. One of them drew a knife across her throat, cutting off her scream. They were built like men trained to fight, and she suspected they were some of the Diamond Guards who'd been on Bautix's side, like the ones in the Center square.

A few minutes later, she turned a corner and the Dom came into view. Lightning flashed, revealing it. Nothing looked amiss on the outside, but all the lights were on. She squared her shoulders, preparing herself for whatever she would find—and what she would have to do.

She would face the Blood King once more.

When she reached the path leading to the door, the entirety of the Thunder tradehouse filtered outside, one at a time. They watched her walk past them to the door without a word. The only one who did anything more than stare straight ahead was their new, youngest employee. He opened his mouth as if to say something to her, tears in his eyes, but one of the other men elbowed him and he hung his head instead of speaking. Arman Kraz stood at the entrance with a smug grin on his face. She barely spared him a glance as she stepped inside.

She entered the hallway and took in the scene in front of her. She wished she could say she'd paused longer, felt a surge of fear or ruthless anger. But there was nothing else Kohl could do that would surprise her.

She spared one glance each for Markus, Johana, and Kushik—their bodies lined up against the walls of the hallway, coated with blood.

Lightning struck once more, further illuminating the hall dimly lit with the silver vine-ensconced electric lamps. Kohl stepped out of the office. He took her in for a moment, his hands hanging loose at his side. His shoes clicked against the jade-and-crystal floor stained red with the recruits' blood as he approached her.

When the lightning's flash died away, only the two closest lamps lit his face, making the hollows on his cheeks stand out like he was a corpse.

A thousand instincts roared up inside her, telling her what to say or do to the man in front of her. But she knew there was only one option left.

A curious glint sparked in his eyes as she sank to her knees.

"Kohl," she said, her voice flat and without hope. "Help me."

35

A long silence passed before Kohl walked toward her, his footsteps the only sound. Aina kept her eyes glued to the floor, afraid to look at him and give away what she thought. He'd told her, not long ago, that one day she would finally admit she needed him.

Today was that day.

He knelt in front of her in the narrow hallway. Bruises that hadn't been there before marked the side of his face now, and pride surged through her at the thought that Markus, Kushik, and Johana had put up a fight. He reached out and touched her chin with his hand, like she was a fine weapon to examine. She let him—he only trusted Blades who obeyed him.

"Bautix tricked us," she said, keeping her voice at the level of an awestruck whisper. "He used the poison against us. Teo, he's . . ." Her voice choked up without her even having to try. "Does he know what we tried to do? That we were trying to take him down?"

Kohl nodded slowly, taking in every tiny reaction on her face, trying to read her as much as she tried to read him. "He's always known."

"What do you mean?" she asked in a soft voice, tilting her head to the side even though a sour taste settled in the back of her throat—telling her she should have known this all along, that this was the way it always was between them.

"How else could I get you to work with me unless you thought we were standing up to him as a team? It was easy to make you hate a Steel like him. He knew you were a threat and wanted to kill you from the start, but I convinced him it would be better if you served a purpose—you would take out his loose ends like Fayes and the smuggler when he no longer needed them, getting you out of the city while he sneaked in his weapons and now, while he takes the Tower. The best way to get you to do all that was to have you work with me."

"To have me work with you," she repeated, her thoughts racing to make sense of his plan. "Does that mean you knew about the bombings?"

"I set off most of them, although I didn't expect you to be caught in the thick of it. The only thing I didn't know about was the fire at the Dom," he said, a sudden darkening in his eyes, and her heart clenched. He'd let so much of the city be destroyed as part of some bigger plan. "Bautix probably suspected I would stop it if I knew."

"Do you want him to win?" she asked slowly, fighting to control her reactions. It made sense, then, why Kerys had fought them on the roof of the train and why it had seemed like she had told Bautix of Kohl's plans—they'd been on the same side the whole time. All this time, whenever he'd been kind to her, or revealed some part of his past or some deep fear . . . she didn't know how much of it was true and how much of it had been to control her, convince her to do exactly what he wanted, like Teo had known he would.

"That's what I let him think," Kohl said with a low chuckle. "I let his plans continue until now, let him think I was tricking you for his benefit. You have to understand, Aina: If you hadn't played along, he would have killed you long ago. I lied to you to protect you. But today, your purpose came to an end, and he wanted me to prove myself. Prove that I could stand against you if needed, to make up for my mistakes in the Tower. He told me to let you die on that ship, poisoned by your own brew like your friend. But I'm close enough to my goals that I don't need his trust anymore. I gave you the antidote to save you." He touched a finger to her lips then, cold as winter and thin like a blade. "He doesn't know you're still alive. But I wouldn't kill you with poison."

Forcing herself to stay still under his touch, she said, "And now that you don't need his trust anymore . . ."

"He's already killed most of the Sentinel and has his men in the Tower now to take it. He'll think he's winning. Once that happens, he'll be the only person in my way. Think of what we can do in the new world that will be left after this. Do you think our people would actually want to follow a Steel, if they had the choice? We can give them a better choice. We can take the south and the whole country together, Aina, and turn things around. We could actually make a difference in the lives of people here."

She kept her face entirely passive, but her mind raced. He'd spent the past month double-crossing her and Bautix at the same time. Kohl alone didn't have the support and weapons to kill the Sentinel and take the Tower on his own, so he'd let Bautix do it. But once Bautix took the Tower, Kohl would fight him for the entire city. The whole breadth of his plan hit her slowly, and it took all her effort to not show her surprise on her face.

"And what do you want with me, Kohl?" she asked, meeting his eyes.

"I want to go back to the way it was. Nothing standing in our way. Me, ruling the south and more. You, working alongside me."

She imagined it in an instant. They would take down Bautix in one swift blow once the Tower was secure, and take over in his place. They would never fear challenge again; they'd have the power of the military and the economy, and the trust of everyone in the Stacks. With the Mothers' magic flowing through her veins, they would even have the trust of the Inosen.

It would be so easy. As easy as it had always been to want to trust him. As easily as he convinced himself he wanted the best for her.

He'd bombed the Stacks and still believed he was the best person to rule. He'd poisoned her best friend and still thought she'd fall in line next to him.

Beneath it all, she knew the real meaning of his words: *You below me, once more.*

"This is better for both of us, don't you think?" he asked. "All we have to do is what we already do best. Our jobs."

The only sound in the room was the ticking clock in the office nearby as he stared at her, waiting for an answer. When a whole minute passed, she turned to face Kohl and took his hands in hers.

"Give me something real, Kohl," she said.

She tilted her head downward as he wrapped his arms around her and kissed her on the forehead. Johana's small, limp hand caught her eye.

"What is the plan?" she asked. "Bautix has almost taken the Tower."

"We need to rout out Mariya Okubo and her allies before I can look for Bautix in the Tower." He lifted a hand to rest on the side of her face. "I know what you can do. The Jackals were able to get in a shipment of weapons today. Guns, bombs, knives. You, Arman, and the grunts from Thunder can help move them from the pickup location to Bautix's men stationed near the Tower. Once he has the weapons, he'll have everything he needs to finish the takeover, and then we can step in."

Aina's thoughts raced, but she nodded once. "I'll do it. Will you be there too?"

"I'll be there later," he said with a small smile. "I have to take care of some things to prepare for the new world ahead of us."

She scanned his face quickly, then turned away. "Then I'll see you at the end of this." If she could use this opportunity of bringing weapons to the Tower to sneak in, take some of those weapons for herself, and find Bautix . . . she could still end this.

She couldn't cut off her shadow, all the dark things that made her who she was, and she didn't want to. She'd embrace it and use it, no matter how weak it made her look. Kohl had always expected her to come back to him in the end, either to fight back and seek revenge or to join him in controlling the country. Because that was what he would do, and he only saw the parts of her that were similar to him.

She drew in a small breath, steeling herself for what she had to say next.

"Thank you for giving me another chance, Kohl. This is where I belong."

He held out a hand to help her stand, and by the relieved breath he exhaled and the hope in his eyes, she could tell he believed her.

36

Once Kohl left, Aina stepped outside to meet with Kraz and the three other members of the Thunder tradehouse. Two of them smirked at each other, as if proud of themselves for having taken the Dom. Their young recruit still looked on the verge of tears. Aina kept her expression neutral, not wanting to give anything away. Whatever information she could get out of Kraz would be useful, so she couldn't have him doubting her before then.

"We're going to the Tower to meet with Bautix and help—"

Kraz pulled out a knife and placed it at her throat so quickly, she barely had time to blink. Trying hard not to gulp or step back, Aina slid her eyes up to meet his.

"We know the plan, Solís. Keep your mouth shut and follow me."

She nodded and gave a conciliatory smile. One of his employees grunted at her and held out a hand. When she raised an eyebrow at him, he pointed at the scythes strapped to her thighs, and she froze.

"Let her keep them," Kraz said, shaking his head. "The Blood King has put her in her place; she won't defy him now. And she'll need her weapons anyway once we're at the Tower."

Trying not to show her relief, Aina stepped in place behind Kraz. His three grunts surrounded her as they walked, like she was a dangerous animal that needed to be kept in a pen.

Good, she thought. *They should be scared of me.*

A moment later, they left the Dom and moved through the Stacks, steadily climbing the hill toward the rest of the city. The rain had mostly stopped, through a few errant drops still landed on her face as they proceeded. It was that thin time of night between full darkness and dawn, and if she looked to the right, she could see the sky lightening a little on the horizon. But even in this deep hour, the streets were still crowded. They passed near the Center and saw more fires, people running from them with their belongings, stores being broken into and raided, fights breaking out in the middle of the street.

Yet no matter where they went, people scattered when they approached, as if sensing they weren't to be challenged.

Aina's thoughts raced the whole way to the warehouse district, her nerves on edge with the chaos in the city. Where had Kohl gone? He'd said he still had work to do. What kind of work could he be doing in the city? It was already a mess, filled with the kind of chaos Kohl loved best. The Tower was taken, the Inosen were being routed out of their homes and killed. . . .

At least, the ones inside the city were. She slowed her pace a little, a new thought prickling at the corner of her mind, but then one of the Thunder grunts shoved her forward to keep moving.

Fighting the urge to punch him in the throat, Aina kept thinking. Kerys had said nowhere in the city would be safe for the Inosen, so all of the ones she'd left near the mines had to be safe. Ryuu had gone to make sure that they were.

But all of Bautix's employees worked in duplicity. What if Kerys had lied, like Kohl had?

Or maybe . . . the thought hit her fast like lightning, and she raced to grasp on to it. Despite how terrible Kerys was, Aina had believed her when she said she didn't want her daughter anywhere that she could be hurt. But would Bautix abide by that desire, even if he cared for Kerys?

No, she answered her own question instantly. He would destroy any of the Inosen's hiding places. They were an opposition to his rule, and he would get rid of them even if he had to lie to Kerys to do it.

"He knows," Aina whispered.

The churning Minos River could be heard around the edge of the nearest building. They were headed toward the outskirts of Kosín, presumably to make their way up to the Tower from the side or from behind, and enter discreetly to help take out the remaining Diamond Guards trying to hold the place.

Bautix knew, and Kohl surely knew, where most of the Inosen were now. And if Mariya had escaped, where else would be safest for her but somewhere provided for by Ryuu and outside the city instead of within its borders? Mariya likely knew of the location of that safe house after last month when Ryuu had explained to her his parents' involvement in protecting the Inosen. Kohl would destroy anyone who got in his way; he needed to get rid of Mariya, and the Inosen wouldn't stand for someone like him to rule. Before he could face Bautix, he'd want to get rid of these remaining obstacles.

The smuggler's words before she'd killed him came back to her now: *The weapons are led through the mine tunnels.* For all she knew, Bautix had even spread the rumors that the safe house at the mines was compromised, like Lill had believed for so long, so the Inosen would leave and he could sneak in the weapons however he pleased. And then he drove them back in after the bombing of all the safe houses in the city . . . so now they were all in one place, easy to get to, and easy to kill. All Kohl had to do was convince the Jackals they were headed to the mines on Bautix's orders, and he'd have plenty of men to help him take out the Inosen.

Panic rose through her, sharp and tasting like rust on her tongue. Forget the Tower. She had to get to the mines now.

She took a quick inventory of her weapons in her mind, recalling where each one was. As they crossed the bridge, she moved.

In one swift motion, she took the scythes strapped to her thighs and slashed them through the throats of the grunt to her right and the one behind her.

The click of a gun. Arman Kraz faced her.

She dodged the first shot, rolling across the bridge as the bullet pinged off one of the handrails. Almost slipping off the edge, she caught herself on the handrail. The wind swept past, lifting the stench of the river toward her where she hung.

As he turned toward her again, she lunged forward, feinting with a strike to the right and then cutting him through the left side. He inhaled sharply when she drew his blood, but recovered faster than she expected.

His other hand not holding the gun flicked a knife out from his sleeve and she barely missed a slash at her chest. She stumbled slightly while getting away from it, then ducked around him. Wrapping one arm around his neck, she used her other hand to disarm him. His gun skidded across the bridge and fell into the churning currents of the river. The young boy from Thunder watched their fight, rapt with attention as Arman threw Aina off him.

He shoved her to the ground and drew another knife. Its blade flashed in the moonlight. She stared up at him, etching his face into her memory: the face of someone who'd always thought Kohl was the better choice of leader.

"Maybe Kohl didn't give me the order to kill you," Arman said, leaning over her so the tip of his knife was half a foot from her face. "But he'll appreciate not having you around anymore. You are nothing, Solís. He told you whatever he had to, to get you to keep following him like a chained dog, but you're just—"

She grabbed the hand with his knife and pulled him forward. His eyes widened, and he aimed the other knife at her face. But before it could reach her, she twisted his wrist so the knife fell into her hands, and she swept it across his neck. As he fell toward her, his blood coating her hands, she grabbed him by the shoulders and shoved him off the bridge. His body hit the water with a loud smacking sound, and a second later, disappeared.

A surge of triumph flashed through her, but it vanished just as quickly. She might have won this fight, but her night was far from over.

The boy from Thunder held his arms over his face as if that would protect him from her next attack. He'd completely frozen on the bridge while she fought his boss. When she approached him and her shadow fell over him, he glanced up through the feeble shield of his arms.

"Did you have fun killing my employees back there?" she asked.

"I didn't kill them, I swear. They made me bring the bodies to the hall, but that's all I—"

"Stop talking." His voice cut off immediately. "Go to the Dom. Bury them, then get some sleep. If you're going to work for me, I can't have you crying every time the job gets hard." His hands fell away from his face then and he looked up at her in confusion. "If I survive the rest of this, I'll meet you there."

The wind swept across the bridge, drying the blood specks

and sweat on her face as the boy took off back toward the Dom. After a quick search of the dead's belongings, she pocketed a pistol and a grenade, then ran.

Dawn had broken, the sky a pale blue in the east. Kohl had already been headed to the mines when she left the Dom, she was sure of it now. His and Bautix's fight for control would tear Kosín apart if she didn't stop it.

Teo's words came back to her: *The city needs you.*

She ran faster, keeping her breaths measured, her strides long. As if she had some map of the city in her head, of where to run to avoid the most chaos, she ran past fires, leapt over broken glass on the ground, climbed a fire escape and ran across it to the next building to avoid a fight in the side street below. Smoke shrouded the moons, so the only light was the flickering orange of flames coming from every corner and the hint of dawn ahead.

Her lungs seared by the time she reached a bridge leading out of the city. It was another three miles to the mines, over the train tracks and through the forest. Countless memories of going there to get illicit diamonds flashed through her thoughts. All those times, she'd never wanted to find Kohl there. Now she could only hope she found him before he destroyed the safe house and everyone in it.

37

Drawing in a deep breath and wiping the sweat off her forehead, Aina ran again. To the left, the cemetery loomed on a slope leading up to Amethyst Hill. The tombstones stood silent sentinel, the only peaceful place in the city, as she ran toward the cover of trees.

She had to slow her pace through the forest to avoid getting snared by branches or tripping over roots. It gave her time to listen for some sign of Kohl, but she only heard the wind and the crickets out here. Her heart ached when she recalled walking through a similar forest toward Amethyst Hill with Teo at her side, and when she breathed in, she thought she caught his scent on the wind.

Instead of thinking of what had happened on that ship, she reminded herself she was doing this for him, and everyone in the city who wouldn't get a tombstone overlooking the fields and trees; those who would die under smoke and flame and be thrown in a mass grave. She was doing this for the people the

Steels underestimated, making them fight for a chance and then punishing them for it, making them follow a path in life they'd never really wanted to; all the people like Teo, who'd only wanted a future in this city that claimed to worship progress, yet only for a chosen few.

Finally, an hour after she'd left the dead bodies of Thunder on the bridge, she exited the fringe of the forest and looked out at the open pit of the Hirai Diamond Mine. The sky had lightened considerably while she was in the forest, heralding a new day. She sprinted across the land, keeping her eyes peeled for some sign of Kohl. Usually, the mines would be filling with workers who started at dawn, but the whole area had emptied this morning. Had the workers been caught in the chaos in the city and been unable to come, or had Kohl already killed them?

A few minutes later, she entered the hidden safe house. The steady rumble of voices quieted to a hush when the door creaked open, but rose again when they saw it was her. Warm candlelight illuminated them, alive and safe for now: the Inosen along with Gevann, two tradehouses—the remaining three must have still been at the Tower—and there, huddled in a corner next to the back door, were Ryuu, Tannis, and Mariya. She searched the crowd for some sign of Raurie and Lill, her heart sinking when she saw them nowhere.

Ryuu and Tannis both waved her over. But as Aina walked toward them, the bosses from the two tradehouses nodded at her. None of them showed any signs of disloyalty—but she couldn't be sure. Kohl might have asked them to wait here and kill all of the Inosen when the time came. She couldn't trust any of them, not the ones in the Tower and not the ones here. The thought made her heart clench, and though she'd been trying to avoid thinking of it, the image of Johana, Markus, and Kushik lying dead in the Dom flashed through her thoughts.

She walked over to the two bosses, knowing she didn't have much time—but she couldn't risk them turning on her.

"Take your people outside," she said. "Defend the perimeter of the safe house in case anyone comes to attack."

They nodded and left without argument. Keeping them at a slight distance, but still close enough to call back if needed, was the only way she could think to test their loyalty now.

As soon as they were out of sight, she turned and continued toward Ryuu, Tannis, and Mariya. "What's the situation with the Diamond Guards in the Tower?" she asked Mariya, whose face was covered in scratch marks and grime. "Are they loyal enough to keep fighting while you're not there, or has Bautix already won?"

"I only kept my most loyal men inside the Tower," Mariya answered, her voice hardening as she took in Aina. "Unlike yours. Bautix didn't even need to pretend to have a negotiation with us. He sent his fighters through the secret entrances and then one of your men, that Arman Kraz, shot Eirhart and Diaso."

Letting out a sharp breath, Aina said, "He's dead now. I'm sorry he turned on you, but we—"

"Whose side are you on?" Mariya interrupted her. "I should have known better than to trust a criminal. What did Bautix promise you?"

Aina let out a humorless laugh, then stepped toward Mariya. "I'm on the city's side, not yours or Bautix's." When Mariya still looked poised to argue, Aina cut off her next words and said, "You're here for a reason: You have nowhere else to go. So work with us."

After a moment, Mariya's shoulders lost. "Your other trade-houses, and my Diamond Guards, helped me escape before that man could kill me too. So I do owe you thanks there. And then I saw your colleague"—she paused, nodding at Tannis—"in one of the back stairwells with the Kaiyanis they were smuggling out. We left through one of the secret entrances together and made our way here. I need to get back there as soon as I can, but I'll need fighters with me."

Aina nodded, feeling a brief surge of relief that Mariya was willing to work with them—she only hoped that the Kaiyanis soldiers would arrive in time to help. Then, knowing she'd wasted too much time, she turned to Tannis and asked, "Were you able to get the Kaiyanis out of the Tower and to the ports?"

"We did, and Mirran took them on the last train out of the city. Are the ports secure now? The soldiers still need to get here safely." Then, biting her lip, she looked at Ryuu. "He told me what happened. I'm sorry about Teo, Aina."

Aina stiffened, trying to push away thoughts of her knife in Teo's chest, her poison in his blood. If she thought any more of it, she would break down right here.

"So then you know Kohl's turned against us. He killed Markus, Kushik, and Johana, and Arman helped him take the Dom."

"He what?" Tannis asked, her voice shallow. They locked eyes and Aina could see all the emotions she'd had to hold back in front of Kohl.

"And it's my fault." Tannis opened her mouth to deny it, but Aina said in a rush, "I trusted him, I went back to him, and this is what happened. He's on his way to kill everyone here too, unless we leave right now."

"Then what are we waiting for?" Ryuu asked, stepping between them. "We need to get everyone out."

As Aina turned to find one of the Sacoren and tell them what was happening, gunshots broke out.

38

The gunfire came from above, where Aina had sent the people from her tradehouses. But straining her ears, she caught the sound of return shots and she breathed a sigh in relief. Her tradehouses were fighting Kohl's men.

Her eyes flicked toward the back of the safe house, where a boarded-up door led deeper into the mines—into the tunnels, where Kohl and the weapons might be. The Inosen might walk right into a trap.

But the only other option was to send them into open gunfire.

"I need to help them up there and get an idea of what we're up against," Aina said in a low voice to Tannis and Ryuu. "Can you get Mariya and the Inosen to the mine entrance and tell them where to go from there, Ryuu? And you can cover them if one of Kohl's men comes to attack through there, Tannis."

They paused for a moment, exchanging a quick look that she couldn't read, and then moved, calling the Inosen to gather in a group. Not wasting another moment, Aina slipped past the Inosen to reach the steps leading outside. She withdrew the pistol she'd stolen from a dead Thunder grunt and checked that it was loaded. As much as she hated using guns, she'd need one for this fight.

Gunshots fired from the trees. The people from her tradehouses went on the defensive, staying low and only shooting when they caught sight of movement within the trees. But even without being able to see all their enemies, the sheer amount of shots fired and the flashes of weapons passing between the trees told Aina they were heavily outnumbered.

Still, she joined them, kneeling behind a crate next to one of the tradehouse bosses. The silver barrel of a gun caught her eye between two trees. She fired first. The bullet struck and the man fell.

But just as she ducked behind another crate to avoid return fire, Tannis and Ryuu joined her at either side.

"You think we'd let you join the fun without us?" Ryuu asked with a raised eyebrow.

"I was always a better shot than you, anyway," Tannis muttered, firing into the trees and eliciting a shocked yelp from whomever she'd struck.

A smile spread on Aina's face as she settled between them, but they were still outnumbered. Her hand went to the grenade she'd stolen from the dead Thunder employees, and she looked over her shoulder at the entrance to the safe house. Gunshots and the screams of the dying built up louder around her. All of this was Kohl's doing. So many things tried to choke and drown them in this city, but all of them were here as living proof that they could fight back with fire and blood too—that they deserved a future, like Teo had before he'd been robbed of it. The Inosen behind her, fleeing for their lives now in the tunnel, deserved a future too. She didn't need to think on it much more than that.

"Get down!" she shouted to Tannis, Ryuu, and the trade-houses fighting next to her—then she uncorked the grenade and threw it toward the tree line.

She dropped, flattening herself to the ground and holding her hands over her head as the explosion rent the air and the heat of flames rose. A moment later, screams and thunderous footsteps joined the din. Jumping to her feet, she saw men running toward them from the south and firing at the fighters in the trees—the grenade had caught plenty of them, leaving bodies and scorch marks on the grass, but more streamed out now.

From the south, though . . . She squinted, trying to make out the faces of the people rushing to help them fight. After a moment, she noticed one thing they all had in common: bright blue hair, streaking across the night.

Tannis gasped and pointed. "The Kaiyanis soldiers. They're here, that means—"

She didn't finish her sentence, and Aina couldn't blame her—she wouldn't get her hopes up about Mirran, Raurie, and Lill unless they showed up themselves, alive and unharmed.

Kohl's men skirted around the trees and fired back at the Kaiyanis soldiers, half of them providing cover as the other half darted toward the mine safe house relentlessly. The moment they found an opening, they'd storm through Aina and her fighters to reach the safe house.

Aina scanned the faces of the fighters in the trees, searching for some sign of Kohl, but it wasn't light enough yet to make anyone out. She only had a moment to decide what to do, but it was simple; they had fewer than twenty people protecting the entrance to the safe house. They wouldn't stand a chance if even half of Kohl's men managed to reach them and attack at close range. Having the Kaiyanis soldiers here would help, but . . . if the Inosen left through the mines and came out into the open again, Kohl's men would shoot them. The only choice was to lure his men away from the open field, so the Inosen could escape into the forest once they left the mines.

"Fall back!" she called out, her voice sending birds flying out of the trees—loud enough for Kohl's men to hear and give chase. A minute later, Aina, Ryuu, Tannis, and the two tradehouses poured inside the dimly lit safe house. It was empty, Mariya and all the Inosen having fled through the tunnels. The boarded-up door they'd left through hung off its hinges.

"Put out the lights and then get in the tunnel," she whispered. They all moved, extinguishing the candles and then filtering through the entrance to the tunnels in the pitch-black. Once they'd all gathered in the tunnel, she moved the door back in place. It wouldn't deter Kohl's men, but hiding the entrance and leaving the room dark would slow them down for a minute.

Their breath and footsteps were the only sound as they raced down the sloping tunnels eastward, deeper into the mines. A sulfur scent reached her nostrils, and she tried not to breathe too deeply. But since oxygen was scarce down here, she soon had to take in as much breath as she could.

It was completely dark as they wandered the tunnels, ears strained for some sound of the other Inosen fleeing. Ryuu led the way, using one candle he'd taken from the safe house. Its light came in flashes, illuminating his face and the rock walls of the tunnels. As they walked, Aina looked toward the dark cracks in the walls and the dirt floor beneath them, remembering how the Mothers came to her in a place similar to this and wondering if they were here now, in some form.

"There's only one way out, so we can't get lost," Ryuu whispered back to them, his voice strangely loud in the silence.

After about five minutes, more light shone from farther down the hall with a reddish glow; someone carrying flares. Aina drew her knives, blinking against the sudden light to see who approached them. Then a voice called out, echoing off the tunnel walls.

"Who is that? Ryuu?"

Ryuu stopped, his eyes brightening at the familiar voice, then called back, "Lill? It's us!" Aina and Tannis followed him at a run just as Lill, Raurie, and Mirran turned the corner ahead and nearly walked into them.

"You're all alive," Aina said, smiling in relief.

"When did you get back here?" Tannis asked, pulling Raurie into a hug.

"About an hour ago," Raurie said. "We saw what was happening and knew we had to act fast, so we sent the soldiers to fight above and came down here to bring you all out. The others made it, but we came here when we didn't see you. Come on, we need to get out of here."

The red light of Lill's flare led the way as the sound of heavy footsteps grew behind them, echoing off the tunnel walls. Kohl's men must have broken through the door. Aina's blood turned cold at the thought. It was too dark here to try to fight; it would be a bloodbath. If she died here, she wouldn't stop Kohl at all. "We're almost there," Ryuu whispered back, his voice tinged with fear. "We'll come out on the first tier of the pit and can climb out from there."

The tunnel sloped upward, opening into a wider cavern. Sunlight filtered into the cavern from up ahead, illuminating a large crate in the center of the room. It sat on a track, as if someone had pushed it into the mines on one of the carts usually reserved for carrying diamonds and ore through the tunnels. Metal glinted from the slightly open lid of the crate: dynamite, pistols, rifles, grenades. Ryuu saw it at the same time she did and slowed, sucking in a sharp breath. Raurie, Tannis, Mirran, and the two tradehouses had reached the mouth of the tunnel and exited, but Lill hung back.

"If they get their hands on those weapons . . ." Ryuu began in a strained voice. "The Inosen are probably still in the mines. They won't be able to escape."

Aina cast one glance back toward the tunnel where the sounds of Kohl's men charging toward them grew louder each second. Turning back to Ryuu, she said, "We're already outnumbered."

Without a break in his step, Ryuu walked toward the crate of weapons and searched through it. Lill called his name in a strained voice as the heavy footfalls of Kohl's men grew closer. Then Ryuu straightened, holding a grenade in one hand, his eyes bright with panic and exhilaration.

"This is more important than me and my family," he said, answering Aina's unspoken question. "You two go ahead."

Aina rolled her eyes and stayed next to him as he backed up toward the mouth of the tunnel where Lill still stood with her arms crossed.

"I'm not going anywhere," Lill scoffed, moving closer to Ryuu.

Together, Aina, Ryuu, and Lill peered into the dark depths of the tunnel, waiting.

Hair rose on the back of Aina's neck and a cold sweat trickled down her spine. She suddenly felt twelve years old again, sitting in a tavern that was about to be blown up right before Kohl found her; right before everything changed.

Kohl's men came into view, racing through the tunnel and toward the weapons, their guns lifting when they saw her. Ryuu uncorked the grenade and threw it. They turned and ran.

Pale blue sky was visible for one brief moment before sound exploded into shreds around Aina and everything turned white.

39

When Aina opened her eyes, the world was on fire.

Shaking herself awake, she saw Tannis kneeling in front of her. A blaze ringed the pit of the diamond mine, climbing the walls and trapping everyone inside. As Aina's hearing came back, so did Tannis's voice shouting at her to get up.

Her ears still rang as she stood, her legs trembling slightly. Tannis yelled at her to make herself useful and then ran to join the fight. Aina forced herself to focus on the scene ahead.

Fire blazed through the mines, set off by the bombs to surround the whole pit. A swirling mass of black smoke prevented her from seeing anything but snatches of movement at a time. Orange flames licked the walls of the pit, building heat around them until she felt like she was inside a furnace. She tried to breathe normally, but ash fell on her tongue and she began coughing.

Gunshots fired through clouds of smoke, hitting targets indiscriminately. Aina flinched when one struck the rock wall behind her, then began moving around the pit in a crouch, her heart pounding in her throat.

They'd collapsed the mines, trapping Kohl's men, but surely not all of them had gone inside the mine—plenty of them were still alive to fight now. Her eyes watered from the smoke, but she blinked it away and searched for any sign of her friends and the Inosen.

After only moving ten feet around the mine, she looked upward, craving some sign of fresh air as it grew difficult to breathe. A bird streaked through a pockmark of gray sky far overhead. An image flashed through her memory of the falcon pendant Teo had worn, its amber eyes staring up at her, and her heart ached. Teo was gone, and the Inosen here barely stood a chance to escape with their lives . . . all because of the fight for power between Kohl and Bautix.

A gust of wind blew away some of the smoke to her left, clearing a narrow path. Ryuu stood at the foot of a ladder, his face sweat-streaked as he gestured for people to climb it. He looked toward the smoke, seeing an enemy she couldn't from here, and then up at the people who'd nearly made it over the lip of the pit. The Inosen who weren't fighting climbed it as fast as they could, ducking and screaming whenever a bullet passed close to them. As Aina watched, two of them were struck and fell from the ladder.

There was a thud in front of her and she nearly tripped over a body. Someone she didn't recognize, likely one of Kohl's men— blood streaked the front of his chest, spilled from his mouth and glassy eyes. A chill swept over her despite the raging heat, but then she felt a spike of determination; magic was one thing these men didn't know how to fight with, for it required faith in something greater than steel and coin.

As Aina crossed the narrow path toward Ryuu, more glimpses

of the battlefield became clear. Raurie and a few of the other Inosen, including June and Sofía, had spread themselves out between the Kaiyanis soldiers and fought back against Kohl's men. They took diamonds from the crates strewn around the pit. Tannis and Mirran fought alongside the Kaiyanis soldiers, shouting orders through the cloying clouds of smoke. Lill stood at the foot of the ladder, in front of Ryuu and guarding the passage of the Inosen trying to escape.

As Aina ran toward the ladder, Mariya Okubo had stepped onto the first rung, her gaze tilted upward. The lip of the pit was only twenty feet up, but it must have seemed like a thousand miles away with the bullets striking the side of the ladder.

"Get to the Tower now with as many men as you can take!" Aina shouted when Mariya looked down, her face covered in ash and sweat. "Go through one of the secret entrances that you haven't closed yet. I'll meet you there as soon as I can."

Mariya gave her a grim nod and resumed her climb, moving quickly as if sheer speed would help her escape the gunshots.

But there was no time to check and make sure she reached the top safely. Aina ducked behind the line of soldiers again and ran, circling around the mine pit.

She still had to find Kohl.

To her right, a familiar voice cried out. Raurie fell to her knees, a bullet having struck her leg, but she lifted a diamond and spoke the same spell Aina had used in the cavern under the Tower— "Cayek inoke." A moment later, a wall of rocks on the other side of the mines crumbled on top of Kohl's men. The world shook and burned around them, and if Aina's thoughts were lining up correctly with the madness in front of her . . . Kohl's men were being butchered.

Keeping low, Aina raced around the edge of the mines, staying behind the line of Kaiyanis soldiers to avoid enemy fire. The whole way, as she passed the swirling clouds of smoke, she felt a storm building up inside her too, one that made her want to stop right here and fight alongside them all to make them pay for what they'd done to her city—what they wanted to do to everyone like her.

A wooden beam fell from the wall of the pit. Aina skidded to a stop, covering her face with her hands as it crashed to the ground and sent a cloud of smoke into her face. But then it cleared, and as a path opened in front of her, she saw him.

Kohl.

He stood at the mouth of a tunnel entrance, flames highlighting him from behind as he fired over and over into the crowd. He was killing anyone in sight whether they were actively fighting him or not. A few of his bullets struck down his own men.

The city needs you, Teo had said.

Maybe Kohl wanted the south to survive and thrive once this battle was won. But his plans had killed Teo, and his bullets were killing Inosen now, people from the place he claimed to love. In his fight to control it all, he would destroy it. And she was done with seeing her home destroyed.

She glimpsed him in snatches as she approached, the smoke passing over him in grasping tendrils. Her breaths came slow and steady now despite the heavy smoke.

When she was a few feet away, the smoke between them cleared, and Kohl suddenly stopped firing. His body tensed, like it could tell something was wrong before his mind realized it. His head turned toward her in one sharp movement, and though she couldn't read his reaction in his eyes, his mouth opened slightly in surprise.

She knew this man. The boy who'd become ruthless to survive, who'd seen that the only way to move forward in this country after the war was to latch on to a scrap of power and build it from the ground up, taking and taking so no one took from you. The man who'd feared losing his home as much as the boy he'd been; the man whose home she'd taken.

The same man who'd both saved and doomed her, and knew exactly how to use that against her even if he'd grown to care for her over the years.

But the only love he knew was control.

He holstered his gun, his chest rising and falling rapidly as he caught his breath. She swallowed down the lump in the back of her throat.

He was just another version of what she could have become. "Aina," he said, his voice flat. "You should be at—"

The metallic screech of her scythes as she withdrew them both from their sheaths told him exactly what she was here for. His bloodshot eyes tightened for a moment, the sapphire blue deepening with the emotion he so rarely showed, and then hardened to ice once more.

"I should have known, shouldn't I?" he asked in a low voice, almost to himself rather than her. "You crave revenge just like I do. You want to rule too but alongside me isn't enough, you—"

She lifted one of her scythes so its blade was level with his throat. The smoke passed over her hand in a serpentine trail, hiding it so all that was visible was the metal against his flesh. Something changed in his eyes then, the monster she'd grown used to over the years rising up yet again—like clockwork.

He drew a dagger faster than blinking. Catching his strike with her scythe, she held fast, both of them grinding their feet into the ground and pushing back. He broke the hold first, pushing hard enough that her weapon almost flew out of her hand, and then he advanced.

They fought hard, their blades glinting sharply in the light, the smoke gathered so thickly around them that the rest of the world disappeared. Sweat dripped into her eyes and her lungs burned with ash settling in her throat. The heat built in intensity as they drew closer to the fire, making every breath a battle.

His dagger slashed across her cheek, a quick, sharp pain, the hilt hitting hard enough that she twisted to the side and nearly lost her balance. His other fist flew toward her face, and she knocked it away with a scythe, drawing a deep cut on his forearm. But as blood flowed from the cut, he didn't even seem to notice—he circled away from the flames, two daggers in his hands now, a wall of smoke at his back and nothing else.

"You refuse to see me as anything but evil, don't you?" he asked, taking a step closer to her—a sudden desperation deepening the blue of his eyes. "You think I couldn't possibly want to help our home."

"You're destroying everything you claim to care about for a chance at power," she said, advancing rather than backing up—not caring how close range or risky it was, as long as he saw in her eyes that this was the last fight they would ever have. "Being the last person standing in this city won't make you good for it, Kohl."

"And so what does that make you?" he asked as she came to a stop in front of him, both of their weapons down at their sides. Despite the roar of flames, she heard his voice clearly. "If you try to kill me now, at least it will prove you're no better than me."

She let out a sharp laugh. "I never said I was. But I'm not doing this for you, Kohl, I'm doing this for Kosín."

A heartbeat later, she met his blades with her own, a clang of metal reverberating through her bones as she gritted her teeth to hold him there. As she pushed him back toward the wall of flames, she knew she was gaining ground, her adrenaline racing as if a crowd were watching and cheering her on. But it was only the two of them. She fought back, forcing an opening—she could strike and kill him there.

But she paused and he slashed a blade across her arm. A look of resignation entered his eyes then. There was no going back from this. And then his fist flew toward her face.

The punch hit her in the jaw and she fell back, vision blacking out for a moment until she landed hard on the ground—her scythes flew from her hands and skidded toward the fire. The flames were so close now, she smelled her hair burning. She was going to die here, alone except for Kohl standing over her body as it turned to ash.

As she tried to roll to the side to regroup at a distance from him, a sharp pain swept across her upper back—a blade had cut through the skin.

She rolled to her knees, ignoring the searing pain on her back, but stopped in place when Kohl approached her, his gun raised and aimed at her face.

He placed his finger on the trigger, but he didn't fire. Hesitation flickered through his eyes, that doubt that always appeared when he came close to destroying her.

In one quick move, she knocked the gun out of his hands.

Pulling a diamond-edged dagger from the brace across her chest, she pressed the blade under his ribs and directly into his heart. He gasped, his hands trying to grab on to her wrist, but his strength faltered by the second.

"Aina," he gasped out.

As Kohl tried and failed to say more, Aina thought only of Teo. His eyes as the life faded out of them, his last words, and the way his head rested on her shoulder. She plunged the knife in deeper.

"You told me to watch while my target's life fades from their eyes," she whispered as they both sank to their knees, his body leaning heavily on her dagger. The smoke gathered around them in wisps and curls, until the rest of the battle faded away. "You told me to check that they are truly dead. So I'm watching and waiting, Kohl, because you taught me well."

His blood-covered hand moved to his jacket with the last bit of strength he had. He lifted it aside, and she thought he was going to draw another gun—he always had multiple on him. Without wasting another moment, she twisted her blade out of his chest and drew it across his throat in one smooth movement. Blood poured down her wrist and arm. The light left his eyes right before he slumped to the ground.

She stepped back quickly, as if expecting him to rise again. Her hands trembled as she looked down at Kohl's blood on them, and then at the dead man below.

Dead. Kohl is dead.

She shook her head, not quite understanding or believing those words. She drew in a shuddering breath, remembering then the moment when she was fourteen and nearly passed out from inhaling glue on the roof of the Dom. It had been hard to breathe then too, like she was suffocating on smoke even with none around. He'd held her up, concern in his eyes, and the next day he'd promised to give her a tradehouse of her own when she was ready. That hope for safety had kept her alive for so long.

And as much as she'd known he'd needed to die for the city to be safe, she knew that his words were true: *We're more alike than you've ever admitted.* All they'd both ever wanted was hope for a future, and in this city, that was as elusive as smoke to hold on to.

After a few seconds passed, she lifted aside his jacket to see what he'd been trying to uncover.

Instead of a gun, it was a glass vial, a familiar one, with a milky liquid inside.

The antidote.

Or perhaps it was the fake. Since Arman had killed the Sentinel himself, and Kohl had used one of the antidotes to spare

Aina from the poison on the smuggler's ship, she had no idea what had happened to the other antidotes and poisons. Frowning, she plucked the vial from his jacket and tucked it into the pouch at her belt.

The raging fire covered all other sounds beyond them. Right after he'd drawn his gun, he'd hesitated. His vision of them ruling together had been shattered and he'd known he was about to die. She'd always thought she'd hear his voice after his death, taunting her and threatening to come back, but right now . . . she heard only her own voice. There was an empty, ghost-like space in her mind that he had always occupied, ever since she was eight years old, before she even knew his name. Even now, when she closed her eyes, she could see shadows in that room, demons that would use his voice again if they ever wanted to get to her.

She opened her eyes. Maybe the shadows would always be there, but she no longer feared them—they were a part of her too.

40

Turning away from Kohl's body and with the fire at her back, Aina faced a wall of smoke ahead of her. Cinders latched on to her hair and singed her skin. Panic flooded her briefly; she couldn't see the ladder the others had used to escape. As far as she could tell, she was the only person still in the mine pit and breathing.

But as she swallowed, her throat itched and burned, and ash got in her eyes. If she didn't get out of here now, she wouldn't be breathing much longer either.

She searched the ground for her scythes, but they must have been swallowed by the fire already. Shielding her face as much as she could, she ran back in the direction she'd come from, willing the smoke to clear. She choked on it, fearing she'd be buried here. The walls of the mine would fall and trap her if she didn't get out soon. More than once, she tripped over debris or bodies, scraping her palms and knees on the ground when she caught herself. After a few more minutes, though, her hand reached out and touched something solid—the rock wall of the pit. She clung to it for a moment, wondering if she might be able to climb it if she couldn't find the ladder. The smoke billowed around her with a gust of wind, and she covered her eyes with her arm. When the wind died down, the path in front of her had cleared of smoke. The rung of a ladder flashed in the light of the flames, ten feet away.

She sprinted to it and jumped onto the first rung, crying out when she nearly slipped right off—her hands were slick with blood. With a blaze of heat at her back, she climbed quickly, keeping her grip on the rungs as tight as she could.

She kept her gaze upward as she climbed, searching for a pocket of sky among the smoke. She was almost there. Ten feet, five feet—when a hand reached down to pull her up.

Grasping it, she hauled herself up the last few rungs and collapsed on the grass, coughing and trying to blink the smoke out of her eyes. "Mariya took the other soldiers and the Inosen," said Tannis, holding up Aina by the shoulders. "We couldn't leave without you."

After another moment, her vision had cleared enough to take in the scene in front of her, and she breathed in deeply, not caring that the air was still thick with smoke—at least she wasn't in that pit anymore.

Under a pale dawn sky, the survivors had gathered. More bodies littered the grass between here and the safe house one hundred feet away. The two tradehouses and about fifty Kaiyanis soldiers were gathered a short distance from the fire, checking for injuries among their fighters. Mirran and Tannis stood next to her, uncomfortably close to the flames, and Aina felt a rush of gratitude toward them; they didn't have to stay here for her, but they had.

"Aina," Mirran said sharply. "Is that your blood?"

When Aina looked down, she stiffened. Dark red, glistening blood still coated her neck, torso, and arms.

"If that were mine, I'd be dead," she said, shaking her head, then looked toward the burning mines—was his body burning there now, disappearing forever? "Most of it is Kohl's."

"So the Dom . . ." Tannis said, her eyes widening.

Aina didn't answer her unspoken question. The Dom might be theirs now, but that no longer mattered. If Bautix ended up taking the city, nothing would be theirs at all, because it would all be gone. "You said Mariya took the other soldiers and the Inosen? She must be on her way to the Tower now. Where are Raurie, Ryuu, and Lill?"

"They went with her," Tannis said in a strained tone. "None of the other Inosen who are able to use magic have fought with it before, so they had to be there. We can go through the same entrance Mirran and I used earlier."

As they walked to the rest of their group, Aina checked her weapons and injuries, noting she'd lost a dagger and two scythes somewhere along the way. Her left arm was still heavy to move around, but adrenaline had carried her through the fight with Kohl and it would get her through the rest of this. The cut Kohl had made on her back still stung, and she knew she'd have to treat it soon or risk infection. Shallow cuts lined her palms and stung when she touched them, but she could still grip a knife handle. For now, it had to be good enough.

Once they gathered the tradehouses and Kaiyanis soldiers, they began their march to the Tower. As soon as the trees cleared ahead of them and the Tower came into view, Aina's exhaustion disappeared, and a new energy replaced it.

Rising thirty stories above the land with sharp spires and turrets, the Tower had always been a source of fear and inspiration for her. She imagined it was somewhat like how the Inosen, including her parents, viewed the Mothers. The morning sun shining above gave her a brief surge of hope. This battle wasn't over, and the city wasn't doomed, nor abandoned, nor lost. And they would see it through to the end.

They all moved northward, cutting across the cemetery toward the Tower. As they did, raindrops dotted the land in front of them. The air grew thick with humidity as everything turned gray and misted.

No Diamond Guards stood in front of the Tower or at the side entrance she could see from here, which sent an eerie chill down Aina's spine. Was it already taken? Were they too late?

Gulping, she gestured for Tannis to lead the way. Following Tannis at the front of the group, Aina searched the grounds for any sign of Diamond Guards approaching to join the fight inside the Tower. They curved around the side of the building and all went quiet except the wind whistling past them and the lashing rain.

Tannis squinted up at the slick wall of the Tower for a moment, then pointed at handholds set along the side. They led twenty feet up into a turret jutting off the side of the building. Aina thought she could make out an opening that had been carved into it, similar to what she'd used to navigate the caves underneath the Tower. The memory of the chill in the water and the rocks that had collided into her made her shiver as she approached the wall and grasped on to the handholds.

Raindrops hit her face and slicked her hands as she climbed. A few times, she nearly slipped, her heart jumping to her throat as she did. She'd never led so many people into a fight before, but nearly one hundred followed her and Tannis now into the Tower. The thought of failing all of them scared her—she'd already failed the recruits at the Dom, and she'd failed Teo. But she kept the image of sliding her knife into Kohl's chest front and center in her mind. He was gone because of her. Bautix didn't stand a chance.

The handholds led to a cramped room barely large enough to stand in, with only a narrow crevice cut into the wall for them to step into. Aina went first, needing to turn her body to the side to fit. She strained her ears to hear what might be happening on the other side of this path. The farther along she got, the more clearly sounds of fighting from within the Tower reached her, distant shouts and the clang of metal. Her breathing came more shallowly, her pulse racing in anticipation of joining the fray.

The path led to a large pantry, with boxes of food stacked along each wall. As her group filed in, she squinted through the darkness to find Tannis and Mirran among all the other heads of blue hair.

"We should go to wherever most of his men will be concentrated so we can take out as many as possible at once," Aina said when she found them. "I think it will be on the lower floors, since the upper ones are smaller and there's not enough room for so many fighters."

"The ballroom would be the best place for a battle," Tannis said in a low voice.

"It's probably a bloodbath," Mirran said, holding out a hand for Tannis to pass her a pistol—and then she smiled. "Let's join it."

Aina clearly remembered the ballroom where she, Teo, Ryuu, and Raurie had stopped Bautix's plans last month. A balcony ringed it with curtains drawn, where she and Tannis had fought Kohl that same night.

"I know where to start," Aina said, and gestured for them all to follow her.

Torches were the only light in the hall they ran through, their boots against the marble floor the only sound. Echoes of shouts grew louder the deeper they penetrated the Tower's walls. Every minute, Aina expected one of Bautix's men to turn the corner and pull a gun on them, but their hunch was right that most of the fighting was concentrated in the ballroom and the other open areas of the lower floors.

Soon, they sped into a hallway where a stairwell continued downward, and another path extended straight toward the balcony surrounding the ballroom.

Aina turned to face the soldiers and they came to a stop, silent as night as they waited for instructions. For a moment, she said nothing, hearing only the din from below. Blades clashed and gunshots fired. Glass broke and people screamed. It would have terrified most people, but right now, all she wanted was to join them.

She needed to be in the thick of it, defending her home and fighting to the last breath.

"Mirran, take the soldiers to line around the balcony and start taking down Bautix's men through the folds of the curtains. Make sure they're careful who they hit; we don't want them to take out our own people by mistake."

As Mirran gathered the soldiers with a quick shout in Kaiyanis, Aina raced down the steps that led to the ballroom, with Tannis and the two tradehouses at her side. With bated breath, Aina led the way to the door and drew a dagger.

It was a massacre inside.

Diamond Guards all fought the same way—in methodical, efficient movements that worked well enough but were obvious to a trained eye. But now they fought one another, the ones who were still loyal to Mariya against those who'd turned to Bautix's side. They were evenly matched, neither side giving ground even as the floor beneath them grew slick with blood.

Bullets flew from the balcony surrounding the ballroom; the soldiers with Mirran taking down as many of Bautix's men as they could. The ones with Mariya fought as well, facing the Jackals who littered the ballroom and striking them down without hesitation. All of the Jackals were new and inexperienced; they dropped with quick shots to the head, blades in their stomachs and knives through their throats. Mariya stood on the stage in the distance, surrounded by a group of Inosen who'd used their magic at some point to raise stone pillars from the ground to cover them in a shield. One at a time, they each used their remaining diamonds to strike at Bautix's men in the crowd. Blood poured out of their eyes and ears and mouths until they collapsed, painting the floor red in front of them.

Aina locked eyes with Tannis for a moment and felt the same energy there; they had a chance to win this. Turning to the tradehouses, Aina pointed to a few of them and yelled to be heard over the gunshots and screams. "You three, stand at the door and don't let any of Bautix's men out. We're outnumbering them now and we need to keep it that way."

She and Tannis ran into the thick of it with the rest of the tradehouses at their back. They ran forward together, clearing a path in the center of the ballroom with their weapons and then turning to face the rest of it, their backs to one another.

A Jackal turned to face Aina, his blade swinging toward her. She dodged it easily and slashed across his chest with her dagger. As he fell back, she slammed him in the back with the hilt of her weapon so he collapsed to the ground. With one more cut through the back of his neck, he stopped moving.

His blood spilled over the floor. The diamonds underneath the glass floor glittered in the ballroom's lights, even with all the fighting and the tight press of bodies engaged in battle.

As she, Tannis, and the tradehouses cleared out the center of the ballroom, the fighting began to spread to the corners. When Aina cut down one of the ex–Diamond Guards, she finally spotted Raurie, Ryuu, and Lill at the nearest corner.

"Aina! We're nearly out of diamonds," Raurie said when Aina ran to join them. Between all the moving bodies and the flashing weapons, bits of the glittering diamond floor were visible. "Do you know if all of those were actually used during the war?"

"Not sure. I think they collected any diamonds they found on Inosen, no matter if they were used or not. A lot of them are probably fine."

Raurie nodded once, as if Aina had confirmed something she needed to know, and Aina realized what she was doing two seconds before she did it. Raurie took one of the diamonds she carried and spoke the same spell Aina had used in the cavern, "Cayek inoke," the spell to crumble earth, and faced the stone balcony surrounding the ballroom.

They jumped out of the way, rolling toward the center of the room as the balcony crashed down onto the glass. Aina shielded her face from the flying shards and the broken stone. Raurie, Ryuu, and Lill ran toward the sparkling gems under the floor even before the crash subsided. The Inosen surrounding Mariya on the stage jumped off to take the diamonds from the newly opened floor.

Just then, someone kicked Aina in the back. The breath knocked out of her, she fell onto the broken glass, scraping her hands and face. Flipping onto her back, she jerked her head out of the way as the Jackal standing above her slashed across her with a dagger. It cut into her collarbone, missing where her neck had been a moment ago. Hissing with the sharp cut, she raised her own dagger to block his next strike.

Raising herself to a crouch, she pushed upward and shoved his blade aside. Another dagger appeared in his hand a moment later and it swept toward her, but right before the knife met her neck, the man gasped. A tip of silver shone through his neck, pierced from behind. Blood spilled from his lips and a choking sound rose from his throat. He collapsed, and Teo stepped into place behind him.

41

Teo pulled her aside and they hid in the shadows of the stage to avoid getting caught in the battle again. Aina stared at him the whole time, thinking he was an apparition, just like the Mothers.

"Teo," she breathed his name, placing a hand cautiously on his shoulder and stiffening when she finally touched him. "Are you—"

But the words wouldn't come out; she had no clue what she wanted to ask.

Are you a ghost, like the Mothers who appeared to me?

Are you going to disappear, like they did?

"I'm here," he said, taking both of her hands in his and stepping in front of her. The rest of the ballroom fell away—the shouting, the clash of weapons.

Not taking her eyes off him, she whispered, "I thought you . . ."

"I know." His head hung a little, dark waves of hair draping around his face. "With the poison, for a moment, I thought I was already dead. But I stopped feeling pain from the wound on my side, and when you used your knife, you, um . . ."

She blinked. "Did I miss?"

When a smile quirked at one side of his lips, she felt that maybe this was real. He wasn't going to leave her again.

"I remember you using a spell before I passed out," he said. "Maybe it actually worked."

She shook her head slowly, the memory coming back to her quickly. Had she actually managed to heal him, when before, she'd only been good at killing with the magic? She'd felt nothing, no sign of the Mothers answering her prayers or the magic working when she tried to heal the wound on his side or stop the poison from spreading. The diamond she'd tried to use had already been spent, and when she'd stabbed Teo, she'd didn't try any spell or draw any of her own blood. Unless . . .

Ryuu's words came back to her then, the day they'd first practiced healing spells and she'd failed miserably: that there were rumors of people able to heal without diamonds or blood. No one really knew how it worked, but Raurie had said it happened after some kind of divine experience. The Mothers appearing to her in the cavern . . . maybe they hadn't disappeared at all. Maybe they'd always been there.

"I had the antidote in my system," she said slowly. "I didn't know it at the time, but Kohl gave it to me before we even got on the train. So when I kissed you, that must have saved you from the poison. And the spell saved you from your wounds. How did you get out of there alive, though? The ship was already on fire when I left."

"Raurie and Lill were still on the ship, searching for the weapons, and they found me a few minutes after you left. We jumped into the harbor and had to swim. I thought I'd die again," he said, shaking his head and staring somewhere over her shoulder. "We couldn't find you or Ryuu, but we waited for Mirran to come in. The Kaiyanis solders arrived, and we all left back to the city together. I headed to the Tower first with a few of the soldiers to get a start on taking it back. I had no idea where you were."

"I'm here now," she said, and then drew him into a tight hug. She could still hardly believe it—she'd actually saved someone rather than doomed them. Looking over his shoulder, she could see the fighting once more. They still had work to do. Pulling back, she said, "We have to get to Bautix."

After a quick scan of the ballroom, she spotted Tannis, Raurie, Ryuu, and Lill fighting together. She waved them over and, when they saw Teo standing there alive next to her, Tannis gasped and Ryuu almost tripped over a broken part of the floor.

"What? You're alive?" Tannis stammered.

"You could act more excited about it," Teo answered with a raised eyebrow.

"We'll explain later," Aina cut in, then gestured toward the exit of the ballroom. "Right now we need to find Bautix."

They traversed the rest of the ballroom, finding it easier to avoid fights than when the battle had started; Bautix's men were much fewer in number now. They left the carnage and made their way through the Tower's corridors.

By the time they reached the upper floors, the Tower had grown quieter. Statues were knocked down and paintings hung in tatters. Bullets had shattered walls and doors. Some office doors were flung open and inside, diplomats and governors lay slumped over their desks or drowned in their own blood. Screams and gunshots still reached them, the sounds penetrating through the walls and echoing off the marble and stone. But with Teo here, she didn't feel as afraid; they'd both faced the worst and the only thing to do was to keep going.

The whole time, she searched for some sign of Bautix, and as they reached the top floors, more sounds of fighting reached them. Beckoning to the others to follow her lead, she peered around a corner of the stairwell into the open floor of the second-highest floor.

A group of Bautix's men fought the few loyal Diamond Guards left. The Guards were outnumbered here, even though they were winning in the ballroom below. One hand trailing to a knife, Aina debated joining to take down Bautix's men here or continuing on to the last floor.

Footsteps pounded up the stairs below them. Teo turned at once, firing a shot into the head of a Jackal who approached them. But more men followed, and Aina's group faced them, weapons drawn.

They broke into small groups, fighting the Jackals in the stairwell. Aina disarmed one by slicing through his wrist so his gun toppled over the railing to the floors below. As he screamed, she crouched and slashed her blade through the backs of the knees of another Jackal who had been about to shoot Ryuu.

A flash of red hair passed by Aina's vision. At first, she thought it was Lill, but when she looked over, she saw Lill had been boxed in by two Jackals and one of them had struck her in the calf with a knife. The men were cut down in seconds, though—Kerys, knives and red hair flashing, had cut through their necks. She stared at her daughter for one moment before running back in the direction she'd come—up the stairs and to the last floor.

Aina raced after her up the staircase, her steps echoing on the stone steps as she left the rest of the fighting behind. If anyone knew where to find Bautix right now, it would be Kerys.

But before either of them could reach the landing, two Jackals stepped out of the hall leading to the top floor and blocked their path.

Aina drew a knife and thrust it into the heart of one of the Jackals. She turned to face the next one, but before she could strike, a knife flew past her and into his throat.

Spinning around, she saw Kerys, her hands raised to show she wouldn't attack.

"Changing your loyalties again?" Aina scoffed, her voice echoing in the stairwell.

"I've spent my whole life jumping to the side of whoever could offer me a chance at safety, and this time, I told myself I'd stick it out, stay by his side and not look back." Kerys swallowed hard. "I did it. For once in my life, I stayed when things got hard, even when all I wanted was to stop. He told me he would leave the mines alone, that he wouldn't touch anywhere Lill was—he knew I still cared for them, as much as he hated it. I believed him. Needless to say, I no longer do. Follow me if you want to get to him."

She turned and walked away without waiting to see if Aina would follow. But after a moment, Aina did, following her to the landing of the top floor and peering around the edge. Six men and women, a mix of ex–Diamond Guards and Jackals, guarded the door to Bautix's quarters.

"I'll help you take them down," Kerys whispered, nodding toward the guards at the door. "You get inside."

Aina withdrew her blowgun. She only had one poison dart left, but it would do the job. As she fired it into one of the guard's throats, Kerys threw a knife at another. It pierced him through the throat, and before the other guards could even react, she and Aina ran toward them from behind the corner.

After cutting down one of the Diamond Guard traitors, Aina moved toward the door they'd been guarding. She sidestepped one more strike and stabbed the attacker in the stomach. As she pulled her dagger from his flesh, footsteps came from down the next corridor: more ex–Diamond Guards ran toward them, guns raised. Kerys stepped into the middle of the corridor and faced them.

In a quick flash, Aina saw what would have been her future had she stayed addicted to Kohl; fighting alongside him until the end, when he would trick her and ruin her until she had nothing left. And then she would have died for him.

As Aina slipped into Bautix's quarters, Kerys stood surrounded by three of the guards with more coming from the stairwell, her knives drawn and eyes fierce.

When the door closed behind Aina with a soft click, effectively shutting out all the sound from the corridor beyond, she heard only her own breath. She scanned the room, which was decorated in gold and deep brown tones. A large oak desk stood near the floor-to-ceiling windows that looked out at the city from a height of thirty stories.

Bautix stood with his back to her, hands folded as he stared out of the window at the city he'd ruined.

Without turning around, he said, "Hello, Aina Solís," and lifted his eyes to meet hers in the window reflection.

She approached slowly, stopping just short of the desk.

"Do you think you're watching your victory or your defeat?" she asked.

The side of his lips she could see tilted upward in a smirk. "Would you have gotten all the way here if your side was losing? Would you have survived the attack on the ship if the traitor Kohl hadn't let you?"

"I have my ways," she said with a shrug. "Even if my side was losing, I would have found my way to you. And I've killed Kohl."

He turned then, a quick pivot of his body that made her tense up. The brightness in his eyes wasn't the look of a man ready to die.

"And I have my ways too, Miss Solís. Would you like a drink?"

She eyed him slowly as he poured a glass of wine for them each. Did he think she was stupid enough to drink something that was obviously poisoned, or was he so confident that he thought he could make her do whatever he wanted? Or perhaps this was his final desperate move when he already knew his men had lost the fight below.

Subtly sniffing the air, she found that hint of her poison: the smell of Kosín, the city burning beyond the windows. Her mind raced as she took the glass from him, slowly closing her fingers around the stem. He didn't seem to know that she was the one who'd brewed the poison. Otherwise, he would know that she would have recognized the scent of it. Bautix probably had an antidote on him, but so did she.

Since Bautix hadn't used the poison on the Sentinel, she assumed he had instructed Kohl to use it all on Aina and her friends while he took out the Sentinel on his own. It would have been something they'd planned together, when Kohl was still pretending to be wholly on his side. But Kohl had only ever fought for himself. He'd wasted two poisons on the ship, kept one for himself, and gave another to Bautix—knowing he would come back to face Bautix eventually. Aina didn't know where the other antidotes were—perhaps Kohl had left them at the Dom—but he'd shown her this one on purpose. He'd wanted her to have it.

The only question was whether she or Bautix had the fake antidote, and which of them would survive.

After staring into the wine for a moment, her thoughts settled into a calm state. She lifted the cup to her lips and drank.

They waited two whole minutes, staring each other down. Aina's pulse raced, like it knew its time was limited. A bitter taste rose in the back of her mouth and she didn't know if it was her imagination or the flavor of death.

As if reading each other's minds, Bautix withdrew a vial of milky liquid from his pocket at the same time Aina reached into the pouch at her belt for her own antidote. In the crease of Bautix's forehead at the sight of her vial, she could practically see his thoughts racing and trying to put it all together. A small smile tilted at the corners of her lips as they both drank their antidotes.

Once it was all gone, she looked at Bautix. He choked on air, one hand gripping his chest. His eyes widened as blood trickled down the side of his mouth, his other hand moving to clutch at his throat.

Aina felt nothing.

After a moment, she walked toward Bautix, then forced him to a kneeling position and turned his body so he faced the window. The skin on his face paled, veins standing out purple on his neck.

"Watch, Bautix," she said, pointing the burning city. "Watch as your forces are destroyed. Watch as your plans crumble around you. You should know something: Kohl would never kill me with poison. He owed me more than that. But with you . . . consider this the end you deserve."

As he choked slowly, his breath stalling and blood flowing from his lips, Aina approached the window to look out at the city. It spread away seemingly forever, toward the river and then the fields beyond that met the horizon. Her eyes trailed toward the south, the Stacks—her and Kohl's domain. She knew he would have done anything to protect that part of the city, up to the point where he nearly destroyed everyone around him—but he'd only wanted it if he ruled it.

"Tell Kerys something," Bautix choked out, his face paling even further with his last breaths. "Tell her I did what I had to do for the good of this country, and I'm sorry if her daughter was caught in it. It had to be done if we were to win."

She could have told him Kerys was likely dead, so it didn't matter—or she could have told him that his plan to get all the Inosen at the mines killed didn't come to fruition. But no matter what she told him, he'd still think what he did was best, even if he used and hurt hundreds of people along the way.

"You're no hero, Bautix," she said instead in a low voice. "You're just as bad as me."

He gave her one more scathing look that she saw through his reflection in the window, probably the most energy he was able to summon at the moment. Then his face relaxed, defeated, calmer somehow.

Bautix fell facedown, finally dead, one hand outstretched toward the window as if he could reach the city by grasping for it.

But that wasn't how Kosín worked. You didn't reach for it. It grabbed on to you and held you fast, sending its darkness through your veins until you either thrived alongside it or choked underneath it.

The only ones who survived were those ready to embrace it, shadows and all.

42

Bright afternoon sunlight shone through the windows, casting a rainbow pattern on the carpet of Ryuu's library. Through the window, Aina could make out the highest buildings in the city. Smoke from pollution curled above them, casting a gray cloud over it all. She much preferred that to smoke from flames.

Aina had spent most afternoons here after Bautix's failed takeover of the Tower a week ago, whenever she wasn't working at getting jobs for Mirran and her new employee, the boy she'd recruited from Thunder. Here, she could stare through the window and hope to see Teo, Tannis, and Raurie return. Every small movement on the path ahead made her look up, expecting to see them, but it was usually a security guard pacing in boredom. A few days after Bautix was dead and the fighting ended, the three of them had left the city, refusing to tell her where they were going. She curled her hand—her good hand—into a fist around the arm of her chair. After thinking Teo was dead, the last thing she wanted was for him to disappear with no indication of when he'd return.

The squeak of a chair nearby made her jump. In the reflection of the window, Ryuu and Lill sat next to her at the table in front of the window.

"You know," Aina said with a sly grin, turning to face them. "If you tell me where they are, you won't have to deal with me hanging around here all day waiting for them to show up."

Lill shrugged. "We don't mind the company."

"You're quite entertaining when you're impatient, actually," Ryuu added.

She let out a grunt of frustration, but after a few seconds, her frustration subsided. Ryuu and Lill knew where the others had gone, but they didn't seem worried, so everything was probably fine.

Probably.

"We have something to tell you, though," Ryuu said, leaning forward and folding his hands together on the table. Lill scooted her chair closer and placed a hand over his, sending him an encouraging smile. This close, it was hard to miss the burn scars on Ryuu's shoulder and Lill's left hand, sustained at some point during the fighting. Then Ryuu took a deep breath and said, "We're moving. To Kaiyan."

Aina blinked. "You what?"

"We're moving to Kaiyan," Lill repeated, her smile only growing wider.

"Yes, I heard you," Aina said, shaking her head in disbelief. When neither of them started laughing to indicate that it was a joke, she knew it was real. Voice softening, she asked, "When did you decide that? Why?"

"I took a few days to think about it," Ryuu began. "After she took back the Tower, Mariya asked me if I wanted to join the Sentinel, and I—"

"He looked like he wanted to run away screaming," Lill interjected.

"It's not for me," Ryuu finished with a shrug. "So instead, she offered to recommend me to the Kaiyanis king as an apprentice of his architect, as long as I agreed to make some business and diplomatic connections while I'm there. I'll probably stay for a couple of years."

"And I've always wanted to see Kaiyan," Lill said. "My father has family in the capital, so I'll bring them his ashes, stay with them for some time, and travel from there. I want to be away from Sumerand for a while." Her eyes trailed toward the window and her shoulders tensed slightly as she spoke. "It'll be easier to move on if I'm away from here."

"What will happen to the mining business, Ryuu?" Aina asked. "Will it all be restored?"

"There is damage, but it'll survive," he said slowly, looking down at the table as he spoke. "My advisors think the mines just got attacked in the fighting, and I don't feel the need to give them any more details." He grimaced then, and Aina remembered him standing in the mouth of the tunnel, a grenade in his hands as he faced the onslaught of Kohl's fighters. "But I'm glad it happened; my parents always cared more about the city and the people here than a business. The advisors will be in charge of operations until I return. And when I come back, I'll have enough skills to steer the business in a new direction. Something that my brother might be proud of."

A long beat of silence passed while Aina took in all they'd said. Though she'd only known Ryuu for a couple months and Lill less than that, she no longer knew what her life looked like without them.

But at the same time, she could see the ghosts of the recent battle in both of their eyes. Her own memories rose up then, making her shudder slightly; the fire at the Dom, the bodies of Johana, Kushik, and Markus spread on the floor, her hands covered in both Teo and Kohl's blood. She couldn't blame Ryuu and Lill for wanting to get away from it all for a while.

"I'll miss you while you're gone," she finally said.

"I'll miss you too," Ryuu said. "But you'll be busy, I'm sure. You and Tannis can finally run the tradehouses properly, with Kohl gone."

She nodded, a brief surge of excitement flooding her at the thought. But it was quickly doused. She and Tannis had finally gotten the prize they'd fought for and no one stood against them, but it didn't feel like the victory she'd envisioned it would be. Something felt off about it all.

Her conversation with Arman Kraz when she and Tannis had recruited Thunder to fight at the Tower came back to her then. *The chaos is what we take advantage of,* he'd said. *Don't do too good a job of getting rid of the chaos, or else we'll have nothing left.*

The tradehouses had first formed in the wake of the old civil war, steered by Kohl, full of revenge and a desire to prove himself. While the newly formed Sentinel had wrestled the country into some kind of order following King Verrain's death, plenty of people had taken advantage.

Her question was how she would handle the chaos, and if it'd be different from the rest. She had a chance now to take the tradehouses in a different direction; a chance to not follow in Kohl's footsteps. But she didn't know how exactly she would handle it yet, so she shook the thought away.

The door opened then, and Aina didn't bother looking up, knowing it would be a maid or butler offering them tea or reporting something to Ryuu. Maybe one of his advisors had stopped by.

But when no one spoke, and no expensive shoes clicked across the wood floor, her eyes flicked up.

Teo, Tannis, and Raurie stood in the doorway. They all looked exhausted, like they'd traveled for days, but pleased with themselves.

Aina shoved her chair back, ran up to them, and pulled them each into a hug, holding Teo for a few seconds longer.

"Finally!" she said, letting go and shaking her head. "Where were you? Nobody told me anything!"

"You managed to keep it a secret from her the whole time?" Raurie called over to Ryuu and Lill.

"She didn't threaten to stab you?" Tannis asked in disbelief.

"Oh, she definitely did," Ryuu replied.

"But we knew she wouldn't," Lill added with a wink.

They all laughed then and Aina rolled her eyes. But a smile tugged at her lips too as they moved toward the table and pulled out chairs. Raurie and Teo walked a little slower than the others, and Aina felt a twinge of pain in her left arm. The pain had started on the burning ship, stabbing jolts that came when she least expected it, numbness and tingling, occasional difficulty to command her fingers to do anything. She had no idea if it would fade with time or not, but she had a good guess where it had come from.

If you use it to kill, you might lose the ability to heal, the Sacoren Gevann had explained. The Mothers had given them a choice, in allowing them to use the magic in violent ways, and now they had their punishment. Ryuu and Lill's burn scars might never go away. Raurie had sustained a bullet wound to her leg the day of fighting and now had to move gingerly on that side. Teo, although he'd never used the blood magic himself, had been saved by it when he should have died. Her poison had attacked his lungs and heart. Now he was sometimes short of breath and took more careful steps. Since he'd never used the magic himself, she hoped his aftereffects would go away soon.

As for her own . . . it might be difficult to fight with her left hand from now on, but she wasn't too worried. The Mothers had told her to embrace her weakness—and she had, learning to use her own strength, to only need herself to win—and perhaps they knew she wouldn't need to fight much more in the future.

Looking around at the group, Aina asked, "Will someone finally tell me where you three went?"

Teo reached over to take her hand, brown eyes bright with whatever secret he kept. "I'll show you."

She couldn't really be mad at him when he looked at her like that.

After leaving the library, she and Teo exited the mansion, passed the maple trees near the entrance, and walked across the grounds. The grass was wet beneath their boots, the sunshine hot on their shoulders—and no taste of ash in the air.

Breathing it in, her frustration disappeared. With the battle over, there wasn't a need to be hurried and impatient and panicked anymore. With Kohl gone, her fear had no place either. It was strange getting used to it, but she hoped the feeling would last.

"Are we going to the mines?" she asked Teo, blushing a little at the fact that they were still holding hands. She hadn't even noticed.

He shook his head with a mischievous grin. "No, much closer than that." Lifting a hand, he pointed at the cemetery ahead.

Aina raised an eyebrow, but Teo just laughed and led the way forward. They reached the tombstones and walked between rows of them for a few minutes before Teo came to a stop. Memories of Kohl would crop up all over the city, and especially at the Dom, even though it looked completely different than when he'd been there.

After a few minutes of walking through the cemetery, Teo stopped in front of a tombstone and pointed at it. Wondering which rich person was buried here and why Teo wanted to show her their grave, she read the names.

For a moment, she was certain she'd stopped breathing. Then she blinked, shook her head, and read the names again. Rafael Solís Galán and Manuela Santos Plata. Only her parents' names, no dates or messages, but a small, white shard was embedded between the two names.

They knelt in front of it, and Aina reached out a hand to touch the stone warmed by the midday sun. Brushing the object between her parents' names, she noted its smooth surface. Porcelain.

"I hope you like it," Teo said quickly, a hesitant look in his eyes like he feared he'd made a mistake. "Raurie told me how her parents used to burn the bodies of Inosen who'd been killed and place their ashes in a hidden shed near the mass graves. A few days ago, when I left with Tannis and Raurie, we went there. We had no idea if we'd find them, so I didn't want anyone to tell you. Tannis said that she'd found the pieces of that porcelain horse that used to belong to your mother. It was broken, and she assumed you did it, but she knew you'd probably regret it later, so she took a piece of it for you. Ryuu had the idea to put it here."

He'd barely finished speaking when she pulled him into a tight hug. Tears pricked the corners of her eyes, but she didn't mind them falling now.

"It's perfect," she said, pulling slightly away as the sun crested to a position directly above them. "It's amazing that you were able to find them. Do you think we'd be able to bring back more? The ashes of people who died during the war?"

"We can tell Mariya Okubo," he said slowly, his forehead creased in thought. "If she wants to announce it to the public, people could go look."

His voice trailed off, and she reread the names, thinking of everything that had led to this moment—and who'd been by her side for it all.

She and Teo looked at each other at the same time. The sun lit his eyes a warm copper tone. It scared her, to sink into this comfort, to be at someone's side without fear—but she wanted to.

"How do you feel?" he asked in a slightly cautious tone. "You killed Kohl. You're free of him now."

The words themselves were hopeful, but she could sense his real question—did she feel free?

"I don't know," she said slowly. Then her gaze turned to the rest of the cemetery. "I came here with him, just a few times. But it's enough to make me remember. It'll be like that all over the city, everywhere I go." Her voice tightened with the realization— she didn't know if she'd ever actually feel free.

Kohl was a ghost wherever she walked, a scar on her heart that would always be there. She tried to believe he would fade over time and she'd stop looking over her shoulder, stop hearing his voice in her head, but she truthfully didn't know if that was possible.

"It's okay if you don't know," Teo said, reaching a hand forward to touch her jaw—and she remembered a time Kohl had gripped her chin so hard, she thought it would break. She tensed, forcing her way through the memory, and thought instead of how different this was. Teo's touch was warm, his grip gentle, his eyes filled only with love. Then he said, "There are two things you know for sure: He's gone."

Aina breathed in deeply, as if she could heal herself with those words alone. "What's the other thing?"

"That I'm here for you." The softness of his voice made her tension slide away then, and she leaned into his touch. "Just because you've been hurt doesn't mean you're broken or have to punish yourself somehow. You deserve love like anyone else."

Her heart swelled at his words—no one had ever told her something like that, and she desperately wanted to believe it.

"I want to figure this all out," she said. "With you, Teo."

She leaned toward him then, weaving one hand through his hair. Teo placed his hand on the back of her head and drew her into a kiss.

But she felt like he was holding back; like he was afraid of hurting her.

She ran her fingers through his hair, cupped the back of his neck and pulled him closer to her—to show him he didn't have to be careful with her. To show him she trusted him. She wasn't a fragile piece of porcelain that might be easily broken, but if there were anyone's arms she wanted to fall apart in, they were his.

He kissed her jaw, trailing kisses toward the back of her ear and then down her neck, one hand on the back of her neck and the other at her waist. His warmth seeped into her, like the sun shone on her from all directions. When he pulled her closer, she leaned into his embrace, feeling safer than she had in years—and wanting to stay there.

43

The Tower still bore signs of the fighting that had hap-
pened there, especially in the entrance hall. The Diamond Guard
leading Aina and Tannis to a meeting with the Sentinel showed
them up the staircase near the ballroom. Peering inside, she
noted that most of it was roped off. Broken glass and blood still
covered the floor. People hired to clean and repair the Tower
were busy fixing the floor, but not in the way Aina had expected.

"Look," Tannis whispered, pointing at one of the men who
hauled out diamonds from the floor in a large crate.

"What are they planning to do?" Aina asked the Diamond
Guard escorting them as they reached the landing to the next
floor.

"Putting a new floor in," he said over his shoulder. "Marble,
I heard. A little pretentious, don't you think? They're going to
renovate the whole Tower."

She and Tannis rolled their eyes at the same time. If he thought
marble was pretentious but a floor of diamonds wasn't, Aina

didn't really know what to say to him. But as long as he wasn't a traitor like all the others, she wouldn't judge him too harshly. There were plenty of open jobs among the Diamond Guards to take the place of the old and support the new Sentinel.

"I'm surprised she invited us to a meeting today," Aina said, frowning as they continued to ascend flights of stairs. "You'd think they'd be busy rebuilding."

"I'm not," Tannis said in a low voice, one hand going to a throwing star—a move Aina recognized as one she did out of habit when she sensed a threat. "She was around after the first war, so she saw what happened. They made sure enough Steels were alive to keep the factories going and give jobs to everyone else, but they didn't pay attention to the rest of the country, and well . . . we both know what happens when people are given free rein in a place that's falling apart."

The Diamond Guard leading them looked back with an uneasy grimace, but said nothing as he showed them into a meeting room. A circular oak table sat in the center, with three people gathered there: Mariya, June, and Sofía. Aina nodded at them all as they sat down, feeling a slight hint of trepidation. All of them knew her, and with two Sacoren in the government, she had hoped the country really was moving into a new future. But Tannis's words spun in her head now, and she had a suspicion of what today's meeting was about.

"Good afternoon, Aina and Tannis," Mariya said with a terse smile. "This is the first chance we've gotten to talk after Bautix's death, so I didn't have a chance to thank you. Without you and everyone on your side, the country would be in Bautix's hands now. I trust you've been busy managing the tradehouses since things have calmed down."

"We have," Aina said, shifting uncomfortably in her seat at the idea of discussing her criminal activities with the highest position of government in the country. But they all knew who she and Tannis were.

"That's actually what we would like to talk to you about," Mariya continued, clasping her hands together atop the table. "We have to decide what is best for the country. The tradehouses began after the civil war, didn't they?"

"It's easy to build profit off instability," Tannis said shortly.

"That's true. However, if we want Sumerand to rise into a new future, and prove to the world that we are advancing as a nation, we need to make an effort to reduce crime and disorder. I hope an agreement will be possible instead of having to act by force."

Her words were soft, but Aina sensed the threat in the air. Aina couldn't blame her; as Tannis had said, Mariya had seen the failures of the Sentinel after the last war, and likely didn't want to repeat them. The photograph of Mariya's daughter on her desk came back to Aina then, and she couldn't help feeling a pang of sympathy for the woman in front of her. She knew Mariya didn't expect any of this to be easy, but her hope was clear in the glint in her eyes as she waited patiently for Aina and Tannis to reply.

"No matter how you try to close the tradehouses—especially if you tried by force—they'll spring up again," Aina said slowly. "Whether we manage them or not. And right now, we are managing them. Crime will never really go away, and we only control a small part of it."

Mariya let out a heavy sigh, and next to her, June and Sofía exchanged a knowing look, as if they could have expected this answer.

Aina turned to Tannis, who nodded at her to let her know they were on the same page.

"I should have known you would be difficult about this," Mariya said, but a small smile twitched at the corners of her lips.

"We won't actually," Aina said. "We think the tradehouses should end too."

It was almost comical how all their eyes widened at once, as if they couldn't believe what they were hearing.

"Not immediately, though," Aina continued, the words coming slow and steady, as if she could hardly believe them herself, but she knew this was the right thing to do. "And not by anything the Sentinel does to try to close them. Whatever you try, it won't work. Like you said, the tradehouses began after the civil war. They thrived in instability and chaos. But it's more than that. They give jobs to people who don't have other options. I want to believe that Sumerand is heading in a new direction and that everything will be happy and prosperous for everyone, but the poor can't survive on hopes and promises. And change in the way that you see it won't happen overnight, not if it's going to last. We want to keep running the tradehouses for a few more years, then we'll transition them slowly into something else; something that might benefit the city. But the Sentinel will not be involved in it."

Mariya nodded at Aina. "You would know best. I think that you, and other young people like you, are exactly what Kosín needs to become a better version of itself." She took a deep breath before adding, "Which is exactly why I'll be stepping down."

Aina's eyes widened, and she looked to June and Sofía for confirmation.

"The new Sentinel will be larger," June explained, "with people from all backgrounds in the country, not just a few."

"I'm here to facilitate a transition," Mariya explained, "while June and Sofía are here to oversee the repeal of any laws and systems that currently disenfranchise the Inosen. We plan to have a new Sentinel put together within a few months, but I won't be a part of it. I am a part of the old order—and I should have done a lot more to fix our country's problems than I did.

I tried my best, but we need something new for the future. Me stepping down, peacefully and publicly, will be a sign of that."

After a brief pause, Aina said, "That's probably the best decision." She looked toward June and Sofía again, feeling a surge of pride. Two Inosen women, from immigrant backgrounds—they all made up Sumerand, so they should all be a part of what it would look like in the future. For the first time, she felt hopeful there might be a future for the people of Kosín like her, who'd so often convinced themselves they'd never have one.

After the meeting, she and Tannis walked together back to the Stacks and stopped at Raurie's uncle's tavern along the way. Raurie stood outside of it, her purple shawl draped over her shoulders, and waved to them.

"Where are you two going?" Aina asked as Tannis walked up to Raurie and kissed her on the cheek.

"One of the initiatives the Sacoren are proposing is to give more business opportunities to Inosen, now that we don't have to hide." Raurie smiled and held up her wrist so her bracelet caught the sunlight. "I'm finally going to open a jewelry store."

"That's great, Raurie," Aina said. "I'll make sure to sell some diamonds there."

"Not that kind of jewlery store, Aina—" Tannis interjected, but stopped when Aina began to laugh.

"Joking," she said with a wink. "Maybe. See you at the Dom later, Tannis? I'm going to train that recruit from Thunder."

Tannis nodded and left to the Center with Raurie, while Aina descended the hills that led farther into the Stacks. The evening had gone quiet apart from the sounds of people cooking and laughing inside their homes.

They all wanted something to hope for, a way to believe they could pull themselves up from nothing and prove to the world what they could really do when they just had a chance. Kohl had loved the Stacks too, but his whole life had been spent fighting, and in the end all his love amounted to was a need to control. The Stacks would stay the same for a while, since a change as big as she and Tannis envisioned wasn't something that could be accomplished overnight. She took a slightly longer route than usual, wanting to take in the Stacks as they were at the end of one era and the dawn of a new one.

One thing that would never change was that this would always be her home.

A few blocks from the Dom, Aina spotted a girl roughly twelve or thirteen years old. She walked behind two older men on the tips of her toes. Both men could easily pick her up and toss her across the street if they wanted to. But neither of them even seemed to notice her, she walked so quietly.

If Aina hadn't been watching, she would have missed the moment when the girl swiped a wallet from the back pocket of one of the men.

The men continued on, laughing loudly about something while the girl darted to a doorway and began to count the kors she'd taken.

Holding back a laugh, Aina walked up to the girl, taking in her lack of shoes, the holes in her clothes, the gaunt hollows under her cheekbones. She didn't blame the girl for shrinking away from her and tightly clutching her prize.

"I have a job for you," she said, and a hint of recognition lit up the girl's eyes when she looked at Aina. "Picking pockets might keep you alive for now, but it won't get you very far here. If you want more, as well as food and a bed, come with me."

Without waiting to see if the girl would follow, Aina continued down the street. When Aina approached the next corner, where she would turn to reach the Dom, the girl would easily be able to guess what awaited her if she chose to join Aina.

Aina waited until she was across the street from the Dom, then glanced over her shoulder. Halfway down the street behind her, the girl she'd offered a job to approached slowly, keeping to the shadows on the side of the street. When the Dom came into view for her, she tilted her head back slightly. A relieved grin flickered on her face, lit up by the sun.

ACKNOWLEDGMENTS

I used to dream of having an "Also by" section at the front of my books that listed my previous books. Now I finally have it and it's one of the best feelings in the world. My duology is out in the world and Aina's story is complete, but it wouldn't have been possible without the support of my team.

Thank you endlessly to Peter Knapp, as well as the whole Park & Fine Literary and Media, for your outstanding work. Pete, your enthusiasm, support, and expertise are incomparable and I'm so glad to call you my agent. Also, Suraurwanda says hi!

An enormous thank-you to Eileen, my editor at Wednesday Books. Your love of stories shines through every time we talk, and I'm so grateful to work with an editor who challenges me to bring out the depth, light, hope, and love in my characters and stories. You are so appreciated, and I'm thrilled to work on my third book with you!

Thank you to my entire team. I love working with you all and creating beautiful books. My endless gratitude goes out to

ACKNOWLEDGMENTS

Tiffany, DJ, Meghan, Alexis, and Brant. A huge thanks to Kerri Resnick for designing the most gorgeous covers I could ask for!

Writing might look, from the outside, like a lonely pursuit. But thankfully, I've always been able to find writing communities that help me stay grounded with friendship and solidarity. Thank you to Las Musas for being my community. And thank you to MSS for always being an amazing writer group chat; Petula, Cindy, Priyanka, Mara, Cassandra, Alisha, Laila, Sabina, Aneeqah, Tana, Jennifer, and Victoria, you're all amazing.

The readers and booksellers who champion books are heroes, and you all deserve endless gratitude. Thank you to all bloggers, booksellers, librarians, and anyone who loves to read and talk about books.

Thank you to my mother, who first taught me how to read and who loves YA! Thank you to Doreen. Thank you to Michelle for always being an amazing friend, and to my friends who've been the best company and support I could ask for: Sonia, Kim, Lyla, Amelie, Molly, Ashley. Thank you to the Crossroads Foundation of Pittsburgh for giving opportunities to young people.